To Win Her Heart

A Players Series Novel

Mackenzie Crowne

LYRICAL PRESS
Kensington Publishing Corp.
www.kensingtonbooks.com

In order to protect her, they'll both have to let their guards down…

Country music's It Girl Jessi Tucker is fed up with her family's stifling security measures. The threat of a dangerous stalker has gotten the men in her life—including her football star cousin, Tuck Tucker—monitoring her every move. To get the freedom she yearns for, Jessi hatches a plan to recruit Max Grayson, Tuck's sexy brawler best friend, to play the role of her new boyfriend. But if her scheme works, will she be forced to hide her true romantic feelings for the sake of her independence? Or will she finally steal the heart of her dream man?...

Max has been pining for Jessi for years and would do anything to protect her, but a professional cage fighter with too many skeletons in his closet has no business being with one of America's sweethearts. Yet while Max does his best to keep Jessi at arm's length, the Tucker family persuades him to accept her offer.

Max believes he can keep Jessi safe from danger, but can he shelter her from his own dark secrets, the media's unforgiving spotlight—and a mutual desire that's harder to resist each day…

Books by Mackenzie Crowne

The Players Series
To Win Her Love
To Win Her Trust
To Win Her Heart

Published by Kensington Publishing Corporation

For Crowne's Crew, my awesome street team, who understand, encourage, and support, and never question my sanity as I entertain the voices in my head.

Acknowledgements

I've been blessed with the most amazing editor. Thank you, Jennifer, for your calm voice of reason and unwavering support.

A special thanks to my critique partners, AJ, V, and Kelly, for their patience, wisdom, talent and humor. They are a bright beacon of sanity in the midst of madness.

Chapter 1

Jessi Tucker needed a man. One with sharp edges. Some bite. A man other men feared.

Not a scary, biker gang kind of guy, of course. Her family would blow a collective gasket if she showed up on the red carpet with a Hells Angel. No, for her plan to work, her supposed boyfriend needed to be someone her father couldn't steamroll and wouldn't reject out of hand. Someone who projected the perfect mix of toughness and respectability—with a little bad boy thrown in for good measure.

Lucky for her, she knew right where to find him.

Slipping the designer sunglasses from her eyes, she scanned the half dozen occupants of the brightly lit fight center. A pair of men squared off on one of three large mats while several others called out encouragement to the combatants inside the netted, octagon ring in the back corner. Bare, well-developed male chests seemed to be part of the dress code, but Max Grayson's muscled body was nowhere in sight. A hum of feminine disappointment vibrated in her throat.

"Can I help you?"

Jessi turned to face the approaching woman. Short, spiky, pink hair covered her head over an angular face. At least a head taller than Jessi's five-four, her slim build didn't detract from the buff and toned arms, legs, and bare midriff between her cut off T-shirt and spandex shorts.

Her big, chocolate brown eyes grew wide. "You're Jessi Tucker! Wow. I mean, wow! My boyfriend and me are huge fans. Your cousin, Tuck, got us tickets when you and Spence were in town last year for your Country Thunder tour." Her teeth flashed in a grin. "Oh, man. Eddie's gonna be so jealous when I tell him you were here. I'm Tina." She stuck out her hand. "I'm the junior self-defense instructor. Are you here to take a class?" Pumping Jessi's hand, excitement increased the volume of her voice with every word. "Oh my God. I can't believe this. You'd want something private, right? I'm available at the moment. The ring is booked for the next two hours, but there's a mat open."

"Actually", Jessi tugged free and cut in before Tina could catch her breath, "I came by to speak to Max. I guess I should have called first to see if he'd be here."

Disappointment damped Tina's smile, but whether because Jessi wasn't interested in her private lesson or she was here to see Max, she couldn't tell. She eyed the painful looking bar piercing Tina's left brow. The thirty-something instructor didn't look anything like the string of Barbie Dolls who clung to Max's arm whenever he appeared at one of her family's frequent gatherings. Then again, according to Tuck, *women* were Max's type.

Jessi wouldn't know, since he mostly ignored her.

Tina's smile brightened almost immediately. "No problem. He's upstairs in his condo."

"Oh." Jessi's gaze flicked to the staircase climbing along the back wall to the second floor. "Is he alone? I wouldn't want to disturb him if he's...ah, busy."

Knowing laughter twinkled in Tina's eyes. "The coast is clear, honey. Max has a way with the ladies, but he keeps things strictly professional during business hours."

She wanted to ask about after hours but thought better of it. If Max agreed to her proposition, she'd be doing her best to find out for herself. After thanking the woman, and promising to send along a signed copy of her latest CD, Jessi crossed to the stairs. The echoing thuds from below quieted as she reached the second floor landing and rounded the corner. A set of double doors beckoned from the end of a short hallway.

She stalked forward, stopped before the doors, and frowned at Spence's voice echoing in her head. *When are you going to stop acting like a scared little girl, afraid to do anything unless Daddy says it's okay?* Irritation simmered, but while her partner's sneering insult pissed her off, the underlying truth in his words rankled. A derisive sniff fluttered her nostrils. Her father would have a conniption if he knew what she was up to but, damn it, Spence was right. It was time she take a stand.

Breathing deeply, she refused to consider what she'd do if Max laughed and slammed the door in her face. Positive thinking was in order. She sucked air through her nose and closed her eyes to visualize the next few seconds, the way she did whenever she was about to step on stage.

Excitement raced through her as the giddy scenario played in her head. Max would open the door. Surprise would light up his long-lashed gray eyes and one side of his mouth would lift in that sexy, crooked smile that made her toes curl. He'd take her hand and tug her inside, and he wouldn't be able to wait until the door was closed before he kissed her. He'd wrap his muscled arms around her, tuck her close, and...

Her eyes flashed open and she slapped a hand to her belly. She was going to throw up.

No, I'm not!

She swiped her damp palms over the thighs of her jeans and, rolling her shoulders, she knocked briskly. No sound came from within. She knocked again. Nothing. The silence taunted her, but she couldn't chicken out now. This was too important. Pressing her ear to the door, she listened intently—and choked on a strangled squeak when the door suddenly swung inward.

Off balance, she stumbled forward and shot out her hand to keep from tumbling over the threshold. Heavy muscle covered by taut skin arrested her fall and scorched her palm with delicious heat. Her fingers tingled with the desire to investigate further, and she might have done just that, but for the deep clearing of a throat.

She snatched back her hand and, focusing on the sight in front of her, nearly swallowed her tongue.

Shirtless, Max's broad shoulders and chest filled the doorway. She blinked at the black tribal tattoo riding one well-developed pectoral. The bold design swirled over his left shoulder and ended in a half-sleeve.

Her gaze flew up, past his face, to the water gleaming in the cropped, ebony hair covering his skull. Helpless, her eyes followed as a droplet trickled down the side of his cheek and jaw to hang suspended from his stubbled, square-cut chin. The sparkling bead plopped onto the center of his chest and slid through the line of short, black curls stepping down the ridges of rock hard abs until it disappeared beneath the towel wrapped around his trim waist.

Her throat clicked on an audible swallow, and she dropped her gaze to his bare feet before making the return trip to his face. If the surprise she'd been expecting had been in his eyes, she missed it. By the time her gaze locked with his, wary disbelief darkened the slate gray orbs.

Arching black brows slammed together. "What the hell are *you* doing here?"

She stifled a wince. Not exactly the greeting she was hoping for. So much for her fantasy. She shrugged inwardly. Knowing Max, that wasn't going to happen anyway, at least not today, but if she pulled this off, she'd live her fantasies soon enough.

She cocked her head and offered him a friendly smile. "Hello, Max."

He leaned forward and turned his head to look down the empty hallway. His lips were flattened in an unhappy line when he straightened and faced her again. "Where is he?"

She blinked. "He who?"

"Your idiot cousin." He raised his voice as he double checked the hall. "Tuck. If you've got a camera running, I'm gonna kick your ass." He straightened once again and pinned her to the spot with a steely-eyed stare. "Look, Squirt, whatever punk he's got going, don't let him suck you into it."

She ground her teeth at the annoying nickname, but was nonetheless relieved. Preoccupied with Tuck's supposed prank, Max was less likely to realize how crazy her plan was. All she had to do was get him to agree before he did. She crossed her arms. "Are you going to invite me in?"

His brows shot up comically. "Hell, no, I'm not inviting you in." Suspicion narrowed his eyes as he shot a quick glance over his shoulder. His head whipped back around, and he fisted his fingers around the knot of the towel. "Did he sneak a camera into my condo?" He dipped his head around the doorjamb once more to shout, "Forget kicking your ass, I'll kill you."

She grinned. Talk about paranoid. "There are no cameras. In fact, Tuck has no idea I'm here. There are, however, several people downstairs who are bound to come running if you keep shouting, so I suggest we move this inside."

"Forget it." He gripped the towel tighter and flicked his other hand toward her in a shooing motion. "Go away. Whatever you Tuckers are up to, I don't want any part of it."

"Fine. We'll have this conversation right here in the hallway, but don't blame me if—"

"Max! Is everything okay?" Feet thudded as one of the men from downstairs took the steps at a run.

She smirked and didn't bother to finish her warning. Ha! As if this six-foot, two hundred pound bruiser needed protection from her.

"Shit."

Her eyebrows shot up as at least part of her fantasy came true. Max grabbed her arm and yanked her inside.

Gripping her elbow, he shoved her behind him and held her there as he spoke to the unknown man. "I'm good. I'm expecting an equipment delivery at two. Make sure Tina goes through everything before she signs. They stiffed us a half dozen sets of gloves last time."

"Sure thing, boss."

Max shut the door on the unseen man and immediately released her arm. He moved several steps away and pierced her with a narrow-eyed glare. "Don't move an inch."

As he stalked across the room in a long-legged stride, her greedy gaze catalogued the muscled expanse of his back. She swallowed, her attention snagging on the adorable set of dimples peeking just above the low slung towel. Heat simmered in her belly, and she found it hard to catch a breath.

Disappearing through a doorway, he slammed the door shut behind him. Her cheeks puffed out on a blowing breath, and she tugged the scarf from her neck. Yeah, that hadn't exactly gone as planned, but at least he hadn't sent her packing. Her shaking fingers fumbled to slip open the buttons of her coat as she glanced around Max's inner sanctum. Having never been invited to his home, she'd been curious at how he lived. She planned to take full advantage of the opportunity to poke into his private space.

Shrugging out of her hip-length, woolen houndstooth coat, she draped it and the scarf over the back of an oversized leather couch. For a bachelor, he had a good eye. A long, black granite island separated the modern kitchen from a comfortable living area. Floors of old-wood planks, aged brick walls, and exposed ceiling beams gave the open floor plan of the converted warehouse a warm, yet masculine, air.

The creamy smooth, mahogany hide of the couch was luxurious under her skimming fingertips as she meandered deeper into his lair. Opposite the couch, orange flames licked at several logs in an inviting brick hearth below a huge, flat screen TV. Beneath the far wall of high windows, a built-in bookshelf caught her attention. Tossing a glance at the closed door where Max had disappeared, she crossed the room and bent to study the titles.

Considering his career, the many health and fitness books made sense, but there was also a wide selection of novels. She plucked one hardbound title from the shelf and scanned the back blurb. A smile tugged at her lips. How about that? Max had a taste for fantasy fiction. Replacing the book, her gaze fell on the heavy bag hanging from a beam in the far corner.

Her heels clicked on the hardwood as she approached the fat, leather cylinder. A vision of Max, sweaty and intense as he worked the bag with fists and feet, honing his fighting skills along with the hardened plains of his athlete's body, flashed in her mind. Heat simmered low in her belly at the idea of a private demonstration. With a hum of anticipation, she balled her hand into a fist and threw her best punch. The bag didn't budge.

"I told you to stay put."

Startled, she jumped and whirled around as Max stalked by her into the kitchen. The towel was gone, which was too bad. The man certainly knew how to wear white terry cloth. She shook off her disappointment. For the coming conversation, the casual jeans and T-shirt covering his muscled frame were probably better than mostly naked and sexy as hell.

"Yes, well." She cleared her throat and trailed after him. "An aversion to orders is why I'm here."

"Meaning?" He wrenched open the refrigerator door and his head disappeared inside.

She slid onto one of the island's four high stools. An alliance with Max, whether real or farce, was her best hope of breaking the chains her family had wrapped around her so tightly she couldn't breathe.

And she was sick of Max looking through her as if she weren't there.

She'd been in love with the big jerk since the first time she met him and, since she was determined to shake up her world, she meant to do something about his habit of giving her the cold shoulder.

She folded her hands in her lap. "Meaning, I have a proposition for you."

His head popped up and a wary frown pulled down the corners of his lips. "I don't like the sound of that." Straightening, he closed the refrigerator door and propped his hips against the counter to unscrew the cap on a water bottle. "Listen, I don't know what your cousin promised you to help him with his game, but I'll make it worth your while to forget it."

Oh, she liked the sound of that, but she wasn't about to *forget it*. She propped her elbows on the counter and leaned toward him. "Worth my while, huh?" Pursing her lips, she dropped her voice to a flirtatious tease. "How would you do that?"

His Adam's apple bobbed on a swallow, and she could have sworn his gaze dropped to her mouth—before he scowled. "Does your father know you're here?"

"Nope." She fluttered her lashes. "There are some things a woman's father doesn't need to know about."

He jerked straight and the wariness in his eyes slid back into suspicion. "Cut that out."

"What?" She blinked and played dumb. If nothing else, she was going to make Max Grayson finally see her for the woman she was.

He bumped out his chin. "Don't try using those baby blues on me. It won't work. I've watched you work your wiles to get your way too many times. What's going on?"

She sat up straight. He'd watched her? That was news. From her perspective, he did his best to ignore her most of the time, but he was wrong about her getting her way. If she did, she wouldn't be here. Okay, that wasn't quite true. If not today, she would have worked up the nerve to approach him eventually. Whether he knew it or not, Max held her heart in his hand, and he was either going to hold it properly, as he did in her dreams, or give it back once and for all.

Bold truth was called for, or at least as much truth as she could afford without tipping him off to the personal side of her agenda. If he agreed to help her, there would be time enough later to ease him into the concept of exploring a real relationship between them.

"I'm here because I need your help."

"With what?"

"With getting my family off my back."

"How am I supposed to do that?" He shook his head and pulled a long sip of water from the bottle.

She fidgeted with the hem of her blouse and had to take a deep breath before she could force the words out. "By pretending to be my boyfriend."

He coughed, spewing water over the counter between them. His thick forearm dragged over his mouth as he stared at her, his eyes full of wary horror. "That's not funny."

"It's not supposed to be. I'm completely serious."

"What you are is certifiable."

She frowned. "No, I'm desperate. The Country Times Awards are in a few days. I need a date." She nibbled her bottom lip. "But what I really need is a man in my life, and you're the only one I know who my family won't be able to run off."

He shook his head. "I don't know what you're up to, but even if I wasn't old enough to be your—"

"Brother?" She offered him an innocent smile.

His dark brows dropped into a scowling V. "I was going to say uncle, and—"

"Women date older men all the time." And the nine-year difference in their ages was no big deal. Not to her, anyway. Hoping to head off his obvious refusal, she let her gaze slide over his solid body and welcomed the surge of excitement in her belly. "Not that you're ancient or anything."

His nostrils flared with his scoffing snort, and her smile slid into a grin.

"My advanced age is beside the point. Your father would rip me a new one if he found out I got anywhere near you." He snatched a paper towel from the holder on the counter and swiped at the wet island.

"I'm sure he'll try." Her smile faded. "But he respects you, and I need a guy my dad can't intimidate, which makes you perfect."

He tossed the towel in the trash and a half smile tipped one corner of his mouth. "Who says he doesn't intimidate me?"

She squinted her eyes in dismissal. "Oh, please. You're not afraid of him or you wouldn't have sacked him last Thanksgiving on the beach."

A smug smile tugged at his lips before he dipped his chin. "The score was tied with time running out, but that's football. You're talking a whole different ballgame here. Ryan's got a dark side when it comes to his *little girl*."

Frustration cranked the band of desperation squeezing her chest. She jammed the fingers of both hands through her loose curls. Failure loomed like a taunting specter, but she couldn't give in. Not without a fight. For close to a year, an uneasy longing had been building in her, stealing the joy she'd always found in her singing. Something was missing. Something vital. If she didn't find it soon, she was going to explode. Or have a breakdown. Either scenario was unacceptable.

"You think I don't know that? I get he's concerned for my safety. I'm not stupid. There are a lot of nuts out there, but he's driving me insane." She swung out her arm. "They all are. I'm twenty-five years old for heaven's sake, yet the family treats me like a teenager without a brain in my head. I can't take it anymore. I won't."

"And you think hooking up with some guy is going to convince them to back off?" He crossed his arms and hiked a doubtful brow.

"I think when they see I'm serious about living my own life, they will. And I'm not hooking up with some guy. I'm hooking up with you." The finger she aimed at his nose emphasized her point. "Think about it. He trusts you, and who better to keep his little girl safe from the crazies he sees behind every curtain than a cage fighting champ?"

A frown tightened his features and his posture stiffened. "What kind of crazies?"

"It's nothing." She waved a dismissive hand. "Weirdo fan mail is part of the business. Dad's just paranoid. The point is, he knows I'd be safe with you around, so he'll back off and give me some space."

"Not likely." He leaned his palms on the counter, holding her gaze. "I'm sorry, but it's not gonna happen. Even if I was willing to go along with your screwy plan, neither your father nor Tuck would stand by while you get involved with a man like me."

Confused by the excuse and more than a little disappointed, she went on the offense. "What do you mean, a man like you? What's wrong with you?"

His eyebrows popped to his hairline as if her question surprised him. "Hell, Squirt, I'm a street brawler from the wrong side of the tracks… among other things."

She rolled her eyes. "Like anyone cares how or where you grew up. Dad likes you and Tuck is your friend."

"Yes, and because we *are* friends, your cousin has a vast understanding of my reputation with women. I'm not stupid, or suicidal enough, to say yes to what would end up a friendship-killing cluster fuck."

With her plan dying a quick death right before her eyes, frustration and hurt made her voice sharp. "You haven't even given me a chance to explain what I have in mind."

He shoved off the counter and crossed to the couch to pick up her coat and scarf. Turning, he held them out. "And I don't intend to."

Chapter 2

Grumbling beneath her breath, Jessi stomped down the stairs and jammed an arm into one sleeve of her coat. As if to pile on to Max's sound rejection, the second sleeve evaded her free hand. She twisted her shoulders and upper body, stabbing blindly at the dangling material. Her three-inch heels wobbled slightly as she stopped short. Reaching back, she punched her hand into the silk-lined sleeve, then flung out her arms in an angry shrug. With a rough tug on the hem, the houndstooth slipped onto her shoulders and settled into place.

The urge to turn around, march back up the stairs, and give Max a piece of her mind burned low in her belly. She tossed a glare back toward the second floor landing and settled for sticking out her tongue. The childish gesture didn't help, but it would have to do. She'd swear off manicures for a year before she gave Max the satisfaction of knowing how much his rebuff hurt.

She'd reached the bottom step before she spotted Dan chatting up Tina at the front counter. Her long-time driver glanced her way and, even from a distance, the disapproval on his normally jovial face was unmistakable.

A growl rumbled in her throat as she crossed the fight center. Thanking Tina, she pushed open the door to the sidewalk. Knowing Dan followed, she headed straight for the town car and slid into the back seat. He shut the door and rounded the hood before sliding behind the wheel.

"For crying out loud, I was gone less than ten minutes." She stared out the window, but in the corner of her eye, caught the dark blue of his suit coat sleeve as he shifted to look back at her.

"I'd be looking at a pink slip if your father learned I'd let you go into a place like that on your own."

"It's Max's place. I was perfectly safe and you know it." She crossed her arms and shot him a smirk. "And Dad would never fire his number one spy."

Straight, white teeth flashed in his unapologetic smile, and she turned back to the window. After nine years, she considered the fifty-something retired marine more family than employee, especially since he and his wife, Aurora, had taken up residence on the bottom floor of the three-story condo she'd purchased earlier in the year. A homebody by nature, Aurora was content in her position as live-in housekeeper, and did her best to give Jessi her space. Dan, on the other hand, took his responsibility as driver-slash-watchdog seriously.

"What are you up to, Jess?"

She cut her gaze to his. With her father jazzed up over a couple of letters from a nutty fan, Dan was on full alert. She latched on to Tina's offer of classes as the perfect explanation for today's visit and lied without qualm. "I'm thinking of taking some self-defense classes."

The glitter in his pale green eyes said he didn't buy her answer for a second, but he shrugged and turned away to start the car. "That's not a bad idea, but if you want to learn how to defend yourself, I could teach you."

"I'd rather have Max."

Though she hadn't meant the comment the way it sounded, especially after the reception she'd just received, the rear-view mirror displayed Dan's quirked lips and knowing eyes. "Now, there's a surprise."

She squirmed in her seat and angled her chin defiantly.

He shook his head. "Where to next?"

* * * *

Jessi tugged the floppy brim of her woolen hat low on her forehead and stepped inside Louisa's Bistro. The chattering buzz of conversation from dozens of patrons competed with the soft bite of pop music drifting from invisible speakers. With her eyes concealed behind dark sunglasses, she scanned the popular restaurant, busy with the lunch hour crowd. An inward sigh shuddered in her chest as she spotted Kris, already seated in a secluded alcove near the back.

Dipping her head, Jessi skirted the crowded tables, looking neither left nor right. Considering her mood, an encounter with a well-meaning fan was the last thing she needed.

The expectant smile froze on Kris's lips as Jessi flopped into the open chair and jammed her oversized purse onto the floor at her feet. She tugged the hat from her head. "I hate men."

"All men or one in particular." Her best friend laughed, leaned her elbows on the table, and arched an auburn brow.

Jessi snatched Kris's untouched glass of water. The chilled liquid did little to douse the flames of embarrassed anger flaring inside. She set down the glass with a decisive thunk. "At this point, all of them." First her father and cousins do their best to lock her up like a child and then Max tosses her out on her ass. Add Dan's annoying smirk and the certainty he would submit a full report to her father before the day was out, and she was ready to write off the entire male population.

"Is Spence still pissed you nixed his songs?"

Jessi flipped opened her menu. How could she have neglected to include her partner's recent nasty attitude in her list of guy grievances?

She rolled her eyes. "You know Spence. He'll bitch and complain, but then he'll get back to work. Once he comes up with a couple of number one hits, he'll calm down." She tossed the menu aside without reading it and dredged up a smile for their usual waitress as she stopped at the table. "Hi, Crystal. I'll have a garden salad and a glass of whatever Kris is drinking." She jerked her chin toward the wineglass in front of her friend.

"Make that two salads." As Crystal headed for the bar, Kris sat back. "If it's not Spence, then it must be your father. What'd he do now?"

Renewed frustration tightened her jaw. "He hired a new bodyguard."

A low hum purred in the redhead's throat, and she picked up her wine. "Is he hot?"

Jessi bit back a laugh. "I'm serious."

"So am I." Mischief sparkled in Kris's hazel eyes. "I know your dad's obsession with security drives you nuts, but do you know how many women would kill to have a muscle-bound hottie following them around wherever they go?"

"I'd sign up for that." Crystal placed Jessi's wine in front of her.

"You'd have to get in line behind me." Kris shared a grin with the waitress.

Jessi fought a smile as Crystal left them alone to answer a hail from three tables over. She shook her head. "I already have enough people sticking their noses in my life, thank you very much."

Sipping at the golden vintage, she savored the dry chardonnay on her tongue while choosing her words. Kris had been pestering her to act on her feelings for Max for years, without success. Well, she'd acted this morning. Talk about an epic failure.

She gulped a large swallow and heaved a frustrated breath. "Besides, the only hot muscles I want around me belong to Max." She scowled at her friend's grin. "But he isn't willing to share them."

"How do you know?" Kris lifted the glass to her lips. "Have you asked him?"

Shifting nervously in her seat, Jessi avoided her gaze. "As a matter of fact, I have."

Wine sloshed over her fingers as Kris froze. "Oh my God. When?"

"About fifteen minutes ago." Jessi squeezed her eyes shut in an embarrassed grimace.

"Well, it's about time. Did you knock on his door naked and offer to be his new sparring partner like I suggested?"

Jessi's eyes popped open on a choked laugh. "Like I'd do that."

"Why not? I would have."

"Of course you would. You're a skanky ho."

"Damn straight." Kris's eyes sparkled with silent laughter as she wiped her fingers with a paper napkin. "Better than a virgin princess."

They shared a grin at the familiar jest, and Jessi smirked. "I might be a princess, but the virgin title doesn't apply."

"Might as well. You've slept with one guy, and that sexy roadie didn't even rate a follow-up."

Jessi winced at the memory of her singular sexual experience. After a disappointing night spent together after a concert in Dallas, Wiley Cotes had been more interested in how she could help his budding singing career than in getting her naked again. As far as she was concerned, he lacked the skill for the former, and as she later discovered lacked the desire for the latter.

She shrugged a shoulder. "Turns out, he's gay. I heard he's in the chorus for a drag show in Vegas."

Kris's mouth dropped open and she huffed out a breath. "I knew he was too pretty to be straight." She shook her head and leaned forward. "Well? I'm dying here. What happened with Max?"

"Nothing good. I wish to hell I hadn't gone to see him."

"What? Why?" A frown wrinkled her friend's brow. Suddenly, her eyes widened in horror. "Oh, Jessi. Don't tell me you went to him with your fake boyfriend idea."

She set aside her wineglass and cocked her chin at a stubborn angle. "Okay, I won't."

Kris groaned.

"It's a good plan," she argued in a low voice.

A wry smirk twisted Kris's lips. "Did Max think so?"

Jessi glanced around, relieved to find their conversation remained private. She pinned Kris with a glare. "That's what I love about you. You're always so supportive." The flash of hurt in her friend's eyes pierced her heart with a spear of regret, and she sighed. "Sorry. That was a bitchy thing to say. No, he didn't, but as I've recently discovered, Max is a jerk."

She curled her fingers around the stem of her glass as Crystal arrived to deliver their salads. Damn Max, anyway. Even if he had no interest in her personally, couldn't he at least have helped her out as a friend?

When they were alone once more, Kris shook her head. "Bitchy is fine as long as you remember I'm on your side. What happened?"

Her shoulders slumped in defeat. "He turned me down flat. You should have seen him. He looked as if I'd asked him to give me a kidney or something. He refused to even listen to my plan and couldn't get me out of his place fast enough." Renewed anger flared in her belly. "What's wrong with me, Kris? Why is he so distant with me when he's always so open and friendly with everyone else? Do I smell? Have bad breath? What?"

"I've never noticed any foul orders coming from you." Kris picked up her fork. "You're beautiful and talented and you know it. The problem is, Max is a guy. They're idiots."

"And jerks." Jessi dug into her salad.

Kris cocked her head as she chewed. "And jerks, but it's not their fault. They can't help the way they think."

Jessi's fork stilled and she stared at her friend. "What's that supposed to mean?"

Dark auburn curls shifted on Kris's shoulders with the emphatic shake of her head. "I know you don't believe me, but I've seen him watching you. He's attracted."

"Max watches everyone. That's just the way he is."

"Maybe, but he doesn't watch the rest of us like he's a starving wolf staring at a juicy steak." Kris bared her teeth in a sly smile. "He wants you, girlfriend, even if he won't admit it."

Jessi speared a slice of tomato and her laugh was derisive. "Yeah, I could see how much he wanted me, right before he kicked me out of his condo."

"CC agrees with me."

Her fork clattered against her plate. "You talked to CC about this?"

"Duh." Kris slipped another bite of salad into her mouth.

Jessi shouldn't be surprised. Cousins as well as friends, Kris and CC had grown up together and shared everything. That hadn't changed since CC married Tuck and the three women had become friends. Still, having her love life, or lack thereof, discussed, even amongst the two women she'd grown to love like sisters, made Jessi uncomfortable. "Thanks a lot."

"Oh, please." Kris waved off her grumbled complaint. "It's not as if your feelings for Max are a secret. Not to those of us who know you, anyway. CC just wants to see you happy."

Jessi picked up her fork and shrugged off her embarrassment. The fact was she sucked at hiding her feelings. Another reason she needed to strike out on her own. It was time she took some chances, experienced the things other women did. How was she supposed to pull that off with well-meaning family members and friends reading her every thought and stepping in to stop her before she ever got started?

"Your cousin is a hopeless romantic these days. She sees daisies and sunshine everywhere now that she's pregnant."

Kris smirked. "Yeah, it's disgusting, but in this case she's right. She knows Max pretty well and says growing up the way he did, your family's acceptance is as important to him as Tuck's friendship. He'd steer clear of anything that would jeopardize either."

A tiny spark of hope flamed to life as she considered CC's claim. That wasn't exactly how Max had put it, but her family's reaction and his friendship with Tuck were at least partly to blame for his refusal to listen. Could it be that simple?

The spark fizzled almost as quickly as it flared. Simple, hell. Nothing was simple when it came to her family, and Tuck was, and always would be, her cousin. That wasn't going to change. Time to face facts. Max was unavailable to her. She'd simply have to put her feelings for the jerk behind her and move on.

"You could try talking to him."

Yanked from her musings, Jessi's laugh held no humor. "Didn't you hear me? He said no." Humiliation heated her cheeks. "Actually, it was more like hell no."

Kris slashed her fork through the air. "Not Max. Tuck. Tell him how you feel. CC's not the only one who's fallen victim to the idea of love and romance."

"Yeah, right." Once he stopped laughing, Tuck would banish Max from any future family gatherings. "He thinks I'm still fourteen. I'll just have to find some other tough guy to help me out."

"Geez, Jess. Maybe you should forget about the boyfriend plan."

"And do what? I tried moving out on my own and ended up sharing my condo with Aurora and Dan, the super spy. The only way I'm truly going to be free of prying eyes is to convince my father I'm safe, without his help."

"I told you, you're welcome to move in with me."

"I appreciate that, but I know you. You wouldn't do well under my father's version of house arrest."

Kris shrugged and grinned. "Depends upon what that bodyguard looks like."

"Knowing my father, he's twice our age and bald."

Kris batted her lashes. "If he looks anything like Bruce Willis, I'm in."

Chapter 3

Max groaned under his breath and shifted his gaze between Ryan's sober face and Tuck's wicked smile. A full twenty-four hours had passed since Jessi had stormed out, pissed as hell at his refusal to go along with her ridiculous plan. He'd slept with one eye open last night, in case one or more of her male watchdogs broke down his door to demand an explanation for her visit.

With the way the Tucker men hovered over the little country star, he couldn't blame her for wanting to free herself from the constant surveillance. Hell, as bold as Jessi was, he was surprised she'd let their aggressive babysitting tactics continue as long as she had, but shit. There had to be an easier way to go about gaining her independence.

For her, and definitely for him.

Ryan cleared his throat. "We're here about Jessi."

"Shit, Uncle Ry, Max knows that." Tuck bared his teeth in a feral smile. "What he's wondering is which one of us is going to throw the first punch."

"Wrong, asshole." Max swung the condo door wider and turned to let them follow him inside. "I was wondering what took you so long to get here. Can I get either of you a drink?"

"I'll pass." Tuck headed for the couch and slumped into a sprawl. "I've got to meet CC for an ultrasound in an hour."

Max paused at the bar and lifted a brow at Ryan.

Jessi's father rounded the couch, sat in the chair across from Tuck, and dropped the manila folder he carried on the coffee table. "I'll take whatever you're having."

Max poured scotch into two glasses. He crossed the room and handed one to Ryan. Settling on the other end of the couch from Tuck, he grinned. "How's the mother-to-be doing?"

Tuck shoved a hand through his shaggy, blond hair. "She's bitching about getting fat, especially since she and Gracie compared bellies the other day. CC can't understand how they're the same size when Gracie's carrying twins."

Max smiled. Gracie's and CC's dual pregnancies had provided plenty of laughs over the past few months or, more precisely, the reactions of their husbands had. The old adage about the bigger they are definitely applied. With more than twenty years of pro football experience between them, both Tuck and Gracie's husband, Jake, had faced down some of the toughest sons of bitches on the planet, but they were pushovers when it came to their wives and complete toast where their future children were concerned.

Ryan cleared his throat, and Max held up his hand. "Before you say anything, I think Jessi may have reached her limit with all the security you have around her. If you don't let up on her a little, she's going to do something stupid."

Tuck's lips flattened in a frown. "Define stupid."

Max inwardly winced. They'd been good friends for five years, but Tuck loved his cousin. In any conflict involving Max and Jessi, Max would be the resounding loser. He respected his friend for that, but he'd been tossed into this situation blind, and the embarrassed hurt in Jessi's eyes as she stormed out of his condo didn't ease his guilt for turning her away when she'd asked for his help.

He shrugged. "You know your cousin better than me."

"Yeah, and she's been making calf eyes at you for years."

Tell me something I don't know.

Beautiful, talented, and barely twenty, she'd been little more than a kid the night he'd first been scorched by the timeless, feminine awareness in Jessi Tucker's big blue eyes. The nine years separating them, not to mention her relation to Tuck, placed her squarely in the "off limits" category as far as Max was concerned.

In the five years since, he'd done his best to avoid Tuck's sexy little cousin, but the blatant invitation sizzling in her eyes whenever they happened to see each other never failed to leave Max sweating. Waking up hard, hot, and singed from all too frequent raunchy dreams starring the petite beauty with a piquant smile and auburn curls didn't help.

When he didn't respond, Tuck's frown slid into a challenging smirk.

"Cut it out, Tuck." Ryan rested his elbows on his spread knees with his glass gripped in both hands.

Tuck smirked and sat back.

Worry darkened Jessi's father's eyes as he studied Max. "Her driver told me she came to see you yesterday. What did she want?"

Max's gaze slid to Tuck, then back to the older man. Unless he flat out lied, this conversation was about to take a turn down the shit hole. He sloshed the drink in his glass, sipped, and braced for the explosion.

"She wanted my help."

"With what?"

"Getting you and the family off her back."

Her father shook his head.

Tuck grinned. "How does she expect to manage that?"

"By pretending we're seeing each other."

Tuck slowly straightened from the couch's back.

Ryan held up a hand, stopping whatever response Tuck would have made. "From what Dan said about how angry she was when she got back to the car, I assume you turned her down."

Max nodded and swallowed another shot.

Tuck grunted, but the older man stabbed Max with an intent stare. "Any chance I can convince you to change your mind?"

The shock on Tuck's face as he whipped his head around to stare at his uncle would have been comical if Max weren't suffering the same astonishment.

He lowered the glass from his lips. "You want to run that by me again?"

Instead of answering, Ryan picked up the file from the table and leaned forward to pass Max the manila folder.

"My daughter gave up a lot for her career, missing out on most of what other girls her age enjoy, including a measure of privacy. I've done what was needed to keep her safe through the years, but she's a grown woman now. She wants control of her life. Under normal circumstances, I'd agree." He sat back and bumped his chin toward the folder. "Unfortunately, now's not the time to back off and let her go off on her own."

Trepidation rippled down Max's spine as his gaze dropped to the file. Although he was sure he wasn't going to like whatever it contained, he opened the flap. Tuck slid across the couch until he was close enough to see the contents over Max's shoulder.

Three letters, hand written in identical, neat block letters, rested on top of a computerized report. A greasy ball of unease grew in Max's gut as he read the first. He passed the sheet to Tuck and read the next two. They contained no direct threats, but the overall message of the short missives was menacing enough to lift the hair on the back of his neck. Whoever had sent them had a definite hard-on for Jessi, and not in a good way.

"What the hell?" Tuck looked up and speared his uncle with an angry glare. He held out the damning letter. "Why am I just hearing about this? Does the rest of the family know?"

"It wasn't until the last letter arrived three days ago, that we knew we had a problem. As her manager, Tim knows, of course. I filled your parents and sister in last night, and asked you to come along this morning so I could tell you both what's happening."

"Has Jessi seen these?" Max met Ryan's steady gaze.

"Seen them and dismissed them."

"Is she out of her mind?" Tuck tossed the letter to the table and burst to his feet. He prowled around the room, then stopped at the bar. The jerking movements of his hands as he poured himself the drink he'd refused only minutes earlier broadcast his irritation.

Ryan shook his head. "She's a public figure, Tuck. You, of all people, know there are a lot of kooks out there who feel entitled to voice their opinion. At least a dozen letters from whack jobs come in every month. She doesn't see these as anything out of the ordinary."

Tuck snorted and threw back the dark malt in a single swallow.

"But you do." Max drew the older man's gaze.

Ryan nodded solemnly.

Max scanned the pages in his hand. None of them were signed, but the last ended with a seemingly random question. "Remember Suzie?"

"Holy shit." Tuck stepped to the couch and held out his hand. "Let me see."

Ryan sighed as his nephew reread the page. "You've got a good eye, Max. The Suzie reference is the reason I'm concerned."

Disquiet churned in Max's gut. "What's the significance?"

Tuck dropped to the cushions at his side. "My grandmother had this antique doll. One of those fancy, dress-up jobs with a porcelain head. When Gram died, she left the doll to Jessi because she'd always loved the thing. She called it Suzie. The doll went everywhere with her when she was little, and when she got older and started touring, she brought it along. About six weeks ago, she returned to her dressing room after a show. The doll had apparently fallen from the shelf where she'd left it. The head was shattered."

Chills pebbled Max's skin. Jessi had claimed her father was paranoid yesterday, but he was right to be concerned. These weren't the musings of a weirdo fan. "Did the letters start before or after the doll was broken?"

Ryan sat back. "The first letter arrived a week later, with two weeks between each of the next two."

"Have you taken these to the authorities?"

"I have a friend in the FBI." Ryan nodded at the file. "The profile he put together is there. The story about the doll was written up in *Country Times*, but the reporter didn't give the doll's name. Which means whoever is responsible for those letters is close enough to have that information."

"You think it's someone she knows?"

"That or someone she knows shared the doll's name with a friend. Either way, Jessi's not safe."

Dread constricted Max's chest like a vice. He nodded. "She needs a professional security detail."

"I agree and so does my FBI friend. Unfortunately, Jessi doesn't."

"Since when do you listen to her when it comes to her security?" Tuck scoffed. "Just line up a team and be done with it."

That sounded like a good idea to Max. Jessi may bristle at the lack of privacy, but the alternative was unacceptable.

"I hired a team yesterday." Ryan met Max's watchful gaze. "You weren't far off when you said she'd reached her limit. She threw a fit when she found out and told me if I hadn't fired them by the time she got back, she'd have no choice but to leave town because she couldn't live her life with one more stranger watching her every move." He arched a brow. "Then she came here. To you."

Max's eyelids slid shut, and he scrubbed a hand over his chin. The short stubble rasped at his palm. "I'm not a bodyguard."

"No, but you know how to handle yourself in a dangerous situation."

He sucked in a heavy breath and fought against the noose tightening around his neck. "I have a business to run."

"Arrangements can be made to have someone on hand to manage the fight center, and didn't you mention taking some time to yourself, since your next match isn't for six months?" Ryan didn't give him a chance to respond. "I need your help, Max, but your services as a bodyguard aren't exactly what I'm after."

Max opened his eyes and glared at the man he considered a friend. "What, exactly, *are* you after?"

"I'd like to know that myself," Tuck interjected.

"Your help." Worry bracketed Ryan's mouth and he sat forward to prop his elbows on his spread knees. "The FBI is investigating. With a little luck, they'll figure this out quickly and we'll all breathe a little easier. In the meantime, the team I hired is still on the payroll, but they'll remain in the background. As far as Jessi knows, I've given in to her wishes, but until this asshole is found, I don't want her alone for a minute."

Tuck's typical, easygoing smile was noticeably absent. "The playoffs start this week, but I'll help where I can."

"I know you will. I'm counting on it. Your father and brother will be around as much as they can, and your sister has offered to help as well, but Jessi has several out of town commitments over the next few weeks." Ryan turned back to Max. "The family and tour security will cover days and evenings, but that still leaves nights."

"And, as Max's *make-believe* girlfriend, she won't spend those alone." Tuck propped an ankle over his opposite knee. "I've got to hand it to you, Uncle Ry, that's genius."

Max shot Tuck a disbelieving stare.

He shrugged, but his cutting smile didn't reach his eyes. "Face it, Max, if she finds a couple of security guards outside her door, she's likely to bolt. If that happens, she's completely on her own with a nutcase on her tail."

"I know it's a lot to ask, son." Ryan's quiet voice drew Max's gaze. "But she came to you. She trusts you."

"And you want me to break that trust. If we do this and she finds out, she's going to be pissed." And no doubt hurt. Neither outcome sat well with him.

"Better pissed than dead."

Max cut his gaze toward Tuck. Although it frustrated him to be pushed into the situation, even if it was for a good cause, he couldn't disagree with his friend's analysis.

Ryan sighed. "I don't like the idea of deceiving her either, but Tuck's right, and keeping her safe is my only concern for the moment. I'll deal with the fallout later, if there is any. If you can come up with some other way to keep her safe, with her cooperation, I'm all ears, but she trusts you. All I'm suggesting is we take advantage of the plan she came up with."

Jessi's father's logic was sound, but pretending to be intimate with a woman who too often invaded his dreams, one he didn't dare allow himself to touch, was a temptation Max would rather avoid. He threw out one last defense. "I already turned her down. She wasn't exactly happy with me when she left here yesterday."

Ryan sighed. "Then persuade her you've changed your mind."

Max dropped his chin to his chest.

"She put this idea in motion, Max, and your cooperation won't go unrewarded. I happen to know you've been frustrated in your attempt to purchase a certain property on the Jersey shore."

Max jerked his head up, and he met the older man's intent stare. The instant racing of his heart thudded against his ribcage. How the fuck did Ryan Tucker know of his interest in Haven Place?

The older man didn't back down from Max's suspicious glare. "I'd have to be blind not to notice the way my daughter watches you. Of course I looked into your background."

Anger and trepidation battled for the upper hand. "Son of a bitch."

"That's cold, Uncle Ry." Tuck shook his head. "Max is a friend."

Ryan sat back. "Tell me that in a few months when your child is born." He turned back to Max. "I won't apologize for doing what I deem necessary to keep Jessi safe. Make no mistake, if I was concerned about anything I found, I wouldn't be sitting here and you wouldn't have been allowed anywhere near Jessi, or the family, all these years. In the meantime, I have connections you don't. I might be able to help with the Jersey…situation."

Understanding glittered in the older man's eyes, and Max swore beneath his breath. The files from his childhood were sealed so the custody shit was hidden, and Elizabeth Krandall had paid a fortune to keep her fight over his inheritance out of the papers at the time. For someone determined, however, the information could be found with a little digging.

Ryan obviously knew more of Max's past than he was willing to say, at least in front of Tuck. That suited Max. His fucked up family ties and the need to exact a measure of justice weren't subjects he normally discussed. With anyone.

Frustration deepened his voice. "I'll talk to Jessi, but if I do this, I do it my way. Without interference from the family." He turned a challenging stare on Tuck. His friend held up both hands. Turning back to Ryan, Max narrowed his gaze so there would be no misunderstanding. "As for the Jersey business, keep it to yourself and stay out of it."

Chapter 4

"What if we throw in a key change there? Bump it up." Jessi tucked the tip of one booted foot behind the rung of the high stool and reached for the water bottle on the shelf behind her.

"That might work." Spence plucked out several chords, adding the change. Leaning over the stand to make several notes on the sheet music, he tossed his head, dislodging the lock of gilded blond hair that slid into his pale blue eyes. He straightened and adjusted the guitar on his thigh. "Let's try it. Starting at the second verse."

Ear trained on the change as they ran through the chords, Jessi hummed in lieu of the lyrics. When they'd finished and he nodded, relief made her smile. Spence was a creative genius when it came to laying down a tune, but he could be a temperamental pain in the ass when things didn't go his way.

He'd been a complete asshole since she'd agreed with her father and refused two of Spence's songs for their upcoming CD. As usual, he'd forgotten all about the songs of hers he'd denied over the years. Since they shared creative say so on what was released, there was nothing he could do about it but bitch...and throw out nasty insults. In her present mood, she was glad she wouldn't have to deal with another heated argument.

He struck the beginning chords for a full play through, and she joined him. Her mind, however, was not on the music. Embarrassment flared in her soul every time she thought of how Max unceremoniously tossed her out of his condo. Bruised and battered, her heart wept at the loss of a dream while her feminine ego demanded pay back for his careless dismissal, but how was she to go about paying back a man intent on ignoring her? For that matter, how was she supposed to face him the next time he showed up at a family event with one of his bimbos?

Okay, that wasn't fair. A couple of the bimbos he'd brought along over the years had been very nice, but still. What was wrong with her, damn it?

Jaw clenched, she plucked at the strings absently. At least her father had backed off on his security team demand, but how long would that last? With Max a definite no, she'd have to find some other guy to help her with her plan, but who?

He'd have to be someone gorgeous…and built. Maybe she should talk to Tuck after all. One of his football buddies with shoulders a yard wide and bulging arm muscles would be perfect. She added a pair of sexy, lower back dimples to the image forming in her mind and smiled.

Oh, yeah. She'd drag her hunky dream-man along to the next family party and make sure to personally introduce him to Max. The rat.

"Where the hell is your head?"

She blinked and her fingers stilled on the strings. "Huh?"

Spence frowned and jerked his chin toward the music stand. "What's the point of me writing down the chords if you're going to make up your own?"

Her gaze flew to the music sheet. She stared as if she'd never seen it before. "Uh, sorry. I have a lot on my mind."

He set aside his guitar and stood. "Yeah, well, so do I. Thanks to you and Daddy, we're two tracks short."

A headache bloomed in her left temple and she sighed. Apparently, she hadn't escaped the argument after all. "Spence—"

"Save it. I'm taking lunch." He turned toward the glass wall separating the studio from the control room. "Looks like we have company, anyway."

She followed Spence's gaze and slapped her hand over the strings of her guitar. With the sound crew off for the day, the control room should be empty but for Dan, who'd been slouched on the couch with a book for the past four hours, waiting to take her home. Unfortunately, he wasn't alone. Max looked straight at her through the glass panel. He dropped his chin in a silent greeting.

"What's he doing here?" Spence turned back.

She glanced down at her lap and hoped he didn't notice the blush heating her cheeks. "I have no idea." Crap. What *was* Max doing here? Hadn't he humiliated her enough yesterday?

"Is he hassling you?"

Her head jerked up and she stared at her partner's intent face. "No. Why would you ask that? He's a friend of the family."

Some of his earlier animosity slid away as he studied her face. "I know he is, but you're not yourself lately. Something's wrong, and to my knowledge, Max has never come by the studio."

She didn't know what to say. Working as closely as they had for so many years, Spence knew her as well as anyone, but something had been wrong with her for months. If he'd noticed, he hadn't mentioned it before. "I don't know why Max is here, and as for the other, I'm just tired, I guess."

Doubt shown clear in his squinted eyes, but she spoke the truth. She *was* tired. Tired of being unhappy when she'd been given so much. Tired of yearning for something she couldn't quite name, and tired of wanting a man who didn't want her in return.

Spence slung the strap of his satchel over his shoulder. "I'm out of here. I told Alicia I'd meet her for lunch."

Jessi sat up straight and a surprised smile spread on her lips. Her assistant had been drooling over Spence since she'd first taken the job three months ago. Jessi understood and could commiserate with the young woman's frustration when Spence failed to pick up on the inviting smiles and blatant invitations she sent his way. Apparently, he'd finally taken notice.

"Well, it's about time. Alicia's been crushing on you for months."

"It's just lunch." Annoyance flashed in his eyes. "Your head's not in the music this morning. I'm calling it a day. We'll pick up fresh in the morning."

She locked her jaw to keep it from dropping open. In all the years they'd worked together, Spence had never called a session short. Never.

"Don't look at me like that." His lips compressed in a tight line. "I'm worried, Jessi. I've never known you to be distracted the way you've been the last couple months. The schedule ahead of us is a bitch. Between the CD, the tour dates, and the Super Bowl gig at the end of the month, neither one of us can afford to lose focus." He crossed the room and paused at the closed door to glance back. "I don't care what you have to do, but for Christ's sake, fix whatever is bothering you and get your head on straight."

He yanked open the door and stormed through the control room on his way out.

Max shifted his gaze between Jessi and Spence's retreating back before he stepped through the open doorway. Dark brows arched above his watchful eyes. "Artistic differences?"

He shut the door behind him, and she stiffened her spine.

"Something like that." Her gaze slid to the control room. No help there. Figures, the one time she wanted him to interfere in her business, Dan left her hanging and buried his nose in his book.

Clamping down on a frustrated growl, she turned back to Max. There was nothing she could do about her flaming cheeks, but she'd be damned if she'd cower beneath his steady gray gaze. They were on her turf now. If anyone was going to be tossed on their ass, it was him.

She stuck out her chin and went on the offensive. "You're the *last* person I expected to see."

"Yeah, I—"

"What's wrong? Did you stop by to remind me of how foolish I was coming to you for help?" She slid from the stool to store her instrument in its case then snapped back around. "Believe me, there's no need. You made yourself more than clear yesterday."

Beneath his bomber jacket, his soft gray jersey shirt stretched against his muscular chest as he shoved his fingers into the back pockets of his jeans. "Actually, I came by to apologize."

"Apologize?" She crossed her arms and hid her surprise. "Are you saying my proposition wasn't as screwy as you made it sound?"

A wry smile curved his lips. "Hell no. Your plan is full-out nuts, but I shouldn't have shut you down the way I did without hearing you out."

Renewed anger simmered in her belly and her laugh was harsh. "My plan was nuts, but you should have asked for details? Right. Don't patronize me, Max. I get it. You think I'm a silly little girl who has nothing else to do but come up with ridiculous larks to fill my time. Believe what you want. I don't care."

Pulling his hands from his pockets, he closed the distance between them in four long strides. She took a tentative step back and her gaze skidded briefly to Dan. He didn't look up from his book, and she didn't bother calling out to him. The studio was soundproof with the intercom shut off. He wouldn't hear her, anyway.

Her pulse sped up as Max dipped his head until his face was only inches from hers.

His sober expression held no hint of humor. "First, don't put words in my mouth. A silly little girl is the last thing I see when I look at you, and second, you do, too, care."

She yearned to ask what he did see, but crowded between the keyboard at her back and his big body, she was too flustered to pull off the question. She settled for a blatant lie. "No, I don't."

"If you don't care, then why this angry little wrinkle?"

The breath caught in her throat as he touched a fingertip to the space between her brows. Shaken, she jerked her head back. "Because I don't happen to like you anymore."

He dropped his hand to his side, but didn't step back. She wasn't sure if that was a good thing or bad. He smelled delicious, but her heart tended to overreact whenever he was near. This close, that foolish organ was going bonkers.

His deep chuckle made her shiver. "Liar. You're pissed. With good reason. I acted like an asshole."

She blinked. Apologizing was one thing, but admitting he'd been an asshole wasn't Max's style. Confused and off-balance, she ratcheted her chin up another notch. "Yes, you did."

"I'm sorry." He rubbed a hand down her arm, and the warmth of his wide palm seeped through the weave of her sweater to scald the blood in her veins.

What the hell? Max had always been one of those touchy-feely guys, forever tweaking her cousin, Patty's hair or hugging the female members of her family, but never with her. What was going on?

She shifted to the side and away from him. "Apology accepted."

One of his dark brows winged up, and she rolled her eyes. It wasn't her fault she sounded suspicious. Including yesterday, when he grabbed her wrist to pull her into his condo, she could count the number of times he'd touched her on the fingers of one hand. Something wasn't right here.

Nerves on high alert, she jumped when the studio door suddenly opened, then relaxed as Craig, their sound manager's teenage son, stopped in the doorway.

"Excuse me, Miss Tucker. Is everything okay?" Craig shifted a distrustful gaze to Max. "Is this guy bothering you?"

On the couch behind him, Dan finally looked up. He shrugged a shoulder as if to say, *what are you gonna do*? Amusement tugged at Max's lips.

She ignored him to offer Craig a smile. At seventeen, the boy was still growing into the lanky body he'd inherited from his father. More long bones and knobby knees than bulk, he wouldn't stand a chance against the honed muscle of Max's fighter's body, but she appreciated the unspoken offer.

"I'm fine, Craig. Mr. Grayson is," she turned a pointed gaze on Max, "one of my *father's* friends."

Max shook his head and silent laughter sparkled in his eyes.

She looked away, focusing on Craig. "What are you doing here? I thought today was your day off?"

He swallowed heavily, making his prominent Adam's apple bob. "Dad said you and Spence were working today so I came in to, uh," he hesitated, as if searching for a reason, then punched a thumb over his shoulder, "organize the instrument storage." Subtle color flushed his cheeks and he shuffled his feet. "I was just going to go pick up some lunch, and thought I'd ask if you wanted anything."

"I brought my lunch."

He dropped his gaze to the floor, and she heaved an inward sigh. Painfully obvious in his interest, his embarrassment each time she spoke to him squeezed her heart with sympathy.

"Thank you, though. It was very sweet of you to ask."

"Yeah. Well." He avoided her gaze and turned toward the control room. "I gotta go." He shut the door behind him and quickly disappeared down the hallway.

"He's got it bad."

"He's a good kid." She met Max's gaze with a tight frown. "I've accepted your apology. Why are you still here?"

He propped his hips against a long table against the wall and crossed his arms. "This plan of yours. How did you see it playing out?"

She narrowed her eyes. "Okay, who are you and what have you done with Max?"

He grinned and twin dimples creased his cheeks above the short bristle darkening his jawline. "I'm curious."

She propped her fists on her hips. "You're up to something."

"I'm trying to understand." The smile slid from his handsome face and his intent gaze held her in place. "Security is an unavoidable evil in your position, and yet I've never known you to complain about the necessity. What's changed?"

She stood rooted to the spot, a captive of the slate gray eyes that had starred in her dreams for years. From the night he'd first walked into her dressing room, she'd yearned for the day he'd look at her and see more than his friend's little cousin. He looked at her now, a man watching a woman with a clear desire to understand in his long lashed gaze. She wanted nothing more than to bask in the moment, to savor the warm glow, but his sober study wouldn't let her.

"I'm suffocating, Max." The admission sprang from her lips before she could think.

His brows slammed together and concern sharpened his features.

What the hell? He wanted to know? She'd do her best to explain the unexplainable.

"Do you know, I can't remember the last time I was alone? While I'm on tour, I understand, but here at the studio?" She shot an annoyed glare at her uncharacteristically inattentive driver before meeting Max's gaze once more. "I'm never alone. I can't go shopping or to a movie without someone tagging along. Even in my own condo, there's always someone else around. Someone who reports back to my father. How pitiful is it I look forward to going to the bathroom, just for a moment's solitude?"

She rubbed stiffened fingers over the dull throb in her left temple. "I'm surrounded by people who are living their lives while I'm marking time as mine passes by." There wasn't a thing she could do about the threatening tears burning at the back of her eyes and nose. Though she tried to stop it, a sob hiccupped in her throat. She pressed her fingers to the bridge of her nose and squeezed her eyes shut.

"Jessi."

His low croon wrapped around her and jostled the control that held on by a thread. She dropped her hand and dragged in several deep breaths, then opened her eyes. Other than uncrossing his arms, Max hadn't moved. Understanding darkened the slate of his eyes.

She shook her head. "Contrary to what my father thinks, I'm not stupid. I know he and the family care about me and are doing what they think is best to keep me safe, but lately, it's like I can't breathe."

A muscle twitched along his jaw. "Have you told him how you feel?"

Her laugh was more of a choked cough. "I've tried." Convinced the reference to Suzie in that creepy fan letter was a definite threat, her father wasn't about to back down. A ragged sigh shuddered through her lips. "It's complicated. In the meantime, I'm about to explode."

Max nodded, hands propped on the edge of the table, bracketing his hips. "What about this fictitious boyfriend you're planning to acquire? I assume you mean to move in together, which means you won't be alone there either. Aren't you trading several pairs of watching eyes for another?"

Put that way, it sounded as if she'd gain nothing for her efforts, but at least she'd be out from beneath her family's collective eagle eye. "That's the beauty of my plan. Dad will be happy knowing I have a big strong man watching over me." She rolled her eyes. "But since the relationship won't be a real one, my *boyfriend* won't be scrutinizing my every move, nor will he care what I do with my time. He'll have his space, and I'll have mine."

Max crossed one booted foot over the other. "Knowing your father, any man you choose will be in for a hard time."

"Probably, but I'm a grown woman, and it's about damn time I started living my life on my own terms. Dad will simply have to accept that things have changed."

A doubtful scoff flared his nostrils. "How long do you think it'll take him to get the message?"

She shrugged. First she had to find her fictitious lover, and with Max out of the running, her search had lost much of its appeal. "Once I find my man, I'd give it a couple of weeks. A month at the most."

He stared at her in silence for several heartbeats. "You really plan to go through with this?"

She crossed her arms and nodded. "It's crazy, I know, but it's either this or leave town and not tell my family where I'm living. I'm not willing to do that."

His eyes slid shut briefly. He straightened away from the table and scrubbed a palm over his bristled chin. "I know I'm going to regret this, but if you're determined to go through with this nutty plan, I'm your man."

She managed to choke back her gasp before it could escape, but it was a close thing. Giddy excitement warred with mistrust. Hidden beneath her arms, she curled her suddenly numb fingers into clenched fists. If he was teasing her, it wasn't funny, and she was going to slug him.

"What about Tuck and the rest of the family? Are you really willing to risk their friendship over a plan you think is nuts?" She jacked up her chin. "Because I have other options, you know. Lots of guys would be willing to help me out."

A sardonic smile lifted one corner of his mouth. "No doubt Craig would be first in a long line, but then, you didn't go to another guy. You came to me."

He had a point. The jerk. "And you refused."

"I changed my mind." He propped his hands on his hips and held her gaze. "I'll deal with Tuck and the family, but if we're going to do this, I have a few terms."

Terms? What kind of terms? She narrowed her eyes. "Like?"

"If we're moving in together, we'll be staying at my place. I have a business to run and a match to train for."

Relief loosened her spine. Now *that* was a term she could get behind. With a little luck, she and Max would eventually end up lovers for real, but in the meantime, fooling Aurora and Dan while sharing her condo would be next to impossible. Her pulse picked up and left her short of breath. "I can work with that."

"Second. I'm not your father, but neither am I some random guy you picked up off the street. I've been around enough to understand Ryan's security concerns, so if you're thinking I'll stand by and let you run off, half-cocked without anyone to keep the crazies at bay, you've got the wrong guy."

He held up his hand when she started to object. "You'll have the space you're desperate for, but if you leave the condo or fight center, Dan or I go with you."

She frowned. His terms didn't sound at all like what she had in mind.

"I mean it, Squirt. You said it yourself. I'm the perfect choice because your father will trust me to keep you safe. I can't do that if I'm not with you. I'm risking his and Tuck's friendship by agreeing to this plan. I won't do that just so you can shop alone."

She didn't want him to risk his friendships at all but geez, was she escaping one cage for another? Fierce with conviction, his eyes had the power to make her legs weak, and her frustration fizzled under anticipation. Cage, my ass! If Max was trapped in there with her, she'd gladly throw away the key. This was her chance to win his heart. Spend all her free time with him? Hell, yeah. She could definitely handle that.

"Done." Her curt nod confirmed her agreement.

Suspicion replaced the conviction in his eyes and a sexy wrinkle creased his brow. She nearly smiled. Poor Max. He'd just delivered the means to make her dreams come true. Her sexy cage fighter had no idea what he was in for.

He shook his head and his lips twisted as if what he was about to say left a bad taste in his mouth. "Lastly, I won't have the paparazzi on my doorstep. If they become an issue, I'll call a halt to the whole thing."

Some of her excitement faded. "That's unfair. I can't control the press."

He sighed, and she wondered if he'd changed his mind when his shoulders slumped. "I don't expect you to. Sorry. I don't have a lot of patience when it comes to the press."

No surprise there. Max was nothing if not loyal to his friends, and having grown up together, Max and Gracie Malone were as close as friends could be. Jessi had been busy building her career at the time, but as Tuck's friend, the press's interest in Jake's custody battle with Gracie had come up with regularity at family gatherings. Matters only got worse when Gracie's connection to Tom Walden was consequently revealed. The press had initially crucified the retired, and very married, quarterback with the discovery of his love child.

As with all scandals, the furor over both stories eventually faded, but for those at the center of the storm, the bitter taste remained. Like Gracie, Jake, and Tom, and Tuck for that matter, Max had distrusted the press ever since.

Jessi rested a hand on the bunched muscles of his forearm. "I understand and don't blame you." She dropped her hand to her side. "I can't promise they won't be a problem at some point, but I'll do whatever possible to minimize any contact."

He studied her in silence for a long moment then, with a dip of his chin, he held out his hand. "Then we have a deal."

Chapter 5

"Breathe, Jessi. They're your family, not a firing squad."

"Easy for you to say." Jessi stopped with her hand on the doorknob of Tuck's Long Island home and shot Max a smirk over one shoulder. "If they freak out and decide to lock me in the basement, you'll be free to walk out the door with a whistle on your lips."

"And a couple black eyes." His dimples made an appearance and his eyes twinkled with mirth.

Less than six hours had passed since they'd shaken hands in her studio, and the speed with which he'd put her plan into motion left her dizzy. As bold as can be, he'd wrapped his arm around her shoulders and led her into the control room. "Congratulate us, Dan," he announced. "We're in love." The comically stunned look on her driver's face, as he scrambled to his feet and followed them to the car, was priceless. Aurora had been no less shocked when they'd arrived at Jessi's condo so Max could help her pack. An hour later, her things were ensconced in his spare bedroom, but to the world, they were living together.

No doubt Dan had already filed a full report. Her father would be in attendance for tonight's family dinner, and if Tuck and the others had yet to hear of her and Max's new relationship status, it wouldn't be long. Yet, instead of the reservations she expected, Max acted as if he was actually looking forward to the coming confrontation.

She frowned and turned back to the door. "Why are you so calm? I'm about to pee my pants."

His low chuckle skittered over her tightly stretched nerves as he stepped closer to her back. He dipped his head to bring his mouth close to her ear. "First rule of battle, Squirt. Never let the enemy see you sweat."

The chilly January evening wasn't responsible for her shiver. His big body surrounded hers, and she had to fight the competing urges to turn and burrow into his arms…or run like hell. A rough sigh lifted her shoulders. "Yeah, but these people aren't the enemy. They're my family, for heaven's sake." Her stare bored into the wooden door inches from her nose. "I'm about to tell my family a gargantuan lie." With a groan, she dropped her head back. It bumped his shoulder. She straightened immediately and scrunched her eyes closed. "Oh, Lord, why the hell didn't that inconvenient truth dawn on me before now?"

He didn't give her a chance to answer her own question. Covering her hand with his, he twisted the knob. The door opened with a quiet snick. Her eyes popped open, and she bit her lip against a guilty whimper. At the far end of the open floor plan, the kitchen teemed with familiar faces, several of whom looked their way. Tuck's dirty blond brows arched to his hairline as his gaze zeroed in on her and Max.

"Too late now. It's show time." Max's deep whisper tickled her ear. Before she could respond, he used the hand on her lower back to turn her until she faced him.

As he lowered his head toward hers, she slapped a hand to his chest. "What are you doing?" The shocked demand came out in a quiet squeak. Her stiffened arm did her little good. He drew her closer.

"Making sure your plan works."

Her world tumbled as he covered her mouth with his. Stunned pleasure liquefied her limbs. With her fingers clenched in the soft material of his sweater, she held on for dear life. The animal heat of his body swirled around her and seeped into her tingling skin as his mouth introduced her to his taste and scent. Spicy man and power. An intoxicating combination.

No simple peck on the lips, this. His tongue swept the seam of her mouth. Helpless to resist, she complied. Opening her lips to welcome him inside, she savored the rich combination of heat and silk as his tongue tangled with hers in a sensual dance. A willing moan gurgled in her throat, and she squirmed in giddy delight as he pulled her tight against the muscular frame that had starred in countless of her fantasies over the years.

Good. So good.

If his plan was to put on a show for the family, he did one hell of a bang-up job. Talk about an Oscar worthy performance. She willingly stepped into the role of supporting actress.

The chiseled contours of his competitor's body molded to her curves, squashing her breasts to the muscled plains of his chest. Her back arched over his strong arm, and he deepened the kiss, bending her to his will and devouring her mouth in a thrilling claiming. Pleasure danced with elation as the bulge of his swelling erection pressed against her lower belly.

A kaleidoscope of color swirled behind her closed eyelids. Tongues of white-hot flame licked through her, all racing toward a common destination. She squeezed her legs together as waves of pleasure suddenly pulsed between her thighs.

Oh dear God. Don't do it. Don't you dare have an orgasm in your cousin's foyer. With your family watching! Horror doused her like the splash of an icy puddle on a wintery Manhattan street.

She squirmed in his arms, unclenching her fingers to press against his chest, and he slowly straightened and broke the kiss. Her eyes popped open. Breathing heavily, she stared into his darkened gaze, but how was she to read what she saw there with her head spinning and her pulse racing?

"Oh, Max. You always did have incredible timing."

Yanked from the sensual vortex, Jessi turned her head and winced as she met the anxious gaze of Gracie Malone across the distance. Beside her, with his large hands slapped over the giggling Malone twins' eyes, her husband, Jake, twisted his lips as he fought a grin. To Jake's left, V, his lifelong friend and publicist, bared her teeth in a smile. CC stood with her mouth open in a comical "Oh." Tuck scowled.

The rest of her family stared at them with varying degrees of shock and humor. Her cousin, Tim, started to laugh. Unable to avoid doing so any longer, she glanced at her father. Expecting condemnation, she was surprised by the steady speculation in his eyes.

"I see Dan spoke the truth." More statement than question, her father directed the comment at Max.

Jessi swallowed a groan and untangled herself from Max's hold. "Dad, I—"

Max stopped her with a hand on her arm. She turned to look at him, but his gaze was locked on her father.

"With all due respect, sir, your daughter and I have had feelings for one another for a while."

Tuck started to cough. CC pounded him on the back. Jessi shot him a glare.

Max ignored them all. "We've decided it's time to explore those feelings and see where they lead. We came here tonight to tell everyone because we didn't want to sneak around behind your backs."

Jessi stared at Max's hard profile. Despite his tough-guy looks, he tended toward carefree and charming. Sure, when bluntness was called for, he had no problem delivering a stinging rebuke, but she'd never known him to be dishonest, with anyone. Yet, he'd made his declaration sound like the honest to God truth.

His intent gaze swept the room, and she held her breath. "If any of you have a problem with that, take it up with me."

Her breath came out in a whoosh at his blatant dare. *Oh, Lord. Here we go.*

Tuck rolled his shoulders, but CC's hand to his arm stopped whatever he might have said. Her father shocked the hell out of Jessi by holding up a hand and dipping his chin in a slight nod. A long moment passed as everyone stared in stunned silence.

"Well, then. Is anyone else hungry?" Gracie's falsely jovial voice pierced the absolute quiet, and she shot Max a strained smile. "Because this preggo is starving."

"Ditto." CC snapped into action, patting her rounded belly, and turning to her husband. "Fire up the grill, Tuck. Your son needs sustenance."

The dual prenatal demands shattered the palsy that had fallen over the room, and everyone began speaking at once. Jessi spent the next ten minutes fielding teasing questions from CC, Gracie, V, and her cousin, Patty, as Max disappeared outside with Tuck.

After the display she and Max put on, she expected her father to march her upstairs to demand answers, but he'd apparently assigned the task to Tim. Her cousin cornered her in the kitchen the moment he got the chance.

Big and blond, he resembled Tuck in more than just looks. Like his older brother, he could be a smart ass, but he also had his serious side. The problem was, she was never sure which Tim would show up.

"You sure know how to make an entrance, Jess."

Okay, she'd be dealing with the smart ass tonight. She jacked up her chin and batted her lashes. "It's a gift."

He chuckled and shook his head. "In the meantime, how am I supposed to handle things for you if I don't know what's happening?"

Her gaze locked on his in an even stare. "You manage my career, cousin. Not my personal life."

He tipped his beer bottle to his lips with a shrug. "In this case, it's kind of the same thing."

"No, it isn't, and I'm telling you right now, my relationship with Max is off limits, so butt out."

He actually looked hurt, and she sighed. As her manager, Tim had more reason to stay on her case than anyone else in the family, yet when it came to her life off the stage, he didn't hover like the rest of them. In fact, he ran interference more often than not.

She rested a hand on his arm and squeezed. "I'm sorry, but you know what I mean."

"Unfortunately, I do, but this is different. If the press gets wind you're involved with a man, any man, it'll have everything to do with your career. Unless you plan to keep Max hidden from the media?"

Her gaze slid to the closed back door. "I'd be wasting my time. Max isn't the type of man who blends into the background."

Tim's grunt drew her gaze.

"From that kiss, I'd say he has no intention of trying."

Since there was no way she could hide the blush heating her cheeks, she didn't bother with an attempt. She jammed an elbow in his side. "Shut up."

He laughed and slung an arm around her shoulders. "Call me tomorrow and we'll work out a press release."

"Um. About that." She peeked up at him with a grimace. "Max has a little bit of an issue with the press, and…."

"And?"

"I sort of…moved into his place this afternoon."

Surprise lit his deep blue eyes and his teeth flashed in a grin. He glanced around, then dipped his head close to hers. "Good for you." His voice dropped to a serious whisper. "It's your life, Jess. Don't let the family or anyone else keep you from grabbing hold of what makes you happy."

His typical, unconditional support made love bubble in her heart, but her smile was wry. "Easier said than done. This thing between me and Max is complicated."

"The important things in life usually are." He straightened and gave her shoulders a squeeze. "I'll talk to Max about the release. We'll keep it as low key as possible, but we're going to have to say something. In the meantime, do me a favor?"

"What's that?"

"The next time you and Max decide to melt each other's circuits, do it in private. If the public witnesses the steam coming off the two of you, we'll have a circus on our hands."

* * * *

"I hope you know what you're doing."

Max stiffened at the quietly spoken accusation and dragged his gaze from his view into the kitchen through the window where Jessi blushed under the bombardment of questions. He faced Tuck and stifled a wince at his friend's narrow-eyed stare.

Damn it, only a few hours into this ill-advised farce and he'd already made a tactical error. Kissing Jessi may have been the most efficient way to stop her doubts in their tracks, but like all bad ideas, it hadn't been thought through. He eyed the three-inch prongs of the barbeque fork in

Tuck's hand. So far, the lethal looking utensil wasn't buried in his chest. Max hoped to keep it that way.

He heaved an uncomfortable sigh. "So do I."

Tuck flicked a quick glance toward the house. "What happened to the imaginary romance idea?"

"Nothing. The plan hasn't changed."

Nostrils flaring in a snort, Tuck winged a challenging brow. "There was nothing imaginary about that kiss, buddy. You looked like you were giving her a tonsillectomy with your tongue."

Guilt prickled at the base of Max's spine. He hadn't intended to take the kiss so far, but his intentions were derailed the moment Jessi melted against him. Midnight fantasies were nothing compared to the reality of holding her in his arms. With her curves pressed close, there had been no room for concerns over the nine-year age span between them *or* their avid audience. The cold hard fact was, seduced by her sultry sex flavor exploding in his mouth, his body didn't give a flying fuck who her family was.

He could only imagine what Tuck and the others saw. He'd been in the grip of an elemental need to stake a claim and to hell with the consequences. Thank God Jessi had come to her senses because he'd lost his, and nothing good would come of letting her believe their time together was anything other than a means to an end. He wasn't the man for her and the sooner he convinced her of that, the better. Unfortunately, spending the next few weeks with the taste and feel of her lingering in his mind would only make the task at hand more difficult.

"It was meant to look convincing. She was having second thoughts." He hated the defensiveness of his tone, but it couldn't be helped. He'd fucked up and knew it. "Would you prefer I'd let her call a halt to her plan and strike out on her own?"

Tuck jabbed the fork at one of several thick steaks sizzling on the grill, his voice a rumble of frustration. "I'd prefer none of this was necessary, but you know my cousin. That kiss is going to give her ideas."

Which was exactly why Max never should have touched her. He scraped at the label on his bottle with his thumbnail. "Ideas she'll have to forget."

Tuck laughed deep in his throat. "Yeah, good luck with that. This is Jessi we're talking about. She's had the hots for you since the day the two of you met and has finally come up with a plan to reel you in. Face it, pal, when she gets an idea in her head, she doesn't let go without a fight."

Panic prickled at the back of his neck. He glanced toward the kitchen window and frowned as Jessi laughed at something Tim whispered in her ear. Tuck's warning wasn't necessary. Her tenacity was the reason Max had gone out of his way to avoid the sexy little crooner for the past five years, and his loss of reason when he'd finally put his hands on her only emphasized the validity of that evasion.

He turned to glower at his friend. "Then why the hell would you agree with Ryan that I should accept her proposition? Aren't you afraid I'm going to hurt her?"

"Do you plan to?"

He jammed a hand through his hair in agitation. "Not purposefully. I care about her, too, you know."

"Good to know." Tuck crossed his arms and the tines of the fork stuck up beside his head like some kind of satanic staff. "But that's not what I meant. That was a very pretty speech you gave but then, a bluff is always more convincing when it contains an element of truth."

Max dropped his arm to his side and bristled at the insinuation that skimmed a little too close to the truth for his liking. "What the hell is that supposed to mean? The plan was to make everyone believe we're a couple. That's what I've done."

Cocking his head, Tuck peeled his lips back in a leering grin. "Jessi wasn't the only one huffing and puffing after that kiss. I've watched you twist yourself into a pretzel in an effort to steer clear of her all these years. There are only three reasons a man goes to that much trouble to avoid a woman. She's either married, ugly enough to choke a dog, or he's attracted and the idea scares the shit out of him."

Since married and ugly didn't apply in Jessi's case, Tuck's meaning was crystal clear…and right. Damn it. Still, what the hell was wrong with him? He knew Max's track record with women. Tuck should be pissed at the thought of his little cousin throwing herself at a man like him, not grinning like an ass.

"What's your point? That your cousin is a beautiful woman?" His snort was short and dismissive. "A man would have to be blind not to notice, but she's far too young for an old street fighter like me. Besides, she's the picket fence and babies type. You know I don't do permanent."

"Be careful, Max." Tuck dropped his arms to flip a steak onto the large platter beside the grill. "Until the day I laid eyes on CC, I sang that same tune."

Unease slithered up Max's spine to wrap around his throat in a chokehold. He grunted. "Fuck you. This situation is entirely different."

Tuck chuckled and shook his head. "Is it? CC and I had a plan, too, remember? A temporary arrangement that didn't include picket fences and babies." He glanced around the sprawling grounds of his suburban home. "Look at us now."

What Max remembered was goading Tuck at every opportunity as he'd watched his confirmed bachelor friend fall hard and fast for his future wife. At the time, their relatively new friendship had included a harmless but intense game of one-upmanship as they chased after the same women. By Max's estimation, they'd been about even in the list of women they'd stolen out from under each other's noses, but when CC arrived on the scene and Max had shown an interest in adding her to his list, the game lost all appeal for Tuck.

Was that what this was about? A little payback? Screw that. If Tuck planned to get a few laughs at his expense by pushing the idea of him and Jessi as a real couple, he had another think coming. "It's not the same. Jessi isn't CC, and the last woman I'd take to bed is the darling princess of those I consider friends."

Surprised understanding flashed in Tuck's eyes as they studied him. He said nothing for a long moment, then cocked his head as if in speculation. "Is that right?"

Gritting his teeth, Max held his friend's challenging gaze. "Damn straight it is. I agreed to help until the asshole threatening Jessi is caught. When he is, I'll deliver her back to the family unharmed *and* untouched."

A sly smile pulled at Tuck's lips. "I've got a C-note that says you'll fold like a bad hand of cards the first time she takes a shower, then has to skip through your condo in a hand towel because she's *forgotten* her clothes."

Unbidden, the image of Jessi, dripping wet and naked, flashed through Max's head and the hard-on that hadn't quite subsided since that gut-wrenching kiss pulsed with new life. She wouldn't dare. Oh, hell. Knowing Jessi, yes, she would.

He slammed his mind's door on the tempting vision. Shit, what had he gotten himself into?

Chapter 6

Jessi swallowed as Max ushered her inside his quiet condo. The night had gone far better than expected, with even her father accepting their surprising status as a couple at face value. However, despite the seeming success of her plan, it appeared Max had been correct in his predictions where they applied to Tuck. Though her cousin showed no discernible signs of anger after he and Max came in from the patio, something uncomfortable had obviously passed between them.

No one but she and Gracie, whose smile remained forced throughout the evening, seemed to notice how tense and withdrawn Max had become, despite the typical laughter and teasing around the table. The evening had dragged on interminably for Jessi. By the time the meal was over and they donned their coats to leave, a headache stabbed at her left temple and guilt bunched her shoulder muscles until they ached.

After that soul-stealing kiss, the last thing she wanted was to call a halt to their deal, but it was no use. She couldn't go through with this farce. Not at the expense of Max and Tuck's friendship. She needed to fix things before they got any worse.

The door clicked shut behind them and she turned. Somber and steady, Max's gray gaze met hers, and a piercing sadness squeezed her heart.

She forced her lips into a smile. "You were right."

"About what?" He stepped farther into the room and shrugged out of his coat.

Pain throbbed behind her eyes. She blinked and dropped her chin to busy herself with removing her gloves. "This." She looked up and swung a hand in an encompassing arch. "All of this. It was a stupid idea, and I'm sorry I dragged you into it."

His bark of laughter had all the humor of a car wreck. "You'll get no argument from me there." He turned away and tossed his coat across the back of the couch. "Anyway, it's done. Your family believes we're a couple. Let's hope your adoring public is as easily fooled."

She stared at his broad back and absorbed the hurt his dismissive words caused. The only man she'd ever truly wanted saw her as nothing but a chore, and an odious one at that. Ego demanded she make him pay for the ache that knowledge caused, but her breaking heart simply wanted this painful episode done.

"That won't be necessary."

He glanced over one shoulder, a question in his intent gaze.

Her throat contracted on a swallow. "I'll call Tuck and explain everything, but if you wouldn't mind me staying for tonight, I'd rather not disturb Dan or my father until the morning."

Turning slowly, he faced her fully and crossed his arms. "You're throwing in the towel?" His question held more than a hint of surprise.

"I wouldn't classify it that way. More like recalculating." She frowned and bumped up her chin. "I know you think I'm a spoiled little bitch, but I don't purposefully hurt the people I care about."

An instant scowl wrinkled his forehead, and he dropped his arms to his sides. "Hold it right there, Squirt. Don't put words in my mouth."

"I'm not." Okay, maybe she was, but he was making her mad, and her head was killing her. She needed a pill and a dark room. The sooner he let her say her piece, the sooner she could find both. "I'm trying to let you off the hook, you jerk."

"Is that right?"

Nodding was a mistake. Tiny knives slashed at her brain.

At her uncontrollable wince, his gaze narrowed in on her face. "What's the matter with you?"

She didn't bother answering. Slipping the purse from her shoulder, she yanked it open. Her hand shook as she dug through the contents.

His sigh was long and drawn out. "So, you're cutting me loose. Then what?"

"I don't know yet, but I'll figure something out." Head bowed and eyes squinted against the throbbing pain, her fingers fumbled with the inner zippered pocket of her purse. "Damn it!"

Before she could find the prescription bottle she knew was in there somewhere, he stepped forward and gripped her arm to pull her toward the couch. "Sit down before you fall down." He lowered her to the cushions. "What is it, a headache?"

She slammed her eyes shut on a white-hot lash of agony. "Migraine."

The purse slid from her fingers, and she slapped her hands over her eyes. She'd waited too long, and now she would pay. The sound of pills clicking in a bottle made her whimper.

"How many?" His deep voice battered about inside her head.

"Please, stop yelling." She dragged in a harsh breath. "One for now."

"Do you need a drink to wash it down?" His low croon was less painful, but the words still cracked against her skull.

She moved her head in an abbreviated shake, and jumped when a warm finger brushed over her bottom lip. Opening her mouth, she stuck out her tongue so he could deliver the pill. Her throat convulsed on a desperate swallow.

She knew from experience the next half hour would be an agonizing waiting game and only luck would keep her stomach from revolting. The odds of that happening increased when Max tucked one arm beneath her thighs and the other behind her back to lift her in his arms. She smashed her lips together as he spun around and they began to move. Jaw locked shut, she didn't bother voicing a complaint. At the moment, she simply didn't have the strength.

Cool and crisp, the pillow cradled her head as he gently lowered her to her back. She squinted through half closed lids to find he'd delivered her to the darkened guest bedroom. She lay still, the pinpoint of her vision on his intent face as he pulled one arm from her coat and then the next. Once he'd slipped off her shoes, he disappeared into the attached bath. She curled into a ball and closed her eyes.

Breathe, Jessi. In and out, in and out.

She didn't open her eyes as he tugged bedding over her shoulders and placed a cool cloth on her forehead.

"There's a basin on the nightstand right beside you. Call out if you need me."

* * * *

Jessi sighed deeply, slid the phone from the pocket of her slacks, and checked the time. One twenty-six. Roughly an hour had passed since Max had tucked her in, and though the migraine had dwindled to a simple headache, experience told her another pill was necessary if she didn't want a repeat of the earlier attack. Tossing aside the bedding, she sat up gingerly and went in search of her pills.

Other than the quiet hum of the refrigerator, the condo was silent. A lamp burned beside the couch. Her purse sat on the stone coffee table. After retrieving the prescription bottle, she padded into the kitchen. Her mouth was as dry as the Sahara, and with the threat of puking less likely, she was willing to take a chance at drinking something. The refrigerator contained several types of juice, but none appealed at the moment. She bypassed them for a bottle of spring water.

Swallowing a pill, her gaze wandered to the closed door of Max's bedroom. The swift onset of her migraine had interrupted the dissolution of their agreement, but what, really, was left to be said? Her boyfriend plan was a bust and the sooner she patched things up between Max and Tuck the sooner she could stop feeling like a total shit.

Unfortunately, that conversation would have to wait until morning. She wasn't about to call Dan at this hour either, but cab companies ran all night. She didn't belong here. It was time to go home.

She rounded the kitchen island to retrieve her coat and shoes from the bedroom but stopped short and stared at the open front door. Unease lifted the fine hair on her arms and neck. What the hell? She distinctly remembered Max closing the door when they arrived. Why was it open now?

A metallic clank reached her ears, and she cocked her head to listen. Someone was downstairs in the fight center. Oh, shit. Adrenaline pumped in her veins and her gaze flew to Max's bedroom door. Oh, God. Was he being robbed on top of everything else?

She tiptoed across the room and didn't bother knocking. Twisting the knob, she stepped over the threshold as the door swung open on silent hinges.

"Max?" Not daring to turn on a light, she made her whisper louder. "Max!"

Only the occasional clink from downstairs met her call. Squinting through the darkness, she eyed his crisply made, empty bed. Fear slid into relief, and she slumped against the doorjamb. Okay, false alarm. Max wasn't asleep after all. She looked over her shoulder. Obviously, the noise from downstairs came from him.

She crossed to the condo's open front door, then moved down the hallway to the stairs on silent feet. Hesitating, she bent at the waist and peeked over the railing on the off chance a crazy exercise nut had murdered Max and was working out before he left.

Nope, no crazies, unless she wanted to count crazy gorgeous. Shirtless, in a pair of washed out shorts that hugged his thick thighs, Max stood with his arms widespread before a floor to ceiling mirror. A pair of large, chunky gray weights were in his fisted hands. The muscles in his back bunched as his arms rose toward the ceiling. With a clank, the weights met high above his head before he lowered his arms once more.

Not wishing to disturb him, but having no choice, Jessi moved down a few steps as he repeated the move in several more reps. He must have caught her reflection in the mirror because he dropped his arms to his sides and turned.

"Feeling better?"

"Much." Embarrassed at more than just his witnessing her at such a weak moment, she forced a smile and descended the remaining steps. "Thanks for helping earlier."

He nodded silently and turned to set the weights on a shelf holding others of varying size.

"I don't mean to interrupt."

He turned his head. "You're not."

She bit her bottom lip. Knowing Max, he wasn't going to be happy when she announced her intention to call a cab, and she wasn't up for an argument. She delayed the inevitable by crossing the room. A single stationary bike sat against one wall. She climbed on as he grabbed a towel from a nearby rack and wiped his face.

Casting about for something to say, her gaze was drawn to the glisten of sweat on his muscled chest. God, he was beautiful. At six foot, he moved with an animal grace that never failed to leave her insides quivering. Like a jungle cat, his sleekly sculpted, olive-toned skin covered a body that whispered of unleashed power.

What would it be like to be held beneath his body as she stared into his soul through those mesmerizing gray eyes? If his kiss was any indication, making love with him would be like touching the sun. Hot, all encompassing, and more than a little dangerous. Danger she'd gladly face, but though she yearned to ask him why he'd kissed her, and beg him to please do it again, what would be the point? He'd made his reluctant acceptance of the situation more than clear, and she was through chasing after a fantasy that would never be.

The cold hard truth was, she'd made a mess of things. They'd never be lovers as she'd hoped, and she'd have to accept that. Though their friendship had never been an easy one, she couldn't stand the thought of losing that, too. She cleared her throat. "Do you always work out in the middle of the night?"

In the low light, his eyes were as dark as a stormy sea as they appeared above the white cloth. "Only when I can't sleep."

"I compose when I can't sleep." She slipped her socked feet onto the pedals and pushed down. The bike's belt began to hum. She tossed him a self-deprecating grin. "The lyrics seldom make any sense in the morning, however."

He rewarded her with a quiet chuckle.

"Sorry about earlier. I shouldn't have waited so long before taking a pill. I know better."

Tossing aside the towel, he straddled the bench beside the bike. "How long have you been having migraines?"

She met his gaze and held it. There was no judgment in his eyes, only curiosity. "About a year."

"Does the family know?"

Of course he'd ask. The family kept tabs on her every move. She shrugged a shoulder as if it didn't matter. "Tim does. I had one about a month ago after a show. He was there, and Aurora found the prescription bottle in my bathroom. Dan immediately informed Dad."

Max didn't comment on her disgruntled tone. He simply nodded. "They're often caused by stress."

Talk about pointing out the obvious. She shot him a sidelong smirk. "Thank you, Doctor Grayson. I wasn't aware of that."

A dimple popped with his smile. She ignored the fluttering in her belly. Tonight was the one and only night she and Max would be spending together, and they'd be doing it fully clothed. She eyed the tattoo riding his muscled shoulder and pec. Correction, *she* was fully clothed—but for her shoes—and the damn butterflies in her belly would just have to learn to live with disappointment.

She shook her head. "How do you know so much about migraines?"

He leaned forward with his elbows propped on his lower thighs, and her eyes were drawn to his big hands dangling between his knees.

"My mother suffered from them."

"Your mother?" Her gaze flew to his face. "I thought you grew up in foster care." She could have bitten her tongue the moment the words left her mouth. Her nose scrunched in a wince. "Sorry, that was rude."

Surprisingly, humor twinkled in his eyes. "It's not rude if it's the truth. I wasn't always a foster kid. My father died when I was twelve. Mom died a year later."

Her legs quit pumping and the bike's belt stilled. "Oh, Max. I'm so sorry."

One of his shoulders jerked in a stilted shrug. "It was a long time ago."

She studied his chiseled face. The subtle remnants of old grief pulled at her heart from his proud features, but she understood the gut-wrenching hole left behind after the loss of a parent. She'd lived with the knowledge for the last fifteen years. Leaning toward him, she rested a hand on his shoulder. "That's just a platitude people use. I lost my mom when I was ten, so I know how it feels."

The muscles beneath her fingers contracted before he visibly relaxed. "The family mentions her occasionally, but I've never heard how your mom died."

She pulled back her hand and looked down at her slacks, fighting against the anger that still fired whenever she thought of her mother's senseless murder. Talking about those dark days made her uncomfortable, but she wanted to reestablish their friendship. He'd shared something she hadn't known about him. The least she could do was reciprocate.

"She was a family counselor for the state. Mostly she worked with battered women." Her gaze lifted to lock on his. "A client's estranged husband caught her and her client one day as they were leaving the courthouse. He shot them both before turning the gun on himself."

"Jesus." His eyes slid shut, and he pinched the bridge of his nose.

"Dad was devastated, and for a long time I was lost." A cleansing breath heaved her chest. "But the family pulled together and propped the both of us up until we were ready to face life again. Like you said. It was a long time ago, but I still miss her."

She began to pedal once more. "Mom was the one who took me to my first singing lesson. Her dream was to see me perform at the Grand Ole Opry."

He dropped his hand to his thigh and opened his eyes. "Which you have."

She nodded and with a smile marred by a familiar sadness, she held his gaze. "Thanks to the family...and Dad. He did what was necessary to help me achieve Mom's dream."

Understanding darkened Max's eyes, and she stilled on the bike.

Her fingers clenched the handlebars tighter. "I owe him more than I can ever repay, Max." Sudden tears burned at the backs of her eyelids, then flooded her vision in an uncontrollable surge. "My stupid plan was an act of desperation. I owe him everything, but I'm losing myself. If something doesn't change, I'm afraid I'm going to disappear." A sob caught in her throat, and she squeezed her eyes shut as the dam inside her broke. "I didn't mean to hurt anyone, least of all you, but I didn't know what else to do."

"Jessi."

His soft croon slammed into the well of confusion she'd been fighting for so many months, and it spilled over into a raging storm of grief. She dropped her head to the bike's bars and willed herself to regain control.

He already thought of her as a silly little girl. Hysterics would only add to his perception.

Strong arms pulled her from the bike as the breakdown she'd feared gained force. He handled her gently, lowering to the bench once more and settling her on his lap with his thick thighs cradling her bottom and his arms holding her close. Surrounded by him, she didn't want to push away. His strength and support were too tempting to resist, like a miraculous lifeline in the midst of a madness that had haunted her for too long. She burrowed closer, unable to contain the wracking sobs.

"Shhh." The shell of her ear heated beneath his whispered reassurance. "It's going to be okay, baby." The endearment only made matters worse, and she choked on a strangled moan.

He rocked her as he dragged a hand down the length of her hair. "Do you trust me?"

Did he have to ask? She nodded against his chest. "You know I do. I wouldn't have come to you otherwise." She pressed even closer when his arms tightened around her.

"Then I don't want to hear any more talk of you leaving. I promised to help you find your way. That's what I mean to do."

A crazy tangle of hope, excitement, and relief twisted in her chest. "But Tuck—" A strangled hiccup cut off her argument.

"Let me handle your cousin. If he's the friend I know him to be, he'll...."

She held her breath when he hesitated. It came out in a whoosh as he rubbed his chin over the top of her head in what her heart insisted was a caress.

"He'll come around."

Chapter 7

Max stared after the town car as it pulled away from the curb. Dan would watch over Jessi while she was at the studio, and the team Ryan had hired wouldn't be far away. She was safe. For now. If only he could say the same for himself.

Tuck was right on when he accused Max of being scared. He was scared shitless. Comforting her in the low light of the closed fight center had been too right, too honest for his own good. He had no business yearning for a woman like Jessi. No business holding her so close he couldn't distinguish between his heartbeat and hers. Tangling himself up with Tuck's cousin would only lead to heartache, for both of them, but for the time being, that was exactly what Max was going to do.

Turning away, he hefted the strap of his duffle over his shoulder, and as he did every morning, headed for the west side. The fifteen block walk to his original business location normally cleared his head. Not so this morning. Images of Jessi falling apart in his arms haunted him.

Forget the asshole threatening her in the letters. Did Ryan know how close to the edge his daughter was teetering? Did she?

For years, he'd watched her work her ass off with a determined focus rare in a girl so young. He didn't have to imagine the horror clawing at her soul with her mother's murder. He'd lived it himself and had a front row seat to his mother's downward spiral after his father had been killed in the line of duty. Learning the source of Jessi's single-minded focus on her career, he now understood why she hadn't simply told her family to fuck off. But at what cost?

I'm losing myself. If something doesn't change, I'm afraid I'm going to disappear.

He recalled her saying she suffered from horrible stage fright on the night he'd first seen her perform, the night they'd first met. He'd scoffed at the idea at the time. No one who owned the stage the way Jessi did could fear it as she claimed, but was he wrong? Were Tuck and Ryan and the rest of the family? Did she perform because it was expected of her? Sing, because her mother had wanted it so? Would she walk away from it all if given the chance or, like her father, did she truly share her mother's dream?

She'd been a child when her mother died, and she had thrown herself into her music career, but had she ever taken the time to consider other options? Probably not. Hell, when would she have had the time? When had she last allowed herself a break from the rigorous schedule required of her?

She'd laughed and insisted Spence would blow a fuse when Max suggested she sleep in this morning to recuperate after last night's migraine and emotional draining. Over the next few days, she and her singing partner had a CD to finish and an awards show performance as well as a concert in Dallas, and that was just this week. From there on, her schedule would take her to a dozen different cities, including a Super Bowl appearance, eight concert stops, and multiple smaller events. Max applauded her work ethic, but something had to give.

Next week was her lightest, but that still left a photo shoot and a fancy dinner to celebrate the opening of a new wing at the Country Music Museum in Nashville. If she didn't take some time to decompress, she would eventually disappear for real, emotionally or literally. With a crazy fan gunning for her, she couldn't afford either.

He frowned as he pushed open the door to his west side location. Behind the front counter, Vern looked up. The twist of the old man's lips that passed for a welcoming smile immediately died on his time-battered face and concern fired in his faded blue eyes.

"What's wrong?"

Max shoved aside thoughts of Jessi to offer his old friend, and his general manager, a smile. "Nothing. Any problems I need to know about?"

"Are there ever?" An affronted snort blew from Vern's bulbous nose as he bent to retrieve a file from behind the counter. "Kid, I've been running fight outfits since long before you were a twinkle in your daddy's eye. I've gone up against more hard-ass cases with fuck-you attitudes than you'll ever meet in your life." He shoved the folder at Max. "You think I can't handle a bunch of yuppie millennials jogging on treadmills?"

Max dropped his head to hide a smile. Though Vern had never made the big time, he'd spent the better part of sixty years laced up in the ring when he wasn't taking on one of his "projects" as he referred to the troubled youth he'd taken under his wing. His face bore the scars of his chosen trade, but the beat and battered bear had the instincts of a mother hen.

As a sixteen-year-old, smart-mouthed punk with a giant chip on his shoulder, Max had been one of those hard cases and credited the rough-edged boxer with saving his life. He'd learned long ago not to argue when the old pugilist was on a tear.

Vern folded his arms against his barrel chest. "Tina called. Said you need an extra body over at your other building for the next few weeks to help man the front." He pointed a gnarled finger, bent and swollen with arthritis, at the file. "That's the monthly report. I had Andy put it together."

Max sucked at his top teeth. Quick to champion those he found worthy, Andy was Vern's latest project.

"He's good with numbers." Vern pressed as if expecting an argument. "And he's got cage fever. He's doing fine here, but he's itching to get over to your other place where the real action is."

Max chuckled. Of course he was. The kid was dying to climb into the cage, but working his way through school, he didn't have the funds to train. Max could empathize. He'd been in Andy's shoes not so very long ago.

He glanced around the busy gym. Close to fifty patrons sweated through their morning workouts. Many more would flow through throughout the day and evening. While he'd worked his ass off to attain success here and was proud of the accomplishment, the traditional gym had been, and continued to be, a means to an end. Lacking the capital to implement his ultimate dream, he'd been forced to put that plan on hold until the income from nearly two thousand gym memberships could supplement the lower profits the cage training facility he envisioned would produce.

Thanks to the unexpected inheritance from his long-dead mother, the wait had been cut down considerably and the reality of his fight center across town, with its second floor living quarters, far exceeded his expectations. The irony of the situation never ceased to bring him a keen sense of satisfaction. With his grandfather's death, what his grandparents had stolen from their daughter in life, had been returned tenfold to their unrecognized grandson.

Dolling out a healthy chunk of cash to the son of a New York cop must have eaten at the old bat's gut. Elizabeth Krandall had done everything in her power to have her husband's will nullified, but in the end, Max's grandmother had been forced to accept defeat. He planned to hand her another with the acquisition of Haven Place.

"If you don't think he's ready..." Disappointment filled Vern's voice as he trailed off.

Max shook off thoughts of justice and met his waiting gaze. "If you believe the kid is ready, send him over."

A grunt growled in the old man's throat. "I'll do that."

"I'll be in my office most of the day. If he can't talk to me before I leave, have him stop by the other building tomorrow morning. Which reminds me. I've got a commitment in the city tomorrow night, but then I'm leaving town for a few days. You have my number if anything comes up."

Vern dropped his chin in a nod. Having never married, Max and the gym employees were Vern's family, and the gym wasn't just a job, it was his home. He ran a tight ship and wasn't one to panic over the small stuff. Max wouldn't hear from him unless something catastrophic happened.

Max greeted several long-time patrons as he made his way to the small office at the back of the building. He tossed the report on his desk as he passed and pulled a water bottle from the small fridge in the closet. Settled into his ancient office chair, he pulled the phone from his pocket and thumbed the keypad. A knock interrupted before he could place the call.

"Are you busy?" Blond curls tucked beneath a chic fedora, Gracie tilted her head through the half-opened door.

His shoulders heaved in a sigh. He should have expected her to show up this morning. They'd been friends too long for her to let last night's fiasco go by without demanding answers. She had, in fact, saved him the effort of calling her, but knowing what was coming, he couldn't help poking her a little.

"If I say yes, will you go away?"

She rolled her eyes and straightened, stepped into the office, and pulled the door shut behind her.

He set the phone aside. "I'll take that as a no."

Although pregnancy had further rounded the womanly curves she'd developed over time, shades of the brave but scrawny little girl he'd met and befriended in the dingy hallway of one of New York's low rent apartment tenements showed in her toothy smirk.

She crossed to the old couch against the wall, sat, and tugged the hat from her head. "You know you're going to tell me eventually, so you might as well spill it. What's going on?"

"I thought I made it pretty clear last night. Jessie and I are dating."

"Why?"

"What kind of question is that?" He dropped his gaze to her impressive baby bump. "Considering your current condition, I would think you'd understand. She's a woman. I'm a man."

Her nostrils flared in an unladylike sniff. "Uh-huh. For years, you've eyed Jessi Tucker like she was the last piece of chocolate cake, yet every time I suggested you do something about it, you told me she wasn't your type."

He twisted his lips in his best imitation of a sheepish smile. "You're right. That was an excuse. The truth is, I'm shy."

An exasperated huff blew through her lips. "I'm serious."

"So am I. You women scare me."

She narrowed her gaze and crossed her arms over her extended belly. "I know the names of at least a dozen women who would say different. Shall I name them?" She didn't give him a chance to respond. "Do you think I didn't know every time you said Jessi wasn't your type that you were really saying you weren't good enough for her?"

A fist of unease balled in his chest and he eased back in his chair, but she wasn't finished.

"I'm sorry. I know your family is a sore spot, but this has to be said. Your blue-blooded bitch of a grandmother did a number on your head, but she's wrong about you. She's so obsessed with bloodlines she wouldn't know a man of quality if one bit her on her wrinkled ass."

Wincing at the direct hit, he curled his lips in what he hoped was a teasing smile. "That's a ten spot for your jar."

She narrowed her eyes at his attempt to throw her off track. Shortly after she and Jake's custody battle had begun, the twins had introduced a system of financial penalties in an effort to clean up Jake's vocabulary. Five bucks per curse. The multi-millionaire tight-end had complained he'd need to take out a loan before he'd learned to curb his tongue around the munchkins. Over time, more pickle jars had been added to the shelf beside Jake's. Max had earned his after missing a spare on a bowling outing with the twins. Tuck had one as well. Gracie's had a pretty pink bow tied around it, and it wasn't empty by any means.

She didn't take his bait. "You're a good man, Max, and more than worthy of a woman like Jessi. Why can't you see that?"

If you only knew. He cursed beneath his breath. Maybe it was time she did. "I appreciate the words of support, kiddo, but I'm not the man you believe me to be."

"That's bullshit." She tossed her head stubbornly.

"Is it? I wasn't always the upstanding citizen I am today. I've done some things, Gracie. Ugly things."

Her eyes glittered with fierce denial. "Whatever they were, I'm sure they were necessary."

Murky images of a dark alley, fear, and a stranger's blood staining his shaking hands slithered through Max's mind. The familiar acidic scorch of bile coated his throat. He slammed his mind's door on the caustic memory and held her gaze. True. The worst of what he'd done had been necessary at the time, but he hadn't walked away unscathed. Life on the street had forged the man he'd become.

"That may be, but it doesn't change the facts. I'm a man who sees an opportunity and takes it, no matter who it might hurt."

She jacked her chin at a stubborn angle. "I've never known you to hurt anyone."

He sighed and sat forward to prop his elbows on his desk. "That's because you don't know the real me." He spoke before she could voice a comeback. "I've told you about my maternal grandmother turning her back on me when my mother died, but did I ever mention her name is Elizabeth Krandall?"

Gracie's eyes went wide. "*The* Elizabeth Krandall?"

He sat back and tucked his hands behind his head. "The one and only."

"But she owns the—"

"New Jersey Hurricanes." He dropped his arms. "I'm her only grandchild. If not for her hatred of my father, and by extension, me, you'd be looking at the sole owner of one of the league's top teams."

"Oh my God." Her shoulders slumped with her breathy huff.

He sighed, hating the pained confusion on her face, but he needed her to understand. "I haven't shared the full truth of my family ties with anyone and wouldn't have today, even with you, other than to make a point."

Anger replaced confusion as the ramifications of his disclosure sunk in. "What's that? That your grandmother denied you your heritage? That she's a fat cow who I hope burns in hell?"

A smile tugged at his lips but died quickly. "She denied me period, with every beat of her non-existent heart, and I wouldn't have it any other way."

"Why didn't you ever tell me?" Gracie whispered, and the hurt in her voice slashed at him like a blade.

He scrubbed a hand over his face and fought the guilt that churned in his gut. "Because I'm a selfish bastard. I pushed you toward Jake when you and he were thrown together in the custody battle because I saw it as a way for you to follow your heart, but it also occurred to me that, through Jake, I'd gain a connection to pro football that might prove advantageous at some point in the future. I didn't tell you my grandmother's name, or about my connection to football, for the same reason I've never told you about a lot of the things I did before we met. I'm damaged goods, kiddo."

Angry flags of color slashed her cheekbones. "No, you're not, and if you ever say anything that stupid again, I'll blacken your eye. So you saw an advantage to Jake and me being together. Big deal. So did I. Are you saying I was selfish for using the custody battle to attain my dream of a family?" She sat forward and her eyes gleamed with militant intensity. "Whatever ghosts continue to haunt you, it's time you let them go. You did what you had to in order to survive and I, for one, am glad you did. How do you think I would have survived if you hadn't? What would have happened to me if you weren't there to stop those boys from...?" Sudden tears glistened and she shook her head. "What would I have done if you weren't there to prop me up when my sister died?"

Aw, shit. An iron band squeezed his chest as the tears spilled over and her face crumbled. The truth was, the scrawny girl with the big frightened eyes had done more to prop him up than he had her. Vern may have been responsible for yanking Max out of the gutter and off the road to hell he'd been on, but with her quirky sense of humor and never-say-die attitude, Gracie had sparked to life the little bit of good left in him.

Those big eyes tore at him, all wet and shiny, and through it all, full of belief. In him.

His mouth twisted in a guilty grimace. "Gracie, this might not be a conversation we should have while you're full of baby hormones."

She sniffed and wiped at her lower lids with her fingertips. "I'm not crying."

"Yeah, I can see that."

A grin cracked through her tears. "You said you're a man who sees an opportunity and takes it. Well, one is right in front of you with Jessi. I say grab it with both hands and run with it."

Jesus, she was like a dog with a bone. He sighed. "Who says I haven't? In case you weren't listening last night, she moved in with me."

"I heard every word. I also saw how tense you were throughout dinner, and don't try and tell me it's because you were worried her family might object because, from what I saw, they don't."

"Tuck does."

"Oh really?" She cocked her head and bared her teeth in a daring leer. "Is that why he bet you a hundred bucks Jessi would have you in her bed before the week is out?"

He sat back with a jolt. "Jesus. He told you that?"

"Actually, I overheard him talking to Jake."

Fucking perfect. With everyone talking about the situation, Jessi was bound to find out why Max had changed his mind about helping her, and he could just imagine her reaction when she did.

His glare didn't faze Gracie in the least.

She crossed one long leg over the other. "My question is, why would a man who is supposedly living with a woman be reluctant to take her to bed?"

"Damn it, you're like a bulldog."

Satisfaction softened her leer into a triumphant smile. "What was it you said when I was still fighting what I felt for Jake and got mad at you for sticking your big nose in my business? Oh, I remember. 'Just doing my job as bodyguard and protector.'"

"If I recall correctly, you told me it was a job for which I hadn't been hired. The same goes, kiddo."

She ignored his valid point, her eyes narrowing slyly. "And I recall a piece of advice you gave me. Good advice, as it turns out. You said, 'You've had a thing for the guy for years. People rarely get the opportunity to realize their darkest dream. It's a sin not to act when a chance like this comes along.'" Her cheeky smile taunted him. "Same goes with Jessi, *kiddo.*"

He ground his back molars and shook his head. "The situations are entirely different."

"Not from where I'm sitting." She tossed her head. "And I'm not about to stand by and watch you be hurt."

While he appreciated her support, she wasn't privy to all the facts and, knowing her, she wasn't going to be happy when she was. "You're worried about the wrong person. I'm the guy who moves on to a new woman every week so none can ever get close, remember?"

Her eyes softened with a twinge of sadness. "None of those women were Jessi. What's going on, Max? You're not making any sense. I like Jessi, but I *love* you. If you're in trouble, I want to help."

"I'm not the one in trouble."

His shoulders shifted in a defeated sigh as he filled her in on the stalker and Ryan's request, leaving out any mention of Jessi's proposition or her precarious state of mind. A wide range of emotions showed on Gracie's expressive face, from surprise to disbelief, and finally, anger on Jessi's behalf.

"Oh, God. What a mess." She combed her fingers through her curls.

He nodded. "Since it seems Tuck has already blabbed to Jake, and now you know as well, I want your promise you won't say a word to anyone, about any of this, especially Jessi. That goes for Jake, too."

"You know we won't. Is there anything we can do?"

"Maybe." The germ of an idea tickled at the back of his mind. "Is the lake house available?"

"Of course. When do you need it?"

He rubbed a palm around the back of his neck. He'd spent a weekend at Jake and Gracie's New Hampshire getaway last month and hadn't seen a soul for three days. "I'm not sure I will, but it's an option. Ryan and his security people may need some time to track down the bastard who's threatening Jessi without having to worry about her in the process."

Gracie dipped her chin in a nod of understanding. "The house is yours whenever you need it, for as long as you do. I'll send the keys over this afternoon."

"Thanks." He tensed when she stood, her eyes filled with concern.

"Will you be okay?"

"Let it go, Gracie." He dropped his head to the back of the chair. "Nothing's changed. I'm not now, nor will I ever be, the man for Jessi Tucker. As soon as this mess is settled, she'll go back to her life, and I'll go back to mine."

Disappointment puckered her brow, but she turned and crossed to the door. He wasn't surprised when she paused with her hand on the doorknob. "Does Jessi know that?"

He scowled at her back. "Probably not, but she'll learn the truth soon enough."

Gracie flashed him a challenging grin over one shoulder. "I'll see Tuck's bet and raise him a thousand Jessi makes you eat those words before this is done."

She walked out the door before he could reply, and Max slumped in his chair. Gracie was wrong. Jessi may believe she had feelings for him, but only because she didn't know the real man. Though she'd brushed against the dark side with her mother's murder, only someone who'd lived amongst the desperate underbelly of society could understand the depths of that darkness.

No matter how successful he became or how many friends in high places he claimed, his soul carried the putrid stench of the street. Jessi deserved better.

Chapter 8

Spence let the last note of the song fade away and lifted his gaze to the boys in the booth. The sound manager flashed a wide smile and a thumbs up, and Spence nodded. Tearing off his headphones, he turned to Jessi with a satisfied smirk. "Think Daddy will approve?"

"Lay off it, Spence. We both know he was right." Jessi discarded her own headgear and rose from the stool. Last night's headache was gone, but not the lingering fatigue. She arched her back before pulling a water bottle from the small refrigerator in the corner. They'd been at it for five hours. As she'd predicted to Kris, Spence had arrived this morning with two new songs that were bound to hit the charts. They'd laid down the music tracks first thing. One of the songs was in the can. They'd record the second after lunch.

"Give us about forty-five?" The sound manager's voice came through the speakers high on the wall.

"Perfect. I'm starving." Spence stood. "Do you want something?"

"No, thanks. I've got a banana in my bag."

He shook his head. "You eat like a bird."

"And you eat like a horse."

His quiet laugh made her grin. With everything else in her life going to shit, tension in the studio was the last thing she needed. In less than two hours the CD would be finished, and if history was any indication, Spence would be riding high for the next few days. Thank God she'd have one less thing to worry about.

They both turned at the knock on the studio door. Alicia's chestnut brown hair swung in a neat bob on her shoulders, and she wore a hesitant smile as her gaze skittered to Spence, then quickly looked away. Her assistant held up several garment bags. Jessi waved her in and turned to Spence. He'd said yesterday's lunch date was just that. Lunch. From the bland look on his face, he meant it. Unfortunately, the shy blush on Alicia's said she'd considered it something more.

"I picked up your outfits for tomorrow night. Here's your dress and shoes, Jessi." She hung one of the bags on a hook beside the door, set a canvas bag on the counter, and patted the remaining bags hanging over her arm. "I'll deliver your costumes for the performance to your dressing rooms before the show."

"Thanks, sweetie."

Alicia's smile went dreamy. "And wait until you see the jewelry Sidney Wiseman is loaning you. God, the set is gorgeous."

Jessi grinned in anticipation. "Sidney's stuff is always spectacular."

"His security detail will deliver the pieces to your condo at five tomorrow afternoon."

"Oh. Hmm." Shoot. This wasn't how Jessi had planned to break the news of her new living arrangements, but the word would get out eventually. She cleared her throat. "Will you get back to him and have them delivered to a different address?"

Without blinking an eye, Alicia pulled a notepad from her purse, and Jessi rattled off Max's number and street.

"That's not your father's place."

It wasn't a question, but there was definitely one in Spence's eyes. Alicia looked up from her notepad as Jessi held Spence's gaze.

"No, it's Max's building."

Confusion wrinkled Spence's forehead. "Why would you have your jewelry delivered there?"

Happiness curled in her belly and tugged her lips into a smile. "Because, as of last night, I'm living there."

"Oh!" Alicia's gasp drew Jessi's attention. Surprised pleasure lit her assistant's soft brown eyes. "Oh, Jessi, that's—"

"Crazy!"

Both she and Alicia turned at Spence's harsh interruption.

Jessi cocked her head and studied him. "Why is it crazy? We're both single. God knows he's sexy as hell, and I've had a thing for him for years."

Spence's blond brows lowered into a scowling V. "From what I've seen, other than yesterday, he's never given you the time of day."

She resisted the urge to kick him in the shin. Okay, that was true, damn it, and if last night had turned out differently, she'd be right back at her condo with Dan and Aurora, but Max had asked her to stay. That had to mean something, and after that kiss and the way he'd held her as she cried out her mini breakdown, all bets were off.

She pierced Spence with a blinding smile. "Well, he has now. He's not only given me the time of day," she turned to Alicia and winked, "he's given me the nights as well."

Alicia returned her grin, until Spence snatched his coat from the peg beside the garment bag. Her lips thinned in practiced indifference, but her eyes told a different story as, oblivious to her heartache, Spence jammed his arms into his sleeves.

"I'm going to get something to eat. I'd like to finish the second song before six so be ready when I get back." The zipper on his coat sang as he yanked it up. "I've got a hot date tonight."

Jessi winced as he marched from the studio and wished she had kicked him. Was he blind? Couldn't he see Alicia had feelings for him? Men could be so dense when it came to matters of the heart. Jessi frowned. Come to think of it, Max suffered from the same poor eyesight. If it was the last thing she did, she was going to change that, even if she had to purchase him his own pair of rose-colored glasses.

She draped her arm over Alicia's shoulders and squeezed. "Don't give up, sweetie. He's under a lot of pressure to finish this CD, and he isn't himself." That was a flat-out lie if she'd ever uttered one, but she didn't want to crush the poor girl's hopes.

Alicia cut her gaze to Jessi's, her eyes darkened with a determined glint. She quickly looked away, her gaze following Spence as he stalked out the control room door. "I don't intend to give up."

Jessi grinned and bumped her assistant's hip with hers. "Atta girl!"

As it turned out, they finished recording the second song much quicker than expected. Spence returned from lunch in a foul mood, but that hadn't stopped them from performing a perfect track on the first take. He left the moment the sound manager said it was a go. Jessi tucked her cell phone between shoulder and ear as she gathered her things to do the same.

Kris's voice was ripe with teasing accusation. "When were you going to tell me you've moved in with Max?"

Jessi laid the garment bag containing her dress over her arm and grinned. "I left you a message."

"I know, but I've been holding a nervous client's hand all day. It's her first photo shoot."

"How's it going?"

"She's already thrown up twice. Now, tell me what happened. Did Max change his mind or did you change it for him?"

Jessi laughed. "Meet me for a congratulatory drink. We finished the CD earlier than expected and, wonder of wonders, I have a couple hours free."

A windy sigh blew through the phone's speaker. "Sorry. No can do. The client is in Seattle, and so am I. Which reminds me, I won't be able to make the awards show. I had to reschedule my flight home and won't get in until late on Friday. In the meantime, if you have time to kill, shouldn't you be doing it with the hot cage fighter?"

"I intend to, but he said he'd be tied up until at least four."

"Then what?"

Jessi slumped against the counter. "Beats me. I guess I didn't think my plan through past asking for his help. I have no idea what to do next."

"Yes, you do. You've just realized that now comes the tricky part. Convincing him the arrangement should be permanent."

"Ugh." She squeezed her eyes shut.

"Start with the tried and true methods. What is it they say? The way to a man's heart is through his stomach? You've got a couple of hours. Plenty of time to put together a romantic dinner."

"This is me, remember? It'll hardly lead to romance if he ends up having to have his stomach pumped."

"Haven't you ever heard of delivery?" Kris's laugh cut off on a groan. "Damn it. I've got to go. The client is turning green again. Good luck, girlfriend."

Jessi disconnected the call and frowned, turning as Dan popped his head in through the open door.

"You ready to go?"

She pushed off from the counter. Kris had a point, but although Jessi had the numbers to several of her favorite restaurants stored in her phone, tonight, she wanted to do something special. Though her experience in the kitchen was almost nonexistent, how hard could it be to make a pot of spaghetti?

Once in the car, she called Aurora for her sauce recipe and had Dan swing by the grocery store on their way to Max's building. She'd dropped the pasta in the boiling water five minutes before Max walked in the door. A flaky loaf of garlic bread was browning in the oven and her salad preparations were coming along nicely.

He stopped short when he spotted her in the kitchen. His gaze flew from the steaming pots on the stove, past the sliced mushrooms on the chopping board, to the small, unlit candle on the island between two place settings. He slid the duffle strap from his shoulder. "What's this?"

I thought we should celebrate the official kickoff of your seduction. Nope. Too bold. Perhaps she should ease into things with something a bit more subtle.

She swirled the knife in her hand in a dismissive wave and offered him a smile. "Just a little something I whipped up. Are you hungry?"

"Famished, actually." He wandered around the island as she returned to her mushrooms. Stopping in front of the stove, he glanced around.

She paused to give him a questioning glance. "What are you doing?"

"Looking for the spoon to stir the pasta."

Her fingers clenched around the handle of the knife. *Crap, I was supposed to stir it?*

"Oh, no you don't." She set aside the knife, wiped her hands on the small hand towel tucked in her jeans, and turned to give him a gentle shove on his lower back. "This is my show. If you want to help, find me a corkscrew."

On his way around the island, he stopped and opened a drawer. He held out a corkscrew. "You sure you don't want any help?"

She snatched the utensil from his fingers and flicked her hand in a shooing motion. "I've got this. Get lost, Grayson." His low chuckle brushed over her like a warm summer breeze.

"Okay, Tucker. I'm going to take a quick shower. Yell if you need anything."

She smiled sweetly—and dove for the row of drawers the moment he disappeared into his room. She eyed the solid block of spaghetti laying like a dead fish in the pot as she stuck the long handled spoon into the boiling water. A groan of dismay escaped her lips. The individual strands of pasta were stuck to each other as if the entire pound had been encased in cement.

Shit! The stupid spoon was useless. All it did was spin the block around in a maddening circle. She tossed it aside and searched through the drawers until she found a long, two-prong fork. It delivered better results, but not by much. She managed to pry only about a quarter of the pound loose in slightly smaller chunks.

Biting her lip, she spun to stare at his closed bedroom door. How long would he be in the shower? Long enough to dump this batch and start over? That would work if he had another package of pasta. Of course he'd have spare pasta. He was a guy, after all, and a bachelor. They lived on the stuff. She dropped the fork to the counter and began rifling through cabinets. Three minutes later, she slumped in defeat.

Why hadn't she thought to buy some fully cooked frozen meatballs? Tim ate them at least three times a week and swore by them. Along with the garlic bread, they would make delicious meatball subs.

"Oh, dear Lord. The bread."

Ripping the hand towel from her waist, she opened the oven door. Thick, black smoke billowed out in a toxic flume that rose to float just below the ceiling. Fanning at the cloud, she folded the towel in half and used it to yank out the baking sheet. She coughed and glared at the two charred logs, then scrambled to switch hands when the heat from the tray seeped through the towel.

"Hot. Hot. Hot!" Her gaze darted about in search of a hot pad. "Oh, come on!" What kitchen didn't have hot pads, or oven mitts for that matter? Aurora's had a whole stack of them.

"How's it coming?"

She spun around to face Max—just as the smoke detector came to life with an eardrum-piercing squeal. He winced and immediately stalked toward the front door. She hesitated for a moment, then dropped the tray of blackened bread on the island. If it scorched the granite, she'd buy him a new slab. She slapped both hands over her ears.

* * * *

Max opened the control panel beside the front door and disengaged the smoke detectors. Blessed quiet returned to the condo. He turned around and found Jessi standing behind the island. Fanning at the smoke floating around her like an angry plume, she twisted her full lips into a pained smile and indicated two halves of burned bread with a graceful flourish of her hand.

"Dinner is served."

He bit back a laugh and, shaking his head, he crossed to the island. "I see you prefer things well done."

She crossed her arms. "Undercooked food can be dangerous. I've never had it, but I've heard botulism is a bitch."

He grinned and, to his surprise, she did, too. She dropped her arms and glanced around his ransacked kitchen. Her gaze paused on the pot of pasta. She gave it the evil eye, then sighed.

"Well, this is a disaster. Who knew preparing a simple spaghetti dinner required a culinary degree?"

He opened the lower cabinet door beside the oven. "Cooking is an acquired art. You just need a lesson or two."

"Good idea." Her gaze rolled up toward the ceiling where the layer of smoke still lingered. "But I think those lessons should be done at the fire department." She lowered her gaze and arched a self-deprecating brow. "Just to be on the safe side."

He bent to retrieve a pair of oven mitts from a hook on the inside of the door and straightened.

"So that's where you hid them." She glared at his hands as he slipped the mitts on to move the pasta pot to the sink.

He chuckled, dumped the entire mess into the basin, and set the pot aside. With a flip of a switch, the disposal chewed through the half dozen bulky lumps. She appeared at his side and stared down at the bubbling pot of red sauce.

Turning her head, she gave him a hopeful look. "Is it salvageable?"

Bending at the waist, he sniffed at the pot's contents. The bitter tang of scalded tomatoes stung his nostrils. He straightened and met her gaze. "I think it's a goner."

Her eyes squeezed shut in an adorable wince, and she stomped her foot. "Epic fail."

A laugh rumbled in his chest. "There's still the salad."

She turned to glare at the pile of mushrooms beside the salad bowl. "If the lettuce hasn't wilted from the fumes."

The bottle of wine on the counter caught his eye. He picked it up and read the label. She may not have a clue what she was doing in the kitchen, but she had the eye of a sommelier. "And we have wine."

"Thank God."

Grinning, he uncorked the wine and poured them both a glass. He tipped his rim to hers. "To the chef."

"Funny." Her eyes sparkled with laughter over the rim of her glass.

While he got rid of the remaining evidence from her failed attempt at an Italian dinner, she sat at the island and finished chopping the salad. He pulled a cooked chicken breast and a small bottle from the fridge and set them beside her elbow.

She looked up. "What am I supposed to do with those?"

"Chop the chicken into strips and throw them in. Add a little homemade dressing and you've got a meal."

She looked doubtful but did as directed. When the improvised meal was ready, she shot him a hesitant look, then pulled a book of matches from her back pocket and lit the candle. She sat back on her stool.

Fork in hand, he arched a brow. "When all else fails, go for ambiance?"

The blush spreading over her cheeks surprised and charmed him. She avoided his gaze. "Something like that." With perfect table manners, she placed a napkin over her lap, then forked up a bite of salad. The moment her lips closed around the tines she hummed in appreciation. Her eyes widened, and she blew any hint of decorum by talking as she chewed. "Oh my God. This is so good!"

Her unpretentious pleasure made him smile as he dug into his plate.

"Where did you learn to cook?"

He looked up and laughed. "It's a salad, Jessi. No cooking involved."

"You know what I mean." She waved her fork, then stabbed another bite. "You're a bachelor. Aren't you supposed to exist on cold pizza and take out?"

"I still eat my share of both, but I didn't always have the funds for restaurant meals. Cooking at home was cheaper." He could have bitten off his tongue when her eyes went all soft and compassionate. His past wasn't something he planned to have on the menu. He shoved the conversation in a more lighthearted direction. "If I didn't want to die of botulism, I needed to learn how to cook."

The diversion worked. She rolled her eyes. "Smartass."

He bared his teeth in a grin. "What about you? I've been to plenty of Tucker family meals where everyone seems to gather in the kitchen, and your aunt Maryanne is a great cook. Why haven't you learned?"

She swallowed a bite. "I'm not a complete novice in the kitchen. I make a mean deviled egg, and I'm a wiz at frosting a cake, but mostly the family keeps me away from the stove."

"I can't say I blame them."

Her fork stilled midair, and she surprised him when she laughed.

"Me either." She shifted her shoulders in a shrug. "My schedule doesn't allow me to attend as many of the family's gatherings as I'd like. When I do show up, someone is always dragging me off to catch up. Learning to cook simply hasn't been a priority, not when Aurora has domain over the kitchen at home, and on the road, everything is catered."

"Then we'll have to remedy that."

She sat up straight. "You'll teach me to cook?"

"Why not? You'll be here for a while. Why waste the opportunity?" And spending time in the kitchen might keep his mind from constantly veering off toward the activities they could explore in his bedroom.

"I think I'd like that, but…."

He cocked his head when she hesitated. "But?"

"I was hoping you'd give me some lessons in self-defense."

Oh, fuck no. Up close and personal while they sweated through wrestling moves would be a bad idea. "Why would you want to train in self-defense?"

"Because this," she jerked her fork back and forth between them, "is just a temporary solution to my ultimate goal. At some point, I'll be out on my own for real, right? When I am, my father will be less inclined to worry about me if he knows I can kick ass and take names."

She had a point. Sort of. He shook his head. "You're confusing self-defense with fight training. The point of self-defense is to hold your own long enough to get away, not take out a potential attacker."

"Can't I do both?"

He couldn't help but smile. "What do you weigh, ninety pounds? The average high school punk would flatten you without breaking a sweat."

"Not if you taught me how to stop him." She angled her chin in that stubborn way he'd always found amusing. "And I weigh one hundred three, if you must know."

He picked up his wine as he laughed. "Face it, Squirt, about the only ass you'd be big enough to kick would belong to a preschooler."

"Fine, then." Her chest heaved in an annoyed huff that only made him laugh harder. "Teach me to hold my own. Like you said, we have plenty of time to waste."

* * * *

Portable keyboard on her lap, Jessi looked up as the door to Max's bedroom opened. As if startled to find her parked on his living room couch, he hesitated, the olive skin of his bare chest gleaming in the low light above a pair of black, drawstring pants.

She waited for him to spin around and hightail it back into his room. Although she'd been sure she'd made some headway earlier, despite nearly burning down his kitchen, it was clear seducing Max was going to be even harder than she thought. Stubborn as he was sexy, he simply refused to cooperate with her agenda.

While she'd pictured a romantic evening on the couch in front of the fire, he had other plans. The moment the kitchen was put back in order after their meal, he couldn't get away from her fast enough. He'd disappeared downstairs to work out, leaving her to twiddle her thumbs.

Obviously, she was going to have to bring her A game if she was going to break through his barriers. Too bad she didn't have one.

The moment stretched as they stared at one another, and she cursed herself for not thinking ahead. First thing tomorrow she was going out and buying some sexy sleep wear. Leggings and a Betty Boop T-shirt didn't exactly scream, *"take me, big boy,"* and Max Grayson was going to take her, even if she had to tackle him to get him to do it.

She tugged the earbuds from her ears. "Sorry. Did I wake you?"

"No. Thirsty." On bare feet, he padded to the kitchen. "What are you doing up?"

She shrugged a shoulder and followed his progress with her eyes. "Couldn't sleep."

He selected a water bottle from the fridge and turned to eye the clock on the stove before his gaze fell on the music sheet by her hip. "It's three AM. Will the lyrics make sense in the morning?"

A smile teased her lips. "No lyrics yet. I had a tune running through my head that wouldn't let go." A big fat lie, but she wasn't about to admit she suffered from insomnia on top of all of her other neuroses.

He nodded and strolled closer. "I meant to ask. How'd things go in the studio today?"

"Great, actually. We finished the CD, which made Spence happy." Or should have. She frowned. "That reminds me. The awards show tomorrow night is black tie. You'll need to wear a tux."

He grunted and sipped at his water.

"If you don't have one, I'll make a call. Will you have a few minutes in the morning to stop in and have it fitted?"

He lowered the bottle from his mouth. "I've got it covered."

"Really, it's no problem. My assistant is a wonder at last minute details."

"I own a tux."

"Oh, good." She blinked. "Wait. You do?"

"Surprised?" His smile suddenly went sharp. "I may be a street rat at heart, but I also hold two cage fighting titles. You'd be amazed at the number of elites who like to go slumming if there's a champion involved. Of course, they insist the riff raff get dressed up first."

His mocking tone stung and she stiffened. This wasn't the first time he'd demeaned himself in an effort to point out the differences in their social standing, and it pissed her off. Geez, did he think this was Victorian England or something?

She gathered her things and stood. "That's not fair, Max. I don't give a shit how you grew up and you know it. And I wasn't talking down at you. I was just surprised. Not everyone owns their own formal wear."

She started to step by him, but he stopped her by gripping her arm. "Wait."

Tingles of heat shot up to her shoulder as he loosened his hold, his fingers moving over the bare skin of her arm in a gentle caress. His somber gray gaze bored into hers.

"Sorry. Sore spot."

She lifted her chin against the pleasurable chill pebbling her skin. "Obviously. Why is that?"

His hand dropped away, and she immediately missed the connection.

He sighed and with the expulsion of breath, it seemed some of his tension faded. "Long story."

She turned to face him squarely. "I'd like to hear it."

A crooked smile quirked one corner of his lips. "I don't think so."

"Why not? I can't sleep, and it appears you can't either." Her gaze roamed down his gorgeous body and up again. She resisted the urge to lick her lips and offered him an innocent smile. "You're a fine looking man, Max. I bet you were an adorable boy."

He arched a wry brow, but there was humor in his eyes as he shook his head. "Adorable wasn't on the list of terms people used to describe me when I was a kid."

"What was?"

"Difficult, delinquent, and my all-time favorite, destined for a life in the federal correctional system."

Her smile slid away, and he blinked as if he hadn't meant to say what he had. He rolled his shoulders as he screwed the cap back onto his water bottle.

"Forget it, Squirt. When little girls can't sleep, the last thing they need is a horror story."

She opened her mouth to point out that whoever had said those things about him had obviously been proven wrong, but he was already walking away.

He spoke over his shoulder before closing his bedroom door. "Get some rest. You don't want to look tired for the cameras tomorrow."

Chapter 9

"Jesus, what a circus." Max stared through the tinted windows as the limo rolled to a stop in front of the theater, the same theater where he'd first seen Jessi and all but fell into her soul-deep blue eyes.

She and Spence were among the nominees tonight, but as the winners of last year's "Song of the Year," they were also expected to perform. Despite himself, Max was looking forward to it. It had been years since he'd watched her on stage, though not from a lack of opportunity. After that first time, when he felt as if her voice had pierced the walls of seclusion he'd erected around his heart, he'd found one excuse or another not to attend whenever the duo were in town for a tour date.

Last night, when she'd briefly slid through the partitions separating his past life from the current, she'd proven her uncanny ability to breach his fortifications hadn't waned with time. In fact, the phenomenon had grown stronger. Other than to Gracie, whom he'd given a sterilized version of his childhood over the years, he'd never voiced such details to another person. Yet, twice in two days, he'd found himself sharing memories with Jessi he'd never spoken aloud.

It was as if her very presence had jiggled the lock on his soul, and if he wasn't careful, sooner or later, the darkness hidden there would be revealed.

"Hell of a way to make a living, isn't it?" Beside him, Jessi heaved a shaky sigh as she stared past his shoulder. The sidewalk teemed with people, split down the middle by a blood red strip of carpet leading to the building's elaborate front doors. "Time to earn my keep."

Dan rounded the trunk and opened the door. Max stepped out and the multitude of flashbulbs nearly blinded him. He lifted his hand to shield his vision, but it was impossible to miss the crowd of press jammed against the velvet stanchions lining the red carpet. The short hairs on the back of his neck prickled against the collar of his tux as he turned to offer a hand to assist Jessi from the limo's low-slung seat.

Her wide smile appeared forced, as if she withheld from her public the genuine pleasure he was used to seeing. Still, her curved lips were better than the nerves stretching her mouth thin for the last fifteen minutes as Dan had wound the car through the busy streets of New York. Stage jitters, she'd explained when he'd asked if she was all right.

She tucked her arm through his and stepped forward on the carpet, reminding him they had a deception to sell. Mindful of his role, that of an attentive lover, he dipped his head closer when she leaned into him. Cameras clicked as her breath bathed his ear with her whisper.

"Picture them in clown noses. It's what I do."

A startled laugh rumbled in his throat, and he made a conscious effort to loosen his stiff shoulders. Shifting his head, he whispered back, "I thought you were supposed to picture the crowd naked."

She paused, bringing him to a stop. Lifting on the toes of her three-inch heels, she pressed her cheek to his. "Chet Bertrum from the *Country Bugle*. He's at two o'clock. No way I'm picturing him naked. I'll stick with clown noses." She brushed his lips in a quick kiss before turning back to wave at the press.

As they passed by Chet, Max stifled a wince. Sweat glistened on the portly reporter's bald head as he called out to Jessi. She greeted him with a flirty, fingertip wave, then turned her face up to Max and fluttered her lashes. He twisted his lips to contain his laughter as they were escorted inside the theater.

A twenty-something woman with brown, shoulder-length hair and large, dark eyes met them as they handed their coats to a uniformed theater attendant. Alicia, as Jessi introduced her, was her assistant. Efficient and calm, she led them toward backstage as she filled Jessi in on what was happening.

"Your things are in a private dressing room. The stage manager is waiting to take you through the drill, but you and Spence will perform last and aren't up until ninety minutes into the show. There will be a commercial break at the hour mark when you'll leave your seats to get ready. Will that give you enough time?"

"That'll be fine. Is Spence here yet?"

"He's already in his seat."

"Is he alone?"

The assistant looked away, but not before Max noted the disappointment in her eyes. "No, he isn't."

Jessi rested a hand on the woman's arm, but if she meant to respond, she didn't get the chance. A flamboyant older man in a deep green tuxedo swept up to them with several other younger men in tow. His dark-eyed gaze skimmed over Max from head to toe before locking on to Jessi. A genuine smile lit his thin face as he pressed a kiss to one of her cheeks, then the other in an old world greeting. He stepped back to give her a similar onceover to the one he'd given Max.

"You look ravishing, Miss Tucker." He spoke in an Eastern European accent that screamed gay vampire as he dropped his gaze to stare at her chest. "These old eyes have never looked upon anything so breathtaking."

Max frowned at the smaller man, but Jessi grinned and slapped a hand to the generous cleavage above her midnight blue gown. "I would blush and say thanks, but I think you're talking about the jewelry."

To Max's surprise, a pale blotch of pink bloomed on the man's high cheekbones. Jessi laughed, and the matching bracelet on her wrist sparkled as she stroked the triple strand necklace of perfect white diamonds adorning her pale skin. "They're Sidney's, and I agree. I only wish I could afford them."

Not likely. Max had nearly choked when the designer's security guards had presented the receipt for the set, which included the earrings dangling almost to her collarbone. She hadn't blinked an eye as she signed her name to the paper, promising to return the collection "as is" at the close of the evening or write a check for a cool one point two million.

Jessi linked her arm with Max's. "Max Grayson, this is Victor. He runs things around here."

The stage manager dipped his head in acknowledgment, offered Alicia a greeting smile, and immediately turned back to Jessi. His lips pulled down in a pout. "I'm not sure if I've forgiven you for neglecting us the last time you were in town."

Laughter sparkled in her eyes. "Come on now, you know Tim handles bookings. I just show up and sing, and I'll be back in a few weeks for a tour stop."

His pout morphed into a smirk. "How is your annoying cousin?"

"A pain in the ass, as usual." They shared a grin. "He'll be in the audience tonight, as will my father. I'll be sure to send him back so you can badger him into apologizing."

Victor sniffed delicately. "That, my dear, will never happen." As if he flipped a switch, the stage manager was suddenly all business. He barked out orders to the three young men waiting patiently behind him, and they scattered like willing minions. Victor turned to Alicia. "Perhaps Mr. Grayson would like a refreshment while I take Miss Tucker through her marks for the evening. Would you be a darling and show him to the green room?"

Jessi squeezed Max's arm before letting go. "I'll only be a few minutes."

Mindful of the stalker, not to mention the more than one million in borrowed diamonds sparkling against her skin, Max curled his lips in a heated smile. While she wasn't aware of his true reason for wanting to stay close, she'd set up this lovers' farce. He'd gladly play up the pretext to keep her safe.

He slid his palm to her waist and let his fingers ride down to caress her hip. "If you wouldn't mind, *darling*, I'd like to stay. You know how jealous I get when you're out of my sight."

"Oh my." Victor's narrow hand fluttered to his chest, and he looked on Max with renewed interest. Alicia wore a pleased smile.

The gleam in Jessi's eyes said he was overplaying it. She batted her lashes. "Why, snookums, you do say the sweetest things."

Max was tempted to kiss her senseless, in retribution, of course. Thankfully, Victor stepped in to save his ass.

He cleared his throat and held out one hand to indicate the stage. "Well, then. Shall we?"

* * * *

Twenty minutes later, one of Victor's minions escorted Max and Jessi to their seats in the second row of the theater. Spence made a show for the audience by rising to his feet and hugging Jessi. His date, a buxom blonde beauty, twittered nervously as he introduced her to his singing partner. The greeting he gave Max was a bit less cordial. A curt nod, a handshake, and the country singer returned to his seat between the blonde and Jessi.

Ryan and Tim were seated in the row directly behind them, but with the show about to start, there was no time for more than a simple hello. Country music's best and brightest were in attendance, many of whom took their turn on stage. The time passed quickly and soon, a soft spoken, female usher appeared to collect Jessi and Spence for their performance. A handsome young couple waited at her side to fill their vacant seats. The usher signaled to another young man when Max insisted on accompanying Jessi backstage.

Jessi gave him no argument, taking the hand he offered with a roll of her eyes, but the arrangement obviously didn't sit well with Spence. He stalked up the aisle and left Jessi and Max to follow. Max wasn't sure what his problem was. Although he didn't consider the man a friend, Spence had seemed friendly enough the few times they'd met.

Max forgot all about her singing partner's foul mood when Jessi emerged from her dressing room several minutes later decked out in a slinky red number. The shiny silk skimmed her curves like a second skin. That is, where there was enough material to cover them. The plunging neckline stopped midway to her navel, and if the hem were any shorter, the folks in the front rows would get more of a show than they'd bargained for.

With the inner curve of her breasts and toned columns of her thighs exposed, the woman strolling toward Max held no resemblance to the talented young girl he remembered from the last time he'd watched her perform. He straightened from his slouch against the wall, vertebrae by vertebrae.

A low whistle blew through his lips. "Jesus, Squirt. That dress should be illegal."

Her purely feminine smile grabbed him by the short hairs, and his balls contracted.

"I think it is in a couple of the southern states." She dropped her gaze and skimmed a hand over one luscious hip, then peeked up at him through her fringe of thick lashes. "Too much?"

His Adam's apple clicked on a pained swallow. "Too little. Your ass is practically showing."

He had to bite back a groan as she spun around and presented him with a view of the sweetest ass he'd ever seen, wrapped up like a gift in shimmering red. She craned her neck to look over her shoulder and tugged at the hem. It didn't help.

Worry darkened her eyes as they lifted to his. "Do you think Dad will be mad?"

Oh, fuck. Ryan Tucker was going to have a stroke when his daughter walked out on stage. "Mad enough to break my jaw."

She spun around. "Why would he be mad at you? I'm the one wearing it."

He crossed his arms. "Have you worn anything like that before? And by before I mean, before you moved in with me?"

"Um. No." She bit her bottom lip. "It's part of the new, independent me."

He dropped his chin to his chest and squeezed his eyes shut. Counting to ten didn't help. When he looked up, she'd chewed the lipstick off the corner of her mouth. "I think it would be better on your father's heart if you eased into your role of Miss Independence. What about the blue thing you were wearing earlier? Can't you wear that?"

His hope of alluding the coming disaster took a fatal hit when Alicia rounded the corner. "They need you at stage right, Jessi."

Jessi drew in a shaky breath. "Sorry, Max. No time. Wish me luck." She stepped around him to join her assistant. They disappeared toward the right stage entrance.

"You're not the one who's going to need it," he mumbled as he hurried after them. Stepping over a bundle of wires, he caught up to her where she stood with Spence. Victor fidgeted with his clipboard as he watched the stage for their cue. Alicia brushed a wand over Jessi's lips in a quick repair job.

Jessi's eyes were closed, and she breathed deeply, as if in meditation. Max's gaze was irresistibly drawn back to her sweetly curved ass above the long length of her legs. The country music world was about to get an eyeful. That costume would have tongues wagging, or simply hanging out, and Ryan was going to lay the blame at Max's feet.

Thank God Tuck was out of town for a game.

"Okay, that's your cue." Victor stepped to the side and beamed a smile at country's sweetheart couple. "Break a leg."

Spence held out one hand. Jessi's eyes popped open and she swallowed. She cast a glance Max's way, her face pale and her eyes full of panic. He frowned, but she looked away, curled her fingers with Spence's, and with a falsely bright smile on her newly repaired lips, stepped into the spotlight.

Startled gasps could be heard before the frenetic roar of the crowd drowned out all sound. Max moved closer for a better view, stopping beside Alicia. On stage, the master of ceremonies greeted the pair and a tall blonde delivered them each a wireless mic before disappearing.

Spence led Jessi to their mark and, lifting their linked hands, bared her palm for a kiss. With her back to him, Max couldn't see Jessi's face, but what he saw in Spence's eyes made him stiffen. Either the man was a consummate actor or he was in love with his singing partner. His earlier behavior suddenly made sense.

Alicia shifted at Max's side, and he turned his head.

She gripped the clipboard tight against her chest. Her eyes remained on the stage as the beginning notes of their latest platinum hit began. "They're so perfect together."

Max grunted and looked back at the couple crooning a heartbreaking tale of love and devotion in front of four thousand adoring fans. He couldn't disagree. The music they made together was fine and pure. Their combined voices created a harmony that seeped into the listener's heart, but Max couldn't quite form the image of physical love between the two.

Perhaps because he didn't want to. He'd become used to the knowledge that, though he wasn't capable of the kind of love he witnessed in others, there was a woman out there who loved him anyway. Like the street scum he'd always be, he'd basked in the glow from Jessi's innocent feelings, skipping close enough from time to time in order to keep her interested, but remaining forever just out of her reach.

For years, she'd been his for the taking. His to deny or claim if he wanted. Selfish and greedy, he kept her hanging when he should have put an end to it long ago. She may not be aware of it, but he owed her for the cruel game he'd embroiled them both in. Her commitment to her career wasn't entirely responsible for her confusion, nor was the loss of her sense of self. A good portion of the fault belonged to him.

As he watched Spence pour his heart out to Jessi through the words of the song, the acid burn of possessive jealousy tore at the lining of Max's stomach. The street in him demanded he stake a claim, take what she offered so sweetly while he had the chance, but she deserved more. So much more.

He'd been given the chance to make things right. Before the bastard threatening her was caught, he'd help her see herself for the incredible woman she was and put an end to their mutual torment once and for all.

Chapter 10

The private charter for Dallas took off mid-morning the next day. Max tucked Jessi into one of the reclining leather seats and suggested she rest through the three hour and fifteen minute flight. She might have pulled herself together after the meltdown he'd witnessed that first night, but the signs of stress were beginning to show elsewhere. Though he'd seen no evidence of another migraine, she wasn't sleeping. When they'd returned home to his condo following last night's show and after party, he'd expected her to crash from sheer exhaustion but, once again, she'd wandered the floors like a ghost until almost dawn. By his estimation, she'd had less than ten hours of shuteye in the three nights she'd spent in his guest room.

He wasn't sure if anyone else saw the signs of her fatigue, but it was only a matter of time before they did.

Concealer only worked so well.

At the stadium, they were met by Bill Stein, the event's coordinator. With Dallas vying for a playoff spot in Green Bay tomorrow, football took a temporary back seat to country music for the hometown crowd. According to Tim, forty thousand fans would soon fill the seats in front of the field-wide stage on the forty yard-line. With the doors opening in less than an hour, the road crew put the finishing touches on the set up while Jessi and Spence ran through a sound check with one of their most popular songs.

Max glanced around, bristling at the amount of people coming and going in the busy sports complex. He spotted both members of Ryan's security team amongst the crew, but he still didn't like the setup. The place was crawling with strangers, all of whom seemed to have a legitimate reason for being there, but who knew? Guilt chewed at his stomach lining. This business of keeping Jessi in the dark where it came to her security was not only dishonest, it was dangerous.

Unfortunately, the hand had been dealt, but that didn't mean he couldn't improvise a little. Claiming curiosity, he gave Jessi's dressing room a thorough inspection before he left her alone with Alicia to prepare for the press conference Tim had called and the following performance.

Parked like a guard outside her door, Max leaned against the wall and forced himself to relax. Although the need pissed him off, the press conference was necessary. He'd been photographed with Jessi last night and would be again before they were done. The last thing he wanted to do was stand before the media's cameras and answer questions, but he knew from experience, with the press, a pre-emptive offense was the best defense. Besides, Jessi was a singer, not a politician or financier. The reporters attending today's presser were all from the entertainment industry. They'd be more interested in where he'd spent his last vacation than his family connections.

With the warm-up band already playing, backstage was a beehive of activity. He catalogued the passersby. No one gave him a second glance until a man in a business suit and wingtips approached. In his early sixties with a narrow face and slicked back, thinning, gray hair, he moved with confidence. He stopped before Max and eyed Jessi's name on the temporary placard beside the door

"Is Miss Tucker here?"

Max rolled his shoulders away from the wall and straightened. "She's getting ready for the show. What can I do for you?"

He hesitated for a moment and briefly glanced over his shoulder. Max stiffened as he reached inside his suit jacket. His entire body went on alert when the man's hand emerged clutching a plain white envelope.

"I need to deliver this to her."

Jesus, could it be this easy? Was her stalker stupid enough to deliver his threats in person with witnesses all around? Max held out his hand. "What is it? I'll give it to her." *And if it contains a block-lettered threat, you're going to need a hospital before the police drag you away, asshole.*

"I need to see she gets it personally."

Max snatched the envelope from his fingers. "I'll bet you do."

"Excuse me, but I…."

Max slid a finger beneath the seal as Tim rounded a corner with Bill Stein at his side. Jessi's cousin wore a smile that faded immediately when his gaze locked on Max.

"Mr. Watson." At Bill's anxious greeting, the guy in the suit turned his head. Bill's smile held an apology. "Security said you'd come back alone. I apologize for not being on hand to meet you."

Shit. Max's fingers stilled in the act of pulling the contents from the envelope.

"Not a problem." Watson shook the coordinator's hand and turned back to Max with what looked like a genuine smile. "Miss Tucker's bodyguard was just checking my credentials."

Max ignored the flat-out lie and Tim's raised brows, then dropped his gaze to the top sheet of the papers he'd pulled from the envelope. His bunched shoulder muscles loosened as he spotted the "Wishes Foundation" letterhead and he scanned the second page, a letter written in a child's uneven script.

Fuck. Jessi isn't the only one on edge. The smiling philanthropist is lucky I didn't deck him first and ask questions later.

Max tucked the sheets back into the envelope and held them out, accepting the man's generous cover for his rude behavior even though he didn't deserve the kindness. "Your credentials are impeccable, Mr. Watson. Sorry for the delay."

The older man nodded but didn't take the envelope. "Completely understandable, son. These days, it pays to be careful." He turned to Bill. "My wife and granddaughters came along with me today. They're big fans, but I know how hectic things can be before a show. They're waiting in our seats." He dipped his chin toward the envelope in Max's hand. "You'll see she gets those?"

Tim stepped in to do damage control. "I'm Tim Tucker, Mr. Watson. Jessi's manager. I'll deliver them to my cousin myself, and if you'll bring your wife and granddaughters backstage when Jessi is finished, I'm sure she'll be thrilled to meet them."

Watson smiled and shook Tim's hand. "That's kind of you, and I'll take you up on the offer."

"I'll see you to your seat." Bill shot Tim a stressed out wince before hurrying to catch up to Watson.

Max pinched the bridge of his nose.

"I wonder if the guy knows how close he came to ending up in traction."

Max slapped the envelope against Tim's chest, his gaze trailing the two men as they headed down the hallway. "Fuck off. You don't have to tell me I overreacted."

Tim took the envelope. "In my opinion, you didn't. I assume you thought it was another letter."

Max whipped his head around to stare at Jessi's cousin.

"That's the reason you're here with her, isn't it?" Sober blue eyes met his gaze. "The reason you changed your mind and said yes when she asked for your help?"

Guilt simmered in his gut, but he didn't back down from Tim's steady regard. Obviously, Ryan had filled him in on the truth of Max and Jessi's supposed relationship, but it was a risk. Of all her cousins, Jessi shared a special bond with Tim. He was her manager, but they were also friends. If anyone was going to object to the deception Max had agreed to, it would be him.

"Sounds like you already know the answer to that."

Tim dipped his head in a nod. "If she finds out, there's going to be hell to pay."

"Don't I know it?" Max scrubbed a palm over the back of his neck. "You gonna tell her?"

"I should." He flicked a quick gaze at Jessi's closed dressing room door before looking back.

Max cocked his head. "But?"

"But Jessi put this potential train wreck in motion, and as far as I'm concerned, getting pissed off is just what she needs." He studied Max with calculating eyes. "She's taken the first step, but until she lets go completely, she'll never be truly happy, and Ryan will continue to call the shots."

What the fuck? Lets go of what? Before Max could ask, Tim knocked on the door and entered at Jessi's call.

Five minutes later, the door opened again and Alicia and Tim emerged, followed by Jessi. Classic and sophisticated, the sparkling, deep blue gown clung to her body from cleavage to toes, the way Max's hands itched to. His gaze licked over her curves to her face. Not a single blemish marred the perfection of her skin, made up for the stage and lights. The dark kohl outlining her large eyes added a touch of exotic to the blue depths, but there was no disguising the nerves lurking in her strained smile as she stopped in front of him.

Holding her gaze, he lifted her hand to brush his lips across her knuckles. "You're beautiful."

Her lashes fluttered and her fingers clenched in his. Pleasure relaxed her smile. Behind her, Alicia sighed.

Tim cleared his throat. "Ready, lovebirds? The press awaits."

Jessi blinked and the odd spell dissolved to reality. Max retained her hand in his as they fell into step beside Tim with Alicia following.

"We'll keep it quick. No more than four or five questions."

Over Jessi's head, Max sent her cousin a wry smirk. "We both know that'll never be enough for the vultures."

Jessi tossed her head of dark auburn curls and her lips pulled tight in an unhappy line. "No, it won't, but it's all they're going to get."

Tim checked his watch and directed them down a second hallway. "Spence is already in there, but I've purposely left only enough time for the basics about the two of you before Jessi and Spence have to be onstage." He eyed Max. "Keep your answers brief and give them a little of what they're looking for."

"What's that?"

"Fluff." He peeled his lips back in a leering smile. "Kiss her on the hand like that again. Most of the reporters are women. They'll be so giddy, they won't notice we've cut them short."

Alicia coughed to cover a giggle, and Jessi rolled her eyes. Tim stopped them before a door and Max was surprised to find Jessi's palm was sweating against his.

She turned to him with an apologetic grimace. "I'm sorry, Max. I know how much you must hate this."

He squeezed her fingers and forced a smile. "This ain't my first rodeo, Squirt. I'll be fine."

She studied him for a long moment, then nodded and turned to Tim. "Okay, let's get this over with." She grabbed her cousin's arm before he could open the door. "But, just so you know. If this blows up in our faces, I'm going to kill you."

Tim flashed a grin and led them into the small conference room. Cameras clicked and flashed as they filed inside. Standing behind a raised dais just inside the door, Spence looked over briefly, then turned back to finish singing the praises of their new CD.

To Max's surprise and relief, the gathering was small. Four women and two men directed their cameras and microphones toward the dais. Before Spence finished speaking, they'd turned their attention to Jessi and Max.

Tim held up a hand. "Sorry for the delay, folks, it couldn't be avoided. We have time for only a few more questions."

A man on the left beat out the others. "Where did the two of you meet, Jessi?"

Jessi glanced up at Max and smiled before answering. "We met officially when Max came to one of my concerts a few years ago, but he's been a friend of the family for years."

"How long have you been dating?"

"Not long."

The second man in the group spoke without looking up from his notes. "There's a Max Grayson listed as holding several cage fighting titles. Is that you?"

Unease itched at the base of Max's spine as the reporter looked up. Beneath a thick shock of dark hair peppered with gray, keen, blue eyes studied him as if searching for the answers to a puzzle. Max nodded as the cameras flashed.

A tall redhead in the middle pinned Max with a smile, though her question wasn't directed at him. "Jessi, you've known each other for a while, yet you just recently began dating. What changed?"

"I've been chasing Max for years." Jessi waited for the woman's gaze to slide her way. "It took me a while to convince him to stop running."

She squeezed his hand as snickers of laughter filled the room.

"More and more women are following the bare knuckle leagues these days," another of the women commented. "Are you a fan? Is that what attracted you, Jessi?"

"I admit, I don't know much about Max's sport. Yet." Jessi turned to eye him with a purely feminine smile. "But all you have to do is look at him to know why I'm attracted."

He squinted in a subtle warning as more laughter followed.

"Your father worked for the NYPD?"

Fuck.

Max whipped his gaze forward as all attention turned to the male reporter with the watchful eyes. Jessi's fingers tightened around Max's. Nausea burned in his throat. So much for fluff. The man was putting together a puzzle, all right, and the picture it formed would lay out the ugly pieces of Max's past.

The muscles in his back and shoulders knotted in apprehension. He dipped his chin in an abbreviated nod. "That's right."

"That's all the time we have, people." Tim stepped forward, partially blocking them from the snapping cameras. "Jessi and Spence have a concert to perform."

Jessi clung to Max's hand and immediately began to pull him toward the exit. Spence turned from the dais to join them.

Disappointed murmurs simmered behind them, cut to stunned silence by a calmly tossed bomb. "That would make you the rightful heir to the Krandall empire, wouldn't it?"

Jessi stumbled to a halt and her gaze flew to Max's. Alicia bit her lip as she hurriedly opened the door. Tim's eyes were shuttered, but like everyone else in the room, he waited for Max's response.

Fury and frustration blasted through him as he turned to spear the nosey reporter with an angry glare. "No comment."

Chapter 11

"They're ready for you, Miss Tucker, Mr. Pierce."

Thanks to Bill's immediate arrival, the quizzical look in Jessi's eyes went unanswered, as did the demand for an explanation in Tim's scowl. Their questions would have to wait. For the moment, anyway. Frustration bunched Max's shoulder muscles as Bill hurried them through the tunnel leading to the field.

Christ. What a cluster-fuck. As if Jessi's request for help had pulled on a loose thread, his carefully concealed past was unraveling before his eyes, along with his hope of closing the deal in Jersey without raising any red flags.

Once he got his hands on Haven Place, he wouldn't give a shit who learned who his parents had been. He wouldn't even care if some enterprising reporter managed to dig up the particulars of his past. Though the details weren't pretty, the worst of his ghosts, as Gracie called them, hadn't been documented anywhere but in his head. The fact was, he would relish watching the Krandall matriarch squirm as she attempted to explain to the world why she'd all but destroyed her own daughter simply for marrying the wrong man, but not at the cost of the home his mother had loved.

He'd covered his tracks the best he could, and yet, no enterprise was foolproof. With his name suddenly linked with the Krandalls in the press, he'd lost the advantage of stealth. Once the story hit the airwaves, he'd once again be on his grandmother's radar. He knew how she operated. She'd immediately start formulating a defense, looking for anything she could use to her advantage in case of any potentially negative fallout. Discovering the small real estate investment firm he'd set up for the sole purpose of making Haven Place his would be difficult, but not impossible, considering the many minions at her beck and call. It was time to up the ante, and the quicker the better. The sooner he sealed the deal, the less chance she'd discover who was behind the purchase before it was too late to stop it.

As they climbed the stairs to the back of the stage, the warm-up band ended their set. Beyond the curtain, the crowd began to chant the headliners' names. Spence checked his appearance in a tall mirror before tugging a showy Stetson low on his forehead. Alicia flitted around Jessi, fluffing her curls into a sexy, windblown look, while Jessi performed what Max had come to recognize as her pre-show meditation ritual.

Her eyes slid shut and she went completely still. For anyone not paying close attention, she looked completely relaxed. The strain around her mouth, however, and the tense line of her back, spoke volumes.

"Ladies and gentlemen, Jessi and Spence."

Her eyes popped open, and she clutched Max's fingers tighter as the crowd roared.

He dipped his head closer so she could hear him. "You okay?"

Her pained smile broke his heart.

"I will be once I start to sing."

She slid her hand free and took the one Spence held out. Her partner's gaze settled on Max. "I'll take care of her."

Max curled his fingers against the urge to knock the smug smile from Spence's face. He turned and led Jessi on stage. A familiar pang squeezed Max's chest as Spence repeated last night's kiss to her palm before they started to sing.

"You're a Krandall?"

Max shoved the unwanted jealousy to the back of his mind and shot Tim a sidelong glance.

"Man, Tuck and Jake are gonna love that." Tim's smile was gleeful, as if he looked forward to their reaction to the news.

"My mother was born a Krandall. She died a Grayson." Max turned back to the stage. While he hadn't lied to his friends, he'd deceived them, and they deserved to know why. But explanations would have to wait. His gaze scanned the stage and floor security. "Where are Ryan's guys?"

Tim jerked his head toward stage left. "One's watching the left back entrance. The other is manning the steps leading to the stage."

"Good." Max pulled his phone from his pocket. "Keep an eye on her from here. I've got some calls to make."

He made a quick call to his lead man in New Jersey. Hopefully, the increased offer on the property would do the trick. If not, he wasn't sure what else he could do, but giving up before he'd exhausted every possibility went against the grain. In the meantime, there was Jessi to consider. She needed a quiet place to unwind and a little time off the grid. Some time away, where he could formulate a plan in case tonight's press conference had lasting repercussions, wouldn't do him any harm either.

His next two calls were to Dan, then Ryan. Jessi's father answered on the second ring.

"Max? What's wrong? Is Jessi all right?"

Max rubbed a palm around the back of his neck. "She's fine. She and Spence are on stage."

"Is the security team nearby?"

"They're doing what you're paying them to do from what I've seen."

"Then what's up?"

"Your daughter."

"After that dress she was almost wearing last night, I don't want to know what else she's done." A weighty sigh drifted through the earpiece. "Do I?"

"It's not what she's done, it's what I'm about to do."

"What would that be?"

Max shut his eyes briefly. Whether Ryan knew it or not, Jessi was at risk from more than a menacing fan. Against his better judgment, he'd agreed to help, and he meant to see it through, but things had just gotten more complicated. "As soon as she's done tonight, I'm taking her somewhere quiet. Somewhere that has nothing to do with country music."

"Are you going to tell me where?"

He hesitated. She'd be safe with him. The point of disappearing was to give her some time free and clear of the pressures she faced on a daily basis, including those from her family. Gracie and Jake would know where they were, but with a nut job gunning for her, he'd rather be safe than sorry.

"Alton Bay, New Hampshire. Jake and Gracie have a place on the lake. It's quiet, and with the summer crowds gone she can work on her music without being disturbed. I don't want anyone else to know where she is. That includes the family and Spence."

"What about her security team?"

Max grunted. "Them, too."

Ryan said nothing for several heartbeats. "I assume you have a good reason for taking her away, but there have been no more letters since we spoke, no contact from the stalker. What's changed?"

"I got a close look at her over the past couple days. Did you know she's been having migraines?"

"Dan mentioned she'd seen a doctor." Ryan's tone held a note of defensiveness. "When I asked her about the pills, she said it was a woman thing."

Max fought a helpless smile. It was pure Jessi to offer a logical explanation most men would accept hands down—before they ran in the other direction. If the account was true, he might have done the same, but she hadn't slapped him down when he suggested stress was the cause, and he wouldn't have bought the woman-thing excuse if she'd given it. Between memories of his mother, two foster homes where he'd been the only male in the house, his friendship with Gracie, and the steady stream of women he'd spent time with over the years, he'd learned to recognize the signs of PMS. The meltdown Jessi suffered the other night hadn't been a byproduct of out of control hormones. Her tears had come from someplace much deeper and infinitely more frightening. They'd come from the depths of her soul.

"That may very well be a part of it, but it's not the whole picture." He gave Ryan a full accounting of all that happened after they'd left the family dinner that first night, including the conversation that dealt with his wife's murder. "And she's not sleeping."

Saying it all out loud reinforced Max's belief that the darling of country music was a woman on the edge of collapse. "If she doesn't find a way to balance the demands everyone has put on her with her own needs as a private person, she's going to break."

"Jesus." Ryan's voice broke. "I knew something was wrong, but I didn't realize it was that bad. How could I have missed it?"

A good question. Then again, Max might have done his best to avoid her whenever he'd visited with the Tuckers, but that hadn't prevented him from watching her every move when he had the chance. He hadn't noticed there was a problem either, not until she'd come to him with her desperate plan.

"Cut yourself some slack. I've rarely seen your daughter when she wasn't wearing a smile. None of us saw it, but the point is, we have now."

"How long will you be gone?"

"She has a run through for the Super Bowl in Tampa next Friday and a tour date in Memphis Saturday. I'll make sure she's there, but I want her schedule cleared for the week. There's a photo shoot on her schedule for Tuesday. Cancel it or reschedule, if you can, and Spence can handle the Thursday dinner in Nashville on his own. You asked for my help. She needs to breathe without the family watching over her shoulder and enough time to find herself. I'll keep her safe while she does."

"What if she can't?"

"Then she can't. Where she goes from there will be up to her."

"Do you need anything from me?"

"Find the bastard who's sending those letters."

"I'm on it." Ryan paused for a moment. "You'll keep me informed?"

"I'll be in touch."

Chapter 12

Jessi reached for the canvas bag on the floor of the limo the moment the door shut. The brewing discomfort behind her left eye hadn't yet progressed to migraine status, but it would before long.

"Another headache?"

Her fingers closed around the prescription bottle and she nodded at Max, seated at her side. Although facing the crowd who would attend the after-concert dinner with a pain-free head was important, he was the main reason for heading off the migraine before it could form.

Lord, he was a treat for the eyes. Max in a terrycloth towel took her breath away and, holy eye candy, was there anything sexier than a dangerous looking man in a tux? If there was, she hadn't seen it and, apparently, the women at the awards party last night after the show agreed with her. Every woman there had dripped with envy, a state of affairs Jessi knew only too well. With perseverance, and a little bit of luck, those days were over but, in the meantime, casually dressed in slacks and a sweater was how she liked him best. This was Max. Her Max, and she planned to enjoy what was left of the evening.

His dark brows lowered as he caught her chin with a fingertip and lifted her face for his study. After a moment, he dropped his hand and faced front. "Change of plan, Dan."

Dan met his gaze in the rear view mirror. "DFW?"

Max nodded curtly.

"Wait. What? Why are we going to the airport?" Confused, she blinked and bounced her gaze between Max and the back of Dan's head.

"That's where the plane is waiting."

"Plane? To where?" She met Max's steady gaze. "I can't go anywhere tonight. They're expecting us in the hotel dining room for the after party."

"Will they put a stop pay on the check if you don't show up?"

"No, but—"

One dark brow lifted. "Kick you out of the country music club?"

"There's no such club, funny guy."

"Then there's no problem."

That wasn't quite true. "Spence will be pissed."

Perhaps it was a trick of the low light, but she could've sworn Max's eyes gleamed with satisfaction.

Beneath his overcoat, his shoulders lifted in a quick shrug. "He'll get over it."

She cocked her head. "Just out of curiosity, where is this plane supposed to take us?"

"To a quiet place." Intent and sober, his gaze held hers captive as he slid the bottle from her fingers and opened it. Shaking out a pill, he offered her his open palm. "A place where you won't be bothered by the pressures of your career or the demands of your family. Someplace you can decompress and find yourself again."

If he hadn't already owned her, heart and soul, she became his at that moment. Her heart fell in a dizzying spiral and settled in a whisper-soft landing. Tears sprang in her eyes as she took the pill from his hand, placed it on her tongue, and swallowed. She spoke without looking away from his beautiful gray eyes. "Take us to DFW, Dan."

The shadow of a smile moved over Max's lips, and she couldn't resist. Fate sealed, she leaned toward him and hoped against hope he would finally see what was right in front of him. Brushing his lips in a brief kiss, she whispered, "You had me at 'quiet'."

* * * *

"Are we there yet?" Jessi opened her eyes and yawned as the wheels of the private jet touched down on the runway of the small, regional airport.

"Almost." Max unclipped his seat belt. "It's about a thirty minute drive around the lake to Alton Bay."

"There's a lake?" She pressed her nose to the tiny window. Other than the runway lights and trees in the distance, there was nothing to see. She spun back around at his quiet chuckle.

"A big, frozen lake. A good portion of Winnipesaukee ices over during the winter months. Like they do in boats during the summer, the locals cross the lake on snow machines come the freeze."

He rose to his feet as the plane came to a stop. She scrambled to follow. Retrieving their bags and her guitar case, which Dan had miraculously pulled from the trunk of the limo, Max shook the pilot's hand before leading her out the dropdown stairs. Frigid wind blasted them as they hurried across the tarmac to an idling SUV.

A tall, muscular boy in his late teens jumped from the driver's seat. He tugged a hat with earflaps over his head at their approach. "Good evening, Mr. Grayson. Miss." He touched the brim of the hat and offered Jessi a dimpled smile.

"Kip, right?"

He nodded at Max and took the bags from his hands. "I left a light on and the fridge is stocked with enough food for a couple days. Mrs. Malone has my number on the small board near the door if you need anything else." He jerked his head toward the open door of the vehicle. "I set the GPS for you. Should deliver you straight to the front door."

Max pulled several folded bills from his pocket and tucked them inside the neck flap of Kip's coat. "Thanks for coming out on such a cold night."

"Oh, man, that ain't necessary." Clearly embarrassed by the tip, the teenager had no way of returning it with his hands full of bags. "The Malones are special people and you being their friend, I'm happy to help."

Max thumped him on the shoulder. "All the same, I appreciate it. You take your girl out for a nice dinner and a movie."

His dimples reappeared with his smile. "I'll do that. Let me stow these in the back and you can take off."

While Kip loaded the bags in the back hatch, Jessi climbed into the passenger seat and Max settled behind the wheel. As they pulled away, she blew the teenager a kiss and grinned when he blew one back.

"There's a heartbreaker if I ever saw one." She turned to catch Max smiling.

"No doubt. From what Jake says, he's a local football star with the talent to make it to the pros someday." They passed through the guard shack and the GPS indicated a left turn. Max guided the vehicle onto the two-lane road. "He's earned a free ride at Boston College starting next fall, but his mom's a single parent and he's ambitious. Apparently, he runs his own handyman and gopher business in the area. Gracie throws him work whenever she can."

"So, this quiet place belongs to Gracie and Jake?"

He nodded. "Jake bought the house as an investment property a couple of years ago. At over two hundred years old, the main structure needed a lot of work, but Gracie took one look and fell in love with the area." He flashed her a grin. "Jake claims he's financed Ivy League educations for half a dozen local kids thanks to all the remodeling they've done, but the results are worth it."

Jessi nodded and chewed on her bottom lip as she studied his strong profile. He hadn't said a word about what had happened at the press conference, and she was dying to ask. Rightful heir to the Krandall empire? Why had he been in foster care if he had a family? An incredibly rich family. If he'd ever mentioned his connection to the famous football Krandalls, she hadn't heard about it. Had Tuck?

Max had to know the press would be all over them when they returned to Manhattan. He'd face further questions, and so would she, which meant she needed to know what was going on. More importantly, she loved him and wanted to help if she could, but from his angry reaction earlier, the Krandalls were another sore spot. A dark and icy mountain road wasn't the best place to bring up an obviously touchy subject, but when they got where they were going....

As late as it was, they met with little traffic on the winding road. Occasional breaks in the dense pines surrounding them afforded Jessi a moonlit view of the snow-covered lake on their left. Small, dark cottages dotted the coastline, mixed in with larger, more modern homes here and there. She counted three bed and breakfasts before they exited the two lane road for a single stretch of blacktop leading deeper into the woods.

The GPS signaled an imminent arrival at their destination, and Max pulled the SUV down a long, tree-lined driveway. They passed by a small outbuilding he said housed a private gym before he brought the vehicle to a stop. A boathouse hung over the frozen lake to their right. A long dock stretched out beside it.

Pale in the bright moonlight, a tall, narrow house sat on a peninsula, the shoreline hugging the rocky strip of land on three sides. Someone, probably Kip, had cleared the snow from the brick walkway leading to the front door.

Max handed her a set of keys. "Go let yourself in. I'll get the bags."

Chapter 13

While Max collected their things, Jessi climbed the gentle rise to the house. A grand old oak clung to the steep strip of land dropping to the water's edge. Bare at the moment, its wide reaching branches would shade the house during the hot days of summer and thrill the Malones, and anyone passing by on the lake, with its brightly colored leaves when fall arrived to cool things off.

Three steps delivered her onto a wide, covered wooden deck wrapping around toward the back of the house. Shivering, she resisted the urge to investigate and pulled open the glass storm door to slide the key into the lock.

The heavy paneled door swung inward. Jessi stepped over the threshold into a well-lit, large modern kitchen. Tucked between glossy white cabinetry, industrial appliances gleamed beneath strategically placed recessed lighting. A gray stone cook island gave way to a charming table nook. Beyond two walls of windows and a set of French doors, a stunning expanse of moonlit lake was visible.

The last wall contained a gas fireplace where cozy flames danced beneath a flat screen TV. A set of stairs ascended on one side and, on the other, another set led to a lower floor. She turned as Max closed the door.

"Would you like a tour?"

She nodded, set aside her canvas bag, and shed her coat to lay it over the slatted back of one of six high stools tucked beneath the island.

Larger than it appeared, the house was like nothing she'd ever seen—built in six staggered levels. Switching back and forth between the front of the house and the back, all but the forth level guest suite contained a single, spacious room. From the basement, at the front of the house, a short staircase led to the Malone twins' bedroom/playroom at the back. Six steps up toward the front once more, a den designed for comfort

Mackenzie Crowne

offered several seating areas as well as a second, larger flat screen above a huge stone fireplace that took up most of the central wall of the house.

They returned to the kitchen, and Jessi collected her coat and canvas bag before they climbed again to the guest floor. Without a word, Max dropped his duffle on the queen bed in one of two modest sized bedrooms. The other, he explained, would soon be converted into a nursery.

Jessi eyed her suitcase, gripped in his hand. Apparently, she'd be sleeping elsewhere, but not for long. Whether he knew it or not, Max had claimed her heart. She would be using this "quiet" time to do some claiming of her own.

He shuffled her down the hallway. She blinked as they stopped in the doorway of the common guest bath. The six head shower stall and oversized Jacuzzi tub would be at home in any five star resort.

"Wow." She shot him a sidelong glance in time to catch his heavy swallow, as if he, too, had some interesting ideas on how to put that tub to good use. She shivered in anticipation.

That's right, big guy. Think about it. You and me, naked and slippery. Soap, water, and steamy possibilities.

He cleared his throat and crooked his head to indicate the stairs at the end of the hallway. "You're one level up."

In the master suite, French doors led to a private deck overlooking the lake and a third fireplace warmed the air. Max crossed the hardwood floor to deposit her suitcase and guitar on the tufted leather ottoman at the foot of the huge four-poster bed. Jessi wandered deeper into the comfortably elegant room and ran her fingers over the smooth wood of a gorgeous antique writing desk.

"If you need anything, give me a shout. Good night."

Jessi turned from her study of a watercolor on the wall above a pillowed lounge as Max headed for the door. Disappointed, she scrambled for an excuse to extend the evening a little longer. "Wait. Are you hungry? I could make us something."

He stopped at the top of the stairs and turned back. "I don't think that would be wise." His lips curled into a teasing smile. "It's late and the local fire department is an all-volunteer force. We probably shouldn't piss them off on our first night in town."

She rolled her eyes but couldn't help returning his grin. "Ha ha." The grin slid from her lips. "About the press conference."

He stiffened visibly and a muscle jumped in his hardened jaw. "It's nearly four AM, Squirt. Get some rest. I'll see you in the morning."

He quickly disappeared down the steps. Growling beneath her breath, she stalked over to the bed and flopped onto her back to stare at the ceiling. Her canvas bag buzzed, and she rolled over to dig for her phone. She'd turned it to vibrate when Spence's first text arrived demanding to know what was keeping her. He'd left three more since, each one increasing in anger. The latest was from Tim.

Just spoke to Spence. He's pissed and worried. R u ok?

"Shit." She'd need to tell the family and Spence something if she was going to enjoy that quiet time Max had promised her, and there were appointments on her schedule that needed attention. Chewing her lip, she thumbed in her reply. *I'm fine. Max and I decided to take some private time. B back 4 the super bowl run-through on Friday. Promise. Will u take care of rescheduling events this week & let Spence know? Alicia & Dad 2?*

Tim's reply buzzed several seconds later. *Sure, throw me 2 the wolves.*

She grinned. *U can handle Dad.*

U r gonna owe me big time.

A laugh gurgled in her throat. *I'll buy you a case of meatballs.*

LOL where r u?

She started to type the answer, then deleted it. Gracie and Jake obviously knew where they were, and she'd have to ask Max if he'd told them to keep the information to themselves. She and Max were less likely to have surprise visitors if no one knew where they were, and that's how she meant to keep it. The whole point of this exercise was to prove to her family she was her own woman, and seducing Max would be difficult enough. An audience would only complicate the issue.

A grim smile played on her lips as her thumbs moved over the screen. *None of ur business.*

Brat.

The emoticon she sent stuck out its tongue.

Shit, Jess. Did u know he was related 2 the Krandalls?

She glanced toward the door and back. *No.*

Has he said anything?

Not yet.

It's gonna cause a stir.

She sighed. *I know.*

At the time, she'd assumed Max's comment about the paparazzi being a problem had to do with what had happened to Gracie and Jake. Now she had to wonder. Had he been concerned about what the press would dig up on him instead? As far as she was concerned, who his family was didn't matter a bit, but he obviously felt differently. Max was a deliberate man. If he'd kept his heritage a secret, even from his friends, he had to have a good reason, but if he thought she'd let him call a halt to their deal now that his concerns about the press had come to pass, he had another think coming.

Unfortunately, she didn't have a clue how she would stop him if he chose to walk away, and she was too tired at the moment to figure it out. *It's late & I'm beat. Talk to you in a few days.*

Ok, b good appeared along with a smiley face.

Her lips curled into a determined smile. Not a chance in hell. She tossed the phone aside and rolled off the bed to dig through her suitcase. She'd been good her whole life—well, with one disappointing exception—and look where it had gotten her. In love with a stubborn man who insisted on keeping her at arm's length. Screw that. The stunning revelation of Max's family connections aside, she meant to make the most of their time alone.

* * * *

Though Jessi dozed, sleep was elusive. After several hours of tossing and turning, she finally gave up. Yawning, she stretched beneath the down comforter, opened her eyes, and quickly squeezed them shut against the bright shards of early morning sun stabbing through the French doors. She reached out blindly for the bedside table where she'd left her phone. The last time she'd rolled over to check, it had been five thirty-eight and not a hint of daylight had shown in the stretch of sky visible from the bed.

Cracking an eyelid, she checked the phone's screen. Seven sixteen. Her stomach growled, and she shoved aside the comforter to pad into the master bath. Once she'd taken care of pressing business, she went to the sink to wash her hands—and yelped at her reflection. Exhausted, she'd fallen into bed without a thought for her usual skin care regimen. Definitely a mistake. The smeared streaks of her stage makeup resembled those of a manic clown.

If her fans could see her now.

She scrunched her nose in a horrified grimace. Forget her fans. If Max caught a glimpse of the disaster she was, all hope for his seduction would be doomed. The T-shirt and socks she'd pulled on to sleep in hit the floor, and she stepped into the shower stall that was a perfect twin to the travertine tile and brushed pewter playground one level below.

Six high power heads blasted the mess from her face and the grogginess from her brain. Wrapped in a towel, she returned to the bedroom to dress and applied a quick coat of makeup before she straightened the room.

Cocking her head, she listened for signs of activity elsewhere in the house. Not a sound reached her ears. In her mind, she pictured Max, his big body sprawled out in slumber one level below. She caught her bottom lip in her teeth as she considered the possibility of tiptoeing into his room to slide under the covers beside him. That kiss they'd shared proved he wasn't immune to her physically, just determined to ignore the pull. Half asleep with his guard down, would his body's natural attraction to hers overrule whatever roadblocks his mind had built?

Eyeing the open doorway, her shoulders slumped with guilt. Sometimes the old clichéd moves worked best, but a quick round of sex wasn't what she was after. If she wanted his heart, she was going to have to win it, and trickery wasn't the way to go. Still, the concept of having nothing on her schedule but implementing Max's seduction left her almost giddy.

Like a shot of adrenaline, anticipation blasted away the fatigue that had dogged her for months. Skipping down the steps, she skidded to a stop in front of his open bedroom door. The room was empty and his bed made.

"Max?" Silence met her call and she descended the stairs into the kitchen. "Max, are you here?" The hum of the refrigerator was the only reply. A glance out the tall window beside the door proved he couldn't have gone far. The SUV sat in the driveway where he'd parked it last night.

She spun around with a sigh. Wherever he'd gone, he'd be back soon. In the meantime, the shiny black, single brew coffeemaker on the counter called her name. Three minutes later, steaming cup in hand and braced for the cold, she stepped beyond the French doors and gasped at the stunning view.

The deck perched thirty feet above the snow-covered lake in a cove of sorts. Not a soul moved about in the cold morning air. The closest shoreline was a half mile across. To the left, the lake opened up for several miles. In a breathtaking backdrop, misty, tree-covered mountains shimmered in the distance. The irresistible serenity was broken only by the whisper of wind through the trees—until her stomach growled again. Shivering suddenly, she returned inside to find some breakfast.

A search of the refrigerator and kitchen pantry proved they wouldn't starve, and the supplies Kip had mentioned offered her a chance to redeem herself after her disastrous attempt at dinner. The small fire extinguisher hanging on the pantry wall made her smile. After a moment's hesitation, she pulled it from its brackets and plunked it down smack dead center on the island.

All volunteer fire department my ass.

Grinning, she gathered the makings of French toast and arranged a half dozen strips of bacon in a frying pan. The front door opened as she placed the first slice of egg-battered bread on the skillet.

Hair damp with sweat, Max dropped a small duffle on the steps leading to the next level. "I didn't expect to see you for a while yet."

She shrugged a shoulder. "I was hungry. So much happened last night, I missed dinner." Subtle lines of returning tension creased his forehead, and she swallowed an inward sigh. A contentious conversation was the last thing she wanted, but this thing with the Krandalls wasn't going to go away. She wanted it over with so they could concentrate on more important things. Still, she hesitated to bring up the subject. "Where'd you go?"

He opened the fridge to pull out the orange juice. "To work out in the gym."

"Want some breakfast?" She added another slice of bread to the batter.

He turned and his eyes squinted beneath lowered brows. She followed his gaze to the extinguisher.

Fluttering her lashes, she offered him a cheeky grin. "Just in case."

His tension melted away as one corner of his lips lifted in a sexy, crooked smile. "I could eat."

He manned the bacon while she browned a tall stack of French toast. When everything was prepared, they ate at the table overlooking the deck and the views beyond. She delayed the topic of the press conference for the moment with questions about the area. Apparently, there were several ski mountains close by, if she was interested, and plenty of trails for the snow machines in the boathouse. The idea of ice fishing left her cold, but the arcade on the other side of the lake sounded like fun.

He polished off a half dozen slices of French toast to her two. When he rose to take their empty plates to the sink, she sucked in a fortifying breath and spoke to his back.

"How did you end up in foster care, Max?"

If her sudden question surprised him, it didn't show. He ran the plates under the water before stacking them in the dishwasher, and turned to prop his hips against the counter. He crossed his arms and met her gaze.

"It's what happens when a minor is orphaned." His casual tone didn't mask the intensity in his eyes.

She leaned her elbows on the table. "If what that reporter said is true, you weren't an orphan."

"It's true, but when my mother died, I might as well have been."

"I don't understand. You had a family."

The angry blow of his wry snort made her wince. He must have noticed, because his shoulders bunched and he sighed.

"My father's parents died a long time ago. Dad had a second cousin I lived with for a while, but she and her husband had four kids of their own and didn't have the time or patience for an angry punk with an attitude to match. I entered the foster care system at fourteen and spent the next four years moving from place to place."

"What about your grandmother?"

His eyelids lowered, shuttering his eyes, but not before she witnessed the flash of heat in them. "Elizabeth Krandall never approved of my parents' marriage. She'd cut all ties with my mother long before I was born."

Jessi swallowed. As annoying as her family could be at times, they were always supportive and stood together as a solid force when hard times struck. She couldn't understand a mother turning her back on her own daughter. "Surely the authorities notified her of her daughter's death."

A muscled jumped along his clenched jaw and he nodded, but didn't elaborate.

"Did she know about you?"

Tension vibrated around him like an aura. "If she didn't before, she did then."

"Then what happened? She's your grandmother. Why wouldn't the state approach her about taking you?"

His barked laugh was harsh as he pushed off the counter and snatched up the skillet. "They did. She declined."

Jessi swallowed against the ache in her throat as if the cruel fingers of his past were wrapped around her windpipe. What kind of monster denied a little boy a place to live and grow? Denied her own flesh and blood?

He turned to the sink and snapped on the faucet. Shoulder muscles and back stiff, he dipped his proud head to the task of scrubbing the skillet. Tears stung her eyes as Jessi rose and crossed the room. She stopped behind him and, with her heart breaking for the little boy he'd been, she wrapped her arms around the man.

He stilled briefly, then shut off the faucet. Wiping his hands on a towel, he turned, forcing her to loosen her hold.

She didn't let go, however. Tucked against him, she buried her head in his chest and sniffed against the tears she couldn't hold back. "She deserves to be whipped."

"Hey." He wrapped an arm around her waist and pressed his palm to her cheek to lift her face. His gaze softened as he studied her eyes. "Don't." He lowered his head, and his bristled cheek scraped at her skin where he pressed a kiss to her temple. "Ah, damn, baby. Don't cry."

Her heart swelled at the endearment, and she turned her head until her mouth was beneath his. The rock hard man he'd become may not need to be comforted, but the little boy he'd been deserved so much more than he'd been given.

Once, twice, then once again, she brushed his lips in whisper-soft kisses as if the gentle caresses could heal the wounds of his past. With a low rumble vibrating in his chest, he accepted her silent offering. He speared his fingers into her hair and cupped the back of her neck. His head dipped and he captured her mouth with his.

Joy and pleasure gushed through her veins. The delicious heat of his body molded to hers and left her dizzy. She clung to him as he deepened the kiss, opening her mouth to his marauding tongue. He pulled her tighter against him, and his erection pressed against her belly. Bold and demanding, his need called to hers. Curling her fingers into his sweatshirt, she willingly answered. She pressed closer and swirled her tongue around his.

Chest expanding on a shudder, he released her neck to drop his hand to the curve of her waist. Pleasurable chills pebbled her skin as his warm fingers dipped beneath the hem of her sweater and rode her side to caress her ribs. Anticipation fired her already heated blood. He captured her moan with his mouth, and his hand came unerringly to cup her lace-covered breast.

With thumb and forefinger, he plucked at the tightened bead of her nipple, peaked with almost unbearable excitement. He shoved a muscled thigh between her legs and a white-hot arrow of pleasure shot in a straight line for her throbbing clit. Unprepared for the speed and power of the pleasurable jolt, the orgasm hit without warning. Her muscles tensed and then quivered like a released bow. She whimpered and hung in Max's arms while her body bucked and shivered.

"Jessi?"

Dazed by the delicious band of waves pulsing through her, she was slow to open her eyes. When she did, Max's face hung inches above hers. His eyes widened and ruddy color rode his high cheekbones. His Adam's apple bounced on a swallow.

"Did you just…?"

Her heavy lids slid shut. "Yes, please."

His low groan vibrated against her chest. "Jesus, you're killing me, Jess."

A latent spasm took her by surprise and she shivered. "Just give me a minute, okay?"

Her leg muscles refused to hold her, and he tightened his hold, lifting her in his arms. Dazed with pleasure and delight, she rested her head against his shoulder as he spun around. An anticipatory smile curved her lips and she snuggled closer. If she had the strength, she'd be embarrassed by the speed with which he'd launched her into orgasm, but she wasn't about to apologize, since he was at fault. Besides, she'd make it up to him in a few minutes.

Still, she was going to have to get control of her rapid-fire response to his kisses. A healthy sexual relationship demanded both parties be present when the fireworks went off.

Her eyelids fluttered open as he bent and deposited her on a hard kitchen chair instead of a soft bed. He straightened and turned away.

She blinked and reached out a hand. "Wait. Where are you going?"

"To take a shower."

Her hand plunked to her knee and her mouth dropped open. She snapped it shut. "You've *got* to be kidding."

He stopped and looked over his shoulder. "I'm here to help you, Squirt, but that's as far as it goes."

She eased back in the chair and eyed the impressive bulge tenting his sweats. Lifting her gaze to his, her smile was keen. "Oh, really?"

He turned away and bent to pick up his bag from the foot of the stairs. "I never would have taken you for a tease, Max."

He straightened and shot her a glare. "Damn it, Squirt. You're a beautiful woman. Of course I'm attracted, but I'm not the man for you."

Every drop of lingering languidness evaporated beneath the scorching flare of frustration. "You can run all you want, but we both know a cold shower isn't going to cure what ails you." She raked her gaze down his body and up again. "Only I can do that."

Chapter 14

The aged wood of the hallway above him creaked. Max looked up from the TV where the Marauders were crushing Seattle to frown at the ceiling. A moment later, the swish and click of cabinet doors opening and closing in the kitchen quickened his pulse.

He scrubbed a palm over his jaw and glared at the empty stairway. Jesus. Tuck would bust a gut laughing if he were ever to learn how Max had run from Jessi like a chicken shit. Especially since the move didn't have the desired effect.

Granted, she'd disappeared while he was in the shower and spent most of the day in her room. The occasional strum of her guitar floated through the house as she worked, and he'd assumed he'd face hurt feelings and pouts when she finally came downstairs for dinner. He should have known better, however. Her innocent smile was a mask for a woman determined to get her way.

A simple meal of grilled cheese and soup turned into a contest of wills. Insisting on helping with the preparations, she took every opportunity to brush up against him in the process. She made little effort to hide her agenda, sliding a slim hand across his back as she leaned for the salt shaker, or bumping a plump breast against his arm so she could sniff at the soup. He spent an uncomfortable half hour pretending that wasn't a hard-on doing its best to break through his zipper.

He'd excused himself the moment the meal was finished and dropped his forehead to the shower's tile several minutes later when she knocked and popped her head inside the bathroom. She laughed, claiming the Malones were going to be surprised when they saw their water bill, before puckering her lips in a wolf whistle and shutting the door.

Jessi Tucker was at war and she didn't fight fair.

If he was smart, he'd pack her up and return her to her father. Now. Tonight. Four more days of the cat and mouse game they'd been playing since that ill-advised kiss in the kitchen and he'd be frothing at the mouth.

The memory of her shattering in his arms didn't help matters.

He'd never had a woman respond to his touch so quickly—or strongly. She'd climaxed for Christ's sake. From nothing more than a kiss and the pressure of his thigh between her legs. The raunchy dreams she'd starred in over the years were tame compared to the scenarios sneaking into his brain in the last twenty-four hours. He could only imagine what it would be like to actually fuck her.

His cock twitched and he broke into a sweat as the shuffle of her slippered feet announced her arrival.

"How much time is left?" Reaching the bottom step, she eyed the TV and crossed the room to set a bowl of pretzels on the coffee table.

"Five minutes. Weren't you watching?"

"I caught most of the first half while I was working," she flopped onto the couch beside him, "but I hate blowouts."

At that moment, Tuck added to the lopsided score of the game with a diving, one-handed catch in the end zone. She pumped her fist in the air and cheered her cousin on as he rolled to his feet to spike the ball.

"Aaaand, here comes Atlas."

Tuck struck his touchdown pose, flexing his chest and biceps for the crowd before his teammates piled on him in celebration.

She laughed and shook her head. "Talk about rubbing it in."

Max shrugged. "They just clinched a spot in the conference final. They have a right to celebrate."

"You know what this means, right?"

He turned his head to meet her gaze.

"There are only four teams left vying for a Super Bowl ring, and one of them is the Hurricanes."

He grunted and looked away.

She kicked off her slippers and propped her feet on the coffee table. "So, I've been thinking about your grandmother."

His shoulders bunched with tension. He'd already said more than he should on the subject of his past, but Jessi had a way of plowing through his defenses. From the sound of it, she wasn't finished prodding.

"I think we should hire a hit man and have her offed."

He flinched, turned his head, and couldn't help but laugh. "You're a bloodthirsty little thing, aren't you?"

She smiled but her eyes were sharp with a militant gleam. "What she did pisses me off. I totally believe in karma, but sometimes it needs a little help."

He propped his feet on the table beside hers. "Trust me, a hit man isn't necessary. As far as I'm concerned, she did me a favor."

Her mouth pulled down into a frown. "How? I don't have any experience with the foster care system, but it couldn't have been easy living with strangers."

"Elizabeth Krandall was as much a stranger as anyone else, and even if the foster families that took me in weren't sure what to do with a punk kid with an attitude, at least none of them actively hated me."

She turned on the couch, tucking one knee under the other. "Your grandmother is a blind fool and a heartless bitch, but hate is a strong word."

"Maybe, but it's an accurate one." He tucked his hands behind his head and looked up at the ceiling. "I was just a kid the one time I met her personally, but even a twelve year old can recognize hate when he sees it."

"Where did you meet her?"

"In a judge's chambers a week after Mom died." And all these years later, his skin still crawled at the memory. "She studied me as if I were a rabid animal that should be put down and, although I can't prove the envelope she dropped on the judge's desk was a payoff, her words made it clear. As the judge picked up the envelope, she told him, 'Take care of this today, and if I hear one word from either the court or the press, you won't like the consequences.'"

A low growl rumbled in Jessi's throat. "Forget the hit man. She belongs behind bars." She snagged a pretzel from the bowl and broke off a piece with her teeth. "But you said she did you a favor?"

He grunted. "Actually, her husband did me the favor. My grandfather didn't step in when my mother died, and maybe he simply overlooked it, but there was an old provision in his will for Mom when he died a few years ago." He rolled his head to meet her eye. "The money came to me, but not before the old bat did everything in her power to stop it."

Jessi's brows arched even as her mouth twisted into an angry line. She popped the rest of the pretzel into her mouth. "I hope it was a lot of money."

The tension drained from his body as satisfaction surged. "Would you consider fifty-eight million a lot?"

Jessi choked, coughed, and sat up straight. "Fifty-eight? Million?"

"And some change."

She blinked and shook her head as if to clear it. "Holy shit!"

His smile was smug. "A drop in the bucket since she's worth billions, but I'm sure my grandmother had worse to say when she had to approve the transfer."

Jessi's mouth dropped open and she sagged into the couch. Suddenly, she narrowed her eyes. "Are you making this up just so I won't do time for capital murder?"

"Scout's honor." He held up three fingers.

She tilted her head to one side, her eyes doubtful. "Were you ever a scout?"

"Hell no. I was a street rat, remember?" He laughed at her scowl. "But it's a cool salute, and I really did get fifty-eight million from old man Krandall."

Her smile started slow and grew into a full blown grin. She sat forward and held up her hand. "Karma, baby!" His palm met hers in a high five. Her soft laughter mingled with his, and she dropped back against the couch. "Wow." Rolling her head, she looked at him. "Still, it's too bad about the team."

His smile faded. "I never cared about the Hurricanes. The Krandalls have only one thing I want, and ironically, I'll use my mother's inheritance to get it."

"What's that?"

Shit. Damn her and her piquant smiles. A frown pulled at his lips as he stared at her without answering. The cat was out of the bag about his connection to the famous football family, but the fewer who knew about Haven Place and his plans, the better.

She rolled her eyes. "Tell me." When he remained silent, she sat up once more. "What? Do you think I'm going to run to the Krandalls and blab?"

"No, but the only way to safeguard a secret is to keep it to yourself."

"A secret, huh? Hmm. With fifty-eight million, you could buy pretty much anything you want, so that must mean they don't want to sell whatever it is." Tapping a fingertip to her lips, she studied him with shrewd eyes. "You said you don't care about the team. I'm guessing...real estate?"

Damn it. What were the odds she'd hit the target on the first try? He looked away.

"I'm right, aren't I?" Her smile was victorious.

"What you are is nosey." He shoved to his feet and swept up the magazine he'd been flipping through before the game. Returning it to the bookshelf, he turned back and pinned her with a stern glower. "And if you share any of this with anyone, I'll...go to the cops and tell them about the hit man."

She sniffed, but her eyes were full of silent laughter as she held up three fingers.

A helpless chuckle rumbled in his chest, and he shook his head. "When my mother graduated from college, her father let her choose from among several of the family's real estate holdings to make her home. She chose a house on the Jersey shore and named it Haven Place."

"What a pretty name."

"It's a pretty house." He shoved his hands into the front pockets of his jeans. "Mom loved it there. She once told me the two years she spent in her house on the shore were some of the happiest days of her life. I think it was because for the first time in her life, she was out from under my grandmother's control, at least partially. My parents met there. Right outside on the beach."

"Oh. How romantic."

Jessi's smile went dreamy and sparked misty memories of the bittersweet longing in his mother's eyes whenever she spoke of Haven Place. He could still remember the yearning in her voice as she talked about the magical summer his parents had met and fallen in love. He rubbed a hand over his chest at the pang in his heart.

"They dated for a couple of months before her parents found out. When they did, they were pissed. They didn't approve of their daughter wasting her time with a blue-collar cop. Her mother gave her an ultimatum. Dump my father or lose Haven Place."

Shocked anger replaced Jessi's smile with a thin-lipped frown.

"Mom married Dad in a civil service the next day, and when she refused to follow their edict and get a quick divorce, they tossed her out of the home she loved and cut her out of their lives."

Moisture shimmered in Jessi's eyes and she shook her head. "Their loss, Max, and your mother's gain." Her voice softened and her eyes filled with empathy. "It sounds like she made the right choice."

He scraped a palm over the back of his neck and nodded. He agreed and from what he could recall, so did his mother. Unfortunately, the happy memories from those early years of his life were in stark contrast to the misery and grief that arrived with the unmarked car pulling up to the curb in his twelfth summer. In the blink of an eye, life changed. His mother had lost the only man she ever loved, and her broken heart was no match for the cancer that killed her less than a year later.

"So, you want to buy your mother's home, but it's not for sale?"

He blinked and shook his head in an effort to shed the dark memories from his mind. "Actually, they're willing to sell it, but no way in hell would they sell it to me."

"Hmm. Yeah, I can see where that might be a problem." Her lips twisted as she considered the situation. "You know, between my music and Tuck's football, my family has a lot of connections. Maybe we could help."

He stared at her. Although he hadn't used the exact words, her father had made the same suggestion. Max didn't like it any better coming from Jessi.

Her brow wrinkled. "What?"

He wiped the suspicion from his face. Ryan's offer had to do with negotiation. He was worried about his daughter and would use every option available to him to keep her safe. Jessi simply wanted to help. She had a soft heart and was a fierce defender of those she loved. It blew him away that she included him in that group.

"Nothing. I appreciate the offer, but I've got it under control." He checked his watch. "Are you finished working for the day?"

Confused hurt darkened her eyes, but she nodded.

He'd heard her moving around upstairs several times last night, which meant she'd spent another night awake. A few hours in the sun and wind would wear them both out. Maybe then she could get some much needed rest, and he could sleep without tossing and turning as his body ached for the woman right down the hall.

"We've got a couple hours of daylight left. I thought a ride on the snow machines might be fun."

"I've never ridden a snowmobile."

"Then it's time for a lesson."

Chapter 15

"Don't you dare laugh."

Bent over the snow machine as he checked the fuel level, Max lifted his head and fought back a smile. Gracie's borrowed insulated ski gear swallowed Jessi's much smaller frame. The unzipped jacket fell open to reveal bib pants, rolled at the ankles. Only the tips of her fingers peeked from the too-long sleeves. Like a North Pole pixie in hot pink, she looked like a kid playing dress up in her momma's clothes—with a couple of notable exceptions.

Despite her petite and slim frame, Jessi wasn't lacking in the curves department. Her breasts filled out the bib nicely, and as she spun in a circle and he got a view of her backside, he blew a silent whistle. The slick pink material accentuated the sweet curves of her hips and ass.

He straightened and rounded the machine. "You'll do, Squirt. Zip up. Where are your gloves?"

She tugged them from a pocket and held them up. "Where's the other machine?"

"It's in the boathouse." He turned back to cap the gas tank. "For your first lesson, we'll ride tandem."

She zipped up her coat and accepted the helmet he handed her. "Where are we going?"

"Out on the lake."

Tugging on the helmet, she eyed the wide stretch of snow-covered water. "Are you sure it's safe?"

"I checked the lake website this morning. The ice pack is plenty thick on this end, and it's flagged where it isn't. We'll be fine. We're not going far." He helped her with the chinstrap and watched as she dropped the windshield in place. "The helmets are wired with an internal radio transmitter so we'll be able to communicate without shouting over the roar of the motor."

She nodded her understanding as he donned his helmet, and jumped when he spoke.

"Can you hear me?"

Her teeth flashed in a grin. "Very cool."

He gave her a thumbs-up and straddled the machine. "Climb on behind me and wrap your arms around my waist. I'll keep the speed down but hold on, and if you get cold, let me know."

Using his shoulder as a brace, she scrambled on and squirmed close to his back until she was set, her gloved hands resting against his stomach. He allowed himself the heady enjoyment of her body pressed to his. Maybe he was playing with fire, but shit, he was human. With each passing hour, his resistance crumbled a little more, and damn it, a man could only take so much. The cheap thrill of her full breasts pressed to his back, even through multiple layers of winter wear, would help to take the edge off.

He slipped the key tether over his left glove and turned the key in the ignition. The machine rumbled to life, vibrating between their legs. Following a previously cut path down to the cove, he set a course close to the shoreline. On their left, fog shrouded the peak of Mount Major, but the sun broke through in patches. For January in New Hampshire, the day was mild.

They rounded a small island marking the entrance to "the broads," or the main part of the lake, and Jessi's gasp filled his ears.

"Oh, wow. Look."

She freed one hand, and he followed her pointing finger to a grove of pines hugging the coastline. Six feet of wingspan suspended a bald eagle on an invisible current. The bird glided through the air. On a graceful spiral, it dropped toward the trees and, with three powerful flaps of its wings, came to a perch on a branch beside a large nest.

"Did you see that?" She tucked her arm around him once more.

Her breathless demand made him grin, and he couldn't help teasing. "They're trees, Squirt. We have them in Manhattan. They're just smaller."

"Not the trees. The eagle. See it? It's right there." She tucked tighter against him to point over his shoulder. "It just landed. I can't believe you missed it. Oh my God. That was awesome." He chuckled, and she tightened her arms in a punishing squeeze, but there was laughter in her insult. "Jerk."

Setting a leisurely course, they crossed a section of "the broads." They passed a half dozen ice huts and Jessi waved to several fishermen working their lines. The traffic on the lake was light, with only a handful of machines passing by in the distance. By the time they arrived back at Alton Bay, the sun had dropped behind the mountains.

"Isn't that the house?" She pointed to the Malones' peninsula.

"Yep."

"We're not going in?"

"There's a restaurant beyond the next jetty. It's one of the few open year round. I thought we'd have dinner before going back."

A dozen snow machines sat quiet in the lot of the small upscale restaurant, along with a couple of cars. A young hostess greeted them as they stepped inside. Her eyes widened and she held out her hands for their helmets and coats. "Miss Tucker. Oh, wow, this is a surprise. We're honored you're visiting us."

Shit. He should have considered Jessi might be recognized. She took the compliment in stride, but Max dipped his head close to the girl. "Miss Tucker is on a short sabbatical. I trust you'll keep her presence here tonight quiet?"

Jessi jabbed him in the small of his back. "Don't mind him. He's overprotective."

A blush colored the young woman's cheeks. "Oh, no problem. I won't say a word."

She stored their helmets and coats, then led them to an open table near the windows overlooking the lake. As she left them alone, Jessi's face lit up at something beyond his shoulder.

Max turned his head as Kip approached their table.

"Good evening, Miss. Mr. Grayson."

"Another of your jobs?" Max smiled.

Kip's dimples flashed. "My girlfriend's parents own the restaurant, and they're short-handed in the winter months. I fill in once in a while." He handed them their menus. "Would you like to see a wine list?"

He rattled off the specials, and Max ordered a bottle of chardonnay. For their meals, he went with grilled cod. Jessi chose the lobster pie. Her choice of appetizer had him swallowing an inward groan. The woman was as persistent as she was beautiful.

A challenging smile quirked her lips, and she offered him an oyster on the half shell. He accepted the shellfish, savoring the peppery bite of the mignonette sauce. Holding his gaze, she followed suit.

Fighting a laugh, he picked up his wineglass. "It's a fallacy, you know."

She set aside her empty shell and took her time selecting another. "What is?"

"That oysters are an aphrodisiac." He watched her over the rim of his glass.

"Oh, I know. That myth is a load of bull."

Metabolically, she might be right, but as she lifted the shell to her pursed lips and the oyster disappeared, it didn't matter. The tip of her tongue appeared for a moment, capturing a bead of moisture from her bottom lip. He hardened in a rush.

"Did you think I was trying to seduce you, Max?"

He forced his eyes from the glossy sheen left behind to meet her gaze. She peeked at him through thick lashes. Although her pose was pure coquette, the glimmer of uncertainty in her eyes ruined the effect.

He blinked and suddenly wanted to slap his palm against his forehead. Bold and brassy, she talked a good game, but she wasn't as confident as she let on. As with everything else she'd gone after in her life, she'd forged ahead with her plans for his seduction with a single-minded determination that overrode any deficiencies in expertise. However, that rapid-fire orgasm she'd experienced proved she had little familiarity with the sexual battlefield, while he had an entire arsenal of knowledge at his disposal.

He'd been playing this wrong from the beginning. With very few exceptions, for the women he'd spent time with over the years, the attraction was about sex. Jessi was a healthy woman, with a woman's needs, but for her, it was all about the heart. To reach her, he had to focus there.

Kip arrived with their meals. "Can I get you anything else?"

"Thanks, Kip. We have everything we need." Max spoke without breaking eye contact with Jessi. He waited until the teenager left them alone. "You've been trying to seduce me since the moment you arrived at my door."

She picked up her fork and didn't bother to hide a coy smile. "You're very observant, if a little slow on the uptake."

Oh, little girl, you're good, but you're out of your league. He pasted on an easy smile. "I'm not slow. I'm particular."

She scooped up a bite of breaded lobster. "Particular?"

"In my taste in women."

The flash of hurt annoyance in her eyes was quick, but he saw it. He pushed back against a stab of guilt. A little hurt now would save them both a lot of heartache later.

She slid the tines of her fork between her lips and hummed in appreciation. Her smile lost some of its gleam as she chewed. "And I'm not to your taste?"

"Nope." He slid his eyes shut briefly as if he savored the tang of lemon pepper and cod on his tongue. The dish might as well have been sawdust. It congealed in his mouth in a tasteless blob.

She cast a furtive glance at some nearby diners and lowered her voice. "The hard-on poking me in the belly on several occasions says different." Though smug, her smile didn't match the growing anger in her eyes.

"That's biology. You're a fine looking woman, Squirt." He scored a direct hit with his use of the nickname. Her lips stretched tight in a frown. Scooping up another bite, he pressed forward, aiming his fork at her. "You have all the right parts for my body, but I'm talking about what my head looks for in a woman."

Her frown slid away beneath a tight smile. "I've met quite a few of your bimb—dates, Max. Most of them were my age or younger, so if you're going to tell me I'm too young, I'll call you a liar."

"No, you're the perfect age."

The little darling had a temper and it showed when she dropped her hand to the table to demand, "Then what's the problem?"

Heat flared in her eyes as he took his time, cutting another bite. "Before Tuck met and married CC, he and I had a little competition going."

"I hardly see how that—"

"When one of us found a new woman, the other did his best to steal her away."

Impatience flashed in her eyes. "What's that got to do with me?"

He slipped a piece of cod into his mouth and chewed before answering. "I'm getting to it."

"Well, hurry it up." She jabbed a fat chunk of lobster and shoved it into her mouth.

He hid a satisfied smile. "We had a lot of fun before CC came along, and so did the women. At last count, I was ahead in the tally."

"I get it. You're a slut, but I don't care about that."

"Good to know." He sipped his wine, then set it aside. "But that's not my point."

She heaved an exasperated sigh. "What *is*?"

"My point is, the women involved didn't much care which of us won the battle. They saw the game for what it was, innocent fun, and in the end, the women got what they wanted. No strings sex in the comfort of five-star accommodations."

She set aside her glass and leaned her elbows on the table. "What are you saying? I'm not slutty enough for you?"

"Not even close."

"That's...just stupid."

And there was the pout he'd expected the other night. He matched her position, crossing his forearms on the table, and pounded the final nail in her seduction coffin.

"My taste in women tends toward those who know the score. Women interested in short-term relationships who shrug and move on to the next guy when I walk away. Because I will walk away, Jessi. That's what I do. I don't stick. Unlike you and your family, I don't collect people. I use them, and when I'm done, I'm gone."

He sat back, picked up his wine, and hoped like hell she was listening. "When this is over, I'll move on to the next woman. If you can live with that, I'm more than happy to accept what you're so determined to give. If not, do us both a favor and stop offering."

Chapter 16

Jessi stomped to the French doors, only to return and flop onto the bed to stare at the ceiling. Sleep was impossible. Torn between marching down to the next level to give Max a piece of her mind and crying, she was driving herself nuts. Couldn't he see how wrong he was? The loner rogue he'd described as they sat in the restaurant wasn't him. Sure, he'd dated a lot of women. Since he was gorgeous and single, that was to be expected, but the user he claimed to be bore no resemblance to the caring man who'd come to her aide when she'd asked.

As for that asinine comment about not collecting people, wouldn't Gracie have something to say about that! Then there was her family. *User, my ass*. For a man with a net worth of close to sixty million dollars, the Tuckers had nothing to offer Max but friendship, so why did he keep coming back?

He'd said he didn't stick, a completely bullshit claim. He did when he cared, like with Gracie, and Tuck and the family, and her, damn it. A man didn't drop everything and put his life on hold to help a woman if he didn't care.

Her mind's eye supplied the picture of the little boy left alone by his mother's death, and the fear and confusion he must have suffered with his grandmother's denial. Jessi didn't need a shrink's degree to guess what drew Max to her family, and if she could get her hands on Elizabeth Krandall at that moment, she wouldn't need a hit man.

She'd do the deed herself.

She rolled her head to the side and glared at the open doorway. He'd all but said he was hers for the taking *if* she was okay with him walking away afterward. Of course she wasn't. How could she ever survive seeing him with one of his temporary women, knowing she hadn't been enough to hold him? How could she survive seeing him period? Then again, being

Max, he'd probably go all noble and cut himself off from the family in order to minimize the hurt, and that would surely break her heart.

Yet, how could she not take the chance? Max was a man worthy of a life full of love and laughter. A life surrounded by family who would share in his victories and help lessen the sting of defeats. Unfortunately, the past and its scars kept him from seeing himself the way others did. A man whose natural charm and giving nature endeared him to those who called him friend and garnered the respect of strangers.

Given time, surely she could help him see that. Time, however, wasn't on her side. He saw their arrangement as temporary but damn it, from the moment she'd met him, she'd wanted Max Grayson, heart and soul. Nearly five years of yearning had taught her she wouldn't win him by sitting back and waiting.

When this is over, I'll move on to the next woman. If you can live with that, I'm more than happy to accept what you're so determined to give.

Though his offer had been intentionally insulting, designed to scare her off, he'd opened a door she hadn't managed to crack, despite trying. She shoved to her elbows and glared at the open doorway. What the hell? Nothing worth having came without a price. If she rolled the dice and lost, she *would* learn to live with it. At least she wouldn't forever suffer from what-ifs.

Scrambling to her feet, she ran her fingers through her hair. She caught her reflection in the mirror and wished she'd brought along something sexier than one of Tuck's old Marauders T-shirts, but it would have to do. Hopefully, she'd be naked before Max realized she'd arrived to accept his terms while wearing his best friend's number emblazoned on her chest.

Frowning, she reached beneath the shirt and shimmied out of her panties. Ha! That ought to save time, in case he tried putting up a fuss.

She padded across the room to the stairs, her bare feet silent on the smooth wooden steps. Tiptoeing down the hall to Max's closed door, she froze when a board squeaked beneath her toes. She held her breath and listened. No sound came from the other side and her shoulders sagged with relief.

She stared at the glossy wooden door. Her palms went damp, and she bit her lip. What was the protocol when a woman decided to call a man's bluff by taking him up on his insulting offer of no-strings sex? Knock or don't knock? And, once inside, what was she supposed to say? *Hiya, Max, I'm here to get laid?*

Should she play it coy? Get her best vamp on? Or should she simply pounce on him and let their bodies do the talking?

She rolled her eyes. *Oh, for heaven's sake. You're not wearing any underwear. Are you going to do this or not?* She grasped the doorknob and stepped inside.

It took a moment for her eyes to adjust to the dark. As the shadows finally shifted and made sense, her gaze fell on the bed. Sound asleep, Max lay on his stomach, a muscled bicep bulging above the forearm tucked beneath the folded pillow. The black swirls of his tribal tattoo rode the well-defined contours of his naked back and shoulders. A light colored sheet tangled around his thick thighs. His ass was bare.

She stared at the firm swell of the smooth mounds and swallowed. "Max."

His head shot up from the pillow, his tone confused and groggy. "What?"

"Max," she spoke a little louder.

Rolling to his side, he turned and looked her way. He blinked and one arm shot out to snatch at the sheet. "Jesus." Yanking the cloth over his lap, he pushed up with an elbow to sit. His fingers clenched the sheet and he glanced around the room, his eyes narrowing as they landed on her once more. "What's wrong?"

She wiped her sweating palms over the hem of her sleep shirt. "Um, nothing." *Oh, yeah. Very vamp.*

Shoulders relaxing marginally, he shook his head. "Then why are you here?"

Get it together, Jessi. It's now or never. Lifting her chin, she took the plunge. "I've decided I can live with it."

His steady gray gaze pinned her to the spot. One moment passed, then another. He dragged a hand over his face. "Don't do this to me, Jessi. Go back to your room."

Disappointment fired her blood. "I can't do that." She wouldn't. Whether he knew it or not, she was doing this for both of them. She'd be damned if she let him talk her out of it.

He dropped his hand to his thigh. "Were you not listening to any of what I said?"

"I heard every word, but the thing is," she sucked in a bracing breath, "I love you, Max."

His eyes slid closed and a pained expression crossed his face.

She stepped forward. "I know that's not what you want to hear, but too bad." She held his gaze as he opened his eyes. "It's *my* heart and *my* love. I'm entitled to give them to whomever I please."

He shook his head and shifted. Before he could rise, she scrambled onto the foot of the bed and crawled toward him. "I heard what you said, and I'm here anyway."

And if you make me beg, I'm going to slug you.

Pressing a hand to his chest, she shoved gently. He surprised her when he didn't resist, falling back against the pillows.

He stared up at her, and his eyes gleamed with a gentle pleading. "I don't want to hurt you."

She didn't want to be hurt either, but she couldn't back down. Not when the stakes were so high. "Then don't."

If she was going to win the game, she needed to play her best hand. She curled shaking fingers under the edge of the sheet and tugged it down his thighs, then gulped as her gaze fell on his growing erection, twitching against his belly. Straddling his hips, she grasped the hem of her sleep shirt, tugged it over her head, and dropped it to the floor beside the bed. He swallowed harshly. Her nipples puckered and she grew wet as his dark gaze catalogued her body.

Lowering her hips until the heated folds between her legs slid against his hardened cock, she didn't bother suppressing her shiver. "I'm a grown woman, Max," she dipped forward to brush her lips against his, "and I'm here by my own choice."

He cupped her face with both hands and, as if he'd finally given free rein to the desire he'd tried to hide from her, his gray eyes flared with a heat so intense, she should have been singed. "Then God help us both."

He dragged her down until their lips fused. The world and its worries held no power against the pleasure of his kiss and touch. His wide palms slid over her shoulders and around her back, sweeping away concerns about the future. Hot and demanding, his mouth claimed hers and banished all thought of family or career and, when he rolled over to tuck her beneath his big body, time and place faded as well—until he reached out to click on the lamp.

Soft light filled the shadows. Panting, she blinked up at his sober face inches from hers. "What's the matter?"

"Nothing." Propped on one elbow, his hot gaze slid down her body. "If we're going to do this, I want to see everything."

The flood of relief left her lightheaded. Her gaze followed his trailing fingertips. They danced over her collarbone to trace the full curve of one breast. Sweet friction made her breath catch as he dragged the rough pad of his thumb over the tightened bead of her nipple. He slid his fingers lower, circling the dip of her belly button. Masculine and tanned against her pale skin, his wide-palmed hand skimmed her lower belly to cup the auburn curls covering her mound.

Wet warmth gushed through her, and she moaned at the telltale throbbing between her thighs. Lord, he was doing it again. Shooting her toward climax with a simple touch. She squeezed her thighs together, and he looked up. Hot and intent, his gaze paused on her peaked nipples before rising to her face.

One corner of his mouth quirked. "So sensitive. Are you that close?"

A blush heated her cheeks and she squirmed beneath his hand. "I can't seem to help it. Apparently, I'm a premature orgasmer."

His deep chuckle and the devilish smile playing on his mouth only made matters worse. Pleasurable forerunners to her impending explosion rippled through her. She whimpered.

Without breaking eye contact, he dipped his head until his lips hovered within a breath of her nipple. "Sex isn't a zero sum game. We'll find plenty more of those before we're done." He stabbed his tongue at the tightened bud and plunged a finger inside her, withdrew, and plunged again. "Go ahead, baby. Come for me."

As if she needed encouragement.

His sensual touch and roughly spoken demand sent her over the edge. Her eyes slammed shut and bright shards of color shattered behind her lids. Harsh waves of pleasure battered her body in a rolling storm of unspeakable delight, and she surged beneath the added stimulation as he massaged her clit with the heel of his palm.

"Max!" His name burst forth on a keening cry.

"I'm here."

Spinning on a manic arc, she was vaguely aware of the rustle of bedding as he shimmied down the bed. A languid heaviness settled in as the sparks of her orgasm faded like stars winking out with the sunrise.

Warm fingers dipped between her tightly clenched legs, gently guiding them apart. Strong hands controlled the jerk of her body as he swept the tip of his tongue over the sensitized bead of flesh between her thighs, then repeated the torturing caress. She tossed her head back and forth on the pillow, helpless against the delicious spasms the loving lashes called forth.

Sliding his hands beneath her, he cupped her bottom, and held her in place for his feasting mouth. His lips and tongue savored and demanded. Relentless in his ministrations, he drove her back to the peak and, when she once again teetered on the edge, he sucked her in, devouring her with an open-mouthed kiss. She shattered with a scream that was his name.

Moments later, the scrape of an opening drawer pierced her lethargic mind. Boneless and replete, her lashes fluttered open. Beside her, Max fisted a condom onto his engorged cock. Taut with unquenched desire, his chest and forehead glistened with sweat. The muscles of his neck stood out in corded relief and, as he turned toward her, fire burned in his eyes. Slipping a muscled thigh between hers, he rose above her.

"I'm sorry, baby. I can't wait another minute." He guided himself into place and, with a single powerful thrust, buried himself deep. His guttural groan bathed the shell of her ear with moist heat.

If she'd had the energy to speak, she would have told him waiting wasn't necessary. As it was, it took some doing to get her wrecked limbs to obey the demands of her brain. Locking her hands behind his neck, she clung to him as he began to rock against her. Amazed she could feel anything when her body was so done in, she shivered at the pull of his thick length against her over sensitized inner muscles.

She wrapped a leg around the back of his thigh, and he lifted his head. Heavy-lidded and intense, his slate gray gaze held hers. The fingers of one hand gripped her chin and jaw. He claimed her lips in an opened-mouth kiss. Driven by long denied passion and need, he consumed her. The stab of his tongue mirrored the pump of his hips. Thrust, retreat, and thrust again.

A rush of liquid pleasure deep in her core signaled her renewed awakening as his passion called out to hers. She strained against him, their bodies entwined. As if they'd danced to this sweet tune a thousand times, her body fell into step with his, arching, falling, twisting toward ecstasy, until her groan of release was nearly drowned out by his shout of completion.

* * * *

Max dipped his chin and pressed a feather-light kiss to Jessi's hair. His eyes slid shut against the sight of her tucked to his side, her slender arms wrapped around him like a vine as she slept. If only the battle raging in his mind could be so easily shut out.

Christ, what a mess. He should have known Jessi would take his comments earlier as an opening instead of the warning they were. Though tiny, every inch of her sexy little body was packed full of the determination and grit that had catapulted her to the top of her industry. Any other woman would have snarled at his insulting proposition and told him to go fuck himself. Not Jessi.

With as little experience as she had in the sex department, she'd stood before him, as bold as can be, and called him out. She claimed she'd heard his message loud and clear, but like Tuck had said, once she got an idea in her head, she didn't let go. Sliding into her hot, mind-blowingly tight sheath, it was impossible to miss the hope of forever in her eyes.

Guilt made sleep impossible, despite the heaviness of his body, his muscles loose with completion. No matter what happened when their time together ended, he was screwed. Although he'd agreed to her plan for a good reason, ultimately, he'd betrayed her trust. There would be hell to pay if she ever found out but, more than that, she hadn't simply offered him her body when she climbed into his bed. She'd handed him her heart.

She loved him. *Him*. A street brawler with blood on his hands. Christ, his heart had nearly stopped in his chest when she'd said those words.

A part of him wanted to shout and dive into the promise in her earnest blue eyes. Cling to the idea of a family with a woman who loved him, a good and giving woman he wanted until he couldn't think straight. He yearned to grab hold of a future where love wasn't ripped away in the blink of an eye. Where a safe place to sleep was a given, and children didn't need to fight for the right to survive…but he knew better.

Security and financial wherewithal would never again be an issue, but love? Love died. Or it judged and found wanting. She loved him, but God knew, he'd done things even the most giving of hearts would find unforgivable. When push came to shove, true colors showed, and his were as black and heartless as the Krandall blood running through his veins. He couldn't, wouldn't taint Jessi's sweet soul with the guilty gore staining his.

She murmured in her sleep, and he tightened his hold. She'd come to him willingly, and he was selfish enough, greedy enough, to take what she offered while he had the chance, but they would both pay a price in the end.

She would end up hating him, and he'd spend rest of his life mourning the death of the love in her eyes and smile. Once this was over and the stalker was found, he'd never again stroke the silkiness of her skin or marvel at the completely unselfish way she gave of herself with no barriers and nothing held back. His taste buds and nostrils would never be clear of her sweet taste and scent. Every woman he met in the future would fall short of the one who fit against him, around him, under him as if she'd been designed specifically with him in mind.

Christ, he'd fucked up. And had no one else to blame.

Chapter 17

"Have they found anything yet?" Max slumped against the deck rail with the phone pressed to one ear and a cup of coffee in his hand.

"Nothing." Ryan sighed. "So far every lead is a dead end."

He grunted, accepting the subtle relief loosening his shoulders. For the moment, the status quo hadn't changed. Once the asshole threatening her was caught, Max would do what had to be done, but for now, Jessi remained his.

"How is she?"

Max flicked a glance through the French doors into the empty kitchen. "Better, I think. She hasn't had a headache since we arrived and, while she still isn't sleeping well, she's out cold at the moment." Thanks to the exhaustive hours they'd spent exploring each other's bodies last night. He wasn't about to share that detail with her father, however.

"That's an improvement. Whatever you're doing, keep it up."

Max choked on his coffee. Keeping it up wasn't going to be a problem. He'd had to force himself to climb from his bed this morning instead of rolling her over and picking up where they'd left off only hours before. The quick, cold shower hadn't worked for shit, not with visions of what they could do beneath those six jetting showerheads or in that deep Jacuzzi tub flooding his mind.

"Will you be returning to Manhattan first or going straight to the Super Bowl warm-up in Tampa? Spence is getting antsy. He's concerned about a low spot in the show and thinks they need to work on it before Friday." Ryan's chuckle came through the phone. "Apparently, she's not taking his calls."

Max snorted. The fact that Jessi had disappeared with Max had to burn the guy's ass. That worked for him. She was too good for her pretty boy partner. "I'll leave that up to Jessi. She's free to go home any time she wants. In the meantime, light a fire under the FBI boys. We need to find this guy."

Disconnecting the call, Max drained his coffee and returned inside. He poured a second cup for Jessi before padding up to his bedroom. A smile teased his lips as he lowered a hip to the edge of the bed. She lay curled on her side with her hands folded beneath her cheek. The sheet left her nude from the waist up and her wild tangle of russet curls played peek-a-boo with sandy pink nipples. At the moment, country music's princess looked like a cross between an angel and a college coed gone bad.

He shifted the mug to his left hand and brushed a fingertip over one puffy nipple, then the other. They puckered immediately as if in greeting, and he smiled. Her lashes fluttered open, closed again, and popped open wide.

If he was expecting shyness or embarrassment over what had passed between them last night, he got neither. She yawned and sat up, the sheet pooled at her waist. "Hi."

"Hi, yourself." He handed her the mug. "How'd you sleep?"

She sipped from the mug and moaned in appreciation. "I think we may have found a solution to my insomnia." A healthy glow tinted her cheeks. "Too bad we can't bottle it. We'd make a fortune."

Her grin was infectious. Because he could, he leaned forward and captured her smiling lips in a long, wet kiss. He sat back before the demands of his body derailed his plans for the morning. "Drink up."

He stood and, pulling off the sweatshirt he'd donned before stepping outside to call Ryan, went to his suitcase.

"Are we going somewhere?"

"Out to the gym. I thought we'd run through a few simple self-defense techniques."

With his self-imposed restrictions on getting too close to her lifted, there was no longer a reason to deny her request. In fact, a few lessons would be smart. Whether she liked it or not, her celebrity would always require enhanced safety precautions, even after the stalker was caught. In the event the formal security around her ever broke down, having a few defensive skills she could employ was a good idea.

"Really?" Excitement gleamed in her eyes.

"You said you wanted some lessons."

"I do."

He bent over the case to select a clean pair of shorts and a T-shirt. "Then get a move on. It snowed again last night. If we have time later, I'd like to get in a few runs at Gunstock. You ski, right?"

"It's been a while, but yeah."

She threw back the covers and scrambled from the bed. Max looked up and almost swallowed his tongue. Apparently, Jessi Tucker didn't have a shy bone in her body. Petite and perfect in all her naked glory, she hurried by him and hit the hall running. "I'll be ready in five."

* * * *

"Keep your arm close to your side. Don't swing wide." Max demonstrated, snapping his elbow back in a sharp jab.

True to her word, Jessi had skipped down the stairs into the kitchen with thirty seconds to spare. The naked siren had been replaced by a sexy cheerleader, complete with swinging ponytail. Sleek black leggings covered her long legs while a cropped midriff left her belly bare. What he'd meant as an added safety precaution for when he was no longer around had turned into an exercise in self-control.

The close contact instruction left him sweating, and not from exertion. No wonder she'd suggested he teach her self-defense. If he hadn't already caved to her charms, he would have been hard pressed to resist her after having his hands all over her body as he adjusted her stance, and the smug smile on her lips for the last twenty minutes said she knew it.

"I thought you were going to teach me some secret ninja moves." Nose wrinkled in concentration, Jessi copied his movement.

He chuckled and tucked her arm closer to her ribs. "Ninjas study for years. We don't have that long."

She repeated the move, this time correctly. "What about that high swing kick thing I saw you do the other day? If someone grabs me from behind, wouldn't it better to clobber him in the head with my foot than poke him in the belly?"

"Again, months to learn and years to perfect." He scratched at his jaw and studied her petite frame. "You're sexy as hell, but you're a tiny thing, and you don't have the time to become an expert. That leaves fighting dirty."

Her eyes lit with interest. "I like the sound of that."

He shook his head and fought a smile, but the topic of her safety was too serious a subject to fuck around. "Pay attention, Squirt. Remaining alert is your best defense. If something feels wrong, assume it is. A predator counts on his victims being unprepared or too shocked to fight back. An elbow jab may not seem like much, but it changes the dynamics. Suddenly, you're not the typical victim, and that split moment of surprise may mean the difference between escape and disaster.

"Keep that pepper spray we talked about where you can access it at all times, and don't hesitate to use it. If the guy has a weapon, your best bet is to scream bloody murder while you have the chance and hope someone comes running to help. Otherwise, there are defensive tools everywhere if you think outside the box."

"Like?"

"Like these." He gathered her hand in his and aimed her fingernails at his face. "Go for the eyes and think gouge. A blind assailant is easier to escape. Be aware of anything at your disposal that will inflict pain. A high heel to the instep or a kick to the front of the knee may not take the bad guy out, but it'll knock him off his game and it hurts like a bitch. A pencil or pen piercing the cheek does, too."

"Ouch." Her face twisted in a pained grimace.

He turned her so that he stood at her back and locked an arm across her chest. "A predator can have you immobilized before you're even aware you're under attack. With enough force, the back of the skull can do a hell of a lot of damage. Snap your head back and aim for the bridge of his nose. Like this." He pressed a palm to her forehead and helped her simulate a head butt. Releasing her, he grabbed her left wrist and pulled her arm down to settle her hand in front of his crotch. "If all else fails, any man will find it hard to keep to his plan when his ball sack is being crushed."

He sucked in a breath as her fingers brushed against the bulge beneath his shorts and he tightened the grip on her wrist. "If you ever decide to employ this move, don't hesitate. Grab hold and squeeze tight, then twist your hand like there's no tomorrow. When he drops to the ground, get the hell out of there fast."

He released her and stepped back. She turned to face him.

"Just remember, none of these moves are by any means meant to replace good, common sense. A good offense is the best defense. Be aware of your surroundings at all times, and don't put yourself in a dangerous situation unnecessarily."

"Got it. When I head to the mall, I'll keep my eyes open and pens and pepper spray at ready." A dimple winked with her grin.

He dropped his chin and narrowed his gaze. "The mall? If I ever hear of you running around on your own like some kind of honky tonk Ninja Girl, I'll paddle your ass so hard you won't sit down for a week."

"Yes, sir." She bumped her fingers to her forehead in a smart salute.

He sighed. "I'm serious, Jess. You may not like it, but facts are facts. I get your need for a little bit of privacy when you're alone in your home, but when you're out in public, some type of physical security personnel is not only smart, it's necessary."

A frown marred her brow. "Now you sound like my father."

"Yeah, well, when it comes to your safety, I happen to agree with him."

The instant hurt in her eyes sliced at him like a physical pain. He cupped her cheek and held her gaze. "Hire yourself a good bodyguard. One you can trust. One who works for you and understands your concerns. Ryan's not an unreasonable man. If he knows you're safe, he'll back off."

She stepped back, out of his reach, and his hand dropped to his side.

"Why do I suddenly get the feeling you're preparing me for your imminent departure?"

He scrubbed a palm along the back of his neck. "Not imminent, but I meant what I said yesterday. Sometime in the not too distant future, I will depart, and I need to know you'll be safe when I do."

The corners of her mouth turned down in an angry frown. "You just had to bring that up, didn't you?"

His shoulders slumped in frustration. "I don't want there to be any misunderstanding between us. What we shared last night was damned good, but it's only temporary."

She stared at him, a crushing disappointment darkening her eyes. "You've made your point quite clear."

"Good."

Her chest expanded on a deep breath, and she nodded curtly. "Okay, what's next?" The chill of her smile dropped the temperature in the room by ten degrees. "Please tell me I get to practice stabbing you with a pen."

* * * *

"I'm sorry, Kris. My phone was turned off." Jessi perched on the long bathroom counter with her feet in the sink and her phone on speaker.

"I know. I left several messages. I finally called your idiot cousin." A soft scoff came through the phone. "I swear, that man has an evil streak."

Jessi rolled her eyes. The snarky barbs flew like missiles whenever Tim and Kris were in the same room, followed by the suggestion of dinner or a weekend in Barbados by Tim while Kris turned up her nose and called him names. Their relationship was like a never-ending game of full-contact foreplay.

"The two of you should just do it and get it over with."

"Ha! Like I'd ever share the goodies with such a dork."

Jessi laughed. "What did he do this time?"

"It's what he didn't do. He refused to tell me where you'd gone."

"How could he when he doesn't know?"

"Oh, please. He's your manager *and* a Tucker. You can't break a nail without him and the entire family knowing about it."

Jessi swished the razor beneath the stream of running water. "True, but that was before. Things have changed, remember? I told you hooking up with Max would work."

"Wait. You're serious? Tim really doesn't know where you are?"

She caught the reflection of her smug smile in the wall-length mirror beside her. "None of them do."

"That son of a bitch!"

Jessi's laugh echoed slightly off the tiled walls. "Uh-oh. What?"

"He said he'd only tell me where you were if I agreed to have dinner with him."

The razor stilled in her hand. "Did you?"

"Of course, I did. A girl has to eat, and he was paying. I ordered the lamb chops, forty-seven fifty, and left when it became obvious he was jerking me around. I cleaned my plate first, of course, and should have dumped that expensive wine in his lap before I left." A derisive sniff blew through the speaker. "So, are you going to tell me where you are or not?"

"We're in New Hampshire and that's all I'm saying."

"Keeping the hunky cage fighter all to yourself, huh?"

Her friend's sly laugh made Jessi smile. "That's the ultimate plan."

"Is it working?"

Heat flooded her as she recalled the pleasurable hours they'd shared in his bed last night, and chilled at the memory of her self-defense lesson. She shut off the water and dried her legs. "The jury's still out, but I'm working on a plea deal. In the meantime, don't tell anyone where we are, including Tim. I don't have a lot of time left before we have to leave for Tampa, and I'll need every minute I can get if my plan's going to work."

"My lips are sealed, babe, but you can bet your ass the moment I hang up, I'll be calling your cousin to gloat. You know how he hates to be left out of the loop. Maybe I'll let him treat me to a lobster dinner before I tell him to piss in his favorite wing tips."

Jessi laughed and hopped down from the counter, cramming the razor into her makeup bag. "You're playing with fire, girlfriend. Just remember, he's a Tucker. We don't fight fair."

"I can handle your cousin. You concentrate on Max and, speaking of him, I saw a short clip from your press conference. Is that stuff about Max and the Krandalls true?"

"Unfortunately, yes." Shit. Other than the ball game yesterday, she hadn't bothered turning on the TV. Busy seducing Max, she hadn't once thought to check and see if there had been any fallout from the press conference. "Why? What are they saying?"

"Not much. I saw it on yesterday's *Country Round-Up*. The networks haven't picked it up that I've seen."

Kris didn't add "yet," but then, she didn't have to. The Krandalls had too big a footprint in the world of sports for the story to remain quiet for long, especially with the playoffs underway. Jessi squeezed her eyes shut on a groan.

"Apparently, the Krandalls had no comment when asked about it."

Her eyes popped open and anger on Max's behalf surged through her veins. "Of course they wouldn't."

"What about Max? He didn't look very happy in the clip I saw. Do you know why he never mentioned coming from one of the wealthiest families in America?"

Jessi hesitated. Max's surprising family ties would be splashed all over the airwaves eventually, but the rest of what he'd told her wasn't hers to share. Still, Elizabeth Krandall's shabby treatment of her grandson was something Kris would understand. After her mother was killed in a car accident and she went to live with CC and her father, Kris had been swept up in her famous rock 'n' roller uncle's single-minded determination to jumpstart his flagging career by capitalizing on CC's kidnapping. As a result, both CC and Kris knew first-hand the cruelty a child experienced at the hands of a selfish parent whose image was all that mattered.

"Max has his reasons. The Krandalls treated him like shit when he was just a little boy, Kris. I don't blame him for not claiming a connection to that family."

"Bastards."

The quiet understanding in Kris's voice warmed Jessi's heart.

"Is there anything I can do? There's a good chance the Marauders will meet the Hurricanes in the Super Bowl. If that happens, with Max's connection to you and Tuck, you know the topic is going to come up. The sports networks will be scrambling to get their hands on some tape. Max really should have a press package ready. I'm slammed at the moment, but I'll rearrange some things and put something together for him if he wants."

Jessi's heart thumped at the further evidence of the fierce loyalty Max inspired in those who called him a friend. *I don't stick.* Geez, the man was blind.

"I appreciate that, and I'll let him know. Tim and I are supposed to work on a statement before the Memphis show. Why don't the two of you get together and...talk strategies over lobster?" She grinned and disconnected the call before Kris could reply.

The door downstairs thumped shut, and Jessi picked up her things. Disappointed over his reasoning behind her self-defense lesson, she'd been too disheartened to go skiing. She'd spent the afternoon working while Max had found something to occupy him in the boathouse.

Fine, so she hadn't had a lot of success at changing his mind about leaving, but she'd be damned if she'd give up. With his workout done for the evening, it was time they got a few things straight.

Padding into the bedroom, she tossed her makeup bag into her suitcase and zipped it shut. She dragged the case behind her, the caster wheels clunking over the hardwood. Hefting it in one hand, she descended the stairs and stalked to Max's room.

His head popped clear of his T-shirt as he pulled it off. He glanced at her bag, then at her. "Going somewhere?"

She settled the bag on its wheels. "Right here, unless you'd rather move your things to the master bedroom. If this is only temporary, I don't want to waste another moment of our time, and I refuse to sneak into your bed like I'm forcing you to sleep with me." She crossed her arms. "So, big guy. What's it gonna be?"

He lifted his eyes to the ceiling. "There's a king bed up there, right?"

She nodded and her heart thumped.

Lips curved in a crooked smile, he crossed to his bag. Tossing his shirt inside, he tucked the duffle under one arm without bothering to zip it, and grabbed the handle of hers. "Lead the way."

Huh. That was easy. Buoyed by the small success, she spun around and left him to follow. "You know the way. Make it fast and, when you're done, I'll be in here." She stepped through the doorway into the guest bathroom, tugged off her sweater, and grinned over her shoulder. "I'm dying to check out that tub."

Chapter 18

Jessi curled against Max's side in the master bedroom's large bed. He ran his rough palm over the curve of her hip, and a pleasant shiver pebbled her skin. She tucked her leg higher, her thigh riding his and her lower leg burrowed between his calves. The last forty-eight hours had passed far too quickly for her liking, but she couldn't find fault with a single moment.

For years, she'd watched Max charm her family members, but though she'd yearned to be allowed inside his circle of interest, he'd kept her at arm's length. Consequently, she'd never experienced the full force of his typically carefree personality. Since he'd joined her in the master suite, he'd relaxed and let down his guard. Quick with a laugh or a teasing smile, he cast aside the wall of distance he'd always kept between them and filled her days with laughter and her nights with passion.

This was the Max she'd longed to know, the man she'd loved for so long. Surely, he saw how good it was between them. Tomorrow morning, they would leave their secluded escape behind for the craziness of her career, but with Max at her side, the missing pieces of her life had been found. She had to find a way to change his mind.

A sigh whispered through her lips. "I had fun today."

He traced his fingertips over her rib cage to cup a breast. "Me too. I need to invest in one of those tubs."

She grinned and pressed a kiss to his neck. "I was talking about the skiing, although the tub part afterward wasn't bad either."

He lifted his head, and she craned her neck to meet his gaze. He arched a brow, and she laughed. "Okay, that part was fun, too." An understatement if she'd ever made one. She was still throbbing from their sensual water adventures.

He grunted and dropped his head back to the pillow as if it were too heavy to hold up, and she resettled her cheek against his shoulder. "When Mom was alive, we used to go skiing several times every winter."

"Why did you stop?" His jaw cracked with a wide yawn.

A subtle sadness poked at her heart. She cuddled closer. "Dad sort of lost interest after she was killed."

A long moment of silence passed. "You didn't go on your own once you were old enough?"

She brushed her palm over the thin trail of hair bisecting his lower abs and smiled at the contracting muscles of his stomach. "By that time, my career was in full swing. It's rare when my schedule allows for several free days in a row."

"When was the last time you went?"

"Kris and I spent a long weekend in Vale the winter after Tuck and CC married."

"Four years ago." He tightened the arm around her back. "That's a long time to go without doing something you enjoy."

Yes, it was. Caught up in the country music rat race, she'd missed a lot of the simple pleasures others enjoyed. She'd forgotten what it was like to have the time to pursue activities that didn't have anything to do with her career.

As if she'd spoken her thoughts aloud, Max tucked a knuckle beneath her chin and forced her to meet his gaze. "Is it all worth it?"

Immediately defensive, though she wasn't sure why, she played dumb. "What do you mean?"

"The schedule. The headaches. The insomnia."

She tensed as he ticked off the negative points she couldn't argue. After days of nothing but pillow talk and laughter, the harsh reminder of reality stung. Pasting a teasing smile on her lips, she fluttered her lashes and attempted to head off the unpleasant direction the conversation had taken. "We've cured the insomnia, remember?"

He didn't smile as she'd hoped. "What about the headaches?"

"Those, too." With the way he seemed to spot whenever a migraine came on, he had to have noticed she'd been headache free since they'd been in the woods. Only time would tell if they would return once she was back onstage, but the tone of his questions made her nervous. "Where's this going, Max?"

He shifted to his side so she came to rest on her back, her head cradled on his forearm. None of the easy laughter of the last few days shown in his somber eyes. "I'm curious. That first night at my condo, you spoke about your mother's death and of owing your father for helping you attain her dream of seeing you on stage, but you said nothing about the dream being yours."

Nerves skidded into unease and her stomach plummeted. With less than twelve hours left before they had to leave, she could think of a thousand things she'd rather do than discuss her career or her meltdown last week. Obviously, Max was of a different opinion.

"What kind of question is that?" Try as she might, some of her tension leaked out, making her answer curt. "I've worked damned hard to make it to where I am."

He leaned over her, his gaze steady as it held hers. "I'm not questioning your talent or your drive. You have more of both than anyone I've ever met. You shine when you stand before an audience, Jess. I've never seen anyone own the stage the way you do, but I've also seen the fear in your eyes before each performance."

She shrugged a shoulder as if the gut-wrenching terror gripping her each time she stepped on the stage was no big deal. "Lots of performers suffer from stage fright. That doesn't mean I don't want to be there." The claim sounded defensive even to her.

He nodded, as if he agreed, but didn't back down from his line of questioning. "And afterward? The headaches and insomnia? Where do those come from? Because there hasn't been a stage in sight for five days and suddenly they're gone."

Damn it. Did he think she hadn't noticed? Didn't wish there was a viable solution to make the stress and unhappiness go away? Angry tears of desperation threatened, and she avoided his gaze by rolling her head to the side. The best defense was a good offense. Several deep breaths helped her gain control and she went on attack. "Why all the questions? Is this another of your attempts to prepare me for when you're gone?"

The question had been a red herring, designed to knock him off track, but the flash of guilt in his eyes told her she'd hit the bull's-eye.

He sighed. "In a way, I guess it is, but you came to me for help. That's what I'm trying to do."

"How? By pissing me off?" She attempted to roll away from him. He threw a thigh over both of hers and held her where she was.

"By asking the questions you should be asking yourself." He swept his thumb over her cheek in a gentle caress. "You claim you're losing yourself. How can you find your way to where you want to be without looking at where you've been?"

Her attempt at diversion had only added hurt to an already uncomfortable conversation. Maybe sarcasm was the answer. "Geez, who are you, Dr. Phil?"

He didn't bite. Saying nothing, he continued to hold her pinned beneath him.

Damn it, why couldn't he just drop it? What was the point? Every dream came with sacrifices and hardships. The important ones anyway. Her mother hadn't survived to see hers realized. That made her dream more important than most.

Jessi slid her eyelids shut against his intent gaze. "I have to sing, Max. If I couldn't, my soul would shrivel up and die." She opened her eyes. "Are you suggesting I give it up?"

His gaze softened, and he shook his head. "Not at all. If singing is what you need, then do it. All I'm suggesting is you take a good hard look at your life and consider your options. Figure out what's holding you back from being happy. Find out what it is you want and then make it happen."

The earnest concern in his eyes warmed her heart. She lifted her hand to cup his bristled cheek. "Haven't I made it perfectly clear what I want?"

"Jessi." He wrapped his fingers around her wrist and tugged her hand away from his face before letting go.

"Max." She held his gaze until he dropped his chin to his chest and sighed.

The marked pain on his face slashed at her like knives. After the emotional jarring he'd just given her, evidence the past two days hadn't made a bit of difference in his plans really did piss her off.

Sliding his arm from beneath her head, he flopped onto his back to stare at the ceiling.

She rolled her head and stared at his profile. "At least I'm honest about what I want."

"Are you? When you're afraid to even look at a reality that's making you ill?"

Her slow, indrawn breath didn't fully deflect the hurt. She rose on her elbow and leaned over him. "What about you, hopping from woman to woman while getting your family fix through *my* family's gatherings."

His gaze sliced to her, full of heat at her cruel words.

Too hurt and angry to care, she pressed on before he could reply. "What kind of existence is that? Don't you want more than a borrowed family? Don't you want one you can call your own?"

He bared his teeth in a smile that didn't come close to reaching his eyes. "I'll stick with borrowed. I've had some experience with real family." He pushed up to sit on the edge of the bed. The muscles of his back bunched as he leaned forward. "In my experience, they're not worth the effort."

Sarcasm aside, the underlying anger in his words cooled hers. She curled her fingers around his arm before he could stand. "I'm sorry, Max. I shouldn't have said that."

Her fingers slid away as he bent to pick up his briefs and stood.

"Your family's friendship means a lot to me. I've never hidden that fact, but they aren't a stand-in for a family of my own." He stepped into his briefs, tugged them up his legs, and over his hips. "Not everyone is cut out for picket fences and kids, Squirt. In fact, in most cases, the world is better off when bad blood isn't passed on." He headed for the door. "Get some sleep. We have an early flight in the morning."

She stared at his back as he disappeared down the stairs. Bad blood? What the hell?

* * * *

At the staccato knock on the door, Jessi turned from the view of the city streets ten floors below their Memphis hotel suite. Max tossed aside the magazine he'd been thumbing through and rose from the couch to answer the summons without a word.

Her heart thumped in an unhappy cadence as her gaze followed him across the suite. After their argument, he'd said nothing about leaving, but he'd been unusually quiet since they'd left New Hampshire. Last night's migraine only made matters worse. Heading for the airport in Tampa after she and Spence had run through their Super Bowl performance, she'd dug for her pills as Max watched her with hooded eyes.

He hadn't said a word, but then, he didn't need to. The physical manifestation of the stress and unhappiness dogging her this past year jabbed at her like an accusing finger. His probing questions and her cruel response hung between them like an out of key song, and she hated the subtle distance that had sprung up between them.

Unfortunately, she didn't know how to bridge the gap she'd opened with her hateful words.

Briefcase in hand, Tim rushed inside the moment Max opened the door, and crossed the room to snatch up the TV remote.

Max arched a questioning eyebrow her way. She shook her head and stalked toward her cousin. "Nice of you to show up. I thought we were going to discuss a press strategy before we left for the stadium."

Tim pointed the remote at the blackened screen of the TV. "Apparently, *Sports Extra* picked up the *Country Times* story, and Elizabeth Krandall decided a preemptive strike was in order. She's holding a press conference."

Instant adrenaline spiked in Jessi's veins as her gaze whipped to Max. Face devoid of emotion, he stopped beside the couch. Tim scanned the channels and Elizabeth Krandall's face filled the screen. Behind a podium emblazoned with the Hurricane's emblem, Elliot Sprig, her nephew and the team's flamboyant owner, stood at her side.

A reporter spoke off camera. "Mrs. Krandall, it's a well-known fact you were left to choose the new team owner when your husband passed so suddenly. According to records, Max Grayson is your closest living relative. Was he in the running when you went through the process of picking a successor for your husband?"

The Krandall matriarch dipped her head forward. "Anyone who follows the world of professional football knows my nephew was quite close to my husband when he was alive."

"The Hurricanes have been in the hands of a direct Krandall descendant since the team's inception," the same reporter pressed. "Why the break from tradition?"

She hesitated, and Elliot opened his mouth as if he was about to speak, but his aunt held up a hand. "I'm confident my husband would have approved of my choice."

Tim grunted and sat on the coffee table. "Classic spin. Notice how she avoids answering the question but still makes her point."

"Shhh…." Jessi stepped to Max's side and wrapped her fingers around the tensed muscles of his arm.

"What about Mr. Grayson? Were he and your husband close?"

Shifting her gaze to the new speaker, Elizabeth's lips drew into a grim line and her shoulders sagged. Suddenly, the powerful matriarch looked more like a frail seventy year-old as she gripped the edge of the podium with one hand. "This isn't a comfortable thing for a grandmother to admit but I'm afraid by the time we gained access to our grandson, it was too late. We couldn't reach him."

A humorless laugh rumbled in Max's chest. Jessi glanced at him. He stared at the TV as if turned to stone.

"Too late, how?"

Jessi looked back at the TV. Max's grandmother covered her mouth with a fluttering hand. As if shielding her from an unseen enemy, Elliot slid his arm around her shoulders and leaned toward the microphone. "According to my uncle, my cousin's juvenile police record read like a blue-print for a thug destined for a life of crime."

Tim glanced over his shoulder at Max, but the Hurricanes owner wasn't finished.

"Apparently, Max Grayson spent a good portion of his childhood running wild on the streets. When my aunt and uncle tried to step in, he wasn't interested in giving up the lifestyle."

Jessi gasped. "That's a lie."

Several voices spoke simultaneously before one stood out. "Max Grayson is your only daughter's son, correct? Why would she let her son run on the streets? Why would you and your husband?"

Elizabeth miraculously found her voice. "You have to understand, my daughter was…." She hesitated and like an expert playing the crowd, the woman who had been at the helm of one of the most successful financial empires for more than four decades blinked and tears flooded her eyes. "My daughter was different."

"Different how?"

Elizabeth's hand shook as she dabbed a linen handkerchief at the corner of her eye. "In the past, emotional disabilities weren't always recognized."

The tendons in Max's arm bunched as he fisted his hands at his side. A muscle jumped in his clenched jaw, but he didn't say a word. He stared at the screen with blazing eyes.

"My daughter didn't see the world as you or I do." Elizabeth shook her head slightly as if the memory saddened her. "She was sweet, and innocent, and…easily swayed. When she graduated from college, she met my grandson's father. Charmed by the smile of a man who saw her as a means to an end, she married against our wishes. While it broke our hearts to watch her be used so cruelly, she was legally an adult. When we made it clear not a penny of her inheritance would be his," her voice broke and she appeared to wilt, "her new husband forced her to cut all ties with the family."

She sagged, and Elliot enfolded her in his arms. "I'm sorry, folks. As you can see, this has been difficult for my aunt."

The press conference ended with a flurry of unanswered questions as Elliot led Elizabeth away.

Tim cued the remote and the TV went blank. Max jolted as if waking from a nightmare.

He turned his head, and Jessi flinched at the fury in his eyes. She couldn't blame him. Bile rose in her throat as renewed anger on his behalf surged through her veins. His grandmother was an evil woman, besmirching her own daughter's emotional state in an effort to cover her selfishness, and she deserved to pay for her cruelty.

Jessi stepped in front of him and wrapped her arms around his waist, pressing her cheek to his chest. "I'm sorry, Max." She gripped him tighter as his arms gathered her close.

Tim spoke behind her. "How much of what was said is true?"

Max stiffened against her, and she turned to glare at her cousin.

He held up a hand before she could blast him and offered Max an apologetic frown. "That's not an accusation, my friend, but the press is going to ask. I can't form an effective rebuttal if I don't know the facts."

Max's chest expanded on a cleansing breath. He nodded and loosened his arms. "As much as I'd enjoy calling her a fucking liar on national television, I'd prefer to stick to no comment."

"That'll only make matters worse." Tim opened his briefcase and retrieved a pad of paper and pen. "Sorry, Max, but we're going to have to come up with some kind of reply. They practically called you a criminal, and while I don't buy that claim, Jessi's fans don't know you from Jack."

Confusion made Jessi frown. She pushed free to look Max in the eye. "I don't understand. Everything she said was the opposite of the truth."

"Not everything. I did run on the streets for a while, and my juvie record isn't pretty." He shifted his gaze to Tim. "Contrary to what you just heard, the Krandalls didn't want anything to do with me from the beginning. Unfortunately, for my grandmother, the timeline disproves her claims."

"How so?"

"When my mother died and I supposedly turned down the Krandalls' offer, I didn't have a record. It wasn't until close to a year later that I had my first run-in with the police."

"What type of run-in?"

"Tim!" She shot her cousin a glare.

Max shook his head and stroked a hand down her arm. "It's okay, Jess. He has a point. I won't let the press smear you over my actions, and the family has a right to know the type of man they've welcomed into their home." He lifted his gaze to Tim. "I didn't do well in the first couple of foster homes I was placed in and took off the first chance I got. It wasn't long before I started getting into the kind of trouble you'd expect from a hoodlum kid. Truancy, vagrancy, petty theft. I'd added a couple of assault charges and did a stint in juvie before I turned sixteen and cleaned up my act."

Jessi's heart pulsed with each charge he ticked off so casually as if reciting the acts of a stranger. "What happened when you were sixteen?"

He looked down at her. "I met Vern."

"Your gym manager?" Tim scribbled notes on the pad in his hand.

Max's face softened with the first genuine smile she'd seen since their argument two nights ago. He nodded, released her, and dropped to sit on the couch. "Turns out, the judge handling my case did a little amateur boxing when he was younger. Vern was a friend of his and managed a gym in one of the roughest neighborhoods in the city. As a requirement of my probation, I spent six months wiping up sweat and blood, and mucking out bathrooms.

"Less than a week after I started, I got into a brawl with one of the punks who hung around out front. Vern must have seen us through the window because suddenly there he was. He grabbed me by the scruff of the neck and pulled me off the kid, but instead of turning me in for breaking the no fighting rule the judge had laid down, he marched me inside and shoved me into the ring with a dude twice my size."

Jessi lowered to the arm of the couch at his side. "He taught you to fight?"

"I already knew how to fight. He taught me to fight smart." One corner of his mouth quirked in a smile. "I didn't know shit about boxing and got my ass kicked that first day, and for several more following, but I learned the basics. How to take a hit and not go down, and when to go on the offensive.

"After the third time I threw a kick, Vern took pity and hooked me up with a mixed martial arts fighter. He said since I'd learned my fighting skills on the street, I might as well use them all." He turned to Tim. "As an adult, my record is clean. My businesses are free and clear. If you want to give the press something, give them that."

Jessi turned to him and scowled. "You can't let her get away with this, Max. She just told a whole pack of lies about you and your parents to millions of people."

A harsh smile slashed his lips. "I don't intend to, but revenge will have to wait."

He arched a brow in silent communication and his reasoning became clear. Until he got his hands on Haven Place, he wasn't going to do anything to make waves.

"Oh." Her confusion evaporated and she narrowed her eyes. "Okay, then. Just promise you'll include me in the party when you expose her innocent act. I want to be right there to see her reaction up close."

Max laughed and ran his palm over her thigh to pat her butt. "Watching her squirm will be better than the hit man idea, huh?"

She grinned. "Something like that."

"Jesus." Tim drew her attention as he stood and closed his briefcase. "Cut it out before you make me hurl."

"What?"

He straightened with an offended wince pinching his handsome face. "The two of you are doing that lovebird secret talk Tuck and CC do all the time. It's annoying."

She pinned him with a squint-eyed glare, but inside, her heart did a rolling flip. She'd envied the private communication between Tuck and CC on more than one occasion, and the realization she shared the same with Max left her almost giddy.

Tim ignored her to eye Max. "You want to let me in on the secret? Why not expose her now?"

Max patted her butt once more before rising to his feet. "Let's just say I've got a project in the works I don't want compromised by a press fight with the Krandalls."

Chapter 19

Jessi swept her thumb over the screen of her phone, scrolling through the latest of the articles that had popped up since Elizabeth Krandall had spread her lies. As Max had hoped, the one paragraph statement he and Tim agreed upon muted the furor to some degree, until the Marauders and the Hurricanes had each won their prospective conferences last Sunday.

As Kris had predicted, the Super Bowl matchup between the teams sparked renewed interest in the story. However, the speculation and innuendo filling the sports publications this morning was tame compared to the all-out snarkiness of the music industry outlets.

Frustrated anger clenched her teeth as she scanned Chet Bertrum's weekly column. *The Country Bugle*'s resident pompous windbag feigned disappointment as he gleefully predicted the downfall of country music's sweethearts in yet another example of talent and fame falling victim to bad choices. She jammed her thumb to the screen and squeezed her eyes shut.

To her joy, the gap between her and Max had disappeared since his grandmother's press conference, but with each negative article, his tension grew. For more than a week, she'd been trying to convince him the interest would wane as soon as a juicier story popped up. Today's rash of articles blew her theory out of the water. And if Max was tense, Spence was pissed. If he'd caught Chet's article before he arrived at the studio, today's photo shoot should be a freaking blast.

"Didn't you say none of the studio crew would be on hand today?"

She opened her eyes as Dan brought the town car to the curb in front of the studio. Following his gaze, she sighed. "What's he doing here?"

A shy smile on his face, Craig waited near the locked door of the building. He lifted a hand in an awkward wave.

"I think that's obvious. The kid has a major crush." Dan twisted in the front seat to look back at her. "But the studio is supposed to be closed to everyone but essential personnel today."

She rolled her eyes. "God, you sound like a marine. It's a photo shoot, not a top secret military exercise."

His teeth flashed in an arrogant smile. "I am a marine, and I'm doing my job. The kid isn't on the list."

"That stupid list." Though the threatening letters her father had been so concerned about had apparently stopped, with no more arriving in the past few weeks, her father had directed Dan to continue the practice of limiting those who had access to her studio. She could see the benefit. The thought of strangers wandering the halls of her private facility left her uncomfortable, but this was ridiculous. "Craig's harmless, Dan."

"Maybe so, but it's my job to be aware of anything out of the ordinary." He keyed the automatic lock on the doors. "If you ask me, the kid's a little too overeager."

He climbed from the car and rounded the hood. Craig hurried forward as if he meant to open her door. With a narrow-eyed, macho-man stare, Dan blocked him and grasped the handle himself. She ignored the hand he held out to help her from the low-slung seat, stepping onto the sidewalk on her own. He answered her glare with a bland smile.

"Good morning, Miss Tucker."

She turned to the smiling teenager. As much as she hated to admit it, Dan was right. Craig was definitely overeager, constantly showing up at the studio or at her local appearances to offer his assistance when he should be dating or hanging out with friends, but he was also sweet. "Hi, Craig. I didn't expect to see anyone from the crew today."

He fell into step beside her. "I thought you might need a gopher once the photographer shows up."

"That's nice of you, but it's a weekday. Shouldn't you be in school?"

He hunched his shoulders as Dan stepped around them to unlock the doors. "My first class isn't until eleven, so I'm good."

She met Dan's arched brows over Craig's shoulder and bared her teeth in a tight smile. It was close to eleven now and the photographer wasn't due until eleven thirty. "That's good, but be sure to head out when you need to." She offered Craig a soft smile. "Your parents won't be happy if your job here is responsible for a slip in your grades."

At the unintended reminder of their differences in age, blotchy color spread across his cheekbones. He dropped his gaze to his big feet, and she heaved an inward sigh. An uncomfortable itch tickled the back of her neck. She hadn't been much older than Craig when she'd first met Max and could empathize with the teenager's feelings. The tug and pull of a healthy crush was a powerful thing. Had she been as obvious? Had

Max been embarrassed by her constant and clumsy attempts to gain his attention? God, she hoped not.

Thankfully, Alicia arrived, saving Jessi from making things worse with Craig. He said nothing, falling into the background as they filed inside and her assistant brought her up to speed on the day's schedule. Craig left ten minutes later, without saying good-bye. Obviously, she'd hurt his feelings, but had no idea how to go about easing them. She settled in the conference room to listen to the new CD while awaiting Spence and the photographer's arrival.

Several minutes later, the door opened and she turned. Tugging the headphones from her ears, she lifted her chin and met Spence's gaze. He didn't look mad, but that didn't mean anything. Temperamental and moody, her partner's attitude could shift on a dime.

Hand on the doorknob, he paused and glanced around the empty room. "Where's Alicia?"

"She ran out to pick up some refreshments for the photo shoot."

He shut the door and shrugged out of his coat. "Have you seen Chet's article?"

Ugh. She set aside the headphones. "Yes, I have. It's a load of bull."

He tossed his coat over the back of a chair. "You know as well as I do, facts don't always matter. What matters is perception. Chet isn't the only one questioning what the princess of country is doing with a man like Max."

"A man like Max?" Every muscle in her body tensed, and she rose slowly to her feet. Hands spread on the table between them, she spoke in a deadly serious voice. "Be careful, Spence. You're about to cross a line you won't be able to uncross."

Frustration rolled off him in waves. "I'll take that chance. I'm not about to keep my mouth shut while my name is dragged through the mud along with yours."

She narrowed her eyes and pinned him with an angry glare. "This isn't about your name. It's about me and Max. From the moment you found out we were seeing one another, you've made it clear you don't approve. What I want to know is why?"

Something flashed in his eyes. Something she couldn't name, and the anger she'd expected darkened his face.

His lips thinned, and his eyes sparked with temper. "Because you have a blind spot when it comes to Max Grayson. Always have. But what do you really know about him?"

Fury flared at the insinuation in his tone. "I know he's a hardworking, successful athlete and business man." She straightened and her voice climbed in volume, along with her temper. "He's also honest and loyal, and while you may not consider him a friend, you've been around him enough to know that."

"Honest?" He shook his head. "I saw your face in Dallas, Jessi. You were as surprised as the rest of us to find out about his connection to the Krandalls. If he's so honest, why didn't you know who he really is?"

She jacked up her chin. "He had his reasons for not advertising his family ties."

His harsh laugh was an ugly facsimile of humor. "I'm sure he did."

"What the hell is that supposed to mean?"

"People lie to cover all kinds of things. To hear his grandmother tell it, he's little more than a thug. How do you know she isn't telling the truth?"

The door opened before she could blast him for believing Elizabeth Krandall's lies. Tuck stood in the open doorway with a wide-eyed Alicia peeking around his shoulder. Cold and intimidating, his cobalt blue gaze raked over Spence before sliding Jessi's way.

"You okay, cuz? Everyone in the building could hear the two of you arguing."

"I'm fine." Flustered, she looked at her assistant. "Is the photographer here?"

Alicia nodded, her nervous gaze shifting between Jessi and Spence. "He and his crew are setting up in the studio. They'll be ready for you both in about ten minutes."

Spence ripped his coat from the chair and jammed his arms into the sleeves. "I'm going for a walk."

Tuck arched a sardonic brow as Spence brushed by him through the doorway. Alicia scrambled back several steps, her teeth gnawing on her bottom lip. Her gaze shadowed Spence stalking through the control room and shoving the door open on his way out.

"Who pissed in his cornflakes?" Tuck turned back.

Jessi shot him a frown, then slid her gaze to her assistant. "Give us a few minutes, Alicia."

She nodded and pulled the door shut behind Tuck.

Residual anger bubbled in her veins and made her voice sharp. "Why are you here?"

His teeth flashed in a grin. "Can't I stop by to visit my favorite cousin without needing a reason?"

"When you've been out of town since Elizabeth Krandall's news conference and you show up here the moment you get back?" She crossed her arms.

He grunted. "Fine. CC and Gracie are baby shopping around the corner. I needed to escape, and CC mentioned you were here this morning." He crossed the room to drop into a chair at the long conference table. "Want to tell me what that was all about?"

She eyed him suspiciously. "You didn't hear?"

"Nothing specific."

Dropping into the chair across from him, she sighed. "He's angry about an article in the *Country Bugle*."

He leaned on his elbows. "I read it, along with others. Your princess tiara seems to have tarnished."

She shrugged dismissively. "I never liked crowns anyway. They cause split ends."

His smile sharp, he studied her with steady eyes. "From the sound of it, Spence isn't feeling as casual about your fall from grace. I'm betting Max won't either."

Instantly defensive, she frowned. "None of those articles are Max's fault. The blame belongs to his grandmother."

"I didn't say he was at fault, but I know Max. It's not like him to be attacked the way he's been and not fight back." His mouth twisted as if in thought. "Unless he has good reason."

She drummed her fingertips on the table between them and chose her words carefully. "He does, but you'll have to ask him if you want to know what that reason is."

Surprise wrinkled his forehead before he narrowed his eyes in that way he did when he was up to no good. "Did I ever mention I have this great picture of you? You were eight and missing a few teeth." Sitting back, he smiled. "I've also got a Twitter account."

She leaned in and matched his smile. "I have pictures of my own. Remember that powder blue tux from junior prom?" She laughed at his pained grimace and sat back. Obviously, Tuck didn't know any more about Max's past than she had, but just to be sure.... "Did you know he was related to the Krandalls?"

He shook his head. "Nope."

She bit her lip. With their conflicting schedules, she hadn't spoken to Tuck in weeks, and Max hadn't said anything about the two of them talking since the news had broken. "Are you mad he didn't tell you?"

Another head shake. "Nope. I've met his grandmother and cousin. I wouldn't claim them either."

Since he was being so accommodating in answering her questions, there was one more thing she wanted to know. She dropped her gaze to her fingers, spread on the tabletop. "Does it bother you we're together? Max and me?"

He leaned forward and covered one of her hands with his. "Should it?"

She looked up, and although a blush heated her cheeks, she met and held his intent gaze. "I'm a big girl."

"You're still my little cousin." He squeezed her fingers. "But, no, it doesn't bother me and won't, unless one or both of you are hurt by the arrangement."

She turned her hand up to entwine her slim fingers with his much larger ones. "I love him, Tuck. A little bad press isn't going to change that."

"I know you do. I love him, too." He pulled his hand back, and his face twisted in a frown, as if he hadn't meant to admit that. "In a best friend, guy sort of way."

She grinned and relief soothed the tension that had knotted her shoulders throughout the argument with Spence. "Relax. Your masculinity is safe." She sobered and leaned on her elbows. "Would you do me a favor?"

Eyes wary, he cocked his head. "That depends."

She smiled. "Go talk to Max. None of this has been comfortable for him. He could use a friend about now."

Chapter 20

Max's overworked muscles screamed with fatigue, and sweat stung his eyes. The clock on the wall ticked off the twenty-minute mark since he'd begun the punishing workout. Grunting, he landed a volley of short, jabbing blows. A bruising snap of his elbow to his invisible opponent's solar plexus, and he spun in a circle, snapping his leg up to shoulder level. His bare foot connected high on the heavy bag with a satisfying thud. Chest heaving, he wrapped an arm around the bag to halt its swing and wiped sweat from his forehead with the wristband on his free arm.

"Impressive. Which one of them were you pummeling, your grandmother or your cousin?"

Max glanced over his shoulder, not at all surprised to find Tuck leaning against the fight-ring steps several feet away. With what seemed like the whole world talking about the truth of his heritage, Max owed Jessi's family an explanation. Tuck most of all, but with him on the road, chewing through teams as the Marauders fought for their chance at a Super Bowl appearance, there hadn't been an opportunity. Victorious at last, thanks to Sunday's conference championship win, Tuck hadn't wasted any time showing up.

"Both." Max yanked a towel from the bar on the wall and scrubbed it over his face. "If you're here to take a swing at me, I'm not in the mood."

"After that demonstration?" Tuck jerked his chin in the direction of the bag and laughed. "I don't think so."

Tossing the towel on the bench nearby, Max turned to face his friend. A heavy sigh lifted his chest. "Look, you have every right to be pissed, but—"

"Damned right I do. Turns out my best friend is a fucking Krandall. Do you know how much shit I'm going to take from my teammates?" Tuck laughed and shook his head. "But hell, if I was related to that pack of jackals, I wouldn't admit it either."

Prepared for anger and condemnation, Max wasn't sure what to say. A lie by omission was still a lie. For years, he'd kept the truth of his identity from the people he cared about and although the need for secrecy had been a valid excuse, his conscience had suffered. Needlessly, it appeared. So far, none of the Tuckers had blinked an eye at learning of his deception. The only people who seemed to care were the members of the press.

"I'm sorry, Tuck. The situation is complicated, but I didn't keep it from you and the family out of any form of malice."

Tuck shrugged. "The thought never crossed my mind, and there's no need for an apology. From what Jessi said when I stopped by her studio, you've got a good reason for keeping quiet." Max stiffened, and Tuck held up a hand. "Relax. She refused to tell me what that reason is, despite my threat to tweet her third grade picture if she didn't." He bared his teeth in a challenging smile. "She's got it bad, buddy."

Max refused to take the bait. "If you're not here to break my nose, why are you here?"

He crossed his arms. "CC and Gracie are on a shopping spree, cooing over baby clothes. I couldn't take any more, and they took mercy on me. I thought we could grab a bite if you aren't busy."

In his current mood, laughing over a couple of beers wouldn't be possible. Then again, a brew—or six—might help him forget the cluster-fuck his life had become. He nodded. "Give me a couple of minutes to clean up." He bent to pick up the soiled towel.

Tuck pushed off the rail and straightened. "I also stopped by to collect on our bet. You owe me a C-note, my friend."

Max slowly straightened and fought the urge to squirm under Tuck's victorious grin. "I never took your bet, and who says you won?"

"Are you kidding? Jessi's face was as red as my classic Corvette." He snickered. "My cousin can't lie for shit. The truth shows on her face every time."

Gritting his teeth, Max turned to take the stairs to his condo. "She'd skin you alive if she knew you were laying odds on her sex life."

Tuck's hurried footsteps thudded on the steps behind Max. "Yeah, yeah. You gonna tell her?"

And be found guilty by association? "No way in hell. I like *my* skin right where it is."

Tuck chuckled and trailed Max into the condo. He headed straight for the fridge, tossed a water bottle at Tuck, and skirted the island to head for the shower. Spotting the filmy scrap of lace draped over the arm of the couch, Max cursed under his breath and changed direction midstride. He snatched up the panties he'd peeled from beneath Jessi's skirt last night, and shooting Tuck a sidelong glance, flat-out refused to think about what had happened next.

Jessi's cousin wore a shit-eating grin. He lifted his gaze from the lacy prize in Max's fist. "I'll take my winnings in cash."

Max shut out his friend's laughter and stalked into his bedroom, stripping as he went. He cranked the handle of the shower and stepped under the spray. He clenched his teeth against a string of curses. Tuck's ribbing over Jessi aside, his assumption the Krandalls were the target of the anger Max had been pounding out in his workout couldn't be more wrong. Sure, given the opportunity, he'd be happy to rearrange Elliot Sprig's homely features, but the focus of Max's fury stared back at him from the shaving mirror on the shower wall.

Jessi wasn't the only one who had it bad. Max knew it, and apparently, so did Tuck. Try as Max might to stay objective about their temporary arrangement, the promise of forever in her eyes whenever he reached for her tempted him until he found it difficult to breathe. The lines between what he knew to be true and what she insisted could be—if only he would reach out and take it—kept blurring.

The more time he spent with her, the more he wanted her, but if the last few weeks had taught him anything, it was that the stench of his past wasn't content to stick to him alone. Although her fierce defense of him stroked his ego as well as his libido, something had to give. It hadn't taken long for the image Jessi had worked so hard to build to fall victim to sly innuendo and outright criticism, with industry insiders asking why country music's sweetheart was shacked up with an obvious thug.

Despite his careful planning, things had spiraled out of his control and, no matter which way he approached the problem, he kept ending up at the same place.

The thought of giving up Haven Place burned like a festering wound, but it seemed fate had stepped in to limit his options. Even if the stalker was no longer a concern, walking away from Jessi now would do little good. Like circling sharks, the press had scented blood in the water, and they wouldn't back off until someone was shredded. He couldn't... *wouldn't* let her take the heat for something that was his fault, but unless he was willing to tell all and produce the evidence to prove his claims, the Krandalls' lies would stand and Jessi would pay the price.

His mother's home was most likely lost to him anyway. Although his lowered bid had been accepted initially, something had gone wrong. The bid was returned as denied the very next day. Instinct told him his cover had been blown.

Decision made, he snapped off the water and wrapped a towel around his waist. In his bedroom, he dressed before keying the false wall panel. His stomach muscles knotted as he opened the safe and removed the file. Striding into the living room, he dropped the folder on the coffee table in front of Tuck.

"What's this?" Tuck looked up, curiosity creasing his brow.

"My past." Max jammed his fingers through his damp hair. "It's time to call a family meeting."

* * * *

Max scanned the avid faces of his friends gathered in Ryan's living room and nodded at the open folder on the coffee table. "What's in that file isn't pretty, but it demolishes my grandmother's false timeline and disproves her claims about my parents."

"Max."

He turned at the softly whispered plea. Perched on the arm of the couch beside CC's cousin, Kris, Jessi stared at him. The knowledge in her eyes of what he risked if he went forward with this plan was shadowed by confused disbelief.

"It's okay, Jess. You were right. I can't let her get away with her lies. I can't let her smear my parents and won't let her drag you down in the process."

For several heartbeats, she held his gaze, then dropped her head to stare at her knees.

A soft whistle blew through Tuck's teeth. He looked up from one of the documents from the file with raised brows and eyes full of concern. "Are you sure you want to give them this kind of ammunition?"

"Lots of kids get into trouble, Tuck." Gracie's eyes sparkled with a determined glint. "And not all of them go on to be an upstanding citizen the way Max has."

"Upstanding citizen might be a stretch." At Tuck's teasing grin, Gracie narrowed her eyes, and he held up a hand. "Calm down, Tiger." He looked at Max. "All I'm saying is, you know how the press works. They'll salivate over some of this."

Probably, but it was a chance Max would have to take. "Holding back my juvenile records will only make them question the rest of what I have to say."

"He's right." All eyes turned to V. With her years of expertise in dealing with the press, Jake's powerful publicist had insisted on being included in tonight's gathering of the family. She straightened from reading the paper Tuck held. "Besides, when going public with this kind of story, it's best to put any potentially damaging information out there from the beginning. If you don't, sure as hell it'll come back and bite you on the ass later." She sent Gracie a wink.

Gracie huffed and rolled her eyes at the reminder of her and Jake's contentious brush with the press. Jake snorted a laugh, and Max stifled a smile.

"Are you sure want to do this, son? You'll be giving up more than your privacy."

Max turned. If he'd been unsure of how much Ryan's investigation had turned up on his stealthy ploy to get his hands on Haven Place, the older man's question and the quiet sympathy in his eyes left no doubt. Oddly, the knowledge didn't anger Max as it should. Instead, it validated his belief that exposing the Krandalls' lies was not only the right move, it was the smart one.

If Ryan could discover Max's connection with the bogus real estate company, Elizabeth Krandall could as well. Considering the constant run-around he'd faced at every turn, odds were, she already had. For months, he'd met with one roadblock after another in his attempt to attain the deed to Haven Place. Rather than dance at the end of the devious strings his grandmother had no doubt been using to jerk him around, without any intention of delivering the prize, he preferred to face her head-on.

"Yes, sir, I am."

Ryan dipped his chin in a nod. Max shifted his feet, uncomfortable witnessing the approval and pride shining in the older man's eyes.

"Of course he's sure." Gracie glanced around the room. "And I say it's about damn time someone stood up to that bit—woman."

Jake chuckled and wrapped an arm around his wife's shoulders.

Max slid his gaze back to Jessi. Head still bowed, she remained silent. Of everyone, her opinion mattered most, but before he could ask what she was thinking, Tuck spoke.

"So, what's the plan?" With his wife balanced on his lap, he looked around at everyone gathered. "I say we run a full-out blitz. We back Max up as a group. All of us against the Krandalls."

A lump formed in Max's throat as, one by one, the others nodded.

"With Gracie and me right up front." CC patted her baby bump.

"Exactly." Gracie's teeth flashed in a keen smile. "No one can a resist a pregnant woman, and what mother-to-be would champion a thug?" Fury darkened the eyes she turned on Max. "I can't believe the worm had the nerve to call you that. If I ever meet Elliot Sprig in person," she shook her head, "well, I won't be responsible for my actions."

Jake's lips twisted in a grimace. "Thank God I'm on the broadcasting side of the sport these days and can no longer be fined. Still, the network might have an issue with my wife knocking a team owner on his ass." He dodged her jabbing elbow and grinned.

"I like the idea of a united front." Tim looked up from the papers in his hand and drew Max's attention. "Max, we'll keep your comments concise as you take apart each of their points, one by one." He tapped a fingertip to the slightly yellowed paper at the top of the file. "Elizabeth Krandall painted your mother as a simpleton and your father a con man. We'll include your mother's college transcripts and your father's decorated service record in the press handout."

Kris crossed her legs. "It's not enough to give them cold, hard facts." She shrugged a shoulder at Tim's frown. "The Krandalls named Max the villain in this situation, and from the tone of the articles over the past week, the press bought the charge." She turned to Max. "To change that perception, they need to see the little boy you were."

His skin crawled at the idea of bearing his soul to the public. "I'm not sure I could pull off a poor-innocent-me sob story. Nor do I want to."

V laughed, cocked her head, and eyed the curled tips of the tattoo peeking above the ribbed collar of his sweater. "No one would think innocent, looking at you, big guy."

"Exactly. So why make the attempt?" Tim wore a scowl as he locked his gaze with Kris's.

She tossed her head, setting fiery auburn curls bouncing, and ignored Tim to smile at Max. "I'm not suggesting a sob story. Just an anecdotal story or two of the three of you as a family to personalize your parents by sharing some details of who they were from your perspective."

"You don't have anything to say, Jessi?"

Every set of eyes turned Jessi's way at Ryan's softly spoken question.

"Nope, it sounds like you all have everything worked out."

She pushed to her feet. Max frowned at the glistening sheen of tears in her eyes. He stepped forward, but she turned toward the hallway.

"Jessi?" Kris arched her neck to look at her.

Jessi continued out of the room. "I've gotta pee."

Max shuffled to a stop, staring at Jessi's back as she walked away. Kris scrambled to her feet and followed.

Tuck was the first to break the uncomfortable silence. "Women." He shook his head and smirked.

CC twisted her head around with a scowl for her husband.

"What?" His smirk disappeared beneath a bland face full of innocence.

"I've gotta pee, too." Gracie scooted forward to the edge of the couch. Jake braced a hand on her ass as she attempted to stand and pushed her to her feet. She smiled at Max, squeezed his arm as she passed, and followed Jessi and Kris from the room.

Chapter 21

Kris shut the bathroom door behind them, and Jessi slashed her index fingers beneath both eyes. Guilt and anger tangled like a hot mess in her chest and her breath came in short pants.

"God. What is Max thinking, Kris? How can he even consider giving up his chance a...." She curled her hands into fists and bit down on her lip.

Kris leaned a hip against the vanity at Jessi's side. "His chance at what?"

She shook her head and avoided her friend's gaze. "A dream. Because, although the family doesn't understand, that's what his announcement tonight amounts to. And for what? To placate a handful of snarky reporters?"

"Snarky reporters can make a person's life miserable." Kris tugged a tissue from the box on the counter and held it out. "And Max isn't the kind of guy who backs down from a fight, especially when the fight is based on lies."

No, he wasn't, but God. She took the tissue and squeezed her eyes shut. If it were up to her, she'd be front and center, exposing Elizabeth Krandall for the evil bitch she was. Given the chance, Jessi would scratch the woman's eyes out for hurting Max with her cruel lies, as well as for the way she'd mistreated him when he was a boy. But the yearning in his voice as he'd spoken about Haven Place and his parents had nearly broken her heart. How could she look at herself in the mirror, knowing he'd given up such a dream over concern for her career?

A tapping knock made her groan, and she met Kris's gaze in the mirror.

"Blow your nose," Kris instructed softly before calling over her shoulder. "We'll be out in a sec."

"Do you mind if I come in?" Gracie's muted voice came through the closed bathroom door. "One of the babies is playing kick ball with my bladder."

Kris cocked her head as if in question. Jessi wiped her nose and cheeks, but the blotchy evidence of her tears was impossible to disguise. She flipped on the water and bent her head to hide her face. "Come on in."

Gracie immediately stepped inside, stopping behind Jessi to rub a soothing hand over her back. "You all right?"

She bobbed her chin in answer and peeked through her lashes at the blonde's reflection in the mirror.

Gracie slung an arm across her shoulders in a brief squeeze. "Stay for a minute, okay? I've wanted to talk to you and haven't had the chance."

Kris pushed off the counter. "I'll wait outside."

"Oh, don't bother. We all know you're going to press your ear to the door." Gracie and Kris shared a grin before Gracie quick-stepped to the toilet.

Jessi smiled wanly. A heart-to-heart girlfriend-therapy session with Kris and Max's best friend—while she peed—wasn't high on Jessi's list of fun new things to experience, but she flipped off the water and used the hand towel nearby to dab her face.

"I swear to God. I spend half my time in bathrooms these days." Gracie danced from foot to foot, reached beneath her dress to tug away her panties, and lowered to the seat.

A tinkling stream sounded followed by a relieved sigh, and Jessi met Kris's gaze. Her friend's teeth flashed in a grin.

Unsure what to say or where to look, Jessi picked up a can of air freshener and studied the nozzle as if she'd never seen one before.

"So, have you told Max you love him yet?"

Jessi's head jerked up, her horrified gaze slamming into the intent, violet-blue eyes locked on her. Heart in her throat, she looked at Kris. Her friend was no help. Expectant eyes watched her beneath arched brows.

"Um. I—"

"You should, you know." Gracie ripped several squares off the roll. "If there was ever a man who needs to hear those three little words, it's Max."

Oh, man. Jessi's throat closed, and the tears she'd only partially gotten under control welled with renewed life. Rolling her eyes, Kris snatched another tissue from the box and shoved it at her. The toilet flushed, and Gracie waddled to the sink, calmly washing and drying her hands before turning to prop her hips against the vanity top.

"He takes the breath away, doesn't he?"

Jessi frowned at the very married woman weeks from giving birth.

Gracie's sparkling eyes reflected her tinkling laughter. "Relax, sweetie, I'm not talking romantically. Well, not in my case, anyway." She bumped her elbow to Kris's, and they shared a sly laugh.

Jessi shook her head, but their humor was impossible to resist.

"Did you know I was fourteen the day I met Max?" Gracie's grin softened into a smile. "He was eighteen and even then, he was larger than life."

Jessi had no problem believing that. He'd raised himself from the time he was twelve. That type of existence forced a person to grow up fast. "CC said you moved into the same building."

Gracie nodded. "God, I was so naïve. I had no concept of the dangers lurking in the corners of the world my sister and I entered when our mom died." The smile slid from her lips and she dipped her chin. "But Max did. He didn't know me from Eve, Jessi, but that didn't stop him from facing down the group of boys who'd cornered me in a dark hallway of the apartment building we'd moved into the day before."

"Oh, geez, Gracie." The tight line of Kris's mouth reflected her horror.

The breath backed up in Jessi's throat. "What happened?"

"He kicked their asses," Gracie's teeth flashed in a wicked grin, "and I fell in love with an unlikely knight in shining armor." She twisted to toss the hand towel onto the counter. "The projects were a scary place, but after that, nobody dared bother me. Not with Max as my champion. A few days later, he gave me my first lesson in the art of street fighting. He said if a kitten was going to live amongst the jackals, she needed to grow some claws."

A helpless smile tugged at Jessi's lips. "He taught me a few self-defense moves while we were at your house in Alton Bay. Thanks, by the way. It's a beautiful place."

Gracie waved off the acknowledgement. "Self-defense lessons, huh?" She rubbed a hand over her belly. "That's Max. He can't resist a damsel in distress."

Jessi sobered at the reminder. "But at what cost?" She had no idea what, or even *if*, Gracie knew about Haven Place but, either way, Jessi wouldn't betray Max's trust. She chose her words carefully and stuck to the concern they all shared. "Because of me, he's being forced to expose the painful pieces of his childhood to the public."

Kris shook her head.

Gracie was more vocal. "Nobody forces Max to do anything. Believe me, I've tried. His concern for you is part of it, but if he didn't believe this was the right way to go, he wouldn't do it."

"That's what I tried to tell her."

Jessi shot Kris a scowl. Okay, they had a point. Max was too deliberate a man to make a decision this important without analyzing it from every angle, but still....

Gracie crossed her arms over her extended belly. "And you never answered my question."

Jessi winced as Kris snickered. Geez. A declaration of love should be a private thing between the parties involved, not fodder for a bathroom discussion.

Tossing her soiled tissue in the trashcan, she played dumb. "What question is that?"

A knowing smirk twisted Gracie's lips, and the heat blooming on Jessi's cheeks must have been answer enough. Gracie pushed off the vanity to pull her into a quick hug.

"Good for you." She stepped back with a wide grin. "How did he react?"

The memory of how she'd climbed onto Max's bed, and all but attacked him, flamed her blush to scorching. A sly laugh gurgled in Kris's throat.

Jessi was quick to abuse her friends' assumptions. "It's not what you think. He wasn't exactly happy to hear it."

"Of course he wasn't." Gracie grinned and flipped the toilet seat cover down to sit. "You no doubt scared the shit out of him."

A dismissive sniff tickled Jessi's nose. "Max isn't scared of anything."

"Don't kid yourself, sweetie. He's scared to death of you."

Renewed frustration simmered in her belly as she recalled the entirety of the evening and his comments during her self-defense lesson the next morning. "Scared isn't how I'd describe his reaction. An hour earlier, he went to great lengths to let me know any romantic relationship between us would be a temporary one."

"Men can be such jerks." Kris's lips arched down in a scowl, and she rolled her eyes.

"You can say that again." Jessi tossed her head. "He said, and I quote, 'When this is over, I'll move on to the next woman. If you can live with that, I'm more than happy to accept what you're so determined to give.'"

"Shut. Up." Gracie narrowed her eyes. "He did not say that."

"Verbatim."

Gracie stared at her in silence for several heartbeats. Disappointment darkened her eyes. "Please tell me you slugged him."

For the first time since she'd listened to Max lay out his plan to call the Krandalls out, Jessi laughed. "I considered it. Instead, I decided to call his bluff." Frustration bubbled, and she clenched her teeth. "I don't understand him, Gracie. I know a guy's sex drive is a powerful force, but hormones and lust don't account for what I see in his eyes whenever he touches me. He has feelings for me, yet, for years, he's acted as if I were invisible."

"That's true." Kris nodded. "He has."

Jessi turned back to Gracie. "I'm beginning to think he avoided me on purpose."

"Ya think?"

She blinked at the sarcastic confirmation. "But why?"

Suddenly, Gracie sucked in a breath and rubbed a hand along her side.

Both Jessi and Kris rushed forward to assist as she shifted her weight to stand.

"What is it?" Kris wrapped an arm around Gracie's waist. "Should I go get Jake?"

"Oh, Lord. Don't do that. He'll panic and I'll end up spending the night in the emergency room." Gracie pushed the heel of her palm against the side of her belly, and Jessi's eyes widened as the mound shifted beneath the clinging cloth.

"Oh my God." Kris pulled her arm free and stared as the mound continued to move.

Gracie laughed. "Cool, huh?"

"Freaky. Does it hurt?"

"Nope, but freaky is an apt description."

"That's amazing." Jessi grinned and couldn't resist resting her hand over the tiny foot-shaped bump that suddenly appeared high on Gracie's belly.

"You should feel it from my perspective. These guys are future acrobats. The bigger they get, the more they complain about the close quarters."

Jessi removed her hand. Gracie's suddenly intense gaze held her in place.

"I love Max like a brother and would never break a confidence, but since he's never technically requested I keep my mouth shut on the subject, I'm going to tell you my theory." She dipped her head closer and bounced her gaze between Jessi and Kris. "And if either of you tell Max I told you, you're going to need a hell of a lot more than a few self-defense lessons. Am I clear?"

Kris snorted, and a helpless laugh escaped Jessi. She nodded.

"Good." Gracie straightened. "It's simple. Max doesn't think he's good enough for you."

Jessi stared at her. Of all the possible explanations she might have imagined, Gracie's theory was the last one Jessi would have considered. Not good enough for her? This from a man who dropped everything to help when she asked? A man willing to share his juvenile police record with the world to protect her image?

"That's ridiculous."

"Agreed, but true nonetheless." Gracie's heavy sigh was tinged with a mix of frustration and sadness. "He has ghosts, Jessi. Ghosts that keep him on the outside, looking in at the happiness that should be his. Perhaps the source is contained in that file in the other room. Perhaps not. Either way, something in his past has him convinced he doesn't deserve the chance at happiness you represent." She reached for Jessi's clenched hands. "He's done everything he could to deny those feelings you see in his eyes, and yet," she cocked her head toward the door, "he's out in the other room right now, proposing an action we both know he never would have considered except for you."

Jessi slid her eyes shut as his reluctant acceptance of their relationship suddenly made sense. "How the hell am I supposed to defeat ghosts?"

Gracie squeezed her hands. "By not giving up on him, and not letting *him* give up on you."

Chapter 22

Jessi stepped through the bedroom doorway and paused. On a stool at the kitchen island, Max sat with his back to her. With his knees spread, his black dress slacks hugged his butt, and the natural colored, weaved sweater enhanced the breadth of his wide shoulders. He bent forward slightly, rereading the sheet of paper containing the statement he'd prepared for the press with Tim and Kris's help. Jessi smoothed a hand over the waist of her slim skirt and crossed the room. Slipping up behind him, she slid her hands around his waist to burrow them under his sweater and pressed her cheek to his back.

"You don't have to do this, you know."

Beneath her fingers, the warm skin over his abs rippled as he straightened and spun on the stool. "Yeah, I do."

Frustration and sadness tangled in her chest like a clenching fist. After last night's family meeting, she'd tried to talk him out of today's press conference. He'd dismissed her concerns, claiming chances were the Krandalls had discovered his plan to attain Haven Place, but even if they hadn't, he owed it to his parents to set the record straight. More importantly, he was done watching the press come down on her for something that was his fault. Before they'd even arrived at his condo, he'd put the wheels in motion.

"Just call Tim and tell him you've changed your mind. He'll handle the details."

Gathering her between his knees, he cupped her hips and dropped a kiss on her nose. "Let it go, Jess. Vern and the guys are already downstairs, and the press is gathering outside. It's done."

A knock on the door cut off further argument. Irritation and guilt fought for supremacy as he gently moved her back and stood to cross the condo and answer the summons. Stepping to the side as Tuck breezed through the doorway, Max shut the door once CC, Jake, Gracie, and V had filed inside.

"Ready to face the vultures?" Winking at Jessi, Tuck helped CC settle on the stool Max had vacated, then headed for the fridge. "From the looks of things downstairs, they've got the place surrounded."

Jessi shot Max a frown. "If it were up to me, I'd lock the front door and post a sign telling them all to go to hell."

"If only it were that easy." V dumped her purse on the island counter.

"Gracie tried something similar when they had the farm staked out years ago." Jake grinned at his wife. "It didn't work."

Gracie pressed a kiss to Max's cheek before moving farther into the room. She blew her husband a raspberry. "It would have if you'd cooperated. Instead, you had to kiss me on the porch—in front of their cameras."

Jake dropped his arm around her shoulders. "As I recall, you kissed *me*, then dragged me upstairs for..." he smiled slyly, "a workout."

V rolled her eyes. "Get a room, you two."

Jake laughed, and Jessi blinked at the surprising blush coloring Gracie's cheeks.

"Jesus. Do you have to bring up sex?" Tuck spun to lean his hips against the counter, a scowl puckering his forehead.

CC rested her hand on her belly. "He's frustrated. Last week the doctor told him he has to keep his hands to himself until after the baby comes."

Immediately concerned, Jessi glanced between her cousin and CC. "Is there a problem with the baby? Why are you here? You should be at home, resting."

CC waved her off with a laugh. "I'm fine and so is the baby. Other than his size." She ran her hand over her baby bump in a circular massage. "Baby Huey is running out of real estate. The doctor is concerned he'll stage a jail break earlier than we'd like."

"Speak for yourself. I'm ready to break him out myself." Tuck shot Max a frustrated glare. "The doc has me on the bench."

"Please." CC rolled her eyes. "You leave for the Super Bowl tomorrow afternoon. You'll be too busy to think of sex at least through Sunday."

Tuck's smile was pure lecher. "Baby, a man is never too busy to think of sex."

Max's lips quirked in a smile, then sobered as he glanced around at his friends. "Thanks for coming. All of you. Considering your past experiences with the press, I would have understood if you'd insisted on staying away."

"As if we'd let you face the mob on your own." Gracie tossed her head and slid onto the stool beside CC. "Don't be an idiot."

Jessi bit her lip against a smile and turned to Max. The awkward wariness stiffening his proud face was so wrong, as if he hadn't actually expected his friends to show and wasn't sure why they had. A piercing sadness squeezed her heart at the further evidence of his blindness when it came to the loyalty and belief he inspired in others.

Gracie was right. Max needed to hear he was loved. By her, definitely, but by others as well. He also needed to be shown. Three short steps allowed her to wrap her arms around his waist. He absently returned the gesture and she smiled.

"Gracie's right." Lifting on her toes, she brushed his lips in a quick kiss. "Don't be an idiot."

He tightened his hold, and some of the wariness slid away as his eyes narrowed in a silent warning. Another knock sounded at the door and, tucking her cheek against his, she squeezed her arms a bit tighter as Jake let Tim in.

He joined the others around the island and eyed Max. "It's almost two. You ready?"

Max tensed against her but nodded.

"Then let's do this."

Max released her to collect his statement from the island.

Jessi turned to Tim. "Where's Dad?"

He briefly shifted his gaze to Max, and the flash of anger in his eyes came and went so quickly she decided she must have imagined it. He propped his briefcase on the counter and retrieved a stack of folders. "He had a meeting. I doubt he'll show."

"A meeting with who?"

Shrugging a shoulder, he closed the case and turned to Max. "I'll give a brief opening and pass out the handouts. Then you're up. Once you're done with your statement, we'll open it up to questions. Answer only the ones you want."

"What if that doesn't work?"

"Leave that to me." V's teeth flashed an eager smile.

Tim snapped his briefcase shut. "If things start to get out of hand, V and I will step in to handle it. Any questions before we start?"

Max shook his head. "Let's just get this over with."

Jessi reached for his hand and, as if he'd forgotten she was there, he blinked. His strained smile didn't reach his eyes. Damn it, she wanted this over with, too, but most of all, she hated it was necessary in the first place. Elizabeth Krandall had a lot to answer for.

The chatter of voices from below hit them as they filed into the hallway. Rounding the corner, Jessi clung to Max's hand and fought back a cringe. The fight center teemed with people. Not surprisingly, the music industry, sports world, and cable news outlets were all represented. As she'd feared, Super Bowl fever and the matchup between the Marauders and Hurricanes had exploded what should have been an obscure disagreement of facts into a front-page story.

Max had insisted on meeting the press on his home turf, and he certainly hadn't gone out of his way to make things comfortable. No chairs were provided, and a half dozen of Max's tattooed and muscled clients stood guard over the stanchions Vern had placed around the center's mats. The precaution left little room for the forty plus reporters, along with several camera crews and their equipment, crammed together like credentialed sardines.

As Max and Jessi descended the steps, followed by Tim and V, Tuck, CC, and the Malones, the noise level dropped and all heads turned their way. Jessi's gaze roamed the faces of the large crowd, concerned but not surprised to find Craig's among them. A shy smile moved over his face as she met his gaze. Apparently, he'd forgiven her for her unintended slight yesterday, but she really was going to have to say something to his father. A crush was one thing, but it was a school day. Skipping class was another matter altogether.

Craig and his crush flew from her mind as Tim gave a brief greeting and passed out the press packets, then signaled to Max. Reluctantly, she released his hand so he could read his prepared statement. In a united front, she and the others stood at his back. He withheld nothing, ticking off the charges listed in his juvenile file. Her anger grew with each harsh detail, juxtaposed against the sweeter memories Kris had suggested he share. Jessi's heart wept as he personalized the parents he'd lost, recalling a family trip to visit the Statue of Liberty when he'd still been young enough to ride on his father's shoulders.

When Max finished, Jessi stepped forward to link her arm with his. Gaze guarded, he looked down at her, and the questions began to fly.

For nearly thirty minutes, he fielded the questions tossed at him. By design and demeanor, he refused to be dragged into a press conference war with his grandmother. Calmly and efficiently, he made it clear he was there simply to set the record straight about his parents. As for himself, the documents in the press packet contained the details of his childhood records. His lack of an adult record, and his business portfolio, spoke for themselves.

"Why did your grandmother and Mr. Sprig make their initial statement?"

Max met the reporter's questioning gaze. "I have no idea. You'll have to ask them."

"Juvenile records are normally sealed," a voice from the back called out. "How did the Krandalls become aware of the contents?"

"Again. You'll have to ask them."

Yet another question tripped over Max's answer. "Your description of your parents' relationship differs greatly from Mrs. Krandall's. Why would she make such claims against her own daughter and son-in-law?"

"You'll have to ask her."

A local sports reporter held up his hand. "With your connection to both the Marauders through your relationship with Jessi and friendship with the Tuckers, and the Hurricanes through your grandmother, who's your pick for Sunday's game?"

Tuck spoke before Max could respond. "You'll have to ask me."

"And me," Jake added.

Not to be left out, CC and Gracie spoke in tandem. "And me."

The scattered laughter lightened the mood and, for several minutes, football took center stage. The handful of sports reporters peppered both Tuck and Jake on the Marauders' chances of earning another championship.

Max's arm muscles gradually loosened beneath Jessi's fingers and relief lightened her heart. When asked how she felt about performing in a Super Bowl in which her cousin would play, Jessi smiled. "I couldn't be more excited." She shot Tuck a wicked grin. "But once it's over, I think my cousin should share his new ring."

The friendlier tone of the questioning was short lived, however, as Chet Bertrum found his voice.

"Jessi, you and your family are obviously supporting Mr. Grayson's attempt to repair his reputation, but how does any of what was said today change the recent negative perception of you from your fans?"

Max tensed and opened his mouth, but Jessi squeezed his arm. She offered Chet a syrupy sweet smile. "I wasn't aware of any negative perception from my fans, Chet. Only spitefully negative articles about whom I choose to spend my time with."

At her blatant reference to his last three articles, Chet's face flushed all the way to his bald forehead, but she wasn't finished.

"But you're right. My fans are interested, so let me clear up any misperceptions." She ignored Max's clearing of his throat and held Chet's gaze. "I support Max Grayson because he's an honorable man. He's not here today because he cares what you all think of him. Like he said, his record speaks for itself. He's here because he's the kind of man willing to share the private details of his life to protect and defend those people he cares about. Like his parents." She turned her head and met Max's concerned gaze. "And me."

Facing forward once more, she brushed her gaze over the crowd. "I write and sing songs for a living. For years, I've entertained my fans with music about love and loyalty, happiness and the heart. Those are the things my fans care about, and they are exactly what I've found with Max." She found Chet in the crowd. "I support Max Grayson because I love him."

At Jessi's side, Max shuffled his feet. She peeked at him in a sidelong glance, but instead of the panic he'd displayed the last time she said those words, wary wonder filled his eyes. His Adam's apple bobbed in a tight swallow as Tim brought the press conference to a close.

Chapter 23

"I always said you were a stubborn son of a bitch, but I never would've called you a coward."

Max dragged his gaze from the top of the staircase where Jessi had disappeared and sent Vern a glare. "I thought you were headed back to the gym."

"And I thought you were driving me because you have shit to do there." The old man's thin lips curled in a sneer. "The next time you need an excuse for acting stupid, leave me out of it."

Guilt ratcheted up Max's spine. Stupid was a stretch, but coward definitely applied in this case. With the press cleared out and the fight center closed for the remainder of the day, Tim's suggestion of a celebratory dinner had been met with approval all around. The hurt on Jessi's face when Max offered his bullshit excuse of driving Vern back to the gym had twisted his guts in a knot, but he was too raw and off balance to trade quips with his friends and Jessi over drinks and dinner.

He needed time to think. Needed the time to get his equilibrium back. Jesus. He knew firsthand how Gracie, Jake, Tuck, and V felt about the press. Yet, along with Jessi, Tim, and CC, they'd stood as one and had his back as if he were part of the family.

"There's nothing needs doing at the gym that can't wait." Vern ripped his coat from the banister. "What the hell were you thinking, disappointing that girl when she just bared her heart to the world defending you? Are you blind, boy, or just stupid?"

Guilt slid toward anger. He jammed his hands into the pockets of his slacks. "Coward, stupid, and now blind. You got any more insults you want to drop on me?"

Vern shook his head, his face a mask of disgust. "Never thought I'd live to see the day Max Grayson would tuck tail and run from a slip of a girl who barely comes to his chin. But you're scared, all right. White knuckled, deer in the headlights, gut in a vice scared."

The bull's-eye assessment hit Max like an uppercut to the jaw, and he clenched his teeth. Fuckin' A, he was scared. Scared shitless of what it would mean to walk away from her and even more alarmed that he wanted to stay. With her boundless belief in him and stubborn determination to wear him down, Jessi Tucker had managed the unthinkable. She'd made him believe he could have things he'd never dared to dream.

Christ. He was screwed. How could he go back to settling for a good-enough-to-get-by existence after having been given a glimpse of a life rich with the kind of love and happiness he'd stopped believing in with the deaths of his parents? Yet, as scared as he was at the thought of a future without Jessi, he was terrified of what would be required of him if he were to take the chance and claim the love she offered. The love he yearned for more than he needed to breathe.

Compassionate, courageous, and sexy as hell, Jessi represented all that was good in the world. When she looked at him, he saw the man he'd always wanted to be reflected in her eyes. How could he survive the blow if the love in those wide blue orbs was replaced with revulsion?

He jammed his fingers through his hair, his gaze swinging to the empty stairs. "It's complicated, Vern."

A windy snort drew his attention.

Vern's eyes gleamed with impatience. "She's a woman. Of course it's complicated."

Max shook his head at the sexist dismissal and, as he studied the rough-edged man who had dragged him from the gutter, he wished things were different. With every fiber of his being, he wished the sins of the past could be erased, but the dark shadows of his childhood never faded and never lost their sting.

"There are things she doesn't know about me. Things I've never shared with anyone."

"Shit, boy, we all have things in our past we ain't proud of." Vern tossed his head toward the empty hallway upstairs. "That girl up there doesn't strike me as the kind who scares off easy." A chuckle rattled in his throat. "Did you see how she ripped into that tight-ass reporter?"

Max's lips curved helplessly. Jessi on a tear was a sight to behold. Like a seasoned pro, she'd sliced Chet Bertrum to pieces with a handful of precision cuts and, if the reactions of the gathered press were an indication, managed to tug at the hearts of her fans in the process.

She'd claimed she found the sentiments with Max but, the truth was, love and loyalty, happiness and heart, were the essence of Jessi Tucker. Her capacity for love and simple joy of life, even in the face of the debilitating stress of her career, were impossible to resist. Whether laughing with her family and friends or whispering her pleasure in the privacy of the night, her inner fire burned hot, torching through his barriers to warm the dark corners of his mind and heart.

"Do you love her?"

Vern's simple question ripped at Max's soul, and he fought the urge to squirm the way he had as a kid whenever the battered old boxer had pinned him on the spot. From the beginning, their relationship been based on the unvarnished truth, with very few exceptions. Vern had always had an uncanny knack for seeing through Max even when others couldn't. Lying would be a waste of time.

Love her? Shit, how could he not? He scraped a palm over the back of his neck. "Yeah, I do."

"Then what's the problem? Why aren't you upstairs telling her you're sorry for ruining her plans?"

Max dropped his arm to his side. "Apologizing won't change who or what I am."

The frown dragging Vern's lips down was reminiscent of the many he'd worn over the years, usually right before he tore into Max for doing something stupid. Today was no different.

"Don't be an ass. In all the years since you staggered into that gym, carrying a chip the size of a boulder on your scrawny shoulders, you've never backed down from a challenge. You fought and scraped and didn't let the shit from your childhood stop you from reaching your goals. Why are you now?"

He yanked on his coat and didn't give Max a chance to respond. "You've done good, boy, building this place and winning a couple of titles, but those things won't keep you warm at night or fill the lonely hours when the years grow long and the body tired." Dipping his chin, he seared Max with faded blue eyes. "That girl upstairs doesn't give a shit who or what you *think* you are. She loves *you*. Max Grayson." He poked a gnarled finger at Max's chest. "Don't screw that up."

Max coughed a humorless laugh as Vern turned and stalked out the front door.

I support Max Grayson because I love him.

He rubbed a hand over his chest, and with a sigh, moved about the center, locking the door, and shutting off the lights. She hadn't repeated the claim since that first night in New Hampshire, and until she'd spoken the words, he hadn't realized how badly he'd wanted to hear them again. Thank God, no one had pressed him for a response to her announcement. Thrilled, humbled, and scared shitless, he wouldn't have been able to utter a word.

She'd called him an honorable man, and the lie burned at his stomach lining like acid. Vern was right. Max owed her an apology, just as he did Gracie, Tuck, and the others, but he owed Jessi more than that. An honorable man wouldn't greedily accept the love a woman offered without giving her the truth.

Dread nearly consumed him as he climbed the stairs on leaden feet. With every fiber of his being, he wanted to be the man she described. He wanted Jessi Tucker. Wanted to grab hold and not let go. To claim forever and experience each and every promise shining like a beacon in her beautiful eyes. But would she still want *him* once she'd heard it all?

Exposing the darkest corners of his soul when she was already pissed wouldn't be a point in his favor, but did the when and where really matter? There would never be a good time for what he had to say. Gut-wrenching fear and desperate hope collided as he opened the condo door. He stopped short after only two steps.

"Jessi?" He shut the door and bent to retrieve a discarded high heel. Its mate lay several feet away. His eyes widened and trepidation was trampled beneath the sudden thundering of his heart. The pounding increased as his gaze traveled across the condo. Like a silky trail of breadcrumbs, the pale peach blouse and slim black skirt Jessi had worn to the press conference pooled at intervals on the wood plank floor.

Moving cautiously, he followed into the bedroom, stepping over the lacy bra she'd dropped. He glanced around the empty room. "Jessi?" Heat slammed into him, and he nearly choked as she appeared in the bathroom doorway.

If she was pissed, she had a devious way of getting even. The clip that held her hair earlier was gone, and her long auburn curls tumbled about her shoulders and bared breasts. A miniscule triangle of black lace was all she wore. While the thong wasn't the face cloth Tuck had once predicted she'd employ, it was just as effective. The thin straps trailed high on her hips, emphasizing the curve of her waist. Her skin gleamed in the low light as she walked toward him, hips rolling in a seductive sway.

He swallowed with an audible click. "Jessi, I—"

"I know. You need your coat but," she stopped before him and rested a hand against his chest, "I was wondering." Her lashes lowered and so did her hand. He sucked in a breath as she cupped his balls through his slacks.

The high heel he'd forgotten he carried slipped from his hand and clattered to the floor.

A purely feminine smile curved her lips. Trailing a finger up the ridge of his swelling erection, she slid his belt buckle from its loop and tugged. It joined the shoe with a clang. Blue eyes, sparkling with sensual intent, peeked at him through a thick fringe of lashes. "Do you think Vern will mind delaying his ride to the gym for a few minutes?"

Max's stomach muscles contracted as she lowered the zipper of his slacks. She dipped her fingers beneath the waistband of his briefs to wrap them around his cock, and his mind went blank. "Vern?"

Her throaty laugh hardened him nearly as effectively as her stroking fingers. She stepped closer and peeled both briefs and slacks down his hips with her free hand. They dropped to his ankles, and she rose on her tiptoes, brushing his lips with hers. She tugged at the hem of his sweater, pushing it up high enough to press her lips to his chest. Electricity arced through him at the nip of her teeth on one small nipple. Silky and warm, her curves slid against his reaching fingers as she shimmied down his body, trailing moist kisses over his chest and abs to drop to her knees.

Lord, have mercy.

His blood surged and he stared down at the erotic picture of her glossy head of curls poised above his straining cock. Sweat broke on his brow, and he grew so hard he hurt. The tip of her tongue, swirling over the head, made him groan, and as she took him in her mouth, he had to lock his legs to stay on his feet.

Damp heat enveloped him. Sucking gently, she drew him deeper, then pulled back with a faint scrape of her teeth.

He slid his eyes shut on a full-body shudder. "Fuck. *Me.*" Her murmur of approval vibrated through him and his balls contracted. Clenching his teeth, he buried his fingers in her curls and gently tugged her free. "Stop, baby. You're killing me."

She tipped her head back and a sultry smile curved her lips. The smoky tenor of her voice sparked over his hypersensitive nerve endings like a live wire. "I've never done this before. Looks like I'm doing it right."

Laughter rumbled in his chest as he slid his hands beneath her arms and lifted her to her feet. Doing it right…hell. She'd brought him to the brink of orgasm in record time, and if he didn't plunge inside her in the next ten seconds, he would lose what was left of his mind.

Clutching her close, he dropped his head, and his mouth dove for hers. She met his hungry kiss and matched him in her urgency. Jamming her hands beneath his sweater, she scored the muscles of his back with her nails.

His tongue sparred with hers as he backed her toward the bed—and nearly toppled them to the floor. Gripping her tighter, he found his balance. She pulled back to meet his gaze, giggling as he kicked free of the slacks shackling his ankles. They stumbled together, falling onto the bed, and he immediately rolled to his back to wrench his sweater over his head and off.

"Hurry." The guttural plea flew from her lips.

She writhed on the bed, shimmying out of her thong. Gaze locked on her movements, he reached blindly for the bedside table drawer and the condoms inside. His fingers closed around a foil packet, and she grabbed his wrist. Scrabbling to her knees, she straddled his hips and snatched the condom from his hand.

She tore at the packaging and cast it aside, then lined up the latex ring with the swollen head of his cock. Lifting his head for a better view, he clenched his teeth and forgot how to breathe. Her slim fingers smoothed the thin rubber over the length of him.

"I meant every word, Max."

His gaze jerked up and locked on hers. The glaze of heated excitement couldn't mask the determination in her blue eyes. Without looking away, she gripped him in her palm and scooted forward to position the tip at the entrance between her folds.

"I love you, and nothing in your past will change that."

She spoke the words as if they were a pledge. As if she'd read his mind and knew what was coming. As if she saw the shadows in his soul and refused to let them matter. Remorse sliced at his heart.

"Don't do that." Her chin lifted, and she shook her head. "Don't go to that dark place where I can't reach you. Stay with me, Max." She lowered her body and took him inside inch by slow inch. "Love me."

I do.

Though the response hovered on his lips, he couldn't speak the words. Not until she understood. Still, the chilling reminder of what he had to do was no match for the plea in her eyes. Explanations and regrets would come later but, for now, he'd give her the only bond he could. Through the physical connection neither of them could resist, he'd make his pledge and hope like hell she didn't throw it back in his face later.

Grasping her hips, he rolled until she lay beneath him. Propped on his elbows, he flexed his hips and slid home. She groaned and wrapped one leg around the back of his thighs.

Pressing his cheek to hers, he began to move while whispering in her ear, "I'm here, baby. I'm here."

Chapter 24

The rustle of clothing interrupted Jessi's silent musings where she stood looking out the bedroom window. Night had fallen as they'd dozed between bouts of lovemaking. She sniffed mentally. Well...Max had napped. She'd been too wound up.

Behind her, reflected in the glass of the bedroom window, he tugged on the slacks he'd worn earlier. The wooden floor creaked a second before he wrapped his arms around her shoulders and dropped his chin to the top of her head.

"You okay?"

She slid her fingers over his forearms where they crossed at her chest, and the sleeves of her robe slipped to her elbows. Sighing, she dropped her head back against his shoulder. "I'm fine. Just restless."

The tensing of his body was subtle, but there. His arms contracted in a gentle squeeze. "We need to talk."

Well, shit. That sounded ominous. So much for thinking a couple of orgasms would help him relax or that a single declaration of love would wipe the shadows from his eyes. She wasn't surprised, though. Far from being relieved things had gone so well this afternoon, he'd been strung as tight as guitar string by the time Tim pronounced the press conference over.

"Normally, when someone says 'we have to talk,' what they really mean is, I'm about to verbally smack you upside the head." She turned in his arms and offered him a wincing smile. "Can't I have a root canal instead?"

One corner of his lips quirked, and he shook his head. Okay, good sign. If he could still smile, all hope wasn't yet lost.

He slid his arms from around her and stepped back, holding out a hand. "Come sit with me."

Gone was the sensual lover of an hour ago. In his place was an intent man with something on his mind. Something she would bet her shoe

closet she wasn't going to like. Beating Max's ghosts would take time…
time she suddenly feared he didn't plan to give her.

She curled her fingers into fists. "Yeah, this doesn't sound good.
Whatever it is, can't it wait until the morning?"

He dropped his hand, and the tight line of his mouth broadcast his
tension. "Waiting won't make this any easier to hear…or say."

Definitely not good.

He swung out a hand, indicating the bed. On shuffling feet, she stepped
by him and climbed onto the mattress before settling cross-legged with
her back propped against the headboard. He sat on the edge, a foot or
so away, which was fine with her. If he was going to break her heart,
she needed a little space. Meeting his sober gaze, she made her voice as
light as possible.

"You're scaring me, and I'm already freaked out over losing
you Haven Place."

His brows dipped with his frown. "This isn't about my mother's house,
and if you blame yourself one more time, I'm going to paddle your ass."

"I can't help it." She returned his frown with a scowl. "Haven Place
wasn't just your dream. It's a part of you."

He scrubbed a palm over his jaw. "Maybe so, but Elizabeth
Krandall was never going to sign over that deed. All I was doing was
spinning my wheels."

She crossed her arms and narrowed her eyes. "I don't believe you're as
calm about losing it as you say."

"Let it go, Jess. It was a pipe dream. An unrealistic one." His shoulders
sagged on a windy sigh. "Hell, if karma is real like you claim, my mother's
home was never going to be mine to begin with."

"What do you mean?"

Wry acceptance quirked his lips. "My mother always claimed the
house was infused with peace and tranquility. A place like that has no
business ending up in the hands of a man like me."

She had no idea where this was going, but it seemed he was deliberately
trying to make her mad. "I hate when you do that."

He arched a brow, a habit that was beginning to get on her
nerves. "Do what?"

"Say ugly things about yourself like 'a man like me' or 'bad blood,'
whatever the hell that means." She dropped her arms and leaned forward
to drill him in the chest with a stiffened finger. "That really pisses me off."

He snagged her hand, wrapping his fingers around her wrist. "Yeah,
well, sometimes the truth *is* ugly."

She tugged her hand free and sat back. Damn his ghosts. Why was it everyone else could see him for the man he'd become, but he couldn't? Dragging in a heavy breath, she softened her voice. "Yes, it is, and you had more ugliness in your life than any child deserves, but you were a little boy, Max. The ugliness was directed *at* you. It didn't come *from* you."

"Didn't it?" He looked away and jammed a hand through his hair.

She stared at his strong profile. A muscle twitched in his clenched jaw. "If you're talking about the stuff in your juvenile file, try again. I read the entire thing and so did the rest of the family."

He lowered his arm and leaned forward, head hanging and elbows propped on his knees. The position was one of defeat—a look she'd never thought to see on him and didn't like one bit.

Her heart squeezed, and she sat forward to rest a hand on his shoulder. "Nothing in that file points to bad blood, Max, or even a particularly bad kid. You were no worse than millions of teenagers who have lost their way for a time."

He turned his head to face her and the hell in his eyes nearly made her cry out. "Tell that to the man I killed."

She had to force herself to breathe. Killed? Suddenly numb, her hand slid from his shoulder. His gaze followed and hardened as she clenched her fingers in her lap. He straightened and lifted his focus to hers. Proud and strong, he watched her, obviously expecting the worst. Her heart contracted at the finality in his eyes and panic replaced shock.

Flinging herself at him, she wrapped her arms around his shoulders and clung to him as he tried to pry her free.

"Did you hear me, Jess?"

Plastered against him, she was surprised to find his heart thudded as heavily as hers. She nodded against his throat. What he said simply couldn't be true. Max could be a hard man, a natural byproduct of the life he'd led. Orphaned and alone, he'd had to fight for everything he'd gained, but a killer? No way.

"I heard. I just don't believe you."

His chest expanded on a shuddering breath. "You'd better believe it because it's true. The *honorable* man you're so hot to support once stuck a knife in a man's chest."

The hurtful, self-disparaging thrust of his words pierced her heart like razor sharp barbs, and she pressed her face to the corded muscles of his neck. "What happened?"

"Jesus." He went still as if he'd turned to stone in her embrace. "What does it matter?"

She loosened her hold and drew back on her haunches to look him in the eye. "I love you, Max. It matters." His eyes slid shut, and she grabbed his hand. Relieved when he didn't resist, she wound her fingers through his. "Tell me. Please."

His lashes fluttered open, and he sighed. "You once accused me of borrowing your family. Of using them to get my fix instead of making a family of my own."

Guilt jabbed her in the stomach. She shook her head in vehement denial of her cruel words, but he continued before she could say a word.

"You were right. You, Gracie, Tuck, Jake, and Tim, the rest of the family...." He dropped his gaze to their joined hands. "The gatherings and friendships I found with all of you fed my desire for the semblance of normalcy."

He lifted his head, his gray eyes shadowed with self-incrimination. "I'm a greedy man, Jess. I built friendships under false pretenses in order to be a part of something I'd given up the right to in a dingy alley years ago, but I can't stand the thought of the filth from my past touching you."

It already had. His memories had stood between them from the beginning, so why tell her now? What had changed? Though he hadn't said so directly, it was clear where this was leading, and she'd be damned if she let him go without a fight.

"I'm not stupid, Max. You're planning to walk away and think painting yourself as a villain will scare me into letting you go. Fine. You opened this can of worms, now finish it. Tell me what happened. You owe me that much."

"Jessi." He sighed her name and attempted to pull his hand free of hers.

She held firm. "Tell me."

Frustration simmered in his eyes, but he did as she asked. "There's not much to tell. I was sleeping in an alley. The guy believed I was fair game for his sexual appetites. I disagreed."

She drew in a sharp breath. "He tried to—"

"Tried and failed."

Tears sprang in her eyes at the remembered fury blazing in his. She gripped his hand tighter. "Oh God, Max. What happened? Did the police believe you?"

"I didn't stick around to find out." He stood, and her fingers slid from his. "I need a drink."

He stalked from the bedroom. Jessi scrambled from the bed to follow. In the kitchen, he pulled a liquor bottle from a cabinet.

She paused behind him, her fingers gripping the edge of the island. "I think I need one, too."

He glanced over his shoulder with hooded eyes, sighed, and pulled down a second glass. After pouring two drinks, he turned and placed one in front of her. He swallowed the contents of his in a single gulp, and she picked up her glass. Although she sipped cautiously, whiskey had never been her drink and she coughed as fire burned the walls of her throat.

Tears stung her eyes. Wrinkling her nose in distaste, she glared at the glass. "None of this is in your juvenile file. Didn't the police ever question you?"

Max poured himself another shot, and over the rim of his glass, he narrowed his eyes.

"Don't look at me like that. You said you didn't stick around. If the police never questioned you, how do you know what happened? How do you know you killed the guy? Maybe he survived."

He tossed back his second shot, grunting once he'd he swallowed. "Not likely. Not with a three-inch blade sticking in his chest."

Stubborn man. He was determined to make himself sound as bad as possible, but didn't he want to know for sure? For all he knew, this particular ghost could be a false one. She chewed her bottom lip. Even if the guy was a John Doe, there would be a record of the death. If she knew the location of the alley.....

The scowl on Max's face said he'd given her all the details she'd be getting. For now.

If she was to have a chance to ask later, he'd have to stick around but, from the look of things, that wasn't the plan. Which meant she didn't have anything left to lose. Swallowing another sip of Dutch courage, she pulled out the big guns. "Do you love me, Max?"

His shoulders slumped, and her heart tumbled. Oh, how wrong she'd been. She had everything to lose. Still, she held her breath and braced for impact. One way or another, she had to know.

He poured himself a third shot but didn't pick it up. Instead, he leaned his hands on the edge of the island and met her gaze. "God help me, but yes. I do."

Her breath came out in a rush. Elated, stunned, and suddenly lightheaded, she sagged onto a stool. She shook her head in wonder. "I've got to tell you, Max. As a declaration of love, that sucked." He straightened and she rushed to finish. "But I'll take it." Her sappy smile couldn't be helped. "I'll take it."

He held up a hand. "Don't say anything for a minute."

"But, I—"

"There's more."

She cocked her head. "More than possibly killing someone? What, did you—"

"Shut up, Jess."

She mashed her lips shut and mimicked turning a key. He might be bossy, but he loved her. Max loved her. Giddy relief and happiness made her dizzy. She blinked when he topped off her glass.

"I know you said be quiet, but I don't want any more."

"Trust me." He set the bottle aside. "You're going to need it."

The giddy happiness fizzled a bit. "Okay, you're scaring me again."

And…there went the brow. She rolled her eyes and shut her mouth.

He said nothing for a moment, and her nerves began to hum. Was he testing to see if she'd remain quiet or was what he had to say that bad?

"I'm sorry my declaration of love disappointed you."

He dipped his chin as if expecting her to argue. She didn't say a word.

His cheeks puffed on a gusty breath. "The truth is, I've never made one before because I've never loved another woman. Not since I sat in a theater downtown and lost my heart to a twenty-year-old country crooner with a voice that touched my soul and eyes that haunted my dreams."

Her nerves fell away as tears flooded her eyes.

He scrubbed his fingers over his forehead and back through his hair. "Jesus. You were just a kid and Tuck's little cousin. I did everything I could to push you out of my mind, but despite my past, your family, and the nine years between us, you were there. Constantly."

Heart so full she couldn't possibly remain quiet, she leaned forward on the stool. "Wow." She swiped a tear from her cheek. "When you say there's more, you really mean it."

He glanced away and swept up his glass. "That wasn't the more."

"O-o-o-kay." Her sappy smile slipped a bit more. "I'm listening."

He drained the shot and his clenched teeth flashed in a grimace. "That morning you showed up here with your screwy plan.…"

A long pause hung in the air. "And you threw me out," she prompted.

He scraped a hand down his face. "And I threw you out. I shoved you out the door without letting you say your piece because.…" He shook his head. "Damn it, keeping my hands to myself when I saw you at the occasional family gathering was one thing. The thought of the two of us sharing a space.…" His hand dropped futilely to his side.

Moisture dampened the folds between her thighs even as her heart threatened to crash through her ribs. Poor Max. She'd never seen him looking so hesitant, so unsure of what to say. Didn't he realize his words stroked her body as much as they touched her heart?

She slid from the stool and moved in front of him. Pressing a hand to the warm skin of his bare chest, she stared into his wary eyes. "I've loved you from the moment you walked into my dressing room that first night."

Although he smiled, there was a sad quality to the curving of his lips she couldn't comprehend. He cupped her jaw in a wide-palmed hand and brushed a thumb over her cheek. "I saw forever in your eyes. It scared the shit out of me."

Her eyes slid shut and she rubbed her cheek against his palm. "And now?"

"Now I'm afraid I've fucked up forever."

Her eyes popped open. The pain in his was like a splash of ice water. She stepped back, and he dropped his hand.

"I don't understand."

He dragged in a harsh breath. "The morning after you showed up with your plan, I had another visitor. Two actually. Your father and Tuck dropped by. Ryan told me about the letters."

And Max hadn't wasted any time coming to the studio to say he'd changed his mind. A chill raced down her spine, and she staggered back several more steps.

Oh, God. He hadn't agreed to her plan for her. He'd done it for Tuck and her father.

Images and pieces of conversations ricocheted through her mind, leaving embarrassment behind and shredding her heart. Max's surprise apology, then the rush to pack her bags and move her into his condo. His seeming calmness as they arrived to tell her family they were a couple. Max holding her so tenderly as she fell apart in his arms.

"Then I don't want to hear any more talk of your leaving. Let me handle your cousin. If he's the friend I know him to be, he'll come around."

A wail of pain clawed its way up from her shattering soul, and she clenched her teeth, refusing to let it loose. Max hadn't been worried about Tuck's reaction any more than he'd been nervous about facing her family because there was no need. They already knew!

"What are you doing?"

"Making sure your plan works."

Nausea gurgled in her throat. The bone-melting kiss they'd shared in Tuck's foyer had been nothing more than a bit of insurance to make sure she didn't back out at the last minute and screw up the plan they'd all devised to keep her in line.

Son of a bitch!

Eyes full of apology, Max stepped toward her and something inside her snapped. She didn't hesitate, didn't bother asking him a single question. Balling her hand in a fist, she landed the hardest punch she could manage to his unprotected stomach. Other than a soft grunt, the hit didn't faze him. Disgusted with herself as much as him, and on the verge of a crying jag, she turned and stomped down the hall before slamming the spare bedroom door behind her.

Chapter 25

Wrapped in a fluffy white robe, Kris swung her condo door open. "What's wrong?" Her eyes went wide. "Holy shit. Are you crazy? It's twenty degrees out there."

Jessi swept inside, shivering but not from the cold. Fury was an effective furnace. If she'd had the presence of mind to think things through before stomping into Max's guestroom in a temper, she would have gathered her clothes from the master bedroom closet first, and sneaking out of Max's condo with only a towel for a coat wouldn't have been necessary. Still, the jeans and blouse she'd pilfered from the laundry room were better than the robe she'd been wearing.

She yanked the black terrycloth from her shoulders and balled it in her hands.

Kris crossed to the couch and snatched up a blanket. "Here. Put this on while I heat up some tea. You look like an ice cube."

"I hate tea." Wrapping the blanket around her shoulders, Jessi followed Kris into the kitchen. "Got any vodka?"

Hand on the teapot, Kris glanced over her shoulder. "Uh-oh. If you're asking for booze, it must be bad."

She smirked as Kris abandoned the stove to dig through a low cabinet. "It's nearly midnight and I showed up wearing a towel for a coat. A request for vodka was your first clue?"

"Give me a break. I'm half asleep." Kris straightened with a large bottle in her hand. A question creased her brow. "Shot glass or fish bowl?"

Jessi slumped into one of the kitchen chairs. "Don't you have any straws?"

Her friend's soft laughter brought forth a small smile. Retrieving several tumblers from another cabinet, Kris brought them and the bottle to the table and filled both glasses. "Spill it. What happened?"

Jessi hunched inside the blanket and gritted her teeth. "That son of a bitch lied to me."

"Max?" Kris slid onto the opposite chair.

She nodded. "My father and Tuck were in on it, too. And Tim, apparently." She scowled. "Although he swears he only found out after the fact. He's on his way here, by the way."

"Now?" Horror flooded Kris's eyes. She jumped to her feet and hurried over to the mirror above the couch. Yelping, she fluffed her hair, then drew color to her cheekbones with a squeeze of her fingers and thumbs.

"I called him after I snuck out of Max's place. You know how Tim is. He badgered me until I told him where I'd be."

Kris marched back to the table and sat. "What did your cousin do? In on what?"

Hurt and anger collided once more, and she clenched her teeth. "A low down, sneaky double-cross."

Kris slid a glass her way. "Start drinking, girlfriend. I think you may be suffering from hypothermia. You're leaving out way too many details."

"There's only one detail that matters at the moment." She dropped her forehead to the table with a thump. "Max agreed to my boyfriend plan because Dad asked him to."

All right, Max hadn't exactly said that, but he didn't have to. Why else would he mention her father and Tuck's visit unless it had to do with her?

Kris said nothing for a long moment, then picked up her drink. "Okay, start from the beginning."

Jessi sat up and freed an arm from the blanket. She reached for her glass, then decided against it. Liquor wasn't what she needed. A good cry was in order—or a solo trip to Tahiti.

"I thought I'd gotten through to him, Kris. After the press conference this afternoon, I thought we'd finally broken into neutral territory."

Kris leaned her elbows on the table. "Tim said it went well." Jessi jolted straight in the chair, and Kris immediately shook her head. "I didn't know anything about a double-cross, so get that thought out of your head."

Her cheeks puffed with her relieved breath. "I thought today went well, too. Max did great, but…." Slumping back in the chair, she proceeded to fill her friend in on what happened afterward. She told Kris about Max declining the celebration dinner, and how she'd taken Gracie's advice, telling him she loved him, then backing up the claim in the age-old language of sex—three times. She spoke of how Max had opened up, sharing details of his past she hadn't known, but left out any mention of what had taken place in that alley all those years ago.

Though she prayed he was wrong, that the creep had survived Max's knife, either way, she'd take his secret to her grave. As far as she was concerned, street justice had settled the matter.

"It was incredible, Kris. He said he loves me. That he's loved me for years."

Kris's lips curved in a smug smile. "Did I tell you or what? Damn, I love being right."

"Yeah, well, don't pat yourself on the back too hard. He said he loved me right before he admitted Dad hired him to babysit me."

The smug smile disappeared. "Babysit you how? And why?"

Renewed anger simmered, and she surged to her feet to pace. "Because of those stupid letters. Remember that bodyguard I told you about? The one my father hired?"

"Bruce Willis?"

Jessi rolled her eyes at Kris's dreamy smile. "I demanded Dad get rid of him. That was the day I went to see Max with my boyfriend plan. The next morning, Dad and Tuck paid Max a visit. Apparently, Dad hired him instead."

"Wait. Your dad *paid* Max to be your boyfriend?"

Embarrassment and betrayal tangled together until she found it difficult to breathe. She growled deep in her throat. "I don't think our having sex was what Dad had in mind, and as far as I know, no money exchanged hands, but it amounts to the same thing. Damn it. I feel like a fool. While I've been doing everything in my power to break through Max's walls, he's been playing bodyguard—with side benefits—keeping me *safe* while my father hunts for a phantom stalker who probably doesn't even exist."

Kris rolled her shoulders. "From what Tim says, the threat is real."

"Geez." Jessi threw the blanket over the back of the chair she'd vacated. "Et tu, Brute?"

Kris's guilty smile flashed and faded quickly. "It's not like that. I just want you to be safe."

Jessi dropped back into her chair. "I know."

Kris covered one of Jessi's hands and squeezed. "What are you going to do?"

"Good question." She sucked in a harsh breath at the pain lashing her heart. "He lied to me, Kris."

Kris slid her hand free and sat back. Eyes full of concern, she cocked her head. "True, but Max wasn't the only one to go into this boyfriend plan with an ulterior motive."

Guilty as charged, Jessi winced.

"He also shared the details of his past with the press. He didn't do that for your father or Tuck. He did that for you, girlfriend."

And lost Haven Place in the process. Jessi scrunched her eyes shut. "Yeah, there is that."

Kris leaned on her elbows. "You're looking at this all wrong. Sure, Max lied by omission, but it wasn't like you were getting anywhere on your own. Look at what you've achieved thanks to your father's interference. You've spent the last few weeks having hot monkey sex with Mighty Max *and* you got him to admit he loves you."

Kris picked up her glass. "As hard as it is for me to admit, it sounds like your boyfriend plan worked. You're angry, with good cause, but we both know once you calm down you're going to forgive him. He says he loves you. Why not give him the chance to prove it?"

They both jumped at the heavy pounding rattling the front door. Kris rose to answer, and Jessi snatched up her full glass, downing the contents. Tim's voice reached her from the other room.

"Is she here?"

"Well, good evening to you, too."

Jessi shook her head at Kris's snarky tone, and when nothing but silence followed, she leaned over to glance into the living room. Her eyes widened, discovering why Tim failed to deliver his typical, snappy rejoinder. He couldn't at the moment. Not with his mouth busy…as well as his arms. Kris's back arched over one of his forearms as he planted a hard and fast kiss on her lips.

Snapping straight in her chair, Jessi choked when her cousin finally spoke in a clipped voice.

"Baby, in the not too distant future, I'm going to call your bluff. I'll have you naked and panting beneath me, and when I do, that sexy, smartass mouth will be singing a different tune. Now, is Jessi here or not?"

Kris's voice was deeper than usual, and a hell of a lot more breathless. "In the kitchen."

Heavy footfalls headed Jessi's way. She looked up as Tim appeared in the doorway, but if he was embarrassed at having his sexy challenge overheard, it didn't show. Brows lowered and eyes intent, he closed the distance. Kris stopped in the doorway, pink flags of color tinting her cheeks.

Tim squatted beside Jessi's chair and rubbed a hand over her knee. "You okay?"

"Hell no, I'm not okay." Tears stung her eyes and nose. "Why didn't you tell me? I expect this kind of bullshit from Dad and the others, but not from you."

He sighed and shook his head. "I'm sorry, Jess. By the time I found out, it was already done."

"You should have said something immediately." She shoved his hand from her knee. "I trust you to watch my back."

Eyes dark with empathy, he balanced on the balls of his feet, knees spread and his hands dangling between his knees. "That's exactly what I was trying to do."

She scoffed a snort and pinned him with a sneer. "How? By standing back and watching while they all made a fool of me?"

The gentle compassion on his face winked out in a flash. His lips pulled tight in a harsh line, and he pushed to his feet. "By keeping my mouth shut and hoping like hell when things blew up in your face, you'd finally get mad enough to face the truth."

"What truth is that?" She tucked her arms around her middle and fought angry tears. "That everyone I care about thinks it's okay to go behind my back and treat me like an imbecile who doesn't have an intelligent thought in her head?"

"Hold it right there." He jammed his hands to his hips. "I've never gone behind your back and you're not exactly innocent in this. You put these wheels in motion when you went to Max instead of facing Ryan head-on and telling him you've had enough."

Oh, so not fair. Okay, so she was partly to blame for coming up with her boyfriend plan in the first place, but for God's sake. She'd been desperate. She shoved to her feet, and her voice rose along with her temper. "I did tell him. He didn't listen. He never listens."

"Why should he when he knows you'll give in?"

"That's not fair! What do you think my going to Max was all about? I was trying to make the point that I'm a grown woman, capable of living my own life."

Ruddy color flagged his cheeks, and his eyes snapped with temper. "Then act like one!"

She gasped and a crushing hurt pierced her heart. "What the hell is that supposed to mean?"

"It means it's time to start living your own life instead of locking yourself in your mother's dream."

As if the blow were physical, she staggered back a step, but apparently, he wasn't finished.

"It's me, Jess. I was there that first time Ryan volunteered you to sing at the fundraiser he organized in your mother's name. I held your hair afterward while you threw up, remember?"

The murky memory of that day not long after her mother was murdered slithered through her head—mind-numbing fear as she stood before her first audience and the subtle easing of the grief in her father's eyes as she started to sing.

Tim's shoulders sagged. "Do you think I don't see the dread on your face every time he suggests a new tour or booking?"

She blinked, the painful images shattering like breaking glass as he stepped toward her.

"He pushed you into a career you never wanted and you let him, but when are you going to realize, none of it will bring your mother back. For you *or* your father."

She couldn't breathe. Pressing a fist to her chest, she dropped into her chair.

"Tim." Kris's quiet admonition broke through the angry tension buzzing between Jessi and Tim like a swarm of bees.

He flicked a sharp glance at Kris. "Sorry, but it's the truth and it's time she hears it." Bracing his hands on the table across from Jessi, he leaned in. "I loved your mother, too. She was a sweet woman with a kind soul, but she's gone. It's time to let go. Do you think she'd be happy knowing you're making yourself sick for a dream that died with her?"

Fifteen years of grief clawed at her lungs and tears flooded her eyes. Tim's pain-filled face shimmered before her.

"For God's sake, Tim." Kris crossed the room to wrap an arm around Jessi's shoulders.

Jessi sucked in desperate breaths. Blinking furiously, she stared into Tim's pleading eyes. The pain in them reflected hers but, as harsh as his words were, they were honest. And true. Hadn't Max voiced a similar sentiment that night in New Hampshire?

Shame gripped her by the throat. All these months…years, actually, she'd let bitterness build inside her, blaming her family for her unhappiness when, the truth was, she'd let cowardice keep her from facing the truth. Afraid to witness the disappointment in her father's eyes, she'd continued along on the course he'd set for her when she'd been too numb to argue. She no longer had that excuse.

"No, she wouldn't." She swiped at the tears leaking down her cheeks with shaking fingers. "Mom would tell me to follow my heart."

Tim's smile was tinged with sadness, but there was relief in his familiar eyes. "She'd want you to be happy."

Max's voice echoed in her head. *Figure out what's holding you back from being happy. Find out what it is you want and then make it happen.*

Her heart thudded against her ribs, but hope trumped her fear. If she truly wanted to live life on her own terms, it would be up to her to take the steps necessary to get there. She wrapped an arm around Kris's waist and squeezed briefly, then turned back to her cousin. "It looks like I've got some changes to make. Will you help me?"

* * * *

"God damn it, pick up." Max held the phone between his shoulder and ear. Shoving an arm into the sleeve of his coat, he yanked open the condo door.

"Hello."

Ryan's sleep-roughened voice only increased the stark fear and frustration clawing at Max's gut. He loped down the steps to the fight center, taking them two at a time. "Wake up. We've got a problem."

Although it was early, two of the mats were already occupied, and Tina manned the front desk. He headed in her direction.

"Max? What's going on?" Instantly clear of grogginess, Ryan's question held a sharp edge.

"Jessi took off." He finished shrugging into his coat. "I was hoping she headed there."

"Why would she come here? What happened?"

"Hold on." He dipped the phone from his mouth as Tina looked up and smiled. "Have you seen Jessi this morning?"

She shook her head. "Nope."

"What time did you get here?"

Confusion tweaked the barbell piercing her brow. "Same time as usual. I unlocked at five. Why?"

He didn't bother explaining. Spinning toward the garage exit at the far end of the center, he called over his shoulder. "Call me immediately if she shows up."

Impatience and concern colored Ryan's voice. "Max. What the hell is going on?"

He punched the bar on the door, rushed into the garage, and wrenched open the SUV door. "I told her the truth about why I agreed to help her."

"Jesus."

"I know, but I had my reasons." He snapped the phone into the hands-free clip and shoved the key in the ignition. Starting the vehicle, he cued the garage door at the same time. "She was pissed, of course. She left sometime between midnight and five this morning."

"Damn it, Jessi." Ryan sighed harshly. "Have you called Tim?"

"I'll let you do that." Shifting in his seat, he looked over his shoulder and backed the vehicle outside, jumping the curb to avoid a double-parked delivery truck. "I spoke to Dan. She didn't go home. I'm on my way over to Kris's."

He ground his teeth and braked at a red light. Rush hour in Manhattan was a slow slog. Walking the three block's to Kris's condo would be quicker but, considering how furious Jessi had been when she slammed the door to his guest bedroom last night, he doubted she'd come with him willingly. Kidnapping was his only option. For that, he'd need wheels.

"What happened with your FBI meeting yesterday?"

"Not a lot. Unless or until another letter arrives, we've got nothing."

Max grunted. "For six weeks, a letter came every other week, then nothing. What changed? Why'd they stop? Has our guy given up or simply gone to ground for the moment?"

"We stepped up her security and she moved in with you, but her security was already tight. I don't know, Max. It doesn't make sense, but I'm not willing to call off the search until we find this guy and know for sure."

Max clenched his fingers on the steering wheel and zipped around a cab picking up a fare. "Neither am I." A soft ping sounded in the background and Max tensed. "Was that your doorbell?"

"Yeah. Jesus, it better be her."

Max ignored the honking horns as he yanked the wheel, crossing two lanes for a last minute turn. "I'll be there in five."

Chapter 26

"Where the hell have you been?" Ryan grasped Jessi by the shoulders and yanked her inside the foyer of his condo. He enfolded her in his arms, squeezing her hard enough to crush her bones.

She blinked, surprised to find he was shaking.

"And why didn't you call and let me know you were with her?"

She pulled back and turned her head toward Tim. Her cousin spread his hands, but she beat him to any excuse he might have made. "I'm fine, Dad. I was at Kris's."

Her father grasped her shoulders. Holding her at arm's length, he studied her face. "God, Jessi. You scared the hell out of me. Max called and said you'd left. I was worried sick."

A lash of hurt whipped across her chest. She stepped back and his hands fell to his sides. "By Max, you mean the man you hired, behind my back, to keep an eye on me?"

Guilt reddened her father's cheeks. "Jessi, I—"

"Save it, Dad." She shook her head. "We have more important things to discuss."

Eyes wary, he slid his gaze to Tim who shrugged and closed the door.

Ryan turned back to her. "What's more important than your security?"

Jittering nerves tangled in her belly. She ignored them, sucked a bracing breath, and officially took control of her life. "My happiness. I'll finish the scheduled concert on Wednesday and perform at the Super Bowl this weekend, but after that, I'm done. The only singing I'll be doing from here on will be in the studio."

His face paled. "You're quitting?"

Tim slapped a hand to Ryan's shoulder. "Hear her out, Uncle Ry."

"When she's talking madness?" His gaze jerked between them as if they were both crazy.

"It's not madness, Dad. Madness is living every day with a gut-wrenching fear of doing your job."

He scoffed in dismissal. "That's just—"

"Stage fright. Yeah, I know. I've told myself to get over it. That lots of performers suffer from it, but most performers put up with the initial fear of walking out on stage because they ultimately love what they do." She swallowed and forced the words from her mouth she should have uttered long ago. "I don't. I hate the stage, Dad. I always have."

His shoulders slumped and confusion clouded his blue eyes. "I don't understand. You've been on the stage for ten years. Why are you only now saying something?"

"Because the stage was Momma's dream, and I loved her, too. When it became your dream after she died…." Tears stung her eyes and her throat threatened to close. "How could I say no?"

Painful memories of those dark days immediately following her mother's murder flashed in her father's eyes as he drew her back into his arms. "Jessi."

She burrowed closer, clinging to him the way she had when she'd been a little girl and her world had been ripped apart. "I'm sorry, Dad. I just can't do it anymore."

He rocked her, his strong arms contracting in a fierce squeeze. "God, sweetheart. I don't know what to say. "

"Say you understand." She pressed her face to his T-shirt and inhaled his familiar scent. "That you won't be disappointed in me for walking away."

"How could I ever be disappointed in you?" His whisper brushed her temple. "You've made me proud every day of your life. Your mother would have loved to see you perform, but she was proud of you, too, even before you started singing professionally."

"I know she was and sometimes, when I was on stage, I felt her there, but I also think she'd understand why I need to stop."

Jessi pulled back and he let go.

He pulled a handkerchief from his pocket and wiped his nose. His chest rose on a deep breath, and he glanced at Tim before turning back to her. "What about the second half of the tour? You have eight cities lined up."

"No." She sniffled and brushed her fingers beneath both eyes. "*You* have eight cities lined up, and I want your word you won't be booking anymore. From here on in, *I* run my life."

Color stained his cheeks, but he nodded curtly. "You have my word."

She released the breath she hadn't realized had stalled in her throat. Relief made her lightheaded, as if a weight had suddenly been lifted from her shoulders and she'd been set free.

Tim gave her a gentle smile, then dove into the sticky details of extracting her from the world of touring. "We'll head over to the studio from here. Spence mentioned he has a new song he wants Jessi to hear. There's a possibility he'll want to run the second half of the tour on his own, and we'll have some logistics to work out with the venues. If not, I'll get to work cancelling the rest of the shows."

Ryan nodded and rubbed a hand over his chin in thought. "It's going to cost a bundle in cancellation fees."

Jessi lifted her chin. "I'll cover them."

"Spence isn't going to be happy."

"Probably not, but he'll get over it. He'll have to." She shrugged to cover her nerves. Spence was the one area where she was uncomfortable with the decisions she and Tim had discussed throughout the hours at Kris's table. Spence had built a career with Jessi at his side. He counted on her, and she was going to let him down. Still, he'd told her to get her head on straight. That's exactly what she was doing. "I'll continue to work with him in the studio if he wants. If that doesn't work for him, he has the talent to go out on his own, and I'll wish him every success."

A heavy sigh lifted her father's chest. "It sounds like you've made up your mind. I'm sorry, Jess. I knew you were unhappy. I should have asked why."

"Don't, Dad. This is on me. I should have said something long ago."

Guilt poked at her as she thought of all the trouble and heartbreak they could have avoided. Then again, if she'd spoken up years ago, she never would have had these past three weeks with Max. Renewed hurt and anger sliced at her like claws.

Her career wasn't the only place she'd be making changes. For years, she'd chased after Max's affections. No more. She'd made her love for him more than clear. The rest was up to him. He claimed he loved her. If that was true, he was going to have to prove it.

Ryan cleared his throat, and his forehead wrinkled in wariness. "You know you have my full support regarding what you've decided to do, but your security is still an issue. Until we know—"

She held up a hand. "We'll get to that as soon as Max shows up. I assume he's out looking for me?"

Her father winced. "He was on the phone when you rang the bell. He's on the way."

As if on cue, heavy knocking shook the door. Tim sent her a questioning glance. She nodded and braced herself as he opened the door.

The heat in Max's eyes scorched her the moment he stepped inside.

"What the hell were you thinking?" Angry tension and relief battled for supremacy on his ruggedly handsome face.

She jutted her chin, but before she could come up with a scathing reply, her father stepped forward.

"Hold on a second—"

"Dad."

He didn't heed the warning in her tone, speaking to Max. "She's quitting the stage."

Max's gaze whipped back to her. The anger in his eyes cooled with his unspoken question. Had she actually come to terms with the source of her unhappiness, or was her sudden decision a knee jerk reaction to all that had happened in the past twelve hours? "Are you sure, baby?"

She steeled against the heat curling in her belly at his smoky murmur. Beside him, her father arched a brow while Tim smirked and rolled his eyes.

She shot her cousin a glare before turning back to Max. "Quitting the stage is about the only thing I *am* sure about this morning."

"Jess." He pinched the bridge of his nose. "I know you're pissed, but—"

"You bet your ass I'm pissed. At myself as much as with you." She shook her head and studied his face. "We make quite a pair, don't we? You're so bogged down with ghosts you can't let yourself be happy, and me...." Her laugh was little more than a harsh cough. "Desperate to win your heart, I couldn't see your sudden interest was just an act." Pain flashed in his eyes, and tears threatened in hers. She looked away, meeting her father's gaze. "I'll put up with your hired babysitter for now, but only until I can make arrangements for my own security."

Heart pounding, she shot Max a challenging stare. Hiring her own security had been his idea, and there was a certain synergy to using his suggestion against him. If what he'd said last night was true, he'd loved her for years, and yet, he'd still planned to walk away once his promise to her father was met. Whether or not his declaration of love meant he'd changed his mind, she didn't know, but she was through asking.

The heat of anger in his eyes was a good sign. Clamping down on the surge of hope, she turned to her father. "In the meantime, find out who is behind those letters because after Sunday, I'm done."

She spun toward her cousin. "You ready?"

Tim nodded and moved to the door.

Max gripped her elbow, stopping her as she stepped past him. "We aren't finished, Jess."

His growled threat delivered a secret thrill. If things worked out like she hoped, they never would be, but until then...

She dropped her narrowed gaze to his fingers on her arm. Lifting her head, she slid the knife a little deeper. "You were hired for the night shift, remember? If you have something to say, you can say it when Tim drops me off. Now, if you don't mind, I have a partnership to dissolve."

* * * *

"I don't believe this." Eyes blazing with anger, Spence shook his head.

Jessi turned to Tim. "Would you give us a few minutes?"

"I'll be in the control room if you need me." He nodded, left the studio conference room, and shut the door behind him.

She turned back to Spence. "I'm sorry. I know this is a surprise. It is for me, too, but it's the right thing to do."

"Jesus, Jessi. After all the work we've done to make it, you're quitting? Just like that?" His face twisted into an angry mask of disbelief. "This is Max's doing."

"No, it's not." She heaved a sigh. "This is my decision and it's long overdue. You said it yourself. Something has been off for months. Years, actually. I simply didn't want to face it."

He shook his head, dismissing her explanation. "I knew it. I knew the day Grayson showed up here something like this would happen."

The heated animosity in his tone made her frown. She hadn't expected Spence to be happy with her decision. In fact, she'd been prepared for an ugly argument, but the target of his anger made no sense. She studied his flushed face. "What's going on, Spence? This isn't about me quitting; it's about Max. Why do you dislike him so much?"

Tight lines of tension creased his brow as he seemed to sag before her eyes. Shoving his fingers into the front pockets of his jeans, he cleared his throat. "Because I'm jealous."

She blinked, confused. "Of Max? We've been at the top of the charts the last three years running and one of your tunes just won song of the year. Why would you be jealous?"

A wry smile tugged at his lips, and he shook his head. The smile slid away almost immediately. "I'm not jealous of his business success. I'm jealous because of the way you look at him."

Unease slithered down her spine, but she cast aside the discomfort as ludicrous. She and Spence had worked together since they were little more than kids. They were friends as well as partners. He couldn't possibly mean that the way it sounded. She cocked her head. "What do you mean? How do I look at him?"

"Like he can't do anything wrong in your eyes."

She bristled at the claim. Up until last night, that might have been true, but this morning, the rose-colored glasses she'd always viewed Max through had lost some of their tint. She huffed a harsh laugh. "Believe me, Max Grayson has plenty of faults."

"I'm glad to hear that."

Her unease catapulted straight into full-blown panic as he closed the distance between them and lifted a hand to cup her cheek.

Oh, shit. "Spence—"

"Let me say this." He shook his head and her throat tightened at the wary need in his eyes. He brushed his thumb over her cheek. "Just listen."

She fought back a groan. *Don't go there. Oh, God. Please don't go there.*

His chest shuddered with an indrawn breath. "I'm in love with you."

Her lashes fluttered closed and the groan escaped.

"I can't help the way I feel, Jessi." He lifted his other palm to cup her face. "Look at me, please."

She did as he asked and nearly wept at the hopeful desperation in his eyes.

"I've loved you for years, but never said anything because I didn't want to chance what we have together professionally."

Shit. Shit. Shit! "Spence, I—"

"I should have told you. I started to a thousand times, but the moment never seemed right. This thing with you and Max...." He dropped his forehead to hers. "Please tell me I'm not too late."

Oh, dear Lord. This could not be happening. Had the entire world gone insane? If the situation weren't so horrifying, she would laugh hysterically. "Spence—"

He stopped the denial on her lips by covering her mouth with his. Shocked, she stood frozen within the cage of his arms. A moment passed, then several more as his searching lips moved over hers. When she didn't respond, he tightened his hold and deepened the kiss, sweeping his tongue over the closed seam of her lips.

Muted laughter from somewhere in the studio jerked her from her shock. She struggled against his hold, pulling back to stare into his earnest blue eyes. The conference door opened, and she shoved at his chest. Stumbling backward, her hand flew to her lips as they both turned toward the door.

Alicia paused in the opening, the laughter draining from her face along with all hint of color. Beside her, Craig stood perfectly still. His wounded gaze clung to Jessi for a heartbeat before he spun around. He bumped into Tim, mumbled an apology, and fled. Alicia backed out of the doorway. Tim stepped to the side, and she hurried through the control room.

Her cousin's eyebrows nearly reached his hairline.

Jessi ignored him, turned back, and held out a beseeching hand. "Spence, I—"

Full of frustrated disappointment, Spence's gaze skittered away. "Don't. I have my answer." He snatched up his coat, jammed his arms into the sleeves, and shouldered his way past Tim to stalk from the room.

Jessi slapped a hand to the top of her head. On legs the consistency of pudding, she stumbled forward and slid into her chair. God, what a mess.

"So, he finally found the balls to make a move on you." Tim shut the door, closing them in.

She dropped her forehead to the table with a groan, then popped back up immediately. "Wait. What?"

He shook his head. "I didn't think he had it in him."

"Excuse me?" She stared at him, slack jawed.

Shoulders lifting in a careless shrug, he stepped from the doorway. "You're always too busy trying to catch your breath when the two of you first walk out on stage, but anyone who's caught that kiss-on-the-hand opening knows it's not an act."

She snapped her sagging jaw shut. "Well, thanks a lot for telling me so I could avoid this disaster. Damn it, Tim." Her gaze flew to the closed door. "God, did you see Alicia's face?"

"Yeah. Poor kid." He dropped into the chair across from hers. "Still, she's hot. She can do a lot better than your uptight partner."

Jessi squeezed her eyes shut.

The chair squeaked as Tim rocked it back on two legs. "So, did he say what he wanted to do about the rest of the tour?"

She opened her eyes and met his gaze with a bland stare. "We didn't quite get to that."

"You're going to have to, and the sooner the better."

"I know." A growl rumbled in her throat. "If he'll even talk to me. In case you didn't notice, he wasn't very happy when he left."

"Neither was Craig." A half smile lifted the corner of Tim's mouth. "Face it, Jess. You're a heartbreaker."

"You're not helping." Snatching up her purse, she dug for her pills.

He chuckled. "I'll call Spence later. Are you going to tell Max what just happened?"

Her fingers clenched on the bottle. Oh, God. Things between her and Max were already precarious enough without adding Spence's declaration of love to the mix. She narrowed her eyes. "I'm not going to say a word about this to him, and if you know what's good for you, you won't either."

A grin was his only response. It faded quickly. "You gonna forgive him?"

She struggled to open the bottle cap. "What do you think?"

He crossed his arms. "I think you've loved him for years, but your pride is involved, so you figure on making him squirm for a while before you let him off the hook."

She shot him a scowl. Exactly, damn it. Tim knew her well enough to know she sucked at holding a grudge, and despite his betrayal, she loved Max. That wouldn't change even if things didn't work out between them. She placed a pill on her tongue and swallowed.

Tim's mouth quirked at the corners, and he eased the chair legs back to the floor. "Just keep in mind, Max didn't do that press conference yesterday for himself. He's a cage fighter, Jess. His grandmother's claims would only enhance his image."

"You don't have to tell me I owe him." She knew better than anyone what he'd given up. If not for her…. *Haven Place.* Her hand froze in the act of returning the bottle to her purse. *His grandmother's claims.* Breathing became difficult as the germ of an idea bloomed in her head. She lifted her gaze and Tim groaned.

"Oh, shit." He leaned his elbows on the table. "I know that look. What are you up to, kiddo?"

Her palms went damp and her heart tripped into an unsteady beat, but she jutted her chin in a determined slant. If she was going to insist Max prove his love, the least she could do was offer him a peace offering once she was done. "What are you doing for the next couple of hours?"

"I'm not sure. Where are we going?"

She swallowed her growing nerves. "New Jersey."

Chapter 27

"Are you sure about this?" Tim's harsh whisper echoed off the imported marble tile. "Blackmail is a federal offense."

"I can do this on my own if you'd rather wait in the car."

On the ride from Manhattan, Jessi had related the full truth of Elizabeth Krandall's actions concerning Max's custody when his mother had died. She'd explained about Max's stealthy attempts to purchase Haven Place and how yesterday's press conference had killed any hope he had of ever claiming his mother's home.

Anger on Max's behalf had outweighed her cousin's concern over the plan she'd laid out, but now that they were here, she prayed he wouldn't take her up on her offer and leave her alone to face the dragon lady. Her knees shook so badly she'd need Tim to carry her back outside once she was done—*if* she wasn't doing a perp walk after Max's grandmother called her bluff.

He tugged a handkerchief from the pocket of his suit coat and wiped at the sheen of nervous sweat glistening on his forehead. "I'm not going anywhere. You're out of your mind, but you'll need a witness to deny her claims should she try to turn the tables on you later."

Jessi rolled her eyes but, in truth, she wasn't as confident in her plan as she let on. From all Max had told her—and what she'd seen with her own eyes—his grandmother was a formidable woman, not above playing dirty. Still, it was obvious maintaining a good reputation was Elizabeth Krandall's Achilles' heel. After ten years on the stage, Jessi was no slouch in the reputation department herself, and she could play dirty as well.

"Mrs. Krandall will see you now."

Jessi jumped as the stern-faced housekeeper who'd admitted them suddenly reappeared. Turning her back on them, the disapproving woman indicated they follow with a curt tip of her head, and led them down a long hall to a closed door. She turned to face them, her lips puckered as if she'd been sucking on something sour. After opening the door, she stepped to the side. The handle clicked in the latch behind them the moment they entered the large, wood paneled office.

Elizabeth Krandall sat in a luxurious leather chair at an enormous antique desk. Her cold gray gaze dissected Tim before sliding to Jessi for a thorough inspection. She crossed her wrinkled hands on the desk blotter and lifted her chin to look down her nose. "I must say I was surprised by your request to see me."

Jessi didn't wait for an invitation. Especially one that wouldn't be coming. The quicker she made her play, the quicker they could leave and she'd be able to breathe again. She slid into one of two wingback chairs facing the desk. "You don't mind if we sit? This will only take a few minutes."

Elizabeth nodded stiffly, and Tim lowered to the second chair.

The Krandall matriarch narrowed her gaze. "You have me curious. After witnessing that farce of a press conference yesterday, I was under the impression the Tuckers were friends of my grandson." Displeasure shone in the eyes she turned on Jessi. "You especially."

"Oh, we are." Jessi bared her teeth in a false smile. "Me, especially." This morning's papers were awash with the contradicting facts Max had presented to the press. No doubt Elizabeth and her minions were already scrambling to come up with a believable spin to explain away the discrepancies. So far, there were more questions than answers, all directed at the Krandalls. Jessi hoped the building pressure would be a point in her favor. "I'm not here to talk about Max, however. I'm here about Haven Place."

Surprise flashed in the old woman's eyes before she covered it with a laugh. "How delightful, and rather ironic, don't you think?"

Jessi ignored her racing heart and cocked her head. "Ironic?"

Elizabeth tapped her fingers on the desk. Her eyes gleamed with satisfaction. "My grandson went to a lot of trouble to refute my claims. Foolishly, it seems. By sending his paramour to achieve what he couldn't manage on his own, he's making my point." She shook her head, her smile smug. "Like father, like son."

Anger eclipsed Jessi's tightly strung nerves. Elizabeth's words made it clear Max was correct when he claimed his grandmother most likely knew of his attempts to buy Haven Place. The bitch had been playing him just as he'd said. Determined to balance the scales of justice, Jessi made her smile sickeningly sweet. "You misunderstand. Max didn't send us. In fact, he doesn't know we're here."

The humor disappeared from Elizabeth's face. "Then what do you want."

"I want Haven Place."

The dragon lady's eyes went hard in a flash. "I'm sorry you wasted your time, my dear. It's not for sale."

Tim softly cleared his throat. Jessi refused to look his way. Like him, she would much prefer if Elizabeth acted against her nature and sold the property in the usual way, but Jessi wasn't leaving until she'd exhausted all her options. Including blackmail.

She sat back and crossed her legs in an effort to hide the anxious shaking of her body. "Are you sure about that? I realize this unfortunate situation has been an uncomfortable one for you." She cast a quick glance at Tim. A muscle twitched in his jaw, and his eyes held a plea for caution. "What, with the press all abuzz because of the Super Bowl, and the opposing accounts of your family history making headlines." She turned back to Elizabeth and, swallowing, pressed past the point of no return. "But there was one detail Max left out of his statement. I would hate to complicate the issue by adding the bribery of a custody court judge to the mix."

Elizabeth slowly sat forward. Although they gleamed with anger, there was no disguising the underlying distress in her eyes. "Be careful, young lady. Blackmail is an ugly business."

Jessi stared at the woman who had made Max's teenage years a living hell. As far as she was concerned, giving up Haven Place was a small price to pay for Elizabeth's heartless treatment of her grandson. Heart pounding, Jessi refused to back down. "I agree. It's almost as ugly as a woman denying her own daughter and grandchild out of spite."

A riot of color flared on Elizabeth's cheeks. "I'm impressed. Your stage image is so sweet, but I'm afraid you aren't quite ready to play with the grownups." She sat back and satisfaction curled her painted lips. "Before you attempt blackmail, you really should check your sources. The judge in question has been dead for at least three years."

Crap. Adrenaline rushed through Jessi, making her fingertips tingle. Hidden from Elizabeth's view by the desk, Tim's foot began to bounce in a frantic beat. A deep breath failed to calm Jessi's racing heart. "Yes, I could see where that might be a problem."

Elizabeth's shoulders loosened.

Jessi forced a smile, presenting a calmness she wasn't close to feeling. "*If* I was planning to go to the authorities." She brushed an invisible piece of lint from the knee of her slacks. "Watching you at *your* press conference last week was an eye-opening experience. I realized how effective a well-placed claim can be when a woman has the right reputation and an avid audience. You're right about my sweet reputation, and this Sunday, at the Super Bowl, I'll have an audience of hundreds of millions." She dipped her chin and lost the smile. "And a live mic."

Elizabeth's eyes narrowed dangerously. "You're bluffing."

"Am I?" Jessi pushed to her feet, afraid she was going to throw up. Tim immediately rose at her side. Holding Elizabeth's cold gray gaze was like staring into ice. Jessi fought a shiver. "Max may not be interested in making you pay for your cruel treatment of him and your daughter, but I am. However, the currency you choose is entirely up to you. Haven Place or a media circus." Slipping her hand in her pocket, she retrieved the slip of paper she'd put there earlier and placed it on the center of the desk. "I'm not interested in robbing you, Mrs. Krandall. I'll transfer the fair market purchase price as soon as I hear from you and expect to receive the deed by courier before kickoff Sunday morning."

* * * *

Tina bumped Max's elbow with hers. "She's back."

Max turned his head, and relief loosened some of the knotting in his gut. Jessi spoke quietly to Tim just inside the fight center doors. Despite her snide jab about Max continuing the night shift, he hadn't been entirely sure she intended to return. She could have just as easily gone back to her place.

From his position beside the fight ring where two of his clients squared off, he studied her face. She looked beat, and no wonder. After everything else that had happened yesterday, hitting her with the truth of why he'd agreed to her plan had been a miscalculation. He should have waited. Should have delayed dropping that bomb in her lap, but Christ. He'd admitted to killing a man, and her unexpected reaction had left him humbled and off balance.

After his one-two punch last night, he should have expected her to do something rash—like slipping out of the condo while he was in the shower. Jessi was unpredictable under normal circumstances. Pissed, there was no telling what she would do, but calling it quits in the middle of a tour?

Crushing guilt weighed on his shoulders like a cement yoke. Though his intentions were good, that last night in New Hampshire he'd practically badgered her to make some changes in her life. Was leaving the stage what she truly wanted? Or would she regret the move later and blame him for fucking with her head once she'd had the chance to think her decision through?

Over her shoulder, Tim bumped his chin at Max in silent greeting, squeezed her elbow, and left. She turned, and without even a glance in his direction, headed for the stairs.

Torn between relief she was safe and frustration over the mess he'd created, a ragged sigh rumbled in Max's chest. "Have you got things here?"

Tina smirked. "Don't I always?"

Max grunted and turned to follow Jessi upstairs. He had no doubt she was angry, with good reason, but was that all there was to her refusal to even look at him? Now that she'd had time to process all he'd told her, was she having second thoughts?

He wouldn't blame her if she was. She was too good for the likes of him. Always had been, but damn it, she'd said his past didn't matter and had made him believe that was true. As far-fetched as the concept was, he, Max Grayson, the street rat who had mastered the art of walking away, no longer wanted to. Having opened his heart to the possibilities shining in her eyes and smile, how could he return to his self-imposed isolation, forever denying himself the healing warmth of her love?

The sad truth was, he might not have a choice. Her cutting remarks earlier at Ryan's condo said she hadn't believed him when he'd said he loved her, but Jessi was the most loving and optimistic woman he'd ever met. Was it just her anger speaking or had he been right all along? Faced with the full truth of his past, would she look at him with fear and disgust? Had he inadvertently found a way to shove her away just when he'd decided to hold her close and not let go?

Was she even now packing to leave or would she hit him with the full force of her temper the moment he stepped inside the condo? Braced for her attack, he cautiously opened the door. He'd gladly face her wrath if it meant he hadn't fucked things up beyond repair, but he'd rather not have the coming conversation with a pen piercing his cheek.

The kitchen and living areas were empty. He cocked his head and listened. Silence reached his ears. "Jessi?"

No response.

Crossing the living room, he stopped in the open bedroom doorway. She'd shed the coat she'd arrived in along with her shoes and was otherwise dressed in the jeans and silk blouse she been wearing this morning at Ryan's. Curled on the bed with her eyes closed, she clutched the sexy red number she'd worn at the awards show to her chest. The rest of her wardrobe lay piled about her in heaps.

The evidence she meant to leave landed a body blow, and he had to force himself to step forward and approach the bed. Her lashes fluttered open as he sat on the edge of the mattress.

Pain hazed her eyes. "I'm mad at you."

"I know, baby." He kept his voice soft and brushed a curl from her cheek. "Headache?"

Her eyes slid shut. "Yes. As soon as it's gone, I'm moving into the spare room."

His surprised breath flew out in a silent rush. Instant relief slumped his tensed shoulders. She wasn't leaving. Not today, anyway. "Have you taken a pill?"

She moaned. "Can't find my purse."

He shifted to study the pile of clothing, doing his best not to jostle the mattress. Her purse was half hidden beneath a pair of jeans. He retrieved the bottle from inside and shook out a pill. "Open up."

She kept her eyes closed and did as instructed. He placed the pill on her tongue.

He eyed the rumpled clothes she wore. "You'll be much more comfortable out of those jeans."

She rolled to her back. "Too much effort."

"I'll take them off for you."

Slits of blue suspicion gleamed at him from between her scrunched lashes, and he nearly laughed. He held up his hand instead.

"I know. You're mad at me. I promise I won't even look."

Her eyes slid shut, and he took her lack of response as assent. Concern grew when she gave him no trouble as he shimmied the denim over her hips and down her legs. Although he watched, she never once checked to see if he kept his word, and her lack of interest proclaimed her level of discomfort. The moment she was free of the jeans, she curled onto her side in a ball.

His heart contracted and he pulled the comforter over her shoulders, then sifted his fingers through the curls spread out on her pillow. "Sleep, baby. I'll be right here when you wake up."

She said nothing in response, and he stood. Gathering an armload of her clothes, he transferred her things to the other bedroom. He'd much prefer they remain where they'd been, right next to his but, if she needed the small victory, he'd gladly give it to her. If things went as he hoped, her clothes would end up back in his closet eventually.

When the task was done, he stood beside the bed. Her cheeks were pale beneath the spray of her thick lashes, but her steady breathing proved she'd given in to sleep. Unable to resist, he shucked his clothes down to his briefs and slid into the bed beside her. His heart thumped a hopeful cadence as she rolled toward him in slumber and burrowed closer with a sigh.

Nothing was settled between them, but she was still here. For now. She planned to take his advice and hire her own security. Fuck that. He had his work cut out for him if he was going to charm her into forgiving him, but if he had anything to say about it, the only bodyguard she'd have from now on was him.

Chapter 28

Jessi opened her eyes with a wide yawn, a full bladder, and a stomach rumbling with hunger. No surprise there. After the press conference yesterday, thoughts of dinner had fallen victim to seduction, and she'd been too frazzled to eat this morning. Spence's declaration of love and tonight's migraine had killed any appetite she might have had for lunch or dinner. After several hours of sleep, she was famished.

She sat up and swung her legs over the edge of the bed to stand. After taking care of business in the bathroom, she padded back into the bedroom. Her gaze snagged on the indentation creasing Max's pillow, and she stumbled to a stop. Murky memories of curling up against his warm body tickled her mind. Had he crawled in beside her? She frowned. The sneak. God knew she had little willpower when he touched her, hell, *looked* at her. If she was going to keep him at arms-length long enough for him to prove he loved her, she'd have to avoid situations that allowed him to catch her off-guard—like when she was too groggy to stay on task.

Blinking, she glanced around the room. Other than the pair of jeans she'd been wearing earlier, all her clothes were gone.

"I was just about to wake you." Her gaze flew to the doorway where Max paused, his brow puckered with concern. "How are you feeling? I was getting worried."

Worried? Why would he be worried? "I'm fine." She snatched up her jeans and stepped into them.

He cleared his throat. "Tim called a couple of times. I told him I wasn't sure you were up to performing tonight."

She froze with her fingers clenched on the zipper and looked up. "Tonight? The Manhattan concert isn't until Wednesday."

"Today is Wednesday."

She flicked her gaze to the darkened window and back. "No, it's not."

He crossed the room. Concerned and searching, his gray eyes studied her face as if looking for signs of illness. "You've been asleep since you got back last night. Nearly eighteen hours. Why do you think I was getting worried?"

Eighteen hours? "Oh my God." She narrowed her eyes. "Why didn't you wake me?"

"Because you were beat, baby, and needed the sleep."

The endearment and his crooning tone threatened her resolve. She mentally hardened her heart and went on attack. "What happened to my stuff?"

He sighed and his shoulders slumped marginally. "Your things are in the guest room closet."

"Oh."

She dipped her head to hide her disappointment, averting her gaze as she zipped and closed the button of her jeans. She didn't *want* to move into the other room. She wanted him to argue with her. Wanted him to admit he hated the idea of sleeping apart as much as she did. Wanted him to rage at her for clinging to her anger over a lie designed to keep her safe while ignoring his declaration of love.

For years she'd been the one doing the chasing, yearning after a future with him. He'd said he was concerned he'd fucked up forever. It was time he man up and fought for the forever they both wanted, and needed, damn it.

She lifted her face and met his gaze. "I'll get out of your way then."

"Wait." He gripped her elbow as she tried to walk past him.

Pausing, she jacked up her chin as the breath caught in her throat.

He released her elbow to cup her neck, massaging her nape with gently caressing fingers. Pleasurable chills chased over her skin.

He stared at her and his eyes darkened with remorse. "I'm sorry, baby. I should have told you the truth weeks ago."

Relief and hope weakened her knees. Okay. Now they were getting somewhere. Suppressing a shiver at his warm touch, she stepped back out of his reach. "Why didn't you? Damn it, Max. I came to you to help me get out from under that type of control."

His forehead wrinkled in a wince. "I know you did, but—"

"A lie by omission is still a lie," she pushed.

"I was trying to—"

"When you love someone, you don't lie to them." She lifted her chin and, in lieu of smacking him physically, she hit him with a verbal punch and prayed for all she was worth she wasn't the one who ended up with the metaphorical black eye. "Then again, maybe you were lying when you claimed to love me."

The disappointment in his eyes took care of the remorse. Her pulse tripped into triple time.

He stepped closer and dipped his head until they were eye to eye. "You're entitled to be pissed because, yeah, I didn't tell you the truth, but I agreed to your plan because I couldn't live with the thought of you being hurt or worse."

She knew that, damn it, but what about later? If he loved her as he'd said, how could he live with her, share his body and heart with her, and not come clean about why he was there with her in the first place?

"You didn't want me to be hurt?" She snorted a harsh laugh. "Do you think your lying to me doesn't hurt?" Bitterness seeped into her scoffing tone, and she crossed her arms. "That first night at Tuck's, did you kiss me to keep me from calling off my boyfriend plan?"

He straightened and his lashes swept down, shuttering his eyes. Although she'd already suspected the reason, his silent confirmation stabbed at her heart. She gulped air as the band of hurt crushing her chest tightened like a vise. "I see. Then tell me why I should believe your declaration of love wasn't just another ruse to keep me in line."

His lashes lifted, his eyes and face going hard. "Everything I said to you the other night was the God's honest truth. Goddamn it, Jessi. I admitted to killing a man. Do you think I'd disclose something like that if it wasn't the truth?" He speared the fingers of one hand through his hair. "You have me so fucking tied up in knots I broke the first rule of the street. I told you shit I've never spoken about to another living soul. Shit you needed to know if we were ever going to have a chance together."

A chance together. Tears stung her eyes, and the breath lodged in her throat.

"Obviously, I misread the situation, but I'm a grown man. I can handle the truth. Don't use doubt over my declaration of love as an excuse." He shook his head and his laugh was harsh. "If you've decided I'm not worth the effort, just say so. It's no more than I expected."

"Max, I—"

"They're waiting for you at the theater." He turned and stalked toward the door. "I'll be downstairs when you're ready."

* * * *

Max broke off from his study of the crowd to slide his gaze to where Jessi and Spence waited to take the stage. Victor, the stage manager Max had met the night of the awards show, spoke to one of his minions. Spence reworked the crease of his Stetson. Pale as a wraith, Jessi performed her pre-show meditation. Though she'd soon no longer have to go through the process, the knowledge obviously gave her little ease. Even from a distance, her tension was evident.

How much of that tension lay at Max's feet, he wasn't sure. When she'd finally come downstairs and they'd climbed into the back seat of the limo, she'd murmured a greeting to Dan before turning to stare out the window. The rest of the short ride had been steeped in an uncomfortable silence with Max left to wonder what she was thinking.

She hadn't corrected his suggestion, that she'd changed her mind about the two of them and, despite what he'd said about expecting her reaction, the reality left him more frustrated than he could ever remember being. Jessi voiced her opinions. It wasn't like her to hold back when she had something to say, and her silence spoke volumes.

Obviously, her repeated claims that his past didn't matter had crumbled to ashes beneath the ugly truth. Ego demanded he accept defeat with a shrug and move on. There were plenty of other women out there. True, none of them were Jessi, but neither would any of them find him wanting when all they required of him was a nice meal, a few laughs, and a good time in bed.

As he'd known from the beginning, love judged. A street rat with shadows in his past was better off avoiding the emotion. Too fucking bad for him, his heart disagreed.

The speakers came to life with the announcement of the headliners. Jessi's eyes flew open, and the fear and panic in her blue gaze as she searched for and found Max was like a fist to the gut. Without her heart and mind in agreement, her instinctive trust in him would quickly fade. It would be best for both of them if he was gone before that happened.

Spence held out his hand. She jumped and looked away. They took the stage to the roar of the crowd. Max gritted his teeth, prepared for the moment Spence would lift her hand for his kiss and was surprised when he skipped the ritual, dropped her hand as they hit their mark, and launched into song.

Max arched a brow. He hadn't had an opportunity to ask Jessi how Spence had taken the news of her retirement, but from the look of things, he wasn't a happy man.

"Where's he going?"

Max followed Tim's gaze and narrowed his eyes on the young man slipping through one of the theater's side doors toward backstage. "Isn't that the kid from Jessi's studio?"

Tim nodded. "Craig. He's the sound manager's son. He's got a thing for Jessi and shows up at her appearances all the time. He even showed up at your press conference, but I didn't expect him to come tonight."

"Why not?" Max slid his gaze back to Jessi. As usual, her tension seemed to have melted away. She held the audience spellbound, crooning in perfect harmony with Spence.

"She really didn't tell you?"

Max turned back to Jessi's cousin. His eyes gleamed with humor. "Tell me what?"

Tim shifted his shoulders and grinned. "I'm not saying a word."

Max shoved his fingers into the pockets of his jeans. He liked Tim, always had, but the vicious mood weighing on his shoulders left him impatient with his typical teasing. "Then why bring it up?"

Tim's gaze flicked back to the door where Craig had disappeared. "Because the kid was pretty upset yesterday."

Every muscle in Max's body went on alert. "Why was he upset?"

Tim's alarmed gaze snapped back. "Fuck. You don't think…?"

"Why?" Max grabbed his arm.

"Shit. When Jessi told Spence she was quitting, he kissed her. I guess he figured it was his last chance to tell her how he feels. Alicia and Craig walked in on it. Craig stomped out of the studio pissed."

Max broke into a run before Tim finished speaking. Catching the eye of one of Ryan's men, he pointed toward the doorway Craig had used. The bodyguard immediately sprang into motion.

Whoever had written the letters was close enough to know about the doll. Max had witnessed the kid's interest firsthand. Why the fuck hadn't the FBI looked at him?

With Tim on his heels, Max rounded the hallway in time to spot Craig disappearing inside Jessi's dressing room. The second of Ryan's men loped toward them from the opposite direction. Max didn't wait for the armed man. He charged into the large dressing room and nearly slammed into the kid. Jessi's assistant stood across the room before the darkened make-up vanity, her face a mask of startled surprise.

Craig spun around, his eyes round as saucers. He clutched a single red rose in his fist.

Max crowded him until Craig backed into the wall. "What are you doing in here?" He shifted his gaze between the rose and the stark white envelope on the vanity top and fury growled in his gut.

Craig's Adam's apple clicked as he swallowed. A tinge of pink slashed his cheekbones. "I...." He held up the rose. "I wanted to leave this for Miss Tucker."

Max flexed his fingers. The need to pummel the kid into the ground was so strong the muscles in his arms quivered. He stepped forward, holding Craig's nervous gaze, and spoke to Tim at his back. "Have the other guy return to stage front, just in case, and get Ryan back here as quietly as you can." He waited until Tim's hurried footsteps retreated into the hall. "And the note?"

"What note?" Confusion wrinkled Craig's brow.

Max shifted his gaze to the vanity, six feet away, and nausea coated his throat. He'd arrived in the dressing room seconds after the teenager. Unless he was a magician, Craig wouldn't have had the time to place the envelope where it lay. Max lifted his gaze to the woman Jessi considered a friend as well as employee. Alicia shuffled her feet and looked away.

A band of helpless rage compressed Max's chest. He had intimate knowledge of the stench of guilty fear. It radiated off Alicia in waves.

He scrubbed a hand over his mouth. Just to be sure, he turned to Ryan's man guarding the doorway. "Has anyone else been in here?"

The young black man shook his head. "Other than these two, no one has come near Ms. Tucker's dressing room since she left to go on stage."

Max absorbed the damning confirmation and bit back the string of vicious curses crawling up in his throat. He nodded. "I'll need some latex gloves."

Ryan's guard nodded and disappeared out the door. The gloves wouldn't be necessary. Opening the envelope could wait for the authorities. Any hope Max might have harbored of Alicia's innocence disappeared as her body tensed and she bolted for the door. He sprung after her, catching hold of her arm before she'd taken three steps. She spun on him and hatred replaced the fear in her dark eyes. Her scream of fury pierced the air as she swiped at his cheek with the nails of her free hand.

He blocked her second attempt, aimed at his eyes, and clamped his hand around her free arm in a grip tight enough to numb the limb.

"Take your hands off me!" Turning her head, she attempted to sink her teeth into his arm.

Tempering his anger was impossible. He shook her like a rag doll, then had to block her flying knee with his thigh.

"Need some help?"

Max ignored Tim's furiously spoken offer. He released one arm and pinned her to the wall with a forearm to her throat. Rage engulfed him, swirling through his mind like acid, and he had to fight the urge to crush her windpipe.

Tears sprung in her eyes, and her body sagged as the fight went out of her. "Please."

"Let her go, son. She's not going anywhere." Ryan's quietly spoken command pierced the fog of his rage, and yet, he had to force himself to loosen his hold.

Jesus. Jessi.

He lowered his arm to his side, and Alicia slid to the floor. He turned away from the muffled gasps of her tears as the returning bodyguard filed into the room behind Ryan and Tim. Craig stood several feet away. His wide-eyed gaze bounced back and forth between Max and Alicia.

A sigh rippled through Max's chest. Clearly, he'd scared the kid with his instinctive slide into violence. With his anger beginning to cool, disgust simmered in his gut. Jessi was right to back away now that she knew the truth about him. Once a street rat, always a street rat.

He held out his hand. "I'll see Miss Tucker gets your gift. You'd best go back to your seat."

His gaze flew to Max, eyes full of wary shock. He nodded, handed Max the flower, and shot one last glance at Jessi's weeping assistant before he scurried out the door.

"I never would have hurt her."

Max turned at Alicia's whisper.

She dropped her hands to her lap. Tears magnified the horror and guilt in the dark-eyed gaze that clung to his. "I swear. I was just trying to scare her into leaving. She already hates going on stage, and I thought…."

Max breathed deep, fighting the urge to tear the dressing room apart with his bare hands. Jessi was going to be heartbroken by the betrayal of her friend, and for what? She'd already decided to leave on her own. Obviously, Alicia hadn't yet heard, and he was tempted to slash her with the news, but she'd learn soon enough.

Her face crumbled. "It's just that, I love Spence and…." A sob shuddered through her body, and she curled in on herself.

Max dropped his head back to stare at the ceiling. "And love makes fools of us all."

Chapter 29

"Are you sure he's here?"

Kris rolled her eyes. "Relax, Jess. I left Max on the sideline surrounded by CC, Gracie, V, and Jake. Jake promised he wouldn't let him go anywhere until the half-time show is over, and Gracie said she'd sit on him if necessary. So did CC and V."

Jessi caught her bottom lip in her teeth. "How did Gracie convince him to come?"

Kris held up a hand. "I didn't ask. He's here. That's all that matters, right?"

Taut with nerves, Jessi paced the closed-off section of the tunnel leading to the field at Tampa's Raymond James Stadium. Her plan to get Max to prove his love had been an epic failure. As if she'd needed proof. He'd given up Haven Place for her, and what had she done? She'd spit on his sacrifice because of her pride and anger. She choked back an inward snort. If anyone had some proving to do, it was her.

"If you've decided I'm not worth the effort, just say so."

God, how could she have been so dense? Though it should have, the thought never once crossed her mind he would read her coolness and anger as a rejection because of the things he'd revealed about his past. Hadn't Gracie warned her? Hadn't Jessi seen with her own eyes how he used the darkness of his past like a shield, belittling himself before anyone else could? He'd expected her to rebuff him once he'd told her the worst of his memories and, like a blind idiot, she'd walked right into his self-defensive predictions.

Between the concert appearance and the painful chaos of Alicia's betrayal and arrest, there had been no time to disabuse him of his faulty assumptions. With the danger to her over, he hadn't returned to his condo that evening, and she had no idea where he'd spent the night. Her hope of clearing the air the following morning as they traveled to the Super Bowl never materialized.

Stunned and hurt by his dismissal, she'd staggered onto the plane. Alone.

Instead of delaying her trip until they settled things between them, *she'd* been the one to walk away, just as he'd expected she would. She'd spent the last two days berating herself for a fool and hoping against hope Gracie could pull off her plan to drag him here today. Though she'd started to dial several times, she couldn't do it. Pleading for his forgiveness over the phone wouldn't be good enough. He needed to hear her apology in person.

The only bright spot since she'd left Manhattan was Elizabeth Krandall's surprising capitulation. Jessi's heart had leaped into her throat when his grandmother had called early Friday morning. In a clipped and angry voice, the Krandall matriarch had agreed to Jessi's demands, with the stipulation she never hear another word from either Jessi *or* her grandson. With the deed to Haven Place transferred to Jessi in what had to be the quickest real estate transaction ever recorded, that shouldn't be a problem—after today.

"Almost show time." Tim stepped through the privacy curtain, looking tanned and handsome in a pair of khaki shorts and a dark blue, short-sleeved golf shirt. He wore a huge smile. "Tuck just scored to put the Marauders up by twenty-one. You should have seen it. It was a thing of beauty."

Kris's lips puckered in a smirk. "You're such a dork."

He leered, stepped toward her, and yanked her to his chest for a steaming hot kiss. Twin dimples scored his grin as he lifted his head. "That's not what you said last night, Sparky."

Kris's gaze skidded to meet Jessi's.

"Sparky?"

A bright pink blush rode Kris's cheekbones. "Yeah, I shared the goodies with your cousin." She rolled her eyes. "He wore me down, all right?"

Jessi smiled, but she was too nervous to offer the ribbing the admission deserved. Tim laughed and, retaining his hold on Kris, turned his head to look at Jessi.

"You know what you're going to say?"

Mostly. She'd gone over the words a thousand times in her mind and, if they fell on deaf ears, she didn't have a clue what to do next. She swallowed. "Aren't you going to try and talk me out of this?"

Anticipation flickered in his eyes. "Hell no. I'm looking forward to it. It's not every day I get the chance to watch my little cousin make a fool of herself on international television."

Jessi groaned and pressed a fist to her belly.

Kris jabbed his midsection with her elbow. "Quit teasing her. She's nervous enough already."

Nervous was an understatement. In a few minutes, she'd be taking the stage and announcing her retirement—in front of an audience of millions. As if that wasn't frightening enough, she would also be laying her heart on the line in the gamble of her life.

Tim cocked his head and held her gaze. "What the hell, Jess. Max deserves a little bit of payback, and you're already guilty of blackmail. It's not like Max's grandmother is going to hate you any worse. Besides, while I can't stand the idea of her coming out smelling like a rose with the press, with everyone slobbering over her generosity she'll be less likely to come after you in the future."

That was the hope but, if this actually worked, Jessi was swearing off screwy plans permanently. Her blood pressure couldn't take it.

Tim obviously took her silence as agreement. He nodded. "Spence is all set in the other tunnel, and the entertainment director will be in to give you your cue." He grinned. "Shit, the guy is so jazzed I won't be surprised if he pisses himself."

Despite the ball of anxiety in her belly, Jessi laughed. The show's director had been delirious over her request. Hoping to surpass the sideline sensation Jake and Gracie had caused five years ago, when Jake had proposed on the field, the giddy man had approved the change to the half-time program on the spot.

Spence hadn't been quite as excited, but he'd eventually given his consent to shorten the last song so Jessi could do her thing. Like her, news of Alicia's actions had hit Spence hard. Since Alicia had been taken into custody, his anger over Jessi's retirement had slid into acceptance, and he hadn't once mentioned the kiss or his declaration of love. Neither had she.

Whether or not they'd continue to work together in the studio, she didn't know, but she'd worry about that later. For now, she had some proving to do—and a certain hunky cage fighter's heart to re-win.

* * * *

Sweating and anxious for the tortuous exercise to be over, Max ignored the arm Gracie wrapped around his waist. Despite himself, he couldn't drag his gaze from Jessi wowing the mesmerized crowd of seventy-five thousand football fans stuffing the stadium to beyond capacity. He breathed a stealthy sigh of relief as the glitz and lasers that had marked the half-time show slowly faded. A single spotlight blinked on. Spence, and the dozens of dancers flying through the air at their backs, disappeared and Jessi stood center stage.

Dressed in white from head to toe like a mystical creature of light, she seemed to glow. Her long auburn curls shifted in the slight breeze, and she hit and held the impossible last note of their latest hit. The moment the song ended, the building erupted with the thunderous applause.

Max's chest shuddered on a ragged breath. Gracie tightened her hold. He glanced her way, and she offered him an innocent smile, but she wasn't fooling anyone. Her bullying tactics to get him to Tampa had little to do with him watching his best friend compete for the championship as she claimed. Jessi was Gracie's agenda and, while he loved her for trying, they'd all be better off when she gave up her push for happily ever after where it applied to him.

As much as the knowledge hurt, Jessi finally understood what he'd tried to tell her from the beginning. Dragging things out would only prolong the anguish.

"Are you happy now?" He arched a brow. "I came. I've seen her. She's beautiful, and I'm still not the man for her."

"Men." V rolled her eyes and winked at Gracie.

"Tell me that in a minute." Gracie bumped his hip with hers, and Jake chuckled at her other side. CC and V laughed outright as Tim and Kris arrived hand in hand.

The hairs on the back of Max's neck stood on end, and he eyed each of them in turn. "You're all up to something. I want to know what it is."

"Shhh." Unholy mischief glittered in Gracie's eyes. "Watch."

She turned back to the field, and Max followed her gaze. From the front of the stage twenty yards away, Jessi patted the air in front of her in an attempt to silence the crowd. Spence appeared from the darkness at her back to stand at her side. She turned her head and blinked as if surprised to find him there.

One of the show crew hurried forward to deliver a hand mic. The raucous, party atmosphere quieted as she lifted it to her lips.

"If you'll bear with me for a moment, I need to say something, and I only have ninety seconds before two incredible teams retake the field."

The crowd roared.

"First." She paused until the applause settled fractionally. "First, I'd like to thank you all, fans or not, for allowing Spence and me to perform today. It was the thrill of a lifetime and the perfect venue to conclude our touring career."

Gasps competed with cries of dismay as a rippling murmur moved through the stands. The breath left Max in a slow sigh. *Good for you, baby*. Though he believed her decision to retire from the stage would ultimately deliver the peace and happiness she longed for, he hadn't been entirely convinced she'd actually go through with it.

Spence leaned in so he could share the mic. "Thank you, everyone. We've had a tremendous run." He slid his arm around Jessi's shoulders. "But all good things must come to an end, and no man has ever had a better singing partner."

She smiled and turned her cheek against his shoulder. He squeezed her briefly and pressed a kiss to the top of her head. The mic picked up his voice just before he released her. "Good luck, Jessi. Be happy."

He exited the spotlight, leaving Jessi alone. Her chest expanded with a deep, bracing breath and, though Max waited for her to take a final bow and follow, she didn't move. Instead, she searched the people standing along the sidelines. Her gaze locked on him, and his shoulders bunched. A surge of energy blasted him like electricity racing through a high-tension line.

Her lips moved in silent communication. *I'm sorry, Max.*

He tensed. Sorry? Sorry for what? Oh, hell.

She didn't smile, and his heart ached at the shimmer of tears in her eyes.

Her shoulders rose on a shaky breath, and she turned back to the crowd. "Before I go, you all know I'm rooting for the Marauders today. If I didn't, my cousin would disown me." She answered the immediate laughter with the stage smile he'd witnessed many times over the past few weeks. Tense and brittle, the false pleasure quivered on her lips and didn't reach her eyes. "But I'd also like to introduce you all to a very special man. Since his grandmother is Elizabeth Krandall, I'll wish the Hurricanes a good and healthy game as well."

More laughter followed and trepidation tiptoed up his spine. What the hell was she doing, calling out his grandmother by name? "Fuck. What have you all done?" he growled out of the side of his mouth.

Gracie jabbed him with an elbow. "We haven't done anything. This is all Jessi, but she has our blessing."

Jessi cleared her throat and drew his attention. "His name is Max Grayson. Some of you may have read his name in the papers lately along with his grandmother's, and as you'll see, you can't believe everything you read."

Dread slammed into him like a fist. He resisted the urge to crane his neck and look up at his grandmother's skybox. Damn it. Jessi's friends and family obviously knew what she was up to. What were they thinking, letting her go through with this? Whatever *this* was.

"Unfortunately, like his grandmother, Max can be a little stubborn."

He cursed and stepped forward, meaning to rush the stage and grab the mic before she could do any more damage. Gracie held him tighter and Jake blocked his path.

Tim crossed his arms. "She's not finished, Max. Trust us, you're going to want to hear this."

"This is Jessi we're talking about. I'm afraid to hear it."

Gracie laughed and waved Jake out of the way so they could see Jessi on the stage.

She cast her gaze over the crowd. "You see, Max doubts my feelings for him, and I need your help convincing him he's the perfect man for me."

The breath left Max as if he'd been sucker punched. Laughter and cheering echoed through the stands as a second spotlight suddenly captured him in its beam. He squinted against the glare and held up a hand to shield his eyes.

"What do you say, everyone? Will you help me out?"

A booming roar of agreement vibrated through the stadium, and her stage smile dropped away beneath a genuine one.

"Okay, then." She turned her head. A sheen of tears glistened in the blue gaze that held him spellbound. "Let Max know with a round of applause if you think he should say, 'Yes, Jessi, I'll marry you and spend forever loving you.'"

His knees threatened to give out. The noise was deafening with a chant quickly immerging. *Say. I. Do. Say. I. Do. Say. I. Do.*

Gracie poked him in the back and yelled over the din of seventy-five thousand matchmakers. She shoved him toward the stage. "What are you waiting for? Say I do, you idiot."

"Well, Max?" Jessi moved to the edge of the stage and held out her hand. "What do you say? Will you make an honest woman of me?"

Speaking was impossible, but a helpless laugh climbed up from his soul. He could only imagine what it had cost her to face her fear of the stage to tempt him with the deepest desire of his heart. Unpredictable, hell. She was insane. Beautifully, maddeningly, charmingly insane. And she was his. Only a fool would voluntarily walk away from her smile or her love, and he'd never been a fool.

The doubt and fears of his past fell away with each step he took toward her, elbowing his way past friend and stranger alike to claim forever. He slapped a hand to the stage to vault up beside her, and cheers of approval rang out. The glistening tears in her eyes spilled over as he gathered her in his arms.

She held the mic to his lips, laughter and love in her eyes.

He tucked her closer, dipped his head, and said, "I do."

The clamor of seventy-five thousand screaming fans was nothing compared to the roar of joy thundering in his head as his mouth claimed hers. With her lips pressed to his, she giggled at the screeching reverberation from the mic trapped between them, and they broke apart.

"Make it quick, kiddo," Tim yelled from the grass at the foot of the stage. "You're out of time, and Tuck has a ring to win."

An adorable blush colored her cheeks as she lifted the mic back to her lips. "Oh, I almost forgot. Your grandmother has an early wedding present for you."

His grandmother? Wedding present?

Tim held up a packet of papers. Max swallowed and took them with a shaking hand.

"Congratulations, my friend." Tim stepped back, a challenging smile on his face.

Max dropped his gaze to the top page of the packet and disbelief nearly brought him to his knees. He whipped his gaze to Jessi and shoved the mic far enough away that it wouldn't pick up his voice. He dropped his mouth to her ear. "Jesus, Jess. This is a deed to...."

"Haven Place. It's yours, Max, with your grandmother's blessing." She rubbed her cheek against his. "Or it will be once I do one last thing." She straightened and looked up at the skyboxes lining the top of the stadium.

Max followed her gaze. High above the field, Elizabeth Krandall's unsmiling face was visible through the glass of the private suite.

The crowd quieted as Jessi spoke once more. "Mrs. Krandall, Max and I can't thank you enough. Gifting us with Max's mother's house is so generous of you and means more to us than you'll ever know."

The crowd went wild. High above them, a grimacing smile moved over his grandmother's face. She slowly lifted her hand in a stilted wave, as if reluctant to do so, but knowing she had little choice.

"Damn it, Squirt." Max dipped his mouth to Jessi's ear. "Do I want to know how you did this?"

"Probably not." She shot him a sidelong grin. "Now, give your grandmother a thank-you wave and let's get out of here. Forever is waiting."

Epilogue

"Your mother would be so proud of you."

Jessi sniffled and squeezed her father's arm. "Stop, Dad. I need to get through this without bawling. Max will think I've changed my mind."

Ryan chuckled, and CC smiled. Gracie coughed a laughing snort.

Kris smirked and her eyes danced with mirth. "After you proposed in front of one hundred and eleven million witnesses? Not a chance, girlfriend."

Jessi beamed a smile. Exactly one week had passed since they'd set the world of sports and music on fire with their fifty-yard line free-for-all, as Chet Bertrum had reported her half-time proposal. It was one week too long as far as Jessi was concerned. If not for Tuck's busy schedule after winning his ring, she would have held the wedding immediately following the game. After years of chasing her cage fighting champion, she'd won Max's heart, and she wasn't taking any chances he would change *his* mind.

Gracie was of the same mind, and along with CC, Kris, and V, had gone above and beyond to have Haven Place ready for the private family service while Jessi dealt with FBI interviews and the dissolution of her partnership with Spence. Her heart was broken over what Alicia had done, but it sounded as if her assistant was taking responsibility for her actions, and a court appearance for Jessi wasn't likely. Spence had declined the possibility of their working together in the studio. Though Jessi wished he felt otherwise, she understood. Her own singing future was up in the air for now, but she looked forward to getting back into the studio eventually.

Neither she nor Max had heard a word from his grandmother, but then, Jessi hadn't expected they would. Her public "thank you" had had the desired effect. Over the past week, the papers had been awash with speculation over the supposed reconciliation of Elizabeth Krandall and her grandson. Max hadn't yet asked Jessi how she'd gotten hold of the deed to his mother's home. She'd save telling him she had sworn off screwy plans for when he did.

As CC handed out the simple bouquets of daisies and greenery, Jessi glanced around the elegantly simple family room leading to the patio. The peace and tranquility Max's mother had attributed to Haven Place had been evident from the moment she and Max had stepped inside for the first time immediately following their return from Tampa. Her gaze paused on the wooden floor in front of the stone fireplace where Max had tossed down a blanket so they could celebrate properly. They'd spent the entire evening wrapped in peace and tranquility, and each other's arms.

Ryan kissed her temple. "Ready, ladies?"

Jessi gulped an excited breath. Gracie nodded and tucked her arm through CC's. Jessi's friends stepped outside in the matching plum cocktail dresses Gracie had pronounced perfect—because they made neither she nor CC look like beached whales. Next went V, then Kris, both stunning in the mid-thigh coral wrap-around dresses Kris had proclaimed would make Tim's tongue hang on the ground.

Ryan squeezed Jessi's hand and led her outside. As if Max's mother smiled down on them from on high, the weather had cooperated. Sunny and in the mid-sixties, a soft breeze blew over the surprisingly spacious patio off the private beach and carried the sweet scent of fresh flowers they'd brought in for the day.

Tuck's parents and Jessi's assorted cousins were in attendance with Tim and Jake acting as groomsmen. As best man, Tuck stood beside Max. They turned together. Jessi's heart fluttered as everyone and everything but Max disappeared.

The black on black tux suited his tough-guy looks, but it was the love in his eyes that brought tears to hers. His sexy, crooked smile curled her toes and stole her breath. Her father placed her hand in her groom's and stepped back. Dipping his head, Max didn't wait for the words to be spoken. He covered her mouth in a voracious kiss to the laughter of the women and catcalls from the men.

Father Mullen, a long-time friend of the Tucker family, finally cleared his throat, and Max lifted his head.

"They're jealous." He winked and held out her hand, his gaze roaming over her in a thorough study. An appreciative whistle blew through his lips. "You're beautiful."

She smoothed a hand down the skirt of her simple white sheath and treated him to the same inspection. "So are you."

A dimple flashed with his grin, and he turned her to face Father Mullen who cleared his throat. "Dearly beloved…."

Lost in Max's smile, Jessi didn't hear a word of the shortened service. It was the little things she noticed, like the way the late afternoon sunlight danced in his ebony hair, and the daisy boutonniere tucked into his lapel, and the warmth of his fingers as he brushed them over her cheek, replacing the lock of hair the breeze tugged from its pins. Rings were exchanged, and she must have given the correct responses because, suddenly, Max was squeezing her fingers.

"I now pronounce you—"

"Jake."

Jessi turned her head at Gracie's whispered plea and her eyes widened. A small puddle of water dampened Gracie's silk heels.

"Oh, shit." Terror blazed in Jake's eyes as he leaped across the distance to grasp his wife's outstretched hand. "Tell me you peed from excitement, Princess."

Her smile looked forced. "Okay, but I'd be lying. My water just broke."

CC wrapped an arm around Gracie's waist. "Oh, sweetie. How long have you been in labor?"

"I've been having contractions for about three hours."

Jake paled as if on the verge of passing out. "And you're just speaking up now?"

Gracie curled a hand under her large baby bump. "Don't yell at me. I didn't want to ruin the day."

He whipped out his phone.

Tuck glared at CC. "Don't get any ideas. The minute Baby Huey starts knocking, you tell me immediately."

His wife curled her lips in a sweet smile. "Knock, knock."

V gaped as Kris squealed and threw her arms around her cousin.

Tuck blanched before color immediately flooded his face. "Are you fucking kidding me?"

"Relax, Daddy." CC's teeth flashed in a grin. "Yes, I'm kidding. I just wanted to see your reaction."

His brows slammed together in a relieved scowl. "That's not funny."

"I thought it was hilarious." V snickered and returned CC's smug smile. Tim laughed and Ryan joined him, shaking his head.

Jake gripped Gracie's elbow and turned her toward the house. He met Jessi's gaze over one shoulder. "Where's the nearest hospital?"

"I think there's one about a mile down the road." Jessi released Max's hand and hurried forward.

"I'm not going anywhere until Max and Jessi are married," Gracie grumbled and Jake groaned.

Jessi stumbled to a stop and spun around, her gaze flying to Max. His lips were quirked in a crooked smile. *Holy crap. What am I doing? We're getting married!*

Jake whipped his head around to glare at Max, flapping his hand in a hurry up motion.

Max's eyes sparkled with restrained laughter. "What do you say, Squirt? Shall we put them out of their misery?"

She grinned and placed her hand in the one he held out. "I thought you'd never ask."

"Father," he said without looking away.

Father Mullen cleared his throat. "I now pronounce you husband and wife. You may kiss your bride. Again."

THE END

Meet the Author

Wife, mother and *really young* grandmother, **Mackenzie Crowne** shares her home with her high school sweetheart husband, a neurotic Pomeranian, and a blind cat. She calls Arizona home because the southwest feeds her soul. Her love of the romance genre has been a lifelong affair, both as a reader and a writer. A bout with breast cancer sharpened her resolve to see her stories shared with others. Today, she's an eight-year survivor, living the dream. Her friends call her Mac. She hopes you will too. Visit her website at mackenziecrowne.com, find her on Facebook, or follow her on Twitter at twitter.com/MacCrowne.

Check out another great read from Lyrical Press

Life beyond the game…

BETTER THAN PERFECT

More Than a Game, Book One

Kristina Matthews

Johnny "The Monk" Scottsdale has won it all on the baseball diamond. He's even pitched a perfect game. Known for his legendary control both on and off the field, his pristine public image makes him the ideal person to work with young players in a preseason minicamp. Except the camp is run by the one woman he can't forget…the woman who made him a "monk."

Alice Harrison once traded her dreams so that Johnny Scottsdale could make it to the Majors—and then her dreams fell apart. Now here comes Johnny back into her life, just when she's ready to finally go after her dreams. This time she's not letting up. Even if she has to reveal what she's kept secret for too long from her son and Johnny. She's can't be sure how things will turn out, but she's not leaving until she swings for the fences…

Visit us at www.kensingtonbooks.com

Chapter 1

"Pitchers and catchers report to spring training in thirteen days, twenty-one hours and seventeen minutes," Hall of Fame broadcaster Kip Michaels announced, and the crowd went wild. "Kicking off today's Fan Fest, I'd like to introduce one of our newest players. Two-time Cy Young Award winner, perennial All-Star, and the last man to pitch a perfect game. Give a warm San Francisco welcome to Johnny 'The Monk' Scottsdale."

Thirty thousand people were expected at the ballpark today. A great crowd—for a baseball game. But instead of working the count, Johnny would be working the crowd. Answering questions. Signing autographs. Putting himself out there in a way he wasn't entirely comfortable with. He was as nervous as the day he'd made his professional debut fourteen years ago. Butterflies? Try every seagull on the West Coast taking roost in his stomach.

Focus. Breathe. Let it go.

"Thank you. I'm thrilled to be here." He'd much rather face the 1927 Yankees than sit in front of a camera and a microphone talking about his game instead of playing it. "I hope I can help the team bring home a World Series Championship."

He tried to relax his shoulders. Tried to hide his nerves. The Goliaths could be his last team. His last shot at a ring. His final chance to prove himself and leave a legacy that went beyond the diamond.

After fielding a few questions about what he could bring to the team, and deflecting some praise about his success so far, Johnny was released to another part of the park to sign autographs. Little Leaguers approached with wide eyes and big league dreams. Tiny tots with painted faces squirmed with excitement about getting cotton candy while their parents shoved them forward to collect an autograph. A shy boy with a broken arm asked him to sign his cast. The look on his face was more than worth the discomfort of being in the spotlight for something other than his on-field performance.

Johnny had signed the big contract. The team paid him a lot of money to pitch every five games. They also paid him to interact with the fans, to be an ambassador for the game he'd loved for so long. The game that had saved him from a completely different kind of life.

He shared a table with another new player, shortstop Bryce Baxter. They were set up near the home bullpen along the third base line. Several other stations were set up around the park, giving fans a chance to get up close and personal with the players. Some tried to get a little too personal.

"So you're the hot new pitcher." A busty brunette leaned over the autograph table, wearing what appeared to be a toddler-sized tank top. The team logo sparkled in rhinestones and she was obviously well aware of the attention she drew. "I'd be more than happy to show you around."

"No thanks. I'm pretty familiar with the city." He held his pen ready, although she didn't seem to have anything to autograph. Nothing he was willing to sign, anyway.

"I could take you places you've never been." She leaned over even more.

Johnny kept his head down, trying to avoid gazing at what she had to offer. He reached for a stock photo, scrawled his signature across the bottom, and slid the picture forward, hoping she'd take the hint and leave.

"You forgot your number." She pouted.

"Sorry. I don't give that out." Johnny wished he could retreat to the locker room. Get away from her and the crowd that seemed to be growing. He never understood why people would wait in line to make small talk and take his picture. He gripped the black marker, needing something to do with his hands. If he only had a baseball, he could roll it around in his palm. Feel the smoothness of the leather, the rough contrast of the raised stitches. Find comfort in the weight and the symmetry of the one thing he could always control.

His teammate inserted himself into the conversation. "Do you know who this is? The one and only Johnny 'The Monk' Scottsdale."

"The Monk?" She drew her gaze over Bryce, then glanced at Johnny before settling on Bryce once more.

"He's a god." He flashed a grin indicating he was more than willing to play her game. "Me? I'm a mere mortal." Bryce leaned toward her, clearly enjoying the interaction.

"You're new, too." She scooted over to his side of the table, dismissing Johnny's rejection as strike one. She must think she had a better chance of scoring with Bryce.

"I am. I think I left my heart somewhere in the city. Could you help me find it?" He slid one of his photos across the table to her.

"I can help you find whatever you're looking for." She took the pen from him and wrote something on the inside of his forearm. Her number, most likely.

Bryce grinned as if he enjoyed having a stranger tattoo him with a permanent marker.

"Bring your friend, too. If he's up for a challenge."

"I'll see what I can do, sweetheart." Bryce tipped his cap and winked at the woman.

Johnny exhaled, realizing he'd been holding his breath during the entire conversation.

"Thanks man, I owe you one." Johnny shook his head, as relieved as if Bryce had just snagged a line drive with two outs and the bases loaded.

"So it really isn't an act." Baxter eyed him carefully. "You really do walk the walk."

"What walk?"

"The celibacy thing. It's for real." A lot of guys thought he was full of it. That it was just for show. A way to get attention, and women. But once they realized he was genuine, most of the other players accepted him. Some even respected him. "You really don't mess around."

"No. I don't. I'm not perfect, but I try to stay out of trouble." Johnny removed his cap and ran his fingers through his hair. Since they were both new to the team, their booth wasn't as crowded as some of the others. They had a chance to catch their breath. He was able to finally sit back and enjoy the perfect weather. It was one of those glorious Northern California days when the sun came out to tease, dropping hints of spring and the fever that came with it.

"You looked like you were a little uncomfortable there." Bryce, on the other hand, seemed to relish the attention.

"I know it's part of the job, but it's not the part I'm good at."

"You let your game speak for itself. That's cool." Bryce reclined in his chair, looking as relaxed as if he was sitting in his own back yard. "Some of us have to use our charm to make up for lack of talent."

Johnny laughed. Baxter had plenty of talent. And more than enough charm to go around.

"She was pretty fine, though." Bryce continued to check her out as she walked away, collecting ballplayer's numbers like kids collected baseball cards. "Exactly what I need to get me in shape for spring training."

"Is that so?" Johnny managed to avoid the whole groupie scene. His entire career had been about control, both on and off the field. The Monk kept his cool. The Monk never got rattled. And The Monk maintained a spotless reputation. He had to, considering where he'd come from.

"There he is. Come on, Mom." A kid, about twelve or thirteen, rushed up to the booth, practically dragging his mother by the arm.

Johnny slipped on his best fan-friendly smile.

"We're, like, your number one fans." The boy was practically bursting at the seams. "Right, Mom?"

The boy's mother stepped forward, taking Johnny's breath away.

He'd had several reasons to come to San Francisco. Eleven million obvious ones, and several others that he'd done his best to articulate to the fans. There was only one reason he should have stayed away.

"Alice." Just saying her name sent a line drive straight to his heart. Even fourteen years later.

"Congratulations on your new contract. I know you're going to have a great year." She sounded like any other fan, wishing him well. She just marched right up to his table to ask for an autograph. A freaking autograph? Like he meant nothing to her.

A slight breeze blew her hair around her face. She tried to smile as she tucked a loose strand behind her ear. Blond, straight, silky—and if he remembered correctly—oh-so-soft. She wore modestly cut jeans and a soft blue sweater that on anyone else would have looked plain and proper. He didn't need to glance at her left hand to know she was off limits. Yet, she still moved him like no other woman ever could. Made him long for what he'd had. What he'd lost. What he'd tried for years to forget.

"Wait." The boy gaped at her. "You guys know each other? For real?"

"Yes. Johnny was…" She held Johnny's gaze just long enough for him to catch a flicker of regret. She turned to her son, who was about an inch or two taller than her. "He was your dad's college roommate."

"You knew my dad?" The boy seemed more impressed by that than the fact that people waited in line for his autograph.

"Yes. I knew him." Johnny swallowed the lump in his throat. "Before he married your mom."

"Cool." The kid smiled and nodded his head, like it was no big deal. "I mean, I know you played for the Wolf Pack when they went to Nevada, but I had no idea you guys were, like, friends."

Sure. Friends.

"Zach." She placed her hand on his shoulder, ready to steer him away. "I'm sure Mr. Scottsdale is a busy man. Let's leave him alone."

They'd once been as close as two people could be. But now he was Mr. Scottsdale.

The boy shrugged, dismissing her and looking up to Johnny with admiration. "It's totally awesome to meet you."

Johnny nodded, giving his most sincere smile, even though seeing Alice, and her kid, hit him like a 97-mile-an-hour fastball.

They started to walk away.

"Give my best to Mel." As if he hadn't already done that.

Alice turned around.

"Mel died. Eight years ago." A pained expression flashed across her face.

"I'm sorry. For your loss." Johnny said the words. He wanted more than anything to mean them, but he'd carried that resentment around for so long, it had become as much a part of him as his right arm.

"Thank you." Alice gave him a sad little smile. It was forced. Polite. The kind of smile she'd give a stranger. "It was good seeing you. Really good."

"Yeah. Sure." He could say the same, but he'd be lying. Seeing her again only reminded him of everything he'd sacrificed.

* * * *

The minute she'd seen Johnny on the stage, Alice's heart had swelled big enough to fill the stadium. There he'd been, larger than life. Damn. The man looked good. Better than on TV. Better than she remembered. He'd gained some muscle. A lot of muscle. Even without the jersey, there'd be no doubt he was an athlete. He moved with the kind of confidence and grace that came with being totally in tune with his body. Like he'd once been totally in tune with hers. She ached at the memory, but shook it off, uncomfortable having such thoughts with her son sitting next to her. Like Johnny had clearly been uncomfortable onstage, addressing the media and the crowds. He never did like to talk about his game. He'd simply let his talent speak for itself.

Just as she'd predicted, women lined up at his booth. They all wanted his autograph. Some of them wanted a little more. She hadn't been able to handle it back then. And now? What he did was his business. Especially since she'd been the one to walk out on him.

"Mom. Are you okay?" Zach was protective of her. And a little too observant.

"I'm fine, Zach." She shook her head to clear the fog of memories that rolled over her. With only the briefest look into his eyes, she couldn't forget the three years they'd spent together, nearly inseparable. Studying. Hanging out. Making love. "I'm surprised to see him, that's all."

"But you knew he'd be here." Zach had that tone, the unspoken *duh*. They'd been coming to Fan Fest every year since Mel's death. She'd known Johnny would be here. She just wasn't prepared for the impact of seeing him again. She'd thought she'd put those feelings behind her. Packed them away with her college sweatshirts and student ID card. "You were so excited when you heard it on the radio. Your favorite player finally becoming a Goliath. Why didn't you tell me you guys were, like, friends?"

"I didn't want you to think it's a big deal." She tried to place her hand on his shoulder, but he squirmed to avoid the contact. That was new. Not unexpected, given his age, but she missed her little boy. The first time they'd come to Fan Fest, he'd held her hand. Until they'd gotten to the miniature version of the ballpark. He'd joined the t-ball game like he was born to play.

"It is a big deal." Zach looked at her like she was hopelessly out of touch. Something he did a lot these days. "Mom, you actually know Johnny Scottsdale."

There it was. The star-struck admiration bordering on worship.

"I *knew* him, Zach." Alice tried to keep her tone neutral. She couldn't betray her emotions. A wave of regret washed over her. The question of what might have been. "But that was a long time ago."

"Wouldn't it be cool if he came to the foundation's minicamp?" Zach couldn't know why it would be such a bad idea.

She'd hoped to avoid him. Avoid digging up the past. And the question that had plagued her more and more as Zach grew. "I already have a pitcher lined up. Nathan Cooper. He's done it for years."

Alice had worked for the Mel Harrison Jr. Foundation since its inception, a little more than a year after her husband's death. The initial donations were privately funded, set up to provide grants to community schools and youth organizations. As the foundation had grown, they were able to provide services for greater numbers of children, but the more successful they'd become, the less contact she had with the kids.

Until a few years ago, when the team had approached her about setting up a minicamp for youth players. It evolved from a Saturday demonstration and meet-and-greet to a weeklong afterschool program where the ballplayers worked directly with the kids, helping them learn fundamentals of the game while boosting their confidence with the attention and mentorship of the pro athletes.

"Cooper's alright." Zach sounded disappointed, bordering on whiny. "But he's not Johnny Scottsdale."

"Zach, we made a commitment to Nathan Cooper."

"And Harrisons always keep their commitments." Zach parroted the family motto. She could tell by the tone of his voice he had to restrain himself from rolling his eyes.

"Yes, Zach, Harrisons keep their commitments." No matter what. She'd made a commitment to Mel, to the Harrison family. She'd hoped her feelings for Johnny would eventually fade. She'd made her choice. A desperate one at the time, but once she'd committed to Mel, she wouldn't look back. She still couldn't. "Cooper's a good player. A good guy. We can't just tell him we don't want him anymore."

"Well, maybe they could both do the pitching clinic," Zach suggested. "Since Cooper's a lefty, maybe it would be better to have a right-handed pitcher too."

"Johnny's a busy man. He doesn't need us bugging him." And she didn't need to be reminded of what she'd given up.

"Yeah, but he probably doesn't know very many people here yet." Zach sounded hopeful. Like they'd be doing Johnny a favor. "It would be good for him to get involved in the community."

"Zach. He doesn't need us." She'd made sure of it.

"But..." Zach couldn't let it go.

"I think it's time for some lunch." Lately, food seemed to be the best distraction.

"I could eat." Zach shrugged. "You want to split some garlic fries?"

"You know I do." The ballpark's signature fries had become a tradition. But if she ate a full order herself, she'd be sorry later.

"Can I get two hot dogs, then? Or maybe some nachos?"

"You're that hungry?" Wasn't it only yesterday that she begged him to eat? Playing airplane with the spoon or bribing him with a toy to take three more bites.

"Yeah. I guess meeting Johnny Scottsdale increased my appetite." He grinned at her. For a second there, he reminded her of someone she used to know.

"Oh, Zach..." She sighed, her emotions getting the better of her. Seeing Johnny for even a few minutes had her all mixed up.

It had been easier when Johnny was on the other side of the country. When he'd been nothing more than a box score. An image on TV. She'd followed his entire career. From his earliest days in the minor leagues, to his first start in Kansas City, to when he was traded to Tampa Bay. She'd watched him. Cheered for him. Wished him nothing but success.

"Oh please, Mom. Don't go there." She was embarrassing him. As she often did whenever she talked about how quickly he was growing up. Becoming a man. Neither of them was quite ready for it, but that didn't matter.

She put her arm around him but felt him struggling with the idea of pulling away. Reluctantly, she let him go, knowing it was only a matter of time before he wouldn't need her at all.

"Order whatever you want. Just don't complain about a stomach ache later."

"I won't." He ordered a hot dog, nachos and a root beer.

She stepped up behind him and ordered her hot dog, the garlic fries and a Diet Coke. She struck up a conversation with the lady behind the counter while they waited for their order.

"Geez, Mom. Why do you have to talk so much?" He'd waited until they were at the condiment station before complaining.

"I was only being friendly. There's nothing wrong with that." She unwrapped her hot dog and placed it under the mustard spout.

"Yeah, then why weren't you very friendly with Johnny Scottsdale?" He kept his head down, concentrating on his food. She'd learned to pay attention more when he seemed least interested in making conversation. "You actually knew him in college and you barely said a word to him."

She hit the pump on the mustard a little too hard and it splattered all over her sweater. She quickly grabbed a napkin to wipe up the stain.

"Is it... Is it because he reminds you of Dad? Does seeing him make you sad?"

"Oh, honey." She put her arm around him, pressing him against her. How could she possibly explain why seeing Johnny again was so painful?

"It seems kind of weird that they didn't keep in touch after college." Zach had no idea how weird it would have been if they had. The three of them had been the best of friends. How many times had they let Mel tag along on their dates? Or how many times had she made herself at home at their place? But Johnny had been at the heart of their little group. And when he'd moved on, she and Mel turned to each other.

"Johnny was trying to make it to the big leagues." She used the same story she'd told herself over the years. "He had to work very hard to get to where he is today. Mel had a job here in the city, and I was busy raising you. We just drifted apart, that's all."

"But, maybe you and Johnny can be friends again." He had a tiny hesitation in his voice. Telling her there was more to the story than he was willing to share.

She waited. Pushing him would never get him to open up.

"Maybe…" Zach took a long slurp of his soda. "Maybe he could tell me more about my dad."